EXPOSED

BOOK ONE OF THE LOVE SEEKERS

MARIA VICKERS

Everyone deserves a chance at love!

Mari Vickers

Exposed

Copyright © 2016 Maria Vickers

ALL RIGHTS RESERVED

Cover Design: **T.E. Black Designs**
www.authorteblack.com

Editing: **Shana Vanterpool**
https://shanavanterpool.com/editing-services/

DEDICATION

Myasthenia gravis is a rare neuromuscular disease that causes muscle weakness. It is called a snowflake disease because no two cases are alike, thus the reason for the symbol I used when formatting this book. They are all fighters. But they aren't this only ones.

This book is dedicated to all of the warriors out there who fight their chronic diseases on a daily basis. I know it is painful, tiring, and can drain you, but you fight on. Regardless of what your disease is, if you have to battle something, anything, you are a warrior in my eyes. MG, MS, MD, ALS, depression, anxiety, GAD, Sjogren's, Reynaud's, arthritis, etc. So many diseases out there, and so many are fighting the good fight so that they may continue to live a full life. I know firsthand how draining it can be and how much it can affect everything. Never give up. If you have to sit down, do it, but get back up and keep pushing forward. I know how often we force a smile or pretend to be okay when we aren't.

KEEP FIGHTING! YOU ARE A WARRIOR!!

CONTENTS

EXPOSED

CHAPTER ONE

EMMA

I was done! Beyond done! As I drove home, I could feel the sting of my tears as they fought to escape their sanctuary. I wanted to cry, but I refused to give into those emotions. Or at least I tried not to give in and let them fall. However, try as I might, a few traitorous ones trailed down my face, taking my eyeliner and mascara with them. I knew by the time I made it home, my face would probably closely resemble a raccoon; and yet, I no longer cared.

I deserved a good cry! Damn it!

Oh God! Why couldn't they have waited until I got home? I was only a few minutes away, and then I could wallow in self-pity, punch a wall, throw my pillows, and scream my head off. Okay, maybe I'd already screamed more than a few times, but after my night, I earned at least that much!

Men suck! That's what I decided tonight. They sucked, and I was probably better off without them. Batting for the other team began to look mighty appealing...if only I wasn't so attracted to the opposite sex. The assholes!

Turning into my apartment complex, I pulled into my assigned parking spot right in front of my apartment and slammed the gear shift into park. No longer would my tears be held back and they began spilling down my face. Sobs wracked my body as I clutched my steering wheel, my knuckles turning white with the force of my grip. I needed to go in, and yet, my body refused to cooperate. I couldn't move.

It wasn't fair! I'd accepted tonight's blind date with the hope that it may lead to something beyond tonight; only what I found waiting for me turned into a nightmare instead of a dream.

I didn't know how long I sat in my car. It could have been a minute, or two, or ten. I sure as hell never kept score, and at that moment, I didn't care. What waited for me inside? Just my dog. Don't get me wrong, I loved my dog, but I craved more. I wanted someone who I could hold a conversation with, someone who would answer my questions instead of staring at me blankly as he tilted his head from side to side. I wanted someone to hold me. As much as I loved Curley's kisses, he wasn't exactly the man I sought. Dogs were great, and my lovable pug's snorts, grunts, and licks were cute, and he had the uncanny ability to put a smile on my face, he just didn't make my list of potential boyfriends. I wasn't into bestiality, thank you very much.

The first thing I looked for in a man was that he had to be human— maybe not the first, but it was important—and of course he had to love dogs. Curley and I were a package deal, and if the prospective guy could not handle that, he needed to move on, because my heart was set on someone else. I preferred my men taller than me, which wasn't a hard feat to overcome since I was only five-seven. Not short, but not too tall. If I described myself, I would have said average all-around. My weight—well, when it came to my weight, I was a little thick, but I didn't believe a size twelve would be considered too heavy. I had long brown hair and brown eyes. Average, average, and average. I didn't care what anyone said, size four was not average.

I didn't think I was ugly by any means, but I wouldn't claim to be a model either. My skin had a little more pink in its tone than it should, but it was healthy and clear of zits and everything else. My bottom lip stood out a little more than the top due to its fullness, and my eyes were wide with a slight almond–shape. My wide forehead was usually covered with bangs, and my teeth were straight thanks to three years of braces as a kid—something a lot of average kids dealt with.

What couldn't be considered average about me? I was disabled.

Four years ago, my life changed when I found out I had a rare disease named myasthenia gravis, some called it a snowflake disease because no two cases were the same, thus that became its symbol. A cane or walker kept me upright and balanced, otherwise, I would fall over. Though I've had enough practice making the ground's acquaintance, I didn't feel it necessary to constantly introduce myself. But I guessed my date tonight hadn't been informed of my "extra leg." Bastard.

I arrived at the pre-arranged meeting place on time, and the hostess informed me my date had already arrived. Butterflies fluttered annoyingly in my stomach like usual when I met anyone new. Would this meeting go well? Not so well? Nervously, I followed her to the table, and as soon as he took one look at me, he got up and attempted to leave me standing there. Who the hell did shit like that? I tried to stop him, but his comment to me felt like a slap in the face. "I don't do handicap. Not even out of pity."

Unable to calm down as I moved through my house, I made my way to my bedroom and patted Curley's head when I finally sat on my bed. My tears continued to fall as I cried over my date, over my night, and over the disappointment I'd endured yet again. This wasn't the first time someone took issue with my disability. Tonight, however, it cut much more deeply, and I was almost convinced no one existed who would be able to accept me and my baggage. My family and friends kept telling me that it would take someone special, that I had to be patient and wait for him, but they didn't understand. Each time this happened, it felt like a little more of my self-esteem—my inner being—was stripped away. What man wanted to deal with someone who wasn't perfect? Apparently no one.

What I really needed and wanted was my best friend beside me, but since we lived in different states, I had to settle for talking to her online. Maybe she could help me gain perspective–or calm me down–because after tonight, turmoil engulfed me. Was she on a date tonight? I couldn't recall. Gia and her husband liked to do date night every other week, and I couldn't remember if tonight happened to be that night. Maybe if I messaged her, I'd feel better. If I texted or called, she'd feel obligated to respond right away, but if I messaged her on FaceSpace, she could respond when she had time. I knew I had to be in a bad place if I chose not to call my best friend immediately.

I was done and embarrassed, and I wanted to quit.

And there it stood, glaring back at me. The real reason I couldn't bring myself to dial her number. While I did want to talk to her, I felt so ashamed about what happened to me that I didn't want to talk to anyone.

Finally giving in, I pulled up the app on my phone and quickly shot her a message on FaceSpace.

Me: *Men SUCK! I'm so done that I don't even know where to begin. Everyone says that I'll meet that special someone who will be able to accept everything. I call bullshit! HA! Fat fucking chance. Men suck!! I don't want to have anything to do with them anymore. I showed up tonight and he tried to leave before I even sat down! I swear if one more person tells me I just have to wait for the right one, that there is someone out there for me who will accept my disability, I will throat punch them!*

I started to put my phone away when I heard it ding. Fuck! Gia's online right now. Which meant, if I didn't answer her immediately, she'd worry, and then she'd call someone. New tears filled my eyes, replacing those I had already cried. The waterworks needed to stop because they were annoying. My date tonight wasn't worth a single drop. My love life—or lack thereof— wasn't worth it. Well, my love life might have been because I began mourning the fact that I would remain a spinster my whole life. In fact, I was convinced of it because I HAVE GIVEN UP!

My lungs expanded with my deep indrawn breath and collapsed when I released it slowly. It was only my best friend. Why did I have to build up my courage? One more breath and I checked her message. OH NO! I didn't! I couldn't have! My eyes widened in shock and fear. I double checked to make sure I had read my screen correctly. I had. Shit!

I still prayed and hoped for the name on the screen to change. Please don't tell me I did what I think I just did! My thumb hovered over the new message that lit up my screen, the one from Bryan Sampson. I hesitated a few more seconds before I tapped on his name to open the conversation.

Scanning the message quickly, I discovered my error. I had indeed sent my message to Bryan instead of Gia. Did I not say I was done with men? How had this even happened? Yeah, we were friends on FaceSpace because we had a mutual friend in common, Mel. And this morning he asked me a question about a wedding gift for Mel and her fiancé...BUT WHY? I hardly knew him. Since he was Mel's friend, I sent him a friend request after he came in for Mel's engagement party, which wound up being a night of karaoke. We had only met in person once almost a year ago, and I had probably only exchanged a couple dozen words with him. On top of that, we'd only talked on FaceSpace twice. Once when I sent him the friend request and this morning. How had this happened? I had to have clicked on the wrong name by accident. My stupid tears were to blame for my clouded vision. He was the last person I wanted to talk to right now.

The man was admittedly hot and could probably model if he wanted to, but instead, he chose to serve our nation and joined the Navy. He's built without being overly big, and he looked sexy as hell with his clean-shaven face and chiseled jaw. His tanned skin, wavy brown hair, and hazel eyes could draw in any woman, and when he smiled, two dimples formed craters on his cheeks that could melt the panties of young and old. HOT! There was no way in hell he would even begin to understand my situation. From what I gathered—and what I saw within ten minutes of meeting him—girls threw themselves at him all the time. He got the pick of the litter and could have anyone he wanted.

Bryan: *Umm, okay. Care to explain yourself? Surely it can't be all bad if you're messaging me...a guy.*

No, I didn't want to explain myself to him. Was he crazy?

Me: *Nope. I'm good.*

Bryan: *Yeah, that's clear from your previous message. Or should I say rant?*

Me: *Harsh.*

Bryan: *Truth. What's going on?*

Me: *And why the hell should I tell you?*

Bryan: *Why not? It's not like we actually know each other. Think of me as the stranger you spill your guts to.*
It's going to be like you didn't tell anyone.
Like a drunk confessing to his bartender.

Me: *Gee thanks.*

But as I gave myself a moment to think about it, he had a good point. Maybe if I vented to him and got everything off my chest, it would help. It wasn't like I would see much of him in the future, so there was no need for me to feel embarrassed by what he thought of me or of what happened. Then again, what if he told Mel, the friend that had introduced us? Honestly, I didn't know why we were friends on FaceSpace other than sometimes you made friends with your friend's friends. Oh...and he was more handsome than anyone should have the right to be! And I wanted to flirt with him, which never happened because I considered him a 10 and me a plain Jane. With so many girls throwing themselves at him, I couldn't bring myself to do more than send a friend request, and when he accepted, it completely surprised me.

Biting my lip, I decided to take the plunge and reply, but first I laid down the rules.

Me: *Don't tell Mel.*

Bryan: *Why would I do that?*

Me: *I don't know...because you know her?*

Bryan: *And your point would be what? Vegas rules, baby. What happens during FS chat, stays in FS chat.*

For the first time tonight, I found my lips curling upward into a smile. I might even admit to a tiny snort as I snickered. I already felt better in a small way.

CHAPTER TWO

EMMA

Bryan: *So are you going to come clean or do I need to call someone in Charleston to come and check on you?*

In my head, his words held a hint of teasing, but I had a feeling deep in the pit of my stomach that if I didn't answer soon, he might really call someone. And the only person I could think of whom he might call would be Mel. I had no choice.

Grumbling, I logged onto the computer to save myself from typing on my phone's small keyboard and finally responded.

_Me:_ *Fine, but if I find out you told anyone, your ass is grass.*

Bryan: *Who am I going to tell? Just be happy my ship got into port two days ago.*

_Me:_ *Where r u at?*

I wasn't sure how many tours he had been on during his Navy career, or how many more he needed to do before he satisfied the government, however, I could picture the faraway places he had visited during his travels and my wanderlust flared. Maybe I should have joined the Navy like my sister, father, and grandfather had, but no, I had decided to go to college and focus on psychology. Yes, I could psycho-analyze myself, however, I hardly ever listened to my own advice.

Bryan: Back in San Diego.

Me: Oh! Mel didn't tell me you were on your way home.

Bryan: It's not home. It's a base in San Diego where I currently reside. Charleston will always be home. LOL.

I imagined his sexy, cocksure smile, and I shook my head. Everything about him screamed confidence and player, and like others who undoubtedly came before me, I had nibbled at the bait he cast. Huffing, I continued to type, my fingers hitting the keys a little harder.

Me: Fine. Fine. Not home, but you're back stateside?

Bryan: Sure am. Now quit stalling!

In my head, I easily heard his command and pictured him ordering his men around. They probably jumped without question, without asking how high. Isn't that what happens when an officer ordered someone to do something? I don't know what it was, but as soon I read his order, I tensed, flinching ever so slightly. He wasn't even in the same room with me, and I found myself doing what he told me to do while thanking my lucky stars that this conversation happened on FS chat instead of over the phone or Skype. I wanted to have that level of protection, my walls and barriers, and chat gave me a little more anonymity. He couldn't see my shame or embarrassment. He couldn't see how much I hurt.

Me: I just had a bad night. Met an asshole for a blind date. That's it.

Bryan: Come on. That can't be all to the story.

Me: Guy was an ass. How much more of a story do you need?

Bryan: Just tell me already.

Me: Why do you want to know so badly?

Bryan: Why don't you want to tell me?

Me: Gee, I don't know. I barely know you, never talk to you, and not sure I can trust you.

Bryan: *Navy trusts me. ;)*

Me: *I may trust you to guard our nation, but other than your handsome face, what are your good qualities? How do I know you won't spill my embarrassing secrets all over your base?*

I knew I was stalling, but could anyone really blame me? The moment I opened my mouth and admitted what happened, typed it in black and white for anyone to see, not only would it be real, but he could and probably would laugh at me. Strangers, people I don't even know, would know of my failures in the love department, which would turn me into even more of a laughingstock than I currently felt I was.

Bryan: *First, I doubt the guys around here would care much for your dating issues. Second, you sound as if you need to talk to someone. I'm available and ready to listen. Third, didn't I already promise not to tell? Finally, I'm bored as fuck. Talking to you gives me something to do. You can tell me or not. Up to you.*

He had a point, and I could admit to myself that I felt scared. Scared to vocalize–or in this case write–what had happened tonight because it chafed and still felt raw. But I needed to talk to someone, to vent and scream at the world and its injustices. So I caved and told him what he demanded to know.

Me: *Don't laugh at me.*

I still feared his reaction.

Bryan: *Already promised that too, honey. :p*

My stomach clenched as I read his last word. I knew a lot of southern men called people honey, sweetie, baby, and a few other choice nicknames without meaning anything by them, but when he called me honey, or baby as he did earlier, it did something to my insides. I melted. The phrase sex on a stick had been made for him.

Fingers shaking over the keyboard, I swallowed hard in an effort to quench my parched throat. I couldn't decide if my throat felt dry from fear, or from his endearment. Maybe a little of both, but either way, I down-played my reaction and mustered all the bravado I could.

Me: *Whatever. I had a date tonight. I'm not sure if you remember or not, but I'm sick/disabled and have to use a cane or walker.*

Bryan: *I remember. The day we met at karaoke, you were using a walker. Mel said you were having a bad day and she made you come out with us anyway.*

Me: *Pretty much, but that wasn't a really bad day. There are some days I can't get out of bed because I'm too weak.*

Bryan: *Got it. And?*

Me: *So...guys don't want damaged goods.*

Bryan: *WTF does that mean?*

Me: *It's true.*

His response didn't come immediately, and I almost wondered if he'd decided to stop talking to me. I waited...and waited some more. Still nothing. Getting up to get a drink, I drank it slowly and refilled my glass before I came back to my computer to find that there was still no response. "Well, I guess that's that," I muttered to myself, feeling a little disappointed that I ran him off so easily.

Just as my fingers moved my mouse to hover over the "X" so I could close the Internet window, a distinctive ding stopped me from doing anything. Someone had messaged me. My eyes darted to the screen and scanned it quickly: Bryan. It had only taken him over ten minutes, but I guessed beggars couldn't be choosers.

Actually, irritation oozed from my pores. I felt irritated at myself for wanting and waiting for his response, irritated at him for taking so long, and irritated that I actually found myself wanting to talk to him some more. Men were supposed to be the enemy!

Maybe he needed a taste of his own medicine.

Bryan: *Sorry about that. My roommate started pounding on my door. He just got home and is fucked up drunk. LOL. I don't think I've ever seen him like this.*

Reading his response, I almost gave in. Lord knows I definitely considered it, however, I stood my ground. I refused to respond immediately and instead clenched my hands into fists so I didn't give into the temptation of typing an answer.

Another ding filled the quietness, and my dog Curley leaped up from where he laid curled next to me and tilted his head to the side in an effort to figure out where the noise was coming from. He made me laugh.

Bryan: Emma?

I watched the clock allowing one more minute to pass before I allowed my fingers to return to the keyboard. But before I could type anything, another ding and this time Curley whimpered at the noise. Patting his head, I snickered, "Don't worry boy. The big bad Navy man in the computer can't get you." My eyes returned to the screen so I could read what he wrote.

Bryan: You there? I said sorry.

His almost begging words, pleading with me to respond to him made me giggle even more.

Me: Sorry about that. I was using the bathroom and got a drink. I didn't realize you were back.

Bryan: Sure you didn't. I know how you girls operate.

The sarcasm was thick with this one, and I laughed some more. It felt good to find humor in the small things and to forget about the bad, even if it was only for a mere moment.

Me: Do tell.

Bryan: We aren't talking about me, we are talking about you right now.

I wished we were talking about him instead of me. The only person that knew how much the complete and utter dismissals bothered me, how much I hated the numerous changes in my life, was my best friend Gia. I think Mel had a clue, but only Gia knew the whole sordid story. We had been best friends since we were kids. She was the only person I told how much it cut when a guy wouldn't give me a second glance for no other reason than I needed to use a cane or walker. I hated using them. I'm 29 and my life has been forever changed all because my body decided to turn on itself. One day I was perfectly fine and healthy, and overnight, I was in the hospital barely able to move and struggling to breathe. At least with the cane and walker, I could continue to be mobile without having to depend on someone else. That would have been even more degrading.

No, in truth it started before my body decided to abandon me. During the summer before I started college in the bedroom of my boyfriend. The panic welling up within me made me feel sick, and I had to push those memories away and bury them again. I didn't want to think about that time in my life.

Taking yet another deep breath, I forced the embarrassment, hurt, and anger threatening to rise, down deep inside myself before I could answer him.

_Me:_ _Guys tend to see me and the last thing they want is to date someone like me._

Bryan: _Why the fuck do you think that?_

_Me:_ _Experience._

Bryan: _Explain._

I supposed if I had resorted to using one-word answers, I couldn't get upset when he did the same thing.

_Me:_ _I've been sick for a little over 4 years. It happened about a month after I turned 25. The guy I was dating at the time couldn't deal with me being sick, so he split. Since then, I've been on exactly 9 dates. 5 from dating sites and 4 from friends with "good intentions" that decided to hook me up with their friends thinking we would be perfect for each other. I've experienced anything from them politely staying through dinner, to my wonderful date tonight. Can you hear my sarcasm?_

Bryan: _What happened tonight?_

_Me:_ _Tonight was my latest bad–I mean blind date. My lovely friend apparently forgot to warn him about my disability, and when the hostess showed me to our table, he got up and tried to leave. He actually turned around as he was about to pass by me, left money on the table, told me "sorry, it's not going to work out," and left. Gone. Finito. My date ended before it even started. And tonight I was only using my cane. Can you imagine if I had been using my dreaded walker? Gasp!_

I attempted to put on a brave face and make light of the situation, but I inwardly admitted, it was getting to me. My nose and eyes stung from the emotions welling up within me. I was hurt and angry, and hated my disease and what it did to me. But talking to him on chat where he couldn't see or hear my tears or pain, and only read about it, was safe. Chat kept him at arm's length away from me and made it all personally impersonal.

So many times I pretended I endured the jeers, comments, whispered insults, and the way men reacted to me. I pretended I handled everything like a trooper with grace and dignity, but the harsh reality was, I felt as if I was breaking on the inside.

The sound of a ding pulled me out of my own head and back to my conversation.

Bryan: *Your walker isn't dreaded, it's a part of life.*

Me: *Yay! Lucky me.*

The sarcasm flowed through my fingers. Some said that the only emotions emails, texts, and chats held (at least the words) were the emotions the reader read into them. Nothing more and nothing less. I was pretty sure he picked up on the fact that my tongue dripped acid right now.

Bryan: *Well, it isn't like you can do anything about it.*

Me: *Gee, thanks for the newsflash.*

Silence. I thought I might have run him off, but before I could type anything, he returned.

Bryan: *I'm not going to pretend to know what you're going through, but I can tell you that you just haven't found the right guy.*

Me: *I've heard that before.*

If Bryan were in the room with me at that moment, I would have throat punched him. I hated hearing—or in this case reading—those words.

Bryan: *From what I remember when I met you, you were shy.*

Me: *Yeah, so?*

Bryan: *So, I think there are guys out there who are interested in you, who* *can look beyond the disability and see you for you. You just have to open up a little more.*

Me: *This is who I am.*

Bryan: *And I think I can help you change.*

Me: *Excuse me?*

Bryan: *You heard me. Did you date a lot before you got sick?*

Me: *Well...*

I accidentally hit enter and paused. Another confession, another thing I had to see in black and white. It was another truth that would glare back at me.

Bryan: *I'm not getting any younger. Did you or didn't you? Not a hard question.*

Me: *Not much.*

I cringed when I typed my response. Vague as it appeared, it screamed the truth.

Bryan: *Was that because you were with your last boyfriend for a while?*

Me: *No, we had only been dating a month.*

Bryan: *Oh.*

Was I supposed to say something, or was he? Did he feel like I was a lost cause? Nervousness had me on edge and feeling cornered and defensive, and while I was trying to hold it all in, I felt like the floodgates would burst open without much effort. And his radio silence after those two little letters appeared on my screen did not help. I almost breathed a sigh of relief when I saw his next message.

Bryan: *What has been your longest relationship with a guy?*

Should I answer him honestly? I really didn't want to, but at the same time, I felt compelled to give him the truth.

Me: A month if we are talking about dating. Friendship wise, I've been friends with a couple of guys since high school.

Bryan: I see. What do you like to do?

He sees? What the hell did he see? I wanted to demand he tell me, however, my fear won in the end and I kept my thoughts to myself.

Me: Do?

Bryan: Hobbies. What do you like to watch? Do you like sports, movies, books? What?

Me: I like to write and read a lot. Love sports, especially hockey and basketball. LA Surf all the way for the hockey, and of course the Dallas Outlaws for basketball. But all sports are fun. One of my guy friends said that I made the best kind of girl because I was just one of the guys. I could drink them under the table, watch sports, and not put up a fuss. He said they didn't have to worry about me griping at them because I'm just another buddy and could never be a girlfriend.

I hit enter and winced. Not only did that statement paint me in a bad light, but it probably also fell under the category of TMI. How embarrassing. I mean, even my closest guy friends didn't consider me datable. Maybe I should tattoo the word 'hopeless' across my forehead.

Forcing myself to scan what I had just sent, I wanted to be like an anime or manga character and facepalm using a brick wall. How in the world did someone ramble in a chat? I'm not sure, but I accomplished that feat. What an idiot, Emma! Smooth operator right here! I was making myself into an utter fool, which dampened my spirits even further thinking about it. Maybe it was better if I closed this chat down before I typed anything else mortifying.

Me: Sorry. I'm tired and I think I just need to go to bed.

Bryan: Wait. Give me a minute.

Me: What?

Bryan: How many guys have you dated...total?

Me: Does that really matter?

What did a number, have to do with anything? Could he not leave me with a shred of my dignity intact?

Bryan: _If it didn't, you would tell me. LOL._

LOL? That did it. My frayed emotions started to run amuck. He mocked me now, and after the night I experienced, that sent me over the edge. Pressing the caps lock on my computer, I did the next best thing to yelling: angry typing.

_Me:_ _LISTEN HERE ASSHOLE! NEWS FLASH, BUT NOT ALL OF US ARE OUT TO BREAK A RECORD TO SEE HOW MANY PEOPLE WE CAN GET INTO BED AND/OR DATE. UNLIKE YOU, I HAD OTHER THINGS TO WORRY ABOUT IN LIFE AND DATING HAD TO TAKE A BACK SEAT! SO YOU CAN KISS MY LILY WHITE ASS AND JUMP OFF THE NEAREST BRIDGE, JERKOFF!_

I slammed my laptop closed with more force than necessary, powered down my phone, and decided to ignore the world for the rest of the night. Maybe I shouldn't have taken my hurt feelings and anger out on him, but right now, I didn't care. I felt more than a little raw and defensive from the snub I received a couple hours ago, and he took the brunt of my anger. Had I overreacted when it came to Bryan? Yes, I probably had. Had he been an ass? Given what little I knew about him and all the assumptions I've made after meeting him and talking to Mel about him, most definitely. But then again, assumptions could be wrong and it was possible he actually wanted to help me.

Whatever. I did not care and did not want to think about it any longer. I was done for the night.

Crawling into bed, Curley jumped up beside me and we cuddled together. In a world where people cared little about me–or others for that matter–I knew I could at least count on my dog. He just couldn't give me everything I craved, and after tonight, I seriously doubted I would ever find a guy who would love me, disability and all. Saying it didn't matter to me, or hoping people would be able to get past it all in order to see who I was on the inside, sounded good, but in reality, nothing was ever that simple or fair.

My eyes closed and shut the world out. I just wanted to wake up and forget tonight ever happened.

CHAPTER THREE

BRYAN

What the fuck just happened? Emma apparently despised answering certain questions. All I asked was how many guys she's dated, and she gave me a dressing down worthy of my commanding officer. What was that?

I tried to send her another message in order to get some answers–or any kind of fucking response–but she went AWOL. Normally if someone was online, I would see a green dot by their name, or if someone switched to the mobile app, it would have a small phone icon, but her name had nothing, which meant she was off the grid.

Technically she couldn't completely disappear. If I really wanted to push the issue and contact her, I could always call Mel, who would conveniently give me Emma's phone number. But I foresaw how messy that would get— with a capital M.

Mel stumbled into my life in high school announcing to the world we were best friends within days of our initial meeting. At that point, I didn't know if I even wanted to be friends with her, but she stuck by me then and ever since. Some thought we were dating in secret, while others placed bets on how long it would take before we crossed the line and became more than "just friends." With Mel? Oh, hell no! I hated to break it to them—not really —but nothing ever happened, nor would anything ever happen between us. There may have been an almost kiss at a party, however, that ended very badly, and it was something that had haunted my nightmares to this day. I could not think about that night without my body breaking out into a cold sweat and my stomach churning.

To distract myself from traipsing down that better left forgotten memory, my thoughts turned from Mel to another girl, one completely opposite of my best friend. Emma Taylor. I'm not exactly sure when I started to hear about her. Vaguely, I recalled Mel saying something years ago that she found a keeper at work, which was her code for a person who wasn't a complete asshole, and a person she could actually tolerate.

Working in the marketing department for a large firm, Mel oversaw and made sure the various regional offices had the latest material and that the sales force did their job. I wasn't sure, but I thought I remembered Mel telling me Emma worked in the training department for the company—whatever that meant.

Emma hadn't been with the company long before she got sick. About a year after that, Mel called to tell me Emma would be moving to her city. Hearing about Emma's move to Charleston was news to me. The way Mel talked, I assumed that she and Emma were buddy-buddy, hanging out every Saturday night. I never realized before Emma moved that they'd never met in person.

But she still battled some sort of illness.

When someone said they were sick, my first thoughts are flu, cold, or strep throat. And if someone said long-term illness, I immediately thought cancer. Apparently, I was always wrong. There were other things in this world that made a person sick. I could not recall exactly what she had or what it did to her, but the first time I saw her, she walked in dragging her feet while pushing a walker. Her whole body and countenance reminded me more of an old person instead of someone in her twenties. Mel told me that Emma was having a bad day and had to use the walker. She also said that sometimes Emma could get away with using a cane, but I had never seen her use one. Then again, we had only been in each other's company that one night.

I had to admit to myself, it unnerved me to see her for the first time. During karaoke, I tried to ignore the walker and just have a good time. Hell, maybe I tried to ignore her, ignore the sick person, but that didn't last long. In the beginning, I couldn't manage to look her in the eye, and then she did something that earned my respect and made me laugh. She leaned forward, slapped the table with her palm, and with a slight slur in her words that had more to do with whatever the fuck she had, and less to do with alcohol—I can't actually remember her drinking a drop—she declared, "Think of it like a portable chair you can take for a joyride without a license. I'm sick, not dead."

That night, she sat in her seat, belted out songs with the rest of us, and held her head up high as she enjoyed herself.

Which brought me to why it surprised me to hear her put herself down

18

so badly. She seemed like a cool girl, and I knew she was pretty. Maybe not stick thin like some girls, but then again, a lot of guys I knew, myself included, wanted something to hold onto. High cheekbones, brown eyes that sparkled as if she were plotting something which could undoubtedly get someone in trouble, silky brown hair, and a quick wit. I was also quite sure she possessed a big brain because I sort of remembered Mel telling me something about Emma obtaining multiple degrees.

Any guy would be lucky to have her. Yes, the walker may put off most men, but not everyone would turn her away just because of something she had zero control over. I'd date her except for two things. One, I didn't date seriously. Emma deserved someone who was searching for a forever type of relationship. And two, she was nowhere near my type. Confidence was key, but I also wanted someone who knew how to use their sexuality. Don't get me wrong, Emma was a nice girl, however, I didn't typically do nice.

On top of that, I had to agree with her friend. She would make a great buddy. Too bad she wasn't a guy. If she was, we could have gone looking for trouble and had some fun.

That being said, I fully intended to help her as promised, and when I was done, guys would be lining up to meet her. I staked my reputation on it.

CHAPTER FOUR

EMMA

Life always had a way of moving on whether you wanted it to or not. As much as I would have liked the world to stop spinning in order to join my pity party or for time to stop so I could lick my wounds, it never did. Everything continued to move forward, ergo I pressed onward as well. That had been one of the hardest lessons I struggled with after I got sick–something I still struggled with a lot. But hey, I was a work in progress.

Ideally, I would have loved to sleep a couple more hours on this glorious, overly bright, Sunday morning, but my sister, Ellie, did not agree. Not that I blamed her...much. I broke the rule she had given me when I moved to South Carolina. I was supposed to text or call her as soon as I got home whenever I chose to go out and about on my own. Sometimes I thought her more of a mother hen than a sister; however, I understood her concern. There had been a couple of times when I had tired myself out and still attempted to drive home. Calling her from a gas station or parking lot on more than one occasion had given her cause for concern.

Last night, I had come home without texting her, got into a fight with Bryan, and shut down my phone. If she tried to call me, which I'm sure she did more than once, I wouldn't have answered because I had every intention of shutting out life. If only I factored in her copy of my key to my house into my diabolical plan, then she would not have tried to shake me awake. Bitch. I love her, but after crying myself to sleep last night, I was still exhausted.

Anyone who had ever experienced the thrilling ride of being on an emotional roller coaster while crying uncontrollably understood what I meant. Sleep became your best friend, wrapping you in a cocoon of warmth and safety and blocking out the world. Actually, it just made you tired as hell and you needed to sleep off the effects of your emotional outburst.

Ergo, when Ellie yelled at me as she attempted to shake me awake at 9 A.M., I might have lashed out by swatting her hands away and pulled my blanket tighter around me. She decided to try another tactic. My blanket left me, ripped away, and I was too weak to fight it. Even with my medicine in my system, the myasthenia gravis did not allow me to fight for too long. I tried though, and I might have groaned, which may have sounded slightly on the cusp of being a moan or a squeal as I tried to swat her hands away again.

She appreciated my efforts about as much as she appreciated my lack of communication. I couldn't help it. I had fallen asleep an emotional mess, and the only thing I had done that morning, was to take my mestinon, muscle medicine so that I could somewhat function when Curley decided he was done waiting for his breakfast. Without that little pill, I would turn into a weak puddle of goo. Not really goo per se, but without it, I felt weak and boneless, unable to speak or hold my head up. Forget walking or doing anything else. I could do nothing without my meds. Too bad they did not chase away my tiredness.

"Get up, Emma," Ellie demanded with her irritation thick in her voice. I knew that tone. It meant she was already at her limit. I wondered briefly if one of the kids had pissed her off this morning, and then all thoughts left me when she jerked the blanket so hard, I rolled to the other side of the bed sans blanket.

"What do you want?" My whines sounded more like a petulant five-year–old than an adult.

Her chest rose and fell with the effort she had exerted, and I could almost see her counting to ten, giving herself time to calm down. And when she finished, her fists slammed down onto her hips and she snapped, "What do I want? Well, considering we had plans for brunch at 10 and you're still in bed, and let's see, you had a date last night and never once called or texted me. How did I know if you made it home all right?"

There was the mother hen I knew and usually loved. "Sorry I didn't talk to you. To sum it up, it was a horrific night and I just wanted to go to bed."

An immediate change overcame her. Her features softened as she moved to sit down on the bed. "Want to talk about it?"

Did she really just ask that? Hell no I didn't want to talk about it. If I didn't call her the night before, I had a good reason, and I did not want to fucking admit that for the umpteenth time, another guy loathed me before I even uttered one tiny peep. "No." My answer was clipped and slammed the door shut on broaching the subject further.

21

Or so I thought. I should have known better.

"Just because he didn't work out—"

I interrupted her as quickly as possible. "Stop. Just stop right there. I'm pretty much done after this one."

"Emmm…" she sang, stretching my nickname out as if it had more than one syllable.

"What?"

"You can't give up on everything because of one bad guy."

My palm itched to slap her. "First, I'm not giving up on everything. Second, it's been nine bad guys. Not to mention the countless others that never made it to the dating round." Have I mentioned I loved my older sister? I do. Seriously. Really. However, she recently retired from the Navy and found herself with extra time on her hands. Time she loved to use to torment…I meant to help and support me. She made it her own personal mission to rescue me or something.

"You just haven't met the one."

Would it be bad if I throat punched my own sister? "The one? I'm pretty much convinced that he doesn't exist for me. That's fine though. I have… umm…I have whatever the hell it is I have. Now can you go away? I'm still sleeping." I curled into a ball on my bed and tried to ignore my sister behind me.

"I know, Curley. She needs to get up," Ellie said to my dog, and he answered with a bark. *Traitor.* To me, she ordered, "No can do. We have brunch plans, and I came to pick you up. So get up, get ready, and let's get the day started."

Curley barked again and jumped on the bed right before he pounced on me. "Oomph. Curley, lay down." He refused to listen and started whimpering. Thanks to my sister breaking in this morning, he was now awake and wanted his food pronto. Maybe I should be happy she waited until after 9:00 A.M. to assault me this morning, considering there had been more than one occasion when she snuck in before seven. I would have killed her this morning if she tried that shit. I still may.

"I know, Curley. Tell your mommy that you're starving and need food." With those words, Ellie successfully got what she wanted.

Slowly sitting up, I scooted off the bed and pushed myself into a standing position using my walker. Not sure why she decided to poke me when she had already won, but she was lucky my legs were unsteady otherwise I would have grabbed her finger and attempted to break it.

I did mention that I loved my sister, right? Maybe I needed to repeat it a few more times like a mantra. "Stop! I'm up already. Why don't you make yourself useful and feed Curley while I take a shower?"

"Sure. Come on, Curley." She turned around and left the room. I didn't miss the victorious expression that lit up her face.

I am so not a morning person.

Like I said, Ellie got out of the Navy almost a year ago after fifteen years in the service. I applauded her work and the sacrifice she made in serving the military because I knew it could not have been easy. We had grown up in a military family, and our dad was absent more than he was present during our childhood. Sometimes, he seemed more like a stranger than a parent. And she had still decided to enlist and serve. Of course, her kids came a few years after she joined, but she managed to make it work.

Now that I looked back on it all, moving from place to place, seeing new things, experiencing things many did not, it was probably one of the best childhoods I could have ever asked for. After my dad retired and we settled in Texas, I met people that had never left the state lines. The world was bigger than that and deserved to be experienced.

When Ellie had been in about five years, she met a guy named Chris and they immediately fell in love. "An instant spark," she told me. For her to talk like that, the one person who probably didn't have one romantic cell in her body, I knew this guy was special to her. I wanted that kind of spark too.

Six years older than me, Ellie had been with her husband for over a decade. Apparently, they were doing something right because they were still together, still in love, and had two ornery children. I loved my nephews. Really, I did, but they could be little heathens at times. One was five and the other seven, so it stood to reason that they could be a little rambunctious with short attention spans…and they hated to listen to anyone and everyone who told them what to do. That being said, her kids had to deal with her leaving a lot, but at least they didn't move as much as we did. Once she returned from the Navy, they remained in South Carolina, which allowed her kids to stay in the same school they had attended since the beginning.

When it became apparent my disease would not be fading quietly into the night, my family held a meeting and decided I needed to move out of Texas and closer to family. My sister won the betting pool. My only stipulation for agreeing to the move was that I had to have my own space. I didn't want to live with family or have people think I needed them to do everything for me. I loathed feeling like I had become a burden. So, when I found an apartment less than a block away for the right price, I moved.

Ellie tried to be understanding of my situation, but she didn't quite get it. In truth, it felt as if no one really related or understood me anymore. I say me, but it was the damn disease. They couldn't understand the disease and the effect it had on me; therefore, they no longer understood me. I became an anomaly. It was okay though. I was all right with that because if they understood exactly what I dealt with, it meant they were dealing with the same thing or something similar. And this…I wouldn't wish it on anyone.

My shower cleared the fog in my head and began to wake me up, and with my alertness came a renewed sense of embarrassment over the previous night. It wasn't only the fact that I'd been looked down upon like I was some sort of pariah, but I also confessed everything to a practical stranger. Why the hell had I divulged everything to Bryan?

Well, it didn't matter. He wasn't here, he didn't really know me, and I could unfriend and ignore him for the rest of my life. Done and planned.

Today greeted me as a new day, and I would take full advantage of it, even if it meant I had to suffer through brunch with my sister, her family, and her friends. *Oh, the joy.*

I love my sister. My mantra repeated itself in my head. I loved her, but I wasn't always keen on some of her friends. At times I felt like they put up with me only for her sake. If I mentioned something to her, she would tell me that I was being paranoid or something like that, but I didn't think so.

There were times when the disease made it harder to speak. My words get slurred and I sounded worse than a drunken sailor. One time, Ellie had a group of friends over, and at her urging, I joined the party. Going to the bathroom that night, I rounded the corner, and I heard a couple of them pretending to slur. It stopped as soon as they saw me. The way they mocked me and my situation felt like an ice bath. My eyes began to burn, but I refused to cry in front of them. How many of their whispered words were about me? How could my sister be completely blind to it?

I knew I had self-esteem issues, and I didn't trust people like I used to, but in all honesty, I'd been burned more than once and lost friends for no other reason than I was sick. When I couldn't do everything I once did with them, they abandoned me, and I never heard from them again. A couple reached out after the dissolution of our friendship, however, behind my back, they teased me and joked about my situation to others. They made fun of the fact I…let's just say, I had changed. I used to play tennis, go for long walks, could drink any of them under the table, partied, and had fun in life. myasthenia gravis robbed me of it all.

Hearing their taunting words, finding out from others—people who were still my real friends—how they mocked me or claimed I was faking, felt like someone stabbed me and left me for dead. It made me leery of new people. Maybe the wall between me and my sister's friends was more me than them. I didn't know, but the wall that I had erected around me, protected me. Or so I thought. It might keep people at bay, however, it didn't stop the hurt feelings.

I stayed in the shower until the water started to turn cold, and when I shut off the spray, my shampoo decided to fall into the tub creating a sound equal to an explosion. It echoed throughout the bathroom, and quite possibly the whole apartment. And what happened next? I was greeted by a pounding on my bathroom door.

Ellie shouted, "Are you all right in there? Did you fall?"

"No, my shampoo fell." Really, can't people tell the difference between a bottle and a body? I would have thought it would have been obvious, but then again, I did just compare the noise to a bomb.

"Are you sure?"

The Bill Engvall *Here's Your Sign* comedy routine popped into my head, and I wanted to be snarky and say, "Nope, I hit my head when I fell and I don't remember a thing. Here's your sign." But I swallowed those words like a giant horse pill taken without water, and instead yelled, "I'm fine." My tone was harder than I intended, but I didn't care too much about offending her at the moment. She pulled me out of bed after a night from hell, this was the best I could do.

"All right. Do you need any help?"

"I got it covered." After I got sick, it seemed as if I needed assistance doing simple things. Shopping, opening jars, and occasionally needing a ride. However, there were some things I would rather do for myself as long as I could. Bathing was one of those things. I would rather not show my naked ass to my family if possible. They saw enough when I was a baby. Thank you very much! It may take me longer, but I managed.

I should have been prepared for her to be lying in wait for me though. As soon as I stepped out of the bathroom and took one small step toward my bedroom, she was there hovering over me from behind. "You want to tell me what happened last night?"

"Bad date. End of story." Unwilling to hash out the details, it was all I was willing to concede. I didn't care if she wanted to know more. I wanted to be cured, but that hadn't happened either.

"That's all I get? I thought you two would hit it off. He seemed like a nice enough guy."

My back went ramrod straight. I leaned against the wall for support and cautiously turned around. Narrowing my eyes, I studied her for a moment before I quietly asked, "Have you actually ever met him?"

"No, but Jenna said..." Her voice tapered off when she caught dark expression.

That's all I needed to hear. Jenna was actually a friend of my sister's that I met shortly after moving to Charleston. Not only did she not have good intentions, but she'd sworn this guy was one of the best she knew and wouldn't care about my disability. I'd also busted pretending to slur. Either she wanted to make fun of me some more, or she assumed that since he worked as a physical therapist, he would automatically accept someone who had to use medical devices in everyday life. I leaned toward the former over the latter. "So basically, you've only heard her side of this guy's personality?"

"Well, yeah, but he seems like a great guy."

"Seems and is are two completely different things."

Maybe it was the hard edge in my tone or my choice of words, but she started to look even warier as she asked, "What did he do?"

"Nothing. That's the problem. He did nothing."

"He had to have done something for you to act like this."

"No, he left before he could do anything else."

"Maybe some sort of emergency popped up."

My sister, the person willing to give her friends the benefit of the doubt —or in this case, a friend of a friend—defended the asshole from the previous night, but I refused to allow her to make stupid excuses for someone else. I had been wronged, and I was done with it all. "He seemed fine until he noticed me walking toward him with my cane, then he got up and started to walk out. But who knows, maybe it was my ugly mug." I tried to laugh it off, but it still stung. I felt raw and exposed.

Her mouth formed a soundless "O." She blinked once, twice, and a third time before she finally changed the subject. "How about some breakfast? My treat. Maybe after, you'll feel better."

Once again, everything was pushed back into the dark corner–or rather back into the closet–and that was the end of it. It was not that my sister wouldn't deal with it. I believed that it was more like she didn't know how to deal with it, or what to say when it got shoved in her face. I didn't blame her completely, because she at least made an effort and tried as much as she could. "Sure. Breakfast sounds good." I gave her a small smile, and once again swept everything under the rug for her benefit.

I knew she wouldn't and couldn't understand where I was or how I've changed. She went to all my doctor appointments, asked her questions, listened to everything the doctors said, and then did her own research. With all of that, she still didn't get it. Then again, my counselor always reminded me that until someone lived it, I could expect sympathy, but not empathy. She might be right, and while I would not wish this on my worst enemy, sometimes I wished people had an inkling of what I experienced.

This whole thing—my new life, the disease—was difficult to deal with, and I always pushed people away. That was on me, but sometimes I felt completely and utterly alone.

CHAPTER FIVE

EMMA

Brunch turned into an awkward affair with my family. My brother-in-law got onto the boys and told them to hold open the doors for me. My sister escorted me to my chair and treated me as if I was an invalid. And the highlight of the morning was seeing Jenna. Happy day. Not!

If the meal had only been my family, I would have been happier and more comfortable, but alas, my sister had invited Jenna, believing we could all discuss my date. I saw Jenna smirk more than once. The bitch knew. My sister wouldn't believe me, though, and thus, I had to endure the meal. I barely touched my food; my defenses were on high alert, and my stomach churned with discomfort. Watching everyone eat as I pushed my eggs around on my plate, I wished Jenna would choke on her sandwich.

When I finally got home from my forced outing, I locked my front door, played with Curley, and then climbed up on my bed with my computer. Curiosity coerced me, making me want to check my email and FaceSpace messages. Had Bryan sent a message after I shut down the night before?

Logging onto the computer, I jumped when that familiar ding rang as soon as I opened FS.

Bryan: *Hey, what happened last night?*

Either his memory had issues, or he was obtuse. I rolled my eyes and attempted to ignore him for a bit, to build anticipation, and to dish out a small punishment. I was still slightly annoyed with him.

Ding after ding could be heard. My phone had been silent during brunch because I had turned off my ringer, however, my computer would not shut up. Even muted, ignoring the messages got harder as his name flashed across the top of my screen, the number of messages increasing…

Bryan: _I know you're there_
Are you ignoring me now?
What are you up to?
_Hi._
I'm still here.
As you can tell, I'm here and not going away.
You may as well talk to me.

Groaning, I realized I had no choice.

_Me:_ _What do you want?_

Bryan: _She lives._

_Me:_ _Smartass._

Bryan: _Well I do have an ass, but it doesn't have a brain, but I've been told I'm smart…so maybe it is too. LOL._

Snorting with laughter, I surprised my dog and he jumped off the bed to curl up on the floor away from me. I wouldn't admit I laughed. That secret stayed between me and Curley.

_Me:_ _Hardy har har._

Bryan: _Does this mean I actually made you laugh?_

_Me:_ _Nope, not at all._

I lied as I continued to snicker. The smile wouldn't leave my face. His dorky answers lightened the load and pressure. Talking to him beat hanging around Jenna any day of the week.

_Me:_ _You really need to try harder if you want me to laugh._

Bryan: _Harder? Well, I am getting harder, but that may be because I'm playing._

I crinkled my nose in disgust and amusement as I giggled.

Me: *Not what I was talking about.*

Bryan: *Masturbation is healthy.*

Me: *Don't need to know.*

Bryan: *Do you ever?*

Me: *Do I ever what?*

Bryan: *Hell. What are we talking about here? Masturbate. Do you masturbate?*

Me: *Not having this convo with you.*

Bryan: *Seriously? Maybe you just need to loosen up and get laid. ;)*

Me: *Not funny! Grrr.*

Now, I was starting to get pissed off again. I could feel my anger and embarrassment growing, and that made for one volatile woman. His conversation, the way he laughed about everything the night before, came rushing back along with all of the emotions. Really, my reaction had more to do with my humiliation than it did him, but I could not bring myself to admit it.

He took a second to respond.

Bryan: *Sorry. I didn't mean to offend. I really didn't.*

Sure he hadn't. I believed him about as much as I believed that my college boyfriend wasn't screwing the clarinet player who sat in front of me in band–and I had walked in on them during the act. Okay, maybe I was overreacting. Probably due to some deep seated issue with men lying and previous experiences, but I refused to psychoanalyze myself.

When he received no immediate reply, he pinged me again.

Bryan: *Look, I really didn't mean to make you mad last night or today. I'm a guy and we can be dicks sometimes. Not gonna lie.*

Me: *You don't say.*

Bryan: *LOL. I do say.*

Part of me felt myself pulling toward him, accepting his candor and words. And yet, the other part still held onto my fear like a protective armor, shielding me from life itself. Did I dare? What could it hurt? I mean, he was in San Diego, in the Navy, and nothing more than a mere acquaintance. It would never build into something more. If anything, Bryan could be the perfect outlet for me to vent to.

Bryan: *Accept my apology?*

Me: *Fine. Whatever.*

I might have been willing to forgive him, but I never said I would make it easy for him.

Bryan: *Wow. So gracious. Thanks.*

I could sense the sarcasm drowning his reply, and decided to play along.

Me: *Yes, I am. As gracious as a princess.*

Bryan: *At least you didn't turn yourself into a queen.*

Me: *Hey, I could've said empress.*

Bryan: *LOL. Yes, you could have.*

Me: *:D hehe*

Bryan: *So your imperial highness, what have you been up to today?*

His latest response surprised me. Were we not going to even broach what happened last night? Was he not going to bring up the touchy subject again? Wait. Why did I want him to?

Me: *Not much. I went to brunch with sis and a few others and now back home.*

Bryan: *How's she doing?*

Me: *Same shit different day. She jerked me out of bed and made me leave the house.*

Bryan: *Might have been good for you.*

Me: *Ha! She does what she wants half the time. LOL.*

Bryan: *LMAO. She does, which is probably why she and Mel get along so well.*

Me: *Don't remind me. I can't believe I introduced them and they hit it off. BTW, how do you know how she is?*

Bryan: *Happens. And Mel tells me stories about her conversations with Ellie and you.*

Me: *Oh.*

Bryan: *Yeah, I've heard that once your sis decides, there is no changing her mind.*

Me: *That's her in a nutshell.*

Bryan: *Mel is the same way. Trust me.*

Me: *True dat.*

Silence descended on his end as the minutes passed, and I worried that I had inadvertently annoyed him or said something wrong. My mind raced with what I could have done to offend. Get a grip! If I continued to think about it, allowed my mind to race down every rabbit hole imaginable–and some that were not–my anxiety would spiral out of control. When it came to the opposite sex, I possessed zero confidence unless I had known the man for years.

To me, Bryan could be nothing more than someone on the other end of the computer. A pen pal, so to speak. Nothing more, and nothing less.

Behind me, my antique alarm clock ticked away the seconds, increasing my annoyance. Since my disability, I periodically underwent moments when I could not control my emotions or anxiety. I felt it bubbling up in my gut, that coil tightening, creating that anxious feeling.

I scrolled through our conversation on the screen, re-reading everything since he popped on this morning, and I saw nothing that should have offended him. Unless he didn't appreciate slang, but I suspected that to be false, since he'd used slang more than once the night I met him.

Tick tock. Unable to stand the radio silence further, I typed my message.

Me: *Hello?*

Bryan: *Just a sec.*

Me: *K.*

If he had something he needed to do, he should have told me he would talk to me later instead of making me wait. Glancing at the clock to see how much time had passed, I rolled my eyes at my own behavior. What had felt like 15 minutes or more to me, had only been five. Once again I had to remind myself, get a grip, Emma!

Instead of waiting for him with bated breath to respond to me, I decided to move on, or act like it didn't matter to me whether he messaged me or not again. He was a crush and that was all he would ever be. And besides, my current goal consisted of trying not to think of him as a guy. A pen pal. Bryan was nothing more than a pen pal. And the sooner I stopped fixating on him, the better. We could be friends, we could talk; however, I wanted someone who would stick by me through thick and thin. Someone who would actually be there for me. Bryan's confirmed bachelor status, excluded him from consideration. According to Mel, he loved the Navy and playing the field. Not exactly an ideal pick for a long-term partner.

Grabbing a glass of iced tea from the kitchen, I settled back onto my bed and picked up my book from my bedside table. My book boyfriend would help to cleanse my mind of all thoughts centering on Bryan.

I immersed myself in a fictional world and my book transported me to a completely different century. I read about time-traveling highlanders who found the loves of their lives in a different century, battled evil, and tried to make the world a better place. They wanted the past to impact the future. And while they did all of that, they still protected the women they had come to love and depend on. A dreamy sigh escaped my lips. Sometimes I hoped, wished, and prayed something like that would happen to me. But until then, I continued to wait for the man who would sweep me off my feet.

My grandmother used to tell me I possessed an old soul. Maybe I did. I always believed the guy should ask the girl—it was how my family raised me–I preferred many things from days gone by, compared to some of the crap out there today. I despised the stupid head games males and females thought they needed to play with each other—I didn't understand them—and I believed kids should play outside more than they played video games.

As a child, I drank out of a garden hose, only played video games occasionally—usually when the weather turned bad—and I learned to use my imagination. Before I could watch television, I had to read for thirty minutes, but that rule never bothered me because I had always loved books. They took me away to faraway places, and let me pretend to be someone else for a short period of time–not that I needed to run away from a bad childhood. Quite the contrary.

I grew up moving from naval base to naval base every one to three years and forced myself to transform from an introvert to an extrovert. Books broke up the stress and allowed me to relax. Plus, I loved imagining how everything played out in my head. There were times reading entertained me more than watching whatever my parents wanted to watch. I was a bookworm of the highest order.

Even as an adult, I loved to read. I could've probably sat there for the rest of the day lost in the world of words until I was interrupted by a certain four-legged creature. I glared at Curley, whose bark distracted me as he stood on his hind legs staring out the low sitting window. After he calmed down, I tried to return to my book, however, someone messaged me on FaceSpace distracting me further, and hearing the ding, Curley decided play time had arrived.

My pooch wanted attention, and he expected to get what he wanted. Taking the toy he brought to me, I threw it so that he would fetch it. This was his favorite game. It always made me giggle when he would hightail it and chased after the toy. There had been a time or two when he wiped out taking a corner too sharply, and this time, he slid across the hardwood floors in the hallway. I didn't know who enjoyed fetch more, him because he got to play, or me because he looked like a clown chasing his toy.

Briefly, my eyes flittered to my computer. While talking to Bryan earlier, I had turned the alerts on my phone back on, which was how I knew someone had messaged me. Did I dare look? Or did I keep whomever it was hanging on for a little longer?

After throwing the toy again, I gave into the urge and unlocked my phone to see Bryan's face appearing in a bubble circle. FS mobile messenger showed their profile picture and names whenever someone messaged, and there, I found his mug smiling back at me. He was finally talking to me again. Now, I could have played hard to get and gone through all of those mind games guys and girls seemed to enjoy playing with each other, but I had already done that the night before and it had ended badly. Plus, my intent was not to attract this particular guy. He might have been a crush, but that is where I drew the line.

Tapping on his circle, I read his message.

Bryan: Sorry about that. We had an issue.

Issue? That sounded serious. My curiosity was piqued.

Me: Everything okay?

Bryan: Yeah, for now.

Me: What happened?

My fingers sped over the keys as they typed out my inquiry when he didn't disclose anything further. Inquiring minds wanted to know.

Me: And what do you mean, 'for now'?

Bryan: Nothing. Really.

Me: Tell me. You want me to spill all my deepest, darkest secrets, so spill some of your own.

There! If that didn't hook him in, I would drop the subject, but it meant my curiosity wouldn't be fed. Besides, quid pro quo.

Bryan: Girl trouble. That's all.

Me: Girl trouble...that's all? Seriously?

I laughed long and heartily, but I chose not to put the LOL in my response. I possessed manners after all and made the conscious decision not to be rude.

Bryan: Do me a favor.

Me: What?

Bryan: Promise me something.

Me: What?

Bryan: Just promise me.

Me: Not promising until I know what it is I'm promising.

Bryan: Don't become the crazy girl.

Me: Bwahahahaha! The crazy girl. Umm. Okay. I think I can manage that.

Bryan: I'm serious here.

Me: I have to know, what the hell happened there? LOL!
And yes, I'm still laughing.

Bryan: U R annoying.

Me: You just told me not to become the crazy girl and I'm annoying?

Bryan: Point taken.

That was all he said, and when he didn't expand, I pestered him for more of an answer.

Me: Well? What happened?

Bryan: Sigh.

Me: That isn't an explanation.

Bryan: My roommate brought his latest gf to the house because he forgot something here.

Me: Okay. And...?

Bryan: She and I hooked up in the past.
All of the sudden she started yelling and then hit me.
Fucking split personality women. She turned batshit crazy.
Don't be her. It took both of us to get her the fuck out of here.
Fuck, now I want a drink! Do. Not. Become. Her.

Me: Haha. I promise not to be her. LOL. ;)
Too bad you aren't here. I'd say let's go down to the bar and grab a beer.

Bryan: Good! And I wish I were there right now.

I cringed realizing what I had done. I really was just one of the guys, wasn't I? No wonder my Prince Charming hadn't shown up yet. Then again,

35

with my disability, he would have to push me as I sat on my walker, instead of riding off on the white horse and all that shit from the fairy tales.

While I contemplated the whole idea of how to get me on a large steed, my phone pinged again.

Bryan: *So are you going to tell me how many guys you've dated.*

There it glared at me in black and white again. Sighing, I finally gave in and typed my response.

Me: *Including the guys after I got sick?*

Bryan: *No, only b4.*

Me: *6*

Bryan: *Total?*

Me: *Yes.*

Bryan: *And your longest was a month?*

Me: *Yes.*

Bryan: *Are you sure your problem isn't that you need to get laid?*

Me: *I hate you!*

Throwing down my phone in exasperation, I grabbed the toy my dog was licking and threw it across the room. It did nothing to relieve some of the tension and anger I felt, but Curley loved it because he chased it like a mad dog.

Bryan seemed to possess the uncanny ability to say the wrong thing and piss me off. I wanted to slap him, however, since he lived across the country, slapping him was impossible. I pictured slapping him, scratching his face with my nails, and punching him in the stomach. I would probably never do any of that, but it made me feel better. I decided that Bryan was an utter asshole of the first degree.

CHAPTER SIX

EMMA

Ding. *Ding. Ding. Ding.*
   I lost count of how many times my phone made that annoying sound. Granted some could've been my friends, the ones I actually called friends—I had a few—however, I knew beyond a shadow of a doubt, the majority were from Bryan. I'd successfully ignored him for over an hour, but those dings began grating on my last nerve thirty minutes ago. And I was adult enough to admit I'd acted more like a five–year–old child throwing a temper tantrum than a woman of twenty-nine whenever he teased me the way he had.

I realized he was jesting because between meeting him once, my discussions with Mel, and my recent conversations with him, I got the impression that was who he was. A single sailor who hadn't a care in the world. In the one night I had spent in his company nearly a year ago, I discovered he had a wicked sense of humor, could out cuss almost anyone, and even when drunk, he won arm wrestling matches. I envisioned the muscles in his arms bulging, his veins throbbing...And I'd gone off track again.

Giving in like I'd known I would, I pulled my computer onto my lap and logged on. Yep, I had been right. Two of my other friends were checking in, but the others appeared under Bryan's name.

I decided to ignore him for now and instead, clicked on Ali's name first. Seeing her message made me smile. I missed all my friends in Texas, but she was special because she had gotten sick about the same time as me, except she had other issues.

Ali: *Hey. Checking in. My new treatment was approved and I start next week.*

Me: *That's awesome! Happy they finally approved you.*

Ali: *How everything going?*

Me: *Bleh. My love life sucks.*

Ali: *LOL. Mine too.*

We continued to laugh and joke a little more, but all too soon she had to go. Moving onto Sammy, I still temporarily pretended Bryan didn't exist. Too bad by the time I answered her, she'd logged off. We had been friends since elementary school and had gotten back in touch thanks to FaceSpace. Now, we talked regularly, making sure we kept in touch.

Bryan could not be ignored any longer. Clicking on his name, I read his messages and shook my head. The moment I opened his chat window, the corners of my mouth pulled up; something so simple had such an impact on me. This was not good.

> **Bryan:** *You know you don't hate me. You love me. LOL.*
> *Well, maybe you dislike me, but prob not. Ha!*
> *Hello?*
> *Where are you?*
> *Come on. You can't be mad at me.*
> *Hey.*
> *Don't make me call Mel.*
> *Okay. Maybe I crossed the line a little, but come on already.*
> *Stop running from the truth.*
> *I promise I can handle the truth.*
> *I thought you wanted my help.*
> *Don't you want advice from the Love Doctor? ;) :P*

His messages cracked me up. Reading what he wrote had me snorting with laughing in a very unladylike way and not caring one iota. Who would have heard me anyway? My dog wouldn't tell on me. He loved me.

With a grin on my face, I continued to giggle as I attempted to respond to him.

> **Me:** *Love Doctor? Since when did you earn that particular degree?*

Bryan: *See, I knew you couldn't stay away. LOL. As for my degree, I have millions of satisfied customers.*

Me: *Millions? A little full of yourself, aren't you?*
Or are you counting each individual sperm? LMAO.

Bryan: *Oh you got jokes.*

Me: *Sure do!*

Bryan: *I haven't heard any complaints from the couples I've helped in the past or from my little swimmers...or the girls I've more than pleasured.*

Me: *Haha! Still full of yourself...or is that full of shit?*

Bryan: *Maybe one day I'll let you take stock for yourself. ROFL.*

A simple joke, a mere jest between two people, and yet, my breath started coming in fast and shallow as my heart rate accelerated. Pressing my legs together, I tried to relieve some of the ache that appeared at the apex of my thighs as I read his words. Damn, this crush was going to be the death of me. I needed to get over my feelings for him and find someone new, and as soon as I managed that, all would be right with the world again. The best way for that to happen would be to take him up on his previous offer. Allowing my "friends" to set me up hadn't worked. Using an online dating service hadn't worked. Maybe if his ideas worked, they could push me through my slump.

Inhaling deeply, I exhaled slowly as I thought about what to type. And then, it came to me.

Me: *You couldn't handle all this. I'm just too good for you.*
Bryan: *Maybe you are.*

I couldn't even begin to tell anyone what those three words did to me. I knew they did not carry the meaning I wished they did, but even so, they made me melt.

Me: *So what sage advice are you going to give me, oh wise one?*
Bryan: *Still with the jokes. But I got you. Should I call you?*

What? No, he couldn't call me. Calling destroyed one of my lines of defense, and if I was going to spill everything to him, I wanted everything to remain as anonymous as possible. A phone or video call became too personal for me.

Me: No, this is fine. I'm slurring a lot today, so it is easier to type.

Bryan: Got it. First things first, we need to work on your self-esteem. Who the fuck cares if you have to use a walker or a cane or that you're sick. Add slurring to the list. It doesn't matter.

Me: Plenty of people. You want a list?

Bryan: They don't matter anymore.

Me: Easy for you to say.

Bryan: Did you have this issue before you got sick?

Me: Not especially.

Bryan: Which is a big fat YES!

Me: Ouch.

Bryan: Truth hurts, don't it.

Me: Don't be a dick.

Bryan: I have a dick, but I don't think I am one. No wants a dick that big. They couldn't use it. Where would be the fun in a 6'1" dick? There isn't... unless we find a giant. If you find a giant, let me know.

Again I laughed. He seemed to be learning when I needed a break and when he could push...maybe. It wouldn't surprise me if he continued to piss me off time and time again in the near future, as well as the distant future. Thinking about it, about the arguments and disagreements we were bound to have, gave me a small thrill. I could not explain it, but it clung to me like a small child holding onto his mother's shirt. Presently, however, it lingered somewhere in the background.

Me: K. If I find a giant, you'll be the first person I tell. If I do, does that mean you will admit you are a 6'+ dick? LOL.

I kept thinking about what it would be like to have this conversation with him in real life. Hearing his voice, seeing his facial expressions, and watching his reactions would have been priceless. Then again, it would wreak havoc on my crush and then my sister would find little bits of me everywhere because I exploded. I had this feeling he was going to become a great friend, which would have been fun if we were closer. On the other hand, I didn't think I could open up in person.

Bryan: If you manage to find a giant, then maybe. Have any beans lying around? A beanstalk may be the only way to find one. :P

Me: Funny.

Bryan: Always.

Me: So back to our discussion earlier, what is this oh so sage wisdom you want to impart?

Bryan: I already told you. You need to work on your self-esteem. The people who tore you down don't matter any longer.

Me: Got it. Anything else?

Bryan: I know it isn't that easy to accept or do, and I'm not expecting you to change overnight...

Me: But?

Bryan: But I know you can do it.
You deserve a good guy who will treat you well and will embrace everything you have to offer–including your illness, disease, handicap, disability, or whatever hell else you want to call it.

Me: Thanks.

Bryan: I'm not done.

Me: Do go on.

Sarcastic? Yes. Interested to see what he would say next? Most definitely. My walls went up, and I peered through a small crack in the mortar.

Bryan: _You apparently had an issue with your self-esteem before you got sick, and after you got sick, it took a huge hit and suffered._

_Me:_ _Maybe._

Bryan: _So, stop._

_Me:_ _Stop?_

Bryan: _Yes! You deserve to treat yourself better._
Until you make some strides in that department, you will not catch a guy, but sometimes catching someone's eye will go a long way in building your confidence.

_Me:_ _You sound like a shrink or Dr. Phil._

To myself, I mumbled, "Been watching some daytime drama and talk shows have we?"

Bryan: _LOL. Maybe I am. Dr. Bryan, or Dr. Sampson, the Love Doctor at your service. Haha._

_Me:_ _LMAO. So confident in your abilities. I bet if I went back in time, I could find a couple of unsatisfied customers. Women you might have left hanging because you completed your mission early. ;)_

Bryan: _Ouch._

_Me:_ _Truth hurts._

My words were meant to taunt him, turning his own phrase back on him.

Bryan: _You got me right in the heart._

_Me:_ _Want me to quote Bon Jovi? 'Shot through the heart and you're to blame...'_

Bryan: _'You give love a bad name.' Well, not you...maybe you do though. LOL. JK._
Good song though.

I chose to ignore his jibe and only respond to his last comment. If I focused on his other remark, I was liable to get upset all over again, and for the moment, we were having fun.

Me: It is.

Bryan: So I know you like Bon Jovi or I assume you at least like that song, what other music do you like?

Me: I feel like I'm filling out a questionnaire for a dating game show or to setup an online profile.

Bryan: A Love Doctor needs to comprehend his clients' quirks and behaviors so that he may make the perfect love match.

Me: LOL.

Bryan: It's true.

Me: Save the BS for some other unsuspecting creature. Haha.

Bryan: Okay. Okay.
But seriously, we need to get down to the nitty gritty and help you get past your insecurities.
So...what music do you like?

Me: And this is going to get me over my issues?

I barked with laughter, and Curley peered at me as if I were crazy before he dropped his head back down on the bed, returning to his nap.

Bryan: Couldn't hurt to practice talking to a guy.

Me: That's not where I have an issue. Much anyway.
I have guy friends and I talk to them perfectly fine. I just group you in with them.
It's guys I'm attracted to or the ones I think are cute or the ones that are here in person that I have an issue carrying on a conversation with.
I'm not very good at flirting, and I'm kind of old school.

Bryan: Old school? What the fuck does that mean?
No offense intended.

Me: LOL. None taken. It means that I think the guy should ask the girl. It means that I want to be courted and I want the guy to take charge.

Bryan: I get that, and honestly, I don't understand why girls want to be all alpha in the relationship. Huge turnoff for me.
I'm not saying I want them to be lie down and take whatever I dish, but yeah. I get you.

His response shocked me. I was completely dumbfounded and only managed a one-word answer.

Me: Huh.

Bryan: What?

Me: Nothing.

Bryan: No, you have to tell me. What?

Me: It's just that I figured you being in the Navy and all, you have girls throwing themselves at you all the time.
Or are you going to tell me that doesn't happen? Or do you ignore them and say, sorry, not interested?

Bryan: I wouldn't say I ignore them per se.

Me: Exactly.

Bryan: But those girls never seem to last, either that or their bravado was only good for the initial approach. LOL.

Me: Takes a lot of courage to approach a hot guy like you.

Bryan: You think I'm hot?

Me: Nope. Not at all. I would hate for your head to get any bigger and explode.

Bryan: Well, depending on the head, it does 'explode' quite often, but something tells me that's not what you were talking about. ;)

I found myself rolling my eyes again. Such a pervert. But I really didn't have a problem with this side of him. If anything, I had to stop myself from attempting to picture that visual image.

_Me:_ _Not exactly._

Bryan: _ROFLMAO._

_Me:_ _A visual I didn't need._

Bryan: _But you enjoyed it._

_Me:_ _Not really._

Maybe I did, but only maybe. Maybe a lot.

Bryan: _Admit it._

_Me:_ _Not gonna happen._

Had he lost his mind? That was a secret I would take to my grave.

Bryan: _LOL._

A lull filled the space between us, but after a minute or two, he filled the void.

Bryan: _So what happened to you before? You said last night that you had other things to worry about other than dating. What happened?_

_Me:_ _Life._

Bryan: _That tells me shit._

_Me:_ _And that's all you're getting for now._
Sorry, but I don't know you from Adam, and I'm not going to share my life story with anyone today.

Bryan: _Tomorrow?_

_Me:_ _Nope._

Bryan: _Day after?_

I chuckled. I had laughed more during this conversation than I had in the past month. What did that say about me and my personal life? Yikes.

Me: Maybe one day. ;) That's all I'll promise for now.

Bryan: That isn't a no.

Me: What about you?

Bryan: Me?

Me: Tell me about you. Who is Bryan Sampson?

Why had I asked him to do that? I slapped at my head in stupidity...or perhaps it had more to do with desperation. Maybe both.

Bryan: Quid pro quo. All right? You tell me something and I'll tell you something.

Me: LOL. Deal, but not now. Tomorrow. My dog is bugging me to take him outside and I just got a text from my sister. Apparently, I'm supposed to go to a BBQ at her house. I already spent the morning with her, but I guess my sisterly duties are not done.

I lied about it all. The walls felt as if they were closing in on me, and I ran away. I had to get offline and decompress, or whatever the hell someone found themselves neck deep and facing shit she never thought she would have to face.

Bryan: I'd make you shake on it if I could, but know this, I will pester you about it tomorrow.

Me: I'm sure you will. TTYL.

Bryan: Later.

Was it bad that the promise of tomorrow gave me butterflies?

CHAPTER SEVEN

BRYAN

As I shut down my computer, I thought about Emma and everything I had learned about her recently. It boggled my mind that she remained single all these years. She gave as good as she got. She didn't believe in playing games. And she could joke with the best of them. Yeah, I said she would make a great buddy to hang out with, and I meant that, but there was so much more to her. A girl that drank beer, liked to watch sports, and appeared smart and witty…she was better than one of the guys.

I wondered if this was what Mel meant when she remarked gay guys made the best type of friend because they represented the best of both worlds. Possible.

Something told me whomever Emma ended up with in the future, she would end up busting his balls if he stepped one foot out of line. I couldn't wait to see it.

Emma was such a strong woman who had been dealt a bad hand. Life had thrown her some curveballs, but somehow, someway, she remained standing. Yes, she had issues to work through, who didn't, but she had proven that she was a survivor. I had only talked to her a handful of times and I already witnessed that.

In my naval career, I had seen and experienced things that would make many quiver. Not everyone could go to war, fight the enemy, or deal with everything we had to deal with as pilots. I understood that. Sometimes I even wondered why I remained in, and then after talking to Emma, I had this urge to do more. I didn't know why either. Her disease and my career were two different things.

Maybe I just wanted to be a better man. How many times had I strung a girl along because we were having fun? How many times had I played games or made the girl do all the work?

I had a plethora of woman at my beck and call. As a single man, who surpassed most men in the looks department, it came with the territory. I didn't do relationships any longer, and yet, after each conversation with Emma, I thought about what it might be like if I shirked off my confirmed bachelor robe and found someone to spend my life with. At the ripe age of 30, my family believed I should start thinking about marriage, however, I knew I wasn't ready to settle down yet. Maybe in another five or ten years.

Fuck me! Emma had me twisted and thinking about things I never thought or wanted to think about. No one had ever made me question my life. I flew planes, had fun, and lived life to the fullest. That was all I needed in life. I needed to remain focused on her, and not on myself or my flaws.

I saw her as a work in progress. If the price of getting her to open up and trust me consisted of sharing a small part of my past—select parts, safe parts —I would do that. It might be fun to learn more about her.

I had my own demons that had been buried years ago. Those would remain buried. This was about her, not me. All her.

CHAPTER EIGHT

EMMA

B lame it on the beer, the barbecue, or the fact my sister Ellie decided to have an 80's movie night, which featured the film *Risky Business*, at her house, but my dreams that night could only be counted as completely loony. I had only been talking to Bryan for about a week, and yet, I blamed my sister for waking up in the middle of the night wondering what the hell I ate that caused the most ridiculous oddball dream no one could ever imagine.

Running a hand through my hair, I asked my dark room, "What the fuck was that?"

This wasn't one of those dreams you thought was weird and yet you really can't remember it to save your life. No, I remembered this dream with full clarity. It had to be my sister's fault.

For the entirety of the dream, I stood there watching as everything happened, only a spectator to this new world. It made me think of A Christmas Carol when the ghosts would take Ebenezer Scrooge to watch something and they were there, but not really part of the scene, only able to observe as everything played out before him.

My dream placed me in the exact same predicament. Appearing in the living room of a strange house, the first thing I noticed was that it seemed eerily quiet. That was until I heard music begin to scream through the speakers right behind me causing me to jump. Furnished nicely, but not too over the top, it reminded me more of a staged prop house that realtors used to sell another house in a cookie cutter subdivision.

I moved behind one of the couches away from the blaring music and something told me to watch the hallway. Instinctively, I knew the hallway just beyond the living room led to stairs on one side and the front door on the other.

Anticipation built as I waited for someone to appear, or for something to happen. And as soon as the lyrics of the song began, Bryan skidded across the floor and into view wearing nothing except socks and Batman Underoos (both the t-shirt and underwear.) Did they even make those in adult sizes? It didn't matter. My eyes remained glued to him as he slid on a pair of sunglasses and started to sing into a wire whisk. His hips swung back and forth as he spun around and shook his ass in front of me. I wanted to reach out and grab it, and then hold on for dear life. Surely the ride would be worth it.

He spanked his own ass and a moan caught in my throat making my voice sound strangled. Why did my subconscious insist on torturing me?

The performance lasted for three songs. I tried multiple times to move toward him, but my feet refused to move. They remained where they stood as if they were glued in place. And after the third song, his gaze landed on me, he licked his lips, pointed, and then turned his palm over and cocked his finger, bidding me to his side. Damn, I wanted him!

Instead of fulfilling his demand and walking forward, I woke up in my bed breathing heavily as if I had run a marathon with my dog licking my arm. No music played, and Bryan no longer danced in front of me.

Flopping back onto my pillow, I stared up at my ceiling and Curley stretched out beside me. I willed my eyes to close so I could return to my dream world. Eventually, they began to feel heavy, drooping lower and lower until I slipped into slumber. However, when I awoke the next morning, I had not received a repeat performance. That sucked.

But what dawned on me as I got out of bed and grabbed a cup of coffee, was that I was going to have to talk to the subject of my fantastical dream at some point that day. Maybe it was a good thing we were only chatting online. I didn't want to imagine how I would react to him, or better yet, how my body would react to his nearness. Although it had only been a dream, when I woke up my body was flushed, my breathing erratic, and I oozed wetness from my lower half. My body wanted him.

With zero doctor's appointments and nothing to occupy my thoughts for the day, I predicted I would remain on edge all day.

Unfortunately, my disability would not allow me to work any longer, and I had to fill my day doing other things. I would write or read when my eyes allowed it, but even that was never an all-day affair because they got tired rather quickly and I wound up with extreme doubled and blurred vision. Audiobooks, television, naps due to constant exhaustion, and playing with Curley occupied much of my normal day.

Therefore, with zero doctor appointments, and nothing concrete to do with my day, the dream I had of Bryan in all of his Batman glory was replayed throughout the day. God help me.

CHAPTER NINE

EMMA

Thankfully, I didn't get the chance to talk to him the day after my crazy dream. His services were needed elsewhere, and I tried not to think of what that meant exactly. It could have been anything from Uncle Sam demanding his attention, his roommate finding another psycho girl to hook up with, or maybe he had his own itch to scratch. Those options were my top contenders, and I leaned toward the latter.

Bryan was a military man who I thought was sexy as hell with his dimpled smile and tats covering one arm. I remembered he said he had more, and I also remembered thinking I wouldn't mind exploring his body. Yeah, I went there. So if he appealed to me to that extent, I knew how much he probably appealed to other girls. I mean the night we went to karaoke, no less than six women tried to hit on him. Mel finally wrapped her arms around his shoulders, lifted a leg to hook around his hips, and pumped her own pelvis back and forth a few times dry humping him. To put a cherry on top of her newly staked claim, she kissed his cheek. Or was it a sort of claim?

In actuality, it couldn't have been a real claim on him since her fiancé, Luke Ransom, stood five feet away from her little performance laughing as girls shot Mel the jealous evil eye wishing she would drop dead right here so their claim on Bryan could be staked. If looks could kill that night, I would be down one friend, and Luke would be without a fiancée.

Bryan and Mel always acted like that according to Luke. The two had known each other since high school and were best friends. I did ask one time why she never dated him, which caused her to practically gag at the thought of it. Correction! She did gag and almost threw up.

Apparently, one night while at a friend's house during their college years, they had been dared to kiss each other. Not ones who typically backed down from a challenge, they gave themselves a pep talk to try and bolster their courage and did what they had to do to succeed. The first clue that this story would end badly, they had to use liquor to go through with it. And the second clue, they got wasted. One shot hadn't cut it. They both had multiple shots of tequila. When they both felt ready, they turned to each other, leaned in for the kiss, and Mel yacked on Bryan. After she threw up on him, he threw up on her, and back a forth a couple of times. Gross.

That night changed things between them. Before, she only considered him a friend, nothing more. After that night, the mere mention or passing thought of kissing Bryan caused her gag reflex to start working overtime. She could kiss his cheek, hug him, and other friendly gestures because they were safe. But kissing him on the mouth...NO GO!

Plus, I didn't think her fiancé would have appreciated it if she had tried to go further with Bryan. Luke accepted their friendship and had known them both since college. Rumor even had it that he witnessed the whole drunken vomit induced night. It never seemed to bother him when they goofed around, or when Mel pretended to dry hump her best friend to chase away the ladies. I gave him props for that because a lesser man would have taken up residence in the middle of Jealous City.

Luke Ransom was a good ol' country boy from Tennessee, and the moment Mel laid eyes on him during her freshman year of college, she decided he belonged to her; however, he refused to go down without a fight. At six feet, he put up one hell of a fight at that. Whenever they were around each other, he pretended to ignore her, always spoke to her as if she were a stranger, and he hardly ever gave her the time of day. If she managed to corner him, he would turn around and leave as quickly as possible.

It sounded harsh, but a couple of his friends had warned him that she liked to play games and loved it when a man played hard to get. And Luke stupidly trusted them. In addition, at the time he was never sure of the exact nature of her relationship with Bryan. Hell, I hadn't known them as long as Luke had, and one night of karaoke even made me question if lingering feelings existed between Mel and Bryan.

The two men were similar in some ways, and yet, very different. Both had brown hair and muscular statures, although Bryan's hair was a couple shades darker...dreamier. Bryan was a little taller, a little tanner, and had a deeper voice than Luke. Where Luke had brown eyes, Bryan had hazel. Okay, other than the brown hair and muscle mass, they were nothing alike unless you counted how much they both cared about Mel. And I included it because according to my granny, a lot could be learned from how a man treated his friends and family.

It had been one of the first things I noticed about Bryan—more like the third or fourth—and I found myself jealous of her and the attention he gave her. Standing next to her, supporting her, stood Luke. A great guy by any standard, and so country I came across as a city girl next to him. After my dad retired and we moved to Texas, I turned slightly country in my attire, attitude, and accent. But Luke had me beat. And then Bryan appeared and suddenly, Mel glued herself to her best friend's side and Luke let it go.

When I asked Luke about it, he chuckled. That chuckle grew. Throwing back his head, he laughed deep from his belly and it was loud. At the time I wondered if he had been driven mad, and placed my hand on his shoulder as a gesture of condolence. He then surprised me when he said, "The moment they start acting normal or weird around each other, that's when I know I have problems." My expression must have told him how confused I felt because he explained, "Trust me. They are more like siblings than anything else. They can't even kiss each other. The day they get over that, then I'll worry."

Scrunching my nose, I shook my head and giggled. "Okay then." I really didn't understand it at the time, but as I continued to watch them throughout the night, I realized that Luke had been right. Bryan and Mel were just Bryan and Mel. They acted and behaved as siblings more than friends...dry humping aside.

I couldn't say for sure when I became friends with Mel. When I could work before I got sick, we always exchanged emails and talked over the phone. After I got sick and had to stop working, she kept in touch and I counted her as one of my true friends. Before I moved to South Carolina, I had never met her in person, however, unlike some friends I had around me for years, she hadn't disappeared when my body decided to turn against me. The day I arrived in Charleston, she had been there to greet me with open arms and a gaggle of people to help us unload the truck. Moving to a strange state where I thought I would have no one except my sister, I was beyond grateful to have another person I could call a friend.

In Dallas, I had several friends. Ones that stood by me and supported me after my life took a one-eighty, and others, who abandoned me and our friendship after I got sick. After good friends shunned me, I feared meeting new people, of seeing the judgment in their eyes. Moving reinforced my defensive measures and my walls were always up. Some of the people I met after I relocated befriended me for no other reason than they were friends with Ellie, while others appeared genuinely interested in getting to know me. In the beginning, I found it difficult to differentiate and it took a long time before I started to lower my walls for anyone.

My other issue was future plans. Some people understood or tried to understand my day to day lifestyle, and some did not. Many did not like the fact I had to cancel on them last minute. Day to day meant day to day. Every day my life was different. Some days, I could walk with only a cane, play with Curley, and do many things I wanted to do for myself. Other days I remained in bed because I could barely walk and sat around like a bump on a log. Turned out that when certain people received a last minute cancellation, they chose to never invite me over for anything again. Parties, game nights, dinners, etc. Nothing. Others accepted it a little more readily and tried to be accommodating, but even their patience could be tested.

I believed most people generally tried to understand me and my condition; and yet, they couldn't really grasp or comprehend it. However, no one really understood how I felt, what I dealt with. Unless someone experienced something similar or the same thing, it was impossible. Maybe that sounded callous of me, but based on my experience, it was what I knew to be true.

The voice of a certain person popped into my head, and I snickered. I imagined Bryan saying, "Blow it off. Their opinions don't matter." Maybe they didn't. That man got me thinking about things I hadn't thought about in years, and I didn't know if that was a good thing or a bad thing.

In high school, I worked hard to make good grades and excel in my academics. I needed scholarships in order to go to college. My family couldn't afford to send me, and I didn't want to be my sister. Ellie joined the Navy like many of our family before her, but that was not the life I wanted. The desire to join the military never called out to me.

It wasn't only the Navy in which I didn't want to follow my sister's footsteps.

Ellie had always been the pretty one with long legs and a small figure. She took after my dad's side of the family, whereas I took after my mom's side with my heavier build. Her strawberry blonde hair hung in gentle waves below her shoulders, and guys rushed to her side every chance they got. At five-seven, I was four inches taller than her with curves to spare. Since middle school, she always had a boyfriend at her beck and call, while I dated here and there, but school took up all of my focus. She liked to have a good time, and I stayed home and studied. We were night and day.

I think the thing that pushed me over the edge, that one defining moment that made me study more than anything happened during my junior year in high school. Ellie had called home from wherever she was stationed at the time, and I informed her that I sat at number four in my class. She told me, "I don't know why you study so much. Even without college, there are guys willing to take care of you if you let them. Besides, you won't attract a guy with your brain. A guy doesn't want to date someone who's smarter than them." Those words sealed it for me. I didn't want to depend on someone else to live my life. That wasn't living. And if a guy didn't want me for me, if I had to dumb myself down for someone, then I didn't want him.

My family was never rich or well–off, but we had enough and did not struggle. I knew if college was going to be an option for my future, I better work my ass off for scholarships. And I did. I wound up with a full ride to North Texas University, one of the best schools in Texas for psychology.

Getting in was only the beginning of my work. In order to keep my scholarships, I had to maintain a certain GPA, the dorms had curfews, and I had a packed schedule. Dating? My love life became secondary to finishing my degree. Yes, I dated here and there, but nothing of any real substance. My experience with guys during college consisted of my roommate forcing me to go on a double date with her because she needed an extra person. I was her last resort. When I gave Bryan my low number, I never included those last resort dates, because I didn't consider them worth mentioning.

After I obtained my Bachelor's, I had to get my Master's. Guys were never the priority until I entered the workforce. Fresh out of college, a large company hired me to work in their marketing department and to develop new training programs for their new recruits. I loved my job. It had not been something I initially considered doing while going to school, but it fulfilled me and paid well. Dating was not an option, and I wanted to date, but I couldn't find a guy who wanted to date me. And when I would find someone, they weren't worth keeping around.

Or so I told myself. Inside, I secretly questioned myself. Was my sister right about men in general? Did they hate girls smarter than them? Ones that were more successful? Did my curves turn them off? Since high school, the men throwing themselves at me were practically non–existent. But when it came to my sister, men flocked to her when she batted her eyes.

I asked my guy friends about it one day, and they all laughed. When their riotous laughter calmed down, Bobby told me I was more like one of the guys than a girl. I was the buddy they all wanted. A buddy, one of the guys. They did not see me as a lovely girl or someone to date.

Self-esteem issues abounded before myasthenia gravis, and after I became disabled, they got worse. Now, men stared at me as if I was a leper. In their heads, I was an invalid, and not what they wanted in a future partner.

I could no longer work, my body quit cooperating with me, and I found myself alone. When I became sick at 25, I should have been living my dream life, but instead, I was worried and trying to figure out where my life was heading. It felt like this disease robbed me of my life. Now that I was 29, there were times I still felt as if my life had been spirited away, however, I had also found a new life through writing, reading, and trying to spread the word about myasthenia gravis awareness.

When people used the saying, stop and smell the roses, or said live for today because you never know what will happen tomorrow...I painfully understood exactly what they meant.

CHAPTER TEN

EMMA

It would be another two days before I would hear from Bryan again for a total of three days without any communication. At times it felt longer than that, especially when my eyes would slowly gravitate toward my phone, or when I happened to be on my computer. I always had FaceSpace messenger open because I didn't want to miss his message. Silly, really, since I couldn't miss his message given all the electronic devices I owned with FS messenger downloaded on them.

Odd that I anticipated his pings with glee when days ago I cringed knowing he waited for me to respond. Who was the person waiting for a response now? Me, and I wanted to slap myself for it. Any time my phone *dinged*, I hurriedly checked it to see whose name or face appeared, and every time Bryan's didn't pop up, I frowned and shook my head in disappointment at him and myself. And after responding to the messenger half-heartedly, I dropped my phone and chastised myself.

The only time I felt apprehensive about talking to him again was when I remembered my dream. Oh, that dream. It did not take much to recall the image of him in Batman Underoos. Sometimes the image created an ache deep within me, but more often than not, the image made me laugh. A big strong navy man with tattoos on his arm dressed in Underoos? Yeah, it was a mental image that did not want to leave once it took root. I attempted to pretend it was not there, but it was always there in the back of my mind ready to pop out at any unsuspecting moment.

Yesterday, my mouth opened of its own accord and confessed the dream to Mel. She fell to the floor laughing like a hyena. Like a fucking snorting hyena. I had never seen her become completely unhinged like this before. I stared at her in disbelief and pondered which was funnier: the Underoos or her in hysterics.

When she finally started to come down from her merry high, I grumbled, "It's funny, but I don't think it's that funny." Then again, I had stewed on the dream for a few days.

"No! No, you don't understand." She gasped for breath, and I worried that she was not getting enough oxygen because her skin began turning blue.

I hesitated but asked, "Okaaaay. Care to explain?"

Taking a deep breath, she tried to sit up but fell back onto the floor again. Her whole body shook with her mirth.

"Well?" I demanded, curious as to the reason behind her acting as if she had completely lost her senses.

She took one more calming breath before she found me with her eyes, a large smile still on her face. "Right after we graduated from high school, I needed to grab something from his house–I don't even remember what it was now. I knocked and thought I heard him say, 'Come in.' He hadn't." Her laughter built up again. "And when…when I walked…ahem…when I walked in, he was dancing to Prince's *1999*."

While it shocked me to hear this, it didn't deserve a reaction as extreme as this. "I see."

"No, that's not all." She guffawed, laughing until she could barely breathe. "He was stripping, and O.M.G…he started to strip. I didn't say anything since I wanted to see how long it would take before he noticed me there. He got down to only his socks and his Captain America underwear before I couldn't take it anymore and started laughing. He heard me and spun around and…and tried to cover up with the curtain, but when he did that, his Captain America ass peeked through the window for all the neighbors to see!" Once again she struggled to breathe from laughing so hard.

And this time, I joined her. I fell backward onto my couch barking with laughter. I was very curious what Bryan Sampson looked like stripping as a teenager. Back before the tattoos or before he joined the Navy. Mel once told me that he played football in school and has always been on the muscular side. Imagining him stripping made my mouth water.

Bad! Bad Emma! If my fascination with him continued, I feared the consequences.

After pulling herself up onto the couch, she collapsed on the couch and we both continued to laugh as we watched a movie and ate takeout. Imagining Bryan in Captain America underwear doing a striptease would forever be ingrained in my head.

I thought about it when I went to bed, and when my dog woke me up from yet another Bryan dream, but this time Captain America Underoos replaced Batman.

And when Bryan finally messaged me the next day, I blushed red and tried to picture him fully clothed instead of in only superhero underwear. I couldn't do it. Once again, chat saved me from embarrassment. I knew if we were on Skype or if he stood in front of me, he would be able to see my pink tinged face. Then again, if we were on the phone, he would probably be able to hear it in my voice.

Bryan: Hey.

His greeting popped up short and simple.

Me: Hey back. Everything okay?

I really wanted to ask him what he had been doing for the past three days, however, I remained polite.

Bryan: Yeah. Have I mentioned u r not allowed to become crazy?

Me: Bwahahaha! Did you get another stalker fan?

Bryan: Fan?

Me: Sure. They're fangirls out for your hot body.

Bryan: Ha! Not even funny. Not laughing.

Me: LOL. So what happened?

I tried not to giggle, but I couldn't help it and wound up holding my side from laughing too much.

Bryan: First, I had to pull extra duty shifts because of some bullshit, and then I come home to find that wacko waiting for me.
Then my roommate brought home a different girl and she tried to convince both of us to fuck her at the same time.
Not into the whole 3some thing. Not my thing.
So between all that shit, I've been staying off the computer.

Me: Damn.

What else was I supposed to say? I sat there blinking at my computer screen in disbelief.

Bryan: U can say that again.

Me: Damn. LOL.

Bryan: Haha. Hilarious. So what u been up to?

Me: Nothing much.

Bryan: That sounds like so much fun.

Me: Yep. My life is the stuff of legends.

Bryan: I see.

Me: :P ;)

Bryan: So r u ready to talk?

Me: About?

Bryan: What do u think?

Me: Weather? LOL.

Bryan: Funny.

Me: I thought we already covered that.

Bryan: We did. LOL. So tell me.

Me: You first.

Bryan: Me first? Okay. I have one younger sister, Rayne. She's 6 yrs younger. When she was born, I tried to sell her to my neighbors. I even made a poster and took it over to them.

Me: LMAO. No, you didn't. Really?

61

Bryan: Really. I don't really remember doing it, but my parents kept that stupid poster and have photographic evidence.
They love retelling that story every time the whole family is together. :P

Me: Your poor sister. LOL.

Bryan: Yeah, and for some reason she still loves me.

Me: I wouldn't. ;)

Bryan: Well, I'm not trying to sell u. :P

Me: Good point. So do you get along with your sister now?
Not trying to sell her anymore?

Bryan: Nah. I guess I'll keep her around for a while. LOL. She is one of my closest friends now, but when she was a baby, she cried, ate, and pooped. That's all she was good for.

Me: Damn babies and their neediness. LOL.

Bryan: LMAO. Does this mean u don't like kids?

Me: I actually love them. U?

Bryan: They ok. Not sure I want any, but u never know.

Me: True.

Bryan: So why did u say life got in the way b4.

Looked like we were going to be jumping into the deep end with both feet immediately.

Me: Because it did.

Bryan: That's not an answer.

Me: Did you ever see something and decide it wasn't for you?

Bryan: Sure. Who hasn't?

Me: *That was me in a nutshell in high school.*
Guys were more interested in my sister.
She basically told me no guy would want me.

Bryan: *WTF?*

Me: *Ok, I typed that wrong. I wanted to go to college and already knew what I wanted to major in. If I wanted college, I needed scholarships.*

Bryan: *Makes sense.*

Me: *I worked my ass off studying and guys were put on the backburner. She joined the Navy and during my junior year in high school, told me that no guy would want someone smarter than him. That I needed to stop studying, dumb myself down, and let a guy take care of me.*

Bryan: *WHAT?*

Me: *I decided I wanted more than depending on a guy.*

Bryan: *U should! WTF? And she was in the Navy, not living off a man?*

Me: *By the time she said that to me, she had met the man she was going to marry. But yeah.*

Bryan: *This is the same sister that Mel is friends with? The same one I met at karaoke?*

Me: *My one and only sibling, Ellie.*

Bryan: *That's bullshit.*

Me: *I know. It's why I worked hard to get scholarships.*
Then I had to work my ass off to keep them, and then I worked on my Master's, which meant grants and loans.
Then working my ass off to finish my graduate degree.
Had a couple of forced dates that my roommate would dump on me and the occasional boyfriend, but none of them were my priority.
That's about it.

Bryan: *Damn. Life huh?*

__Me:__ Life.

__Bryan:__ I can see why u didn't date much, but that doesn't explain ur self-esteem issues.

__Me:__ Do we have to talk about that?

__Bryan:__ Yes. U need help and I'm gonna help, but I need to know.

__Me:__ Do you have security clearance for that?

__Bryan:__ Haha. I've got ur clearance.

__Me:__ I don't know if you do. I'm not a giant and I haven't found one yet.

__Bryan:__ Rofl

__Me:__ :D hehe

__Bryan:__ I'm shaking my head at u. :P Talk to me.

__Me:__ What's there to tell? Guys never really paid much attention to me.
In high school, I was the geeky girl who always had her nose in a book.
In college, more of the same.
When I started working, I thought I would finally meet someone, but I only met losers.

It felt as if the heat in my cheeks increased. Typing might have been impersonal, but the feelings of embarrassment, trepidation, and fear lingered. I wanted to close the chat and pretend none of our conversations ever happened, but at the same time, I reasoned with myself that this would be good for me. I hoped it would.

__Bryan:__ So u didn't date much.
Just a sec. Phone dying. Switching to computer.

I waited for his return, silently praying he would be called away, and laughing at myself because that went against everything I had decided to do with my life.

__Bryan:__ Back.

Me: Welcome back.

Bryan: Back to the conversation. You didn't date much.

Me: Nope. I always thought the guy should ask the girl, and I always wind up tongue-tied around guys.

Bryan: You don't with me.

Me: You're different.

Bryan: How?

Me: You're just Mel's friend.

And that's the way it needed to stay, I thought to myself. It may not have been the only reason, but it worked sufficiently enough. My crush wanted to grow and flourish. The last thing it needed was any further prodding or encouragement. So, I reminded myself of his status and told myself he would remain safely in the friend zone. By keeping him on FS chat instead of actually talking, I remained distant enough and out of reach. Not that he wanted to reach for me.

Bryan: Ouch.

Me: No, it's just...

Bryan: I get it.

Me: I guess I never had confidence in myself. My sister could get a guy at the drop of a hat, and they would take one look at me and never quite understood how to talk to me or act around me.
Sometimes I wondered if she was right.

Bryan: She isn't. I would rather date someone who knew how to use their brain than a complete bimbo.
Shudders.

Me: Why the military?

I decided a change in subject was in order. I needed a break from my situation, from the memories threatening to break free before I found myself back in that bedroom with people laughing at me, teasing me, and my boyfriend doing nothing to stop them. No, not right now. I didn't want to deal with those memories.

Bryan: *My turn?*

Me: *Yep.*

Bryan: *Why not? I wanted to serve our country, to fight for it, and protect it.*

Me: *And why did you join the Navy?*

Bryan: *I grew up near the beach and loved the ocean. It felt like the perfect fit.*
Plus there is nothing like racing up into the air and soaring free when I pilot my jet.

Me: *I can only imagine the rush.*

Bryan: *It is. I guess I'm a bit of an adrenaline junky too.*

Me: *LOL. I can see that.*

Bryan: *What about you? What did you do for an adrenaline rush before? What about now?*

Me: *I used to skydive.*

Bryan: *Wait. Really? You?*

Me: *Yeah me.*

I understood what he meant about soaring free through the sky because I have felt that incomparable feeling whenever I used to skydive. Not many people knew about my penchant for jumping out of planes, especially my family. They would have probably thought I was crazy. However, I actually had several jumps under my belt.

I missed the feeling of the air rushing over my skin and hair, of gazing into the distance and being able to see for miles where heaven met earth. Up in the sky, there were no worries about tests, school, making the grade, or my job. It was me and the feeling of pure bliss. My heart would race, and as I fell back down to earth, my adrenaline would spike and that familiar anxious feeling would arise. I never wanted the feeling or the rush to end.

But it did.

After I got sick, I stopped jumping completely and hadn't been up since. I longed for that experience again, to feel the air whipping past me. Sadly, as much as I longed to soar through the sky again, I understood what the phrase pipe dream meant. Skydiving was my pipe dream.

My obsession began in college. During the first semester during my Master's program, one of my friends persuaded me to go up in the plane, and then once I strapped myself to an instructor, I fell out of the plane and experienced nirvana. One time and I was hooked. After that, I would save up extra money from my part-time job and jump as often as I could. Of course, after graduation and finding a full-time job, I went more often. Up there, I felt free without a care in the world. I was flying.

Bryan: And now?

Lost in my own little world, I had left him hanging for several minutes. Oops. But what did he mean now?

Me: Now? Nothing. I write but haven't done much with it. That's not really an adrenaline fix though.

Bryan: Why not go jumping again?

Was this man serious? Did he not understand? His question felt like a slap in the face.

Me: I can't.

Bryan: Why not?

I decided Bryan was either delusional or plain mean. Rubbing my chest where a familiar ache started to form, I pressed my other hand against my eyes in an effort to prevent the tears from falling. When I thought I was more in control, I responded again.

Me: Hello? MG?

Bryan: What the hell is MG?

Me: Myasthenia gravis. In layman's terms, I'm constantly fatigued and

weak. My muscles don't absorb the chemical from the nerve properly, and therefore, do not work as they should.
It can affect any voluntary muscles in the body. Throat, eyes, legs, arms, mouth, breathing, etc.

Bryan: *Oh.*

Me: *Yeah.*

Now he would realize how broken I really was and bid me farewell like so many others before him. If he didn't, his gaze would be filled with pity, and I would hate him for that.

Bryan: *So why can't you jump again?*

Wait! What? Did he really ask that stupid question again? Did he have rocks for brains? Did he like hurting me?

Me: *Because I'm sick.*

Bryan: *You have a disease, you're not dead. You might not be able to land on your own, but you can do a tandem jump with someone. It is possible.*

What? I hadn't thought of that. A tandem jump? When I first started skydiving, I did several tandem jumps in order to learn how to skydive and then to train. Why hadn't I thought of a tandem jump? Oh because after MG took over and claimed my body, my life changed and I never considered alternate possibilities for things like skydiving.

There were other issues though. I struggled to breathe most days, so I didn't know if they would allow me to go up or not. I'm not on oxygen or anything, but my normal breaths were shallower than normal.

I would have loved to skydive one more time. To free fall and glide through the air. Nothing beat that feeling.

Me: *I don't know. Maybe?*

Bryan: *You asking me?*

Me: *LOL. Maybe.*

Bryan: *LMAO. I gtg. Have a date tonight and I need to get ready.*
I'll talk to you tomorrow. Think of more questions, little birdy.

A date? That stung, but I reminded myself that he did not belong to me. We hardly knew each other and lived on opposite sides of the country. His only obligation, if I could call it that, was to advise me on how to get over my little (big) slump. That was all.

Scrunching up my nose after re-reading his comment, I snickered.

Me: Little birdy? :s

Bryan: Yes.

Me: Fine. TTYL.

I kind of liked the thought of him calling me little birdy, even if I didn't know why he did it. The nickname was something between us, something only we shared, and that made me feel special.

And later that night when my phone chimed with that annoying FS chat alert, I shot up in bed, startled out of slumber, because for some reason my ringer had been turned up to full volume, and squinted at my phone. My irritated expression switched to bewilderment almost immediately. Bryan messaged me. Odd, considering he was supposed to be out on a date.

Bryan: What up?

Me: Uh...nothing. Do you realize it 2am here?

Bryan: It is?

A couple of minutes passed and I thought maybe he had decided to disconnect the conversation when he realized how late it was. But that became wishful thinking.

Bryan: Huh. U r right.

Me: Are you drunk?

Bryan: Maybe. LOL

Me: Goodnight.

Bryan: Wait! Bad date. Didn't even make it past dinner.

I rolled my eyes and ran my hand through my hair. At that moment, I knew I was going to ask because he expected it and because I was curious, even if I wanted to slap him too. Slap or kiss? Both? No. No kissing. I would not allow myself to feel anything for him only to have my heart crushed.

Me: What grievous sin did she commit?

Bryan: Slurped her soup and tried to give me a foot job in the restaurant. Her feet stank.

I tried not to laugh, but I couldn't help it. Curley only lifted his head and dropped it down again, but I was pretty sure my dog shot me a look of annoyance.

Me: Oh, how horrible.

Did that sound sympathetic enough? I hoped so because I could not quell my laughter. Good thing he was either drunk or really buzzed.

Bryan: It was! If u r going to give a foot job, make sure ur feet are nice, groomed, and don't stink.
Promise me you'll groom ur feet.

Me: Got it. I solemnly swear...LOL.

Bryan: R u mocking me?

Me: Nope. Not at all. Maybe a little.
Yes. Yes, I am.

Bryan: I thought so. And here I thought you were my friend. :P

Me: I am, but that is funny.

Bryan: U wouldn't think so if u had smelled them. Worse than the city dump.

Me: EWWW!

Bryan: Now you get me.

Me: Go to bed.

Bryan: I guess I do have duty tomorrow at 6am. Will you sing me a lullaby?

Me: lalalala. There. Now goodnight.

Bryan: Wait.

Me: What?

Bryan: So have u had sex? U hardly dated. Did u ever have sex?

Me: Goodnight.

Bryan: Night.

Something told me he would probably bring that question up again. Had I? Yes. Good sex? Never. Of the two guys I had slept with, one I didn't want to think about because it was a painful memory, and the other, I felt nothing going in. Maybe he used a toothpick?

My first experience had not been like people wrote about in books. It hurt emotionally and physically. If possible, I never wanted to think about it again. My second experience had been a little different. He took steroids and acted proud of the fact he juiced, but his dick had shrunk smaller than my hand. Or maybe it had never been that big to begin with. Either way, while my virginity had been taken, my experience in the sex department was lacking.

CHAPTER ELEVEN

BRYAN

Lying in my bed, I stared blankly up at the ceiling. A plain white ceiling with an almost smooth surface and nothing interesting on it or about it. My head still spun from the alcohol I guzzled when I got home and the cold medicine I swallowed before I left for my disaster of a date. Thinking about the foot job and the smell made me cringe and gag.

Each toe had chipped nail polish and at least three had jagged edges. But all of that did not compare to the smell. I wasn't lying to Emma when I said it smelled worse than the city dump. Patrons from the furthest corners of the restaurant started to frown as they sniffed the air trying to figure out where the putrid smell originated from.

Damn, I fucked up. This date was a contender for top ten worst dates of my life and currently battled for the number two spot. Why not first? The first belonged to a woman and her daughter. One night, I found myself at a bar, drank a little too much, and decided to hit on an older woman. When she invited me back to her place, I quickly agreed, needing to use something other than my hand to engulf my dick.

We got to her place and another woman stood in the doorway waiting for us. Without me knowing, the woman had invited her daughter to join us. It happened to be the daughter's eighteenth birthday, and I was dear old mom's birthday present to the younger woman. As if that did not take the cake for awkwardness, the woman's daughter kept calling me daddy and begging "daddy" to take her cherry. I got out of there as quickly as possible, but not before I stepped on a roller–skate, sailed two feet forward, and crashed into a wall, which woke up the baby. I didn't even know there had been a baby in the fucking house.

My date tonight battled for number two because I couldn't decide which one was worse: a foot job with stinky ass feet or dumpster diving to get my keys. I've had some bad dates. How did I keep getting into these messes? Did I attract the crazies?

I groaned remembering my dumpster diving escapade. My date that night drank too much at dinner and thought it would be funny to steal my keys and throw them into the huge dumpster behind the restaurant. Fuck me! It took me days to get rid of the smell. I thought because I was a newly named ace fighter pilot hotshot, I needed to celebrate and show off. My date probably had a bottle and a half of wine all on her own, and I only had a glass or two.

I was starting to lean toward stinky feet winning number two. Some women were fucking weird.

I breathed a sigh of relief that I forced Emma to promise me she would not become one of the crazies. I wasn't sure why I had done that, but I didn't want to see her go down the road toward Crazy Town. She was better than that and too nice of a person to become that type of woman. If I needed to tie her up and lock her in the basement to prevent her from going psycho, then I would. Mel too. Although, it might already be too late for Mel. By the time I met her, she was already well on her way. Thankfully, Emma promised.

Even before I got home tonight, my thoughts drifted to Emma. I wanted her to be the first person I told about my date. I wanted her to be the person I laughed, or cried, with. I didn't want to think about the whys of it, but something about her had me confiding in her. Maybe that sounded odd, and it was for me because I had never been inclined to talk to anyone about my dates or my life before. Mel knew, but I had known her since high school and our families were friends. Emma was different. Normally outside the select two or three, I kept most things to myself, and this one little slip of a girl made me want to reach out to her.

What happened to her? Would she even tell me the whole story when she finally decided to confide in me? I somehow doubted it, and that bothered me. I wanted her to trust me enough to tell me anything. Not only due to her relationship with Mel, but because I genuinely liked her and wanted her to find her happiness. Before any of that could happen though, we had to get down to the heart of the matter.

My mind wandered and conjured various reasons for her self-esteem and trust issues. Each and every fictional reason I imagined, had my anger increasing. My hands balled into fists at my sides, and I lifted them right before I brought them down hard on either side of my body, hitting my bed.

She deserved better. I didn't know what happened, and yet, I instinctively wanted her to have better.

Turning over, I peered out of the window of my bedroom. I lived near the beach, and if I opened my window I would be able to hear the crashing waves over the sounds of traffic. But looking out the window, inky blackness greeted me, matching my mood perfectly.

I heard my roommate getting in from his own date, and sighed. Maybe I was the one that needed to get laid instead of Emma. I hadn't had sex since we pulled into port in South America a couple months ago. Fuck, I needed something. Too bad I didn't know what I needed, and yet, I had this niggling feeling in the back of my mind that I should know.

Tonight had sent me over the edge and made me forget why I should not mix cold medicine and alcohol. As I left earlier tonight, I felt almost guilty for going out on a date. Why? I wasn't in a committed relationship and was single and carefree. But the feelings of guilt would not leave, then the date turned sour, and when I got home I grabbed the new bottle of whiskey, put it to my lips and guzzled a quarter of it before I set it down on the counter. I had convinced myself talking to Emma would be unnecessary and wrong. And yet, after drinking a few more gulps, I drunk chatted her.

Why the hell had I done that? Maybe talking to her lately made me feel closer to her than almost anyone else. Maybe it was the promise to share with her if she shared with me. Maybe I wanted to talk to someone who didn't know me, who wouldn't push me too much. Emma would understand that.

My life was beginning to spiral, but for some reason, thinking of Emma allowed me to believe I had an anchor somewhere in the world. Because finding out from your little sister that your parents had made the decision to get a divorce, on top of funky feet, equaled one hell of a night.

CHAPTER TWELVE

EMMA

I didn't know how much Bryan drank the night before, or how early he had to get up in the morning in order to make it to his duty station on time, however, I did know when he finally managed to get online later in the day, the first thing he typed had me guffawing and wiping tears away. I had a hard time trying to tamp down my laughter in order to answer him.

Bryan: _I'm giving up alcohol for Lent._

Re-reading that one sentence still threw me into a fit of giggles.

_Me:_ _Lent is done. Easter was two months ago._

Bryan: _I don't care._

_Me:_ _Are you even Catholic?_
Because isn't it only the Catholic religion that practices Lent?

Bryan: _No, they aren't, and no I'm not. I'm Baptist. Don't care though._

_Me:_ _Riiiiight._

Bryan: _What's that supposed to mean?_

_Me:_ _Nothing. LOL._

My chuckles filled the air, echoing throughout the room, which in turn startled my dog, who immediately ran out of my bedroom and down the hall. I could hear his little feet pounding on the hardwood floor in the hall. Between the two incidences, I laughed some more. Tears spilled down my face; I couldn't stop. My sides began to hurt and I could hear the dings of his response, but I still did not stop laughing.

Several minutes later, breathing heavily, I wiped my tears again and blew my nose. Sniffling, I giggled a little more and grabbed my computer. His irritation oozed from the computer.

> **Bryan:** *Are you laughing at me?*
> *What the fuck are you doing over there?*
> *Whatever. I don't need to deal with you right now.*
> *I'm logging off.*

The little green circle next to his name had disappeared, which meant he actually logged off, and for whatever reason, I found that hilarious as well. His alcohol consumption must have been off the charts if he was saying stuff like he was giving up alcohol for Lent. Why had that even popped into his head?

After my bad manners, I FaceSpace stalked him, waiting for the moment the green circle appeared again, and when I saw the green light, I jumped on him like a ninja snatching up her prey. Okay, not literally since we were in two different states, but I clicked on his name faster than I've ever clicked before.

> **Me:** *SORRY!*

FaceSpace always told me when someone looked at my messages because it changed from a clear circle next to the name to a grey circle with a time stamp. He either had not seen my message, or he ignored it. Well, he was about to learn that I knew how to play the message bombing game just as well as he did.

> **Me:** *Don't be a big baby.*
> *SORRY again.*
> *Hello.*
> *I'm not stopping until u talk to me.*
> *How much did u have to drink last night?*
> *Lent is a year away. If u give it up now, ur ahead of the game. LOL.*
> *I really am sorry.*
> *Please?*

I couldn't stop laughing. It wasn't you though.
It's not you, it's me. :P LOL
It was something else that happened at the exact same time.
I swear!

He still ignored me, and I made the same threat he used on me multiple times.

Me: *Don't make me call Mel.*

Bryan: *U wouldn't because u don't want her to know we're talking.*
I'm what's hiding in ur precious closet ready to spring free.

Me: *I would.*

Bryan: *Nope. U r too chicken shit to call her.*

Me: *Pulling her up on my phone right now.*

Actually, no I wasn't and I wouldn't. He called it accurately, but he didn't have to know that.

Bryan: *Ha! U wouldn't dare.*

Well shit! Now it had turned into a dare of sorts. That changed things completely. Something about him made me want to rise to the challenge and prove him wrong. Plus it was fun. Now I had to call my friend. Unlocking my phone, I found her number and hit *TALK*.

Me: *It's ringing.*

Two rings and then it sent me to voicemail. Damn. My eyes glanced at the clock briefly and it knew it was early. Only 8:16 P.M. She was off work, however, no answer usually meant Luke had her otherwise occupied doing something.

Me: *You're in luck, my friend. Voicemail.*
Bryan: *I can't believe you called her. Please tell me you didn't really go through with it.*
Me: *I did. Why?*
Bryan: *It's Luke and Mel's anniversary.*
Me: *Oh shit.*

77

Bryan: Yep.
Me: Fuck. I might be in trouble when she sees I called.

Mel could be funny about certain things, and big events or special dates fell into those unique categories. And since I knew what those dates were, heads could potentially roll the next day. Sometimes she was gracious, but not always. Their anniversary was at the top of the "do not disturb unless someone dying" list, and Mel was scary.

Bryan: Pretty much.

Me: Asshole.

Bryan: LOL. Excuse me?

Me: Haha. You read that right. This is all your fault.

Bryan: How is this my fault?

It sounded as if he started to loosen up and that made me feel more comfortable and less anxious. I didn't want him to be mad at me.

Me: You practically dared me to call her.

Bryan: I don't remember daring u to do anything.
And I don't remember forcing the phone into ur hand.
Nor do I remember putting a gun to ur head or making u call her.
Did I? Hell, maybe I have a clone somewhere running amuck doing shit like that.
ROFLMAO.

Me: No, but you still dared me.

Bryan: Not really, but using ur backward logic, if I dared u to jump off a cliff, would u?

He had me there, and the butthead knew it. Trapped in a trap of my own making.

Me: No, but still.

Bryan: Ha. U r so busted. LMAO.

Me: Ok, ok. I concede. My hands are up in surrender. Haha.

I found myself snickering.

Bryan: I'll see what I can do to head Mel off at the pass and give u time to gird ur loins.

Me: Gird my loins???

Bryan: Isn't that what they say in books and shit?

Me: LMAO. Maybe. Just funny to see that from you.

Bryan: I'm a man of many talents and surprises, baby.

My stomach flipped and my inner muscles clenched deep inside me. Swallowing hard, I cleared my throat before I typed. I prayed he couldn't see how much I desired and wanted him with just one word: baby.

Me: I'll take your word for it. :D

Bryan: ;)

Before I attempted to crawl through the computer so I could jump his bones, I changed the subject.

Me: How much did you have to drink last night?

Bryan: Enough.

Me: How much?

Bryan: Enough that I won't be drinking for a while and may actually be giving it up for Lent next year starting today.

Me: Ouch.

Bryan: I got to work and almost threw up. After some aspirin and dry toast, I felt a little better, but I really don't remember the last time I ever felt this bad after drinking.

Me: Sounds loverly.

Bryan: Want to answer my question?

Me: Question? I don't remember you asking anything.

I had an inkling that he meant our prior conversation from the night before, but that did not stop me from praying he had forgotten all about it in his drunken haze.

Bryan: Sex. Have you ever had sex?

Crap! He came back around to the exact subject I wanted to avoid like the plague. Like with most things in my life, admitting my lack of conquests to this man embarrassed me. Item whatever on a list of about 500 items long. I may have opened up about some of my insecurities, but that did not mean I was ready, or willing, to become a completely open book. However, somewhere deep inside, I knew it would only be a matter of time before he pried all of my secrets from me.

Me: How long did your longest relationship last?

Bryan: Turning it back on me?

I was stalling. He knew it. I knew it. But that did not stop me as I attempted to misdirect him from his interrogation.

Me: Why not? You said an answer for an answer.

Bryan: Fine. 2 years.

Me: Wow. Really?

Bryan: Yes, really.
Senior year in high school to first year in college.
I found out she was cheating and we broke up. Now u.

Me: I have.

He must have been waiting for me to continue because when I did not expand on my answer, he got demanding.

Bryan: That's all I get? U should at least give me a little more. I'm a sick man.

Me: *You are sick but too bad it is all in your head. LOL.*

Bryan: *Tell me.*

Me: *Two different guys and neither were any good.*
I mean I read all these romance novels and I'm starting to think everything is exaggerated.
I'm told sex can be good, and Mel thinks it's explosively amazing, but I don't get it. I've never experienced that.

I could already imagine his laughter and felt my anxiety and fear start to spike, causing bile to burn the back of my throat. Before I got sick, men called me an oddball because I didn't jump into bed with as many guys as possible. They were put out by the fact I made them wait instead of having sex on our first date. Typically, they started out nice enough, but soon their personalities changed and they tried to either pressure me or make some excuse as to why they fucked someone else. I wanted more than just a physical relationship.

After we mended fences, Ellie told me one time about six months before I got sick that I wanted it all. Maybe I did. I wanted a mental and physical relationship. The man of my dreams would talk to me as an equal, make me laugh, and think me beautiful. He would want me for my mind and body. Where were those guys?

Bryan Sampson's image appeared in my mind and I couldn't shake it out. Sure over FaceSpace he would talk to me and we could joke, but in person, I would be no more than a friend or less. I'm not saying he would ignore me in front of others, but I was definitely not his type.

And if he did ignore me, well he wouldn't be the first. Going out with Mel or my sister, people naturally approached them. They were whole and carefree. When it came to me though, I was the elephant in the room that everyone chose to pretend didn't exist. Heavier than some and pushing a walker or using a cane to balance made people uncomfortable. I understood that, but it still hurt my feelings.

Ellie always told me to ignore those people. Not hard to do considering they ignored me first. Mel would tell me to make myself over the top and that I needed to add bling to my walker. I chose to make it black with pink skulls thanks to duct tape. I was never the audacious person who craved the spotlight. I could pretend to be that person, but when the other party doesn't want to be around you anyway, it makes it difficult to be the life of the party.

My hand rubbed my chest where it suddenly burned. Bryan and I would work together until I found someone and then…what? I didn't want to say goodbye, but what exactly were we? Friends for the sake of our friends?

Bryan: Ouch! U really been gypped out of some shit.

If he only knew. Moving from place to place as a kid, I learned to make friends fairly easily, and when we moved, I left them all behind. Every couple of years, my life started over. Sometimes I wished I could have one more restart.

I might say that, but I didn't mean it. The truth of the matter was, getting sick opened new doors for me. I've met people I would never have met, made new friends through my online support groups, and started to write more. And as sad as it sounded, because the reason sucked, my family grew out of this experience together and we are all closer than we used to be. As with everything in life, there was good and bad to be had. I didn't want to be sick, but since I had no choice in the matter, I chose to do what I could to help raise awareness and I found a new way to live a good life for me.

Me: It is what it is.

Bryan: Hell no. We really need to find u someone that will show u exactly what u r missing. Trust me, it's a fucking lot. But first, we need to get u over ur issues.

Me: My issues?

Bryan: Low self-esteem and ur fortress of solitude that no one can penetrate.
U have issues.

Me: Does that mean you have issues too?

Bryan: We aren't talking about me.

Me: Quid pro quo.

He didn't respond. I waited a couple of minutes with my fingers hovering over my keyboard before a message popped into the chat window.

Bryan: Sorry, pee break and needed more aspirin.
Yeah, I have issues. Everyone does, but urs r practically impenetrable.

Me: You ok?

Bryan: Yep. Only a hangover headache. Backlash from binging.

Me: Why did you binge?

Maybe I missed the mark or failed at picking up the right cues, but a bad date did not equal a reason to get so drunk, a hangover became your best friend the next day.

Bryan: Because.

Me: Because?

Bryan: It wasn't intentional. I drank some whiskey and then drank some more. I had already taken cold medicine b4 my date, so it probably added to it and BAM.

Me: I thought you weren't supposed to drink while on cold meds.

Bryan: Thank u for the public service announcement. No, u should not.

Me: Got it.

I decided it was best to ignore his sarcasm, or I might reach through the computer and slap him. Talking to him put me on edge, and it would not take much to push me right over the cliff.

Okay, maybe I wouldn't do that to him since he was out of it, and he was helping me with my "situation."

Bryan: But seriously for a sec cause I'm about to crash. Ur better than that. Ur better than comparing yourself to someone else, better than putting yourself down, and better than u give yourself credit for. U need to see it for yourself. U deserve to treat yourself better than u do.

Me: I know.

Bryan: Do u? Because when I look at u, I see a beautiful woman with a pretty smile, who's a great person on the inside and out.

My cheeks burned red with his high praise as butterflies danced in my stomach. He thought me beautiful?

Me: *Thank you.*

Bryan: *Don't just thank me, believe it. I've gtg. I'll ping later.*

Me: *K. Feel better.*

I didn't know if I believed him or not. For so long I had been unsure of myself in a lot of different aspects. Getting over the hurdles I had placed in my own path, might be one of the hardest things I've ever faced.

My sister wasn't really all bad. In truth, she wasn't bad at all...only sometimes, but I loved her to death. Since we had entered adulthood, our relationship drastically improved; and when I got sick, she tried to step up to the plate and help me. She checked on me all the time, went grocery shopping for me whenever I asked, or if she thought I needed groceries, and took me to every single one of my doctor appointments. Not only had she become my part-time caretaker, but she had become a good friend as well. That being said, as a sister, Ellie still annoyed me to no end.

Having my sister take care of me, sometimes made me feel like a burden to her. She has cooked for me, dressed me, and helped me with basics when I struggled. I hated depending on her or anyone for so many things. It shouldn't, but it made me feel like less than a person. She always told me it never bothered her to do things for me, and perhaps it didn't, but it bothered me. What person actually wanted to have her sister dress her or brush her teeth? No one I knew.

And then there were the times when she tried to speak for me, only to give out false or inaccurate information. Or the times when she overreacted. Of course on that front, my parents were the king and queen of overreacting.

Being around me all of the time, Ellie had a level of knowledge my parents did not possess. They made me feel like I was five again when they were around. My mom cut my food into bitesize pieces, tried to carry me from point A to point B, and constantly asked if I needed help in the bathroom. Fuck no.

On a couple of occasions when they came in to visit and stayed with me, I accidentally dropped the shampoo bottle. Unlike Ellie, who called through the door to check on me, my mom barged into the bathroom and ripped the shower curtain open. Not her finest hour. Not mine either since I yelled, screamed, and told her to get the fuck out.

The truth of the matter was I struggled. I was still learning how to cope and live with my new body, with my disease, even four years later. And the funny thing about that was, I think Bryan made more headway in a few conversations than anyone else had in years of knowing them. I might also admit he made more progress than me on my own.

My walls cracked and light started to peek in. Maybe, and I wasn't saying for sure, but maybe not everyone around me sucked—and that included me.

CHAPTER THIRTEEN

BRYAN

For almost two weeks, Emma and I talked on a daily basis, and for some reason, I felt like I had hit the glass ceiling so to speak. I needed to break through her defenses and slap some sense into her, but I couldn't figure out how to do it.

Curious about what another guy would say or think, and dreading it at the same time—I would not be exploring that particular emotion—I showed her picture to my roommate, Evan, and filled him in on a few details of her personality, leaving out her disability temporarily.

"I'd do her in a heartbeat and maybe more than once," he proclaimed, grinning widely.

It was time to hit him with the other half of the truth. I realized exactly why she thought the way she did about men. "What if she used a cane or a walker? Would it change things for you?"

Hesitating, he finally admitted, "I don't know, but I can say this, if I saw her in a bar, I wouldn't give her a second glance with that shit. Sorry."

He wouldn't give her a chance just because she used medical devices to help her walk? No other reason? It made me want to punch him in the face. I resisted though.

And then he said something else that gave me pause and made me think. "Are you telling me that if you went into the bar and saw her with a walker, you would stroll right on up to her and try your hand at picking her up? It doesn't matter how pretty or cool she is, we see that shit, we pretend we don't see her, we turn, and walk in the opposite direction. You would too. So don't give me that crap that you would fuck her no questions asked. You are the same as the rest of us shallow fuckers because when it comes down to it, we don't want to bother. Hell, I've seen you do that."

"Me? What are you talking about?"

"Do you remember when Danny asked us to meet his fiancée, Lila, and she brought that other girl with them?"

"She did?" I honestly could not recall meeting anyone else that night.

"And my point is made. Not that she was all that cute, but Lila's friend or sister or whoever the fuck that girl was, was deaf and had braces on her legs. You gave one split second glance and turned away."

"No, I didn't." I tried to brush off his words, to remember the girl in question, except I drew a complete blank.

"Do you remember her?" Evan demanded. His smirk said he had me backed into a corner, and he knew it.

I hesitated, and then finally gave him my quiet answer, "No."

"There you have it. Look. Emma may be the greatest person on the planet. Hell, she could have fucking Mother Theresa's personality with Marilyn Monroe's body, but with that excess baggage, no one would try to get in her pants or give her a second glance. With that shit, someone is going to have to get to know her first, and that is mighty hard to do at social events when people judge on appearance first before they ever consider a person's personality."

Furrowing my brow, I thought about what Evan had said, and while I hated to admit it, I had to concede that he had a point, but I still needed to know something. "Now that I've told you about her, would you still do her?"

"Hell yeah. She's hot and sounds like a lot of guy's wet dream, but she's not just some stranger at a bar now. Is she?"

"No, I guess not," was the only answer I could come up with because it contained nothing but the absolute truth. Emma was more than a mere stranger to both of us.

I marinated on mine and Evan's conversation over the next 24 hours. He was right, and it made me both sad and angry for Emma. But at the same time, I was ashamed to admit that if I walked into a bar, if she was just another face in the crowd, I wouldn't give her the time of day.

In my holier than thou "I know everything" attitude, I had actually tried to convince her she was wrong, been telling her to get over her insecurities and her self-esteem issues, and now I realized how full of shit I was.

Slowly, too slowly to an impatient ass like me, she had been opening up to me, and it took my roommate knocking me down a couple of pegs before I realized the uphill battle she faced on a daily basis. Dealing with her illness and disability, her mountain got steeper and taller with every step she took, and she fought the battle alone.

It was weird, less than a month ago, Emma was barely a blip on my radar, and now I talked to her almost daily, and I looked forward to those conversations. I lived the life of a single Navy pilot and enjoyed it immensely. Sometimes it felt like it lacked something, however, I knew how to shut down those feelings fairly quickly. I wasn't ready for something serious, something that required a commitment. The Navy had the only commitment I wanted to make to anyone.

I flew planes for a living, it was every little boy's dream come true. Nothing else compared to the rush of takeoff and zooming through the air. When I wasn't deployed or up in the sky, I flittered from one woman to the next and found a lot of the crazies. Even if I wanted a long-term relationship, I would never consider any of them for that role in my life. The only person who came close enough to fit the bill—if I was actually looking—was Emma.

No, I loved my life the way it was. I'd been stationed in San Diego almost a year and a half ago, and had been gone for the past nine months on deployment.

My roommate Evan and I had met each other back in junior high when his Army father had been stationed in Savannah for less than a year. We kept in touch and when I called with the news that I got transferred to San Diego, he offered me a room in his house. He had tried to follow his father's footsteps and joined the Army, but after four years when it came time to re-enlist, he opted to leave. It wasn't where he saw his life going. Although, I wasn't exactly sure he saw his life taking the turns that it had.

After getting out of the Army, he didn't know what to do and eventually decided to use his expertise and business degree to open a dojo. Now he taught little kids, and anyone else who wanted to learn, how to defend themselves. He said it was fulfilling and he loved the hours, so he never complained.

I counted him as one of my closest friends, even though there were times I've wanted to gut him and throw his body in the ocean for the sharks. I was pretty sure he would say the same thing about me. Over the years, he had become one of the people I turned to for advice, and when I needed a boost to my conscience. That little voice in me liked to talk, but I didn't always listen when I should. I trusted him to be honest with me, and help me see reason. He always did. The Emma situation was just one example.

I was an ass.

I needed some sort of edge with Emma. Something that would break her shell and crumble her walls faster, instead of chipping away at them one small sliver at a time. Truth be told, I needed a fucking sledgehammer for her defenses. Maybe I was too cocky for my own good. I knew I was impatient, but this had to be done, and I felt as if I had to be the one to do it.

Picking up my cell, I called the one person I knew who could help shed some light on the puzzle that made up Emma Taylor. "Mel! How's my third favorite girl?"

"Third?" She snickered. "You must want something because I'm climbing higher up the list. Normally, I'm number four."

"Bullshit at home," I grumbled.

"My parents told me." I hated how her voice got softer, how it had that almost pitying tone. Would Emma have the same tone of voice if she knew how my family stood on the precipice of falling apart?

"Fuck!"

"You know our parents are friends and that kind of secret cannot be kept considering they play bridge every week together."

My hand raked through my hair and pulled. Maybe the pain would make everything disappear. It didn't work and I huffed, "I know. Did you know they haven't even called me? I found out from Rayne."

"What? Please tell me that's some sort of sick joke."

"You know how things are with them. Can you really ask me that? But to answer you, this is not a fucking joke. I've only spoken to them once since I got back to San Diego, and that conversation lasted less than ten minutes." The only thing that kept me from blowing my stack during my conversation with Mel right now was that Emma popped online, and we started to chat with each other. To some, I might be considered a rude ass jerk for carrying on two different conversations at the same time, but it did not matter to me. One consisted of only typing and one required I speak aloud. Easy.

I heard her sigh before she said, "Sorry Bryan. That's messed up."

"Yep, it is."

She didn't say anything for a minute or two and neither did I, and then she cleared her throat. "So, I know you didn't call me to complain about your parents' lack of communication skills, considering they've hardly kept you informed since high school. What's up?"

"You're right. That isn't why I called. I really called to ask you about Emma. What's her story?"

"Why? You interested?"

"No," I rushed loudly.

"Don't be so quick to answer," she mumbled. I could almost pick up notes of irritation in her voice, but when it came to masking her feelings, Mel was the master.

Rolling my eyes, I retorted, "Don't be a bitch or I'll spread your dirty secrets to Luke. I really like him and would hate to see him run away screaming."

"You can't scare me. He knows everything."

"Everything? Does he know about the Barbie graveyard? Or about what you did to Raggedy Ann?"

"You don't even know if that's true or not. We didn't meet until later, dumbass."

"Your mom has pictures. And besides, I don't need proof. The fact that you and I are so close, that our friendship is so tight, will be enough proof for him. I'm sure he'll believe everything I say. Damn, I could probably make shit up and I'd still have him eating out of the palm of my hand. Another thing, you're awfully defensive there. Plus, you've never really denied anything in the past, which by my standards is proof enough for me."

A growl from deep in her throat echoed through the phone. I had touched on a nerve. "Asshole."

"But you love me anyway."

"I do, but I could also shank you right now."

"Watching prison dramas again?"

"Hooked on 'em," she chortled. "Now, what do you want?"

"What's Emma's story?" I accidentally chuckled out loud at something Emma typed in our chat window.

"What the hell are you laughing at? You ask me about my friend and then you laugh at her?"

"No, I'm not laughing at her. The TV is on and that funny puppet guy is on. He's hilarious. So what's her story?" I crossed my fingers that she believed my lie.

"Okaaay." She sounded as if she didn't quite believe me, but she moved past it. "She's been burned a few times."

"I got that." I itched to ask her about her sister, but since Ellie and Mel were friends, in addition to Vegas rules applied to all conversations I had had with Emma up until this point, I kept that particular line of questioning to myself. "I've just talked to her a couple of times, and she seems…I don't know. Closed off?"

"She is. Her best friend, Gia, told me one time that she's had some crappy relationships with guys, and after she got sick, some of her friends started treating her like shit. She also said Emma has had trust issues for a while, but she wouldn't tell me why. Gia told me Emma puts on a happy face and does anything for anyone, even on days she is struggling or when she wants to cry. So, I don't know. I've known her almost five years, and we're close, but she doesn't share everything with me."

"Oh." I laughed out loud again and winced when I realized what I had done.

"Interested?"

Thankfully, she didn't ask about my outburst—either that or she chose to ignore me. "No, just curious," I quickly replied.

"Good, because she deserves better than someone who practices love 'em and leave 'em."

"I know. Besides, she's a friend of yours. I won't touch that."

She paused for a moment, and then Mel spoke softly, "I hope she finds someone that will treat her right."

"Me too."

Dead silence descended between us. Had I said something I shouldn't have? Thinking over my conversation with her, the last words I had spoken, I didn't think so, but I wasn't sure. Mel's mind worked differently than others—at least I always believed it had.

"You do?" Her question came across the line, sharp, and yet, quiet at the same time.

"What? She's your friend and seems like a nice enough person. She deserves someone good." I still refused to admit how much we talked, what we talked about, or how much I looked forward to my conversations with Emma.

And then, once again, Emma's wit struck again. I really should have waited to talk to her because she kept making me laugh.

"Seriously, what are you laughing at? And don't give me that bullshit about puppets on TV. Do you have someone over there, doing a piss poor job at giving you a blow job or something? If you can talk on the phone, get blown at the same time, and laugh about it, she sucks...or maybe she doesn't. Does she need lessons?" She laughed so loudly, I had to pull the phone away from my ear.

"What? I would never have called you if I had a girl over here," I growled. Mel was not funny. Okay, maybe that joke had been a little funny.

"No, but you have called during sex before."

Leave it to her to bring up something so embarrassing. "That was an accident and you know it."

"Might have been, but listening to you having sex is not something I ever wanted to hear. It's hard to forget too. Oh, oh, Bryan. Harder. Spank me." She mimicked the breathless voice of the girl I happened to be banging right after I moved to San Diego. It was over a year ago, and I still couldn't live that shit down. "Right there. Oh faster! Oh God! More!"

I threw my head back and it banged against the back of the couch before I snapped, "Fine! Fine. If you must know, I'm talking to Emma right now. I told you, we've talked a few times."

"Wow. I..." her voice trailed off.

"I'm just trying to help her. Nothing more than that. Trust me. So, don't go reading anything into it."

"I realize give you shit and stuff, but you're a good guy no matter what your sister says," Mel snickered, and I could hear the smile in her voice.

"Gee. That's so nice of you to say."

"You know you love me."

"I do. I'll let you get back to whatever it was you were doing…or blowing. I need to go."

"K. Behave and have fun talking to Emma."

"Never. Behaving is overrated." I stuck out my tongue and chuckled as I disconnected our call, choosing to respond to only the first part of her comment. After my conversation with Mel, if anything, I had more questions than answers. Too bad I didn't know Emma's best friend, Gia. Focusing on my computer screen, I decided to let it go for the time being and enjoy my chat with a friend.

CHAPTER FOURTEEN

EMMA

The more I talked to Bryan, the more I found I dropped my guard and shared a little more of myself. Parts of me I had only shared with my best friend before. This lone man had a knack for making me feel completely at ease, like I could be myself with him. Of course, the fact that we only talked online helped contribute to my comfort with him. We were friends on FaceSpace only, and that is how it would remain for the foreseeable future.

FaceSpace gave us a small level of secrecy and protection. Without hearing his voice, without seeing his face, I remained hidden and separate in a way. FS became our own little world, and no one had to know we were communicating with each other or what we talked about. To some, it probably sounded more like a dirty little secret, however, the things I shared with him, I would not share with others. In a short period of time, he had become my confidant, and I told him things I had not even confessed to my best friend. It was safe. I could share my fears, anger, bitterness, hopes, and dreams without worrying he would tell anyone else. For me, typing in our chat window became an electronic journal. That's what he was: a diary.

He didn't judge me when I finally told him I was afraid of dying. One of the women, Ruth, I knew from the support groups had passed away. Though Ruth and I had never met in person, she had tried her best to encourage me and others who suffered from myasthenia gravis. In fact, she had made it her life's mission to spread awareness and to help others who struggled to fight on a daily basis. Finding out about her death had left me shaken, and I had tried to blow Bryan off and forgo our conversation, but he wouldn't let me. Instead, he stayed online and talked to me for two hours about my friends and some of my fears.

Our conversations never got too technical, but he understood the disease made me weak and that I struggled sometimes. He also finally got me to confess that one day I wanted to publish a book. Instead of laughing at me, he encouraged me to pursue my dream. Times like that when my defenses were at their highest, he surprised me with his responses.

Day in and day out I sat at home and was unable to do much. I went out periodically, but taking Curley on a long walk hasn't happened since I got sick. Everything I did to maintain an active lifestyle, disappeared when the myasthenia gravis appeared.

As time passed and I finally faced the fact that my life had forever changed, I sank into a deep depression, and it finally took my sister calling around and sending me to a counselor before I started to make an attempt at embracing my own life. And then one day Ellie said, "Why don't you write again? You don't have to work on a set schedule. You can do it as much or as little as you want, and if your eyes start to see double, then take a break." Her words that day lit a small spark in me, and I began writing again. Something I hadn't done in years.

My days were filled with doctors, infusions, playing with Curley, writing, and reading. Yippee. Not really. The number of days I had to use my walker versus my cane had increased, but luckily my doctor decided to try doing IVIG more often. The IV medicine I got had helped me remain independent, however, the doctor decided once every two weeks was not enough for my body. Insurance received the request from my doctor to increase my dosage to every week, but we hadn't heard back from them yet. I learned that when insurance companies are involved, it always became a waiting game, which sucked for the sick people who depended on them. They held all the power.

And the person I shared all of that frustration with was Bryan. He always seemed to be there when I needed him, even when I refused to share, or hesitated to answer. Somehow, he dragged whatever he wanted to know out of me...most of the time. There were still some things I would not share, could not share. Those would remain locked and hidden in my past.

I foolishly thought everything would remain between us, but it turned out that I had been very wrong.

A couple weeks after we started chatting, Mel approached me, cornering me like a caged animal with no means of escape. The door to freedom stood on the other side of her, and she knew with my lack of coordination, slow moving feet, and inability to remain upright without help, she had me right where she wanted me. Deep down in my bones, I knew she wanted something from me, but there was no telling what that something could be.

"What's up, Mel?" I decided to go for the casual approach instead of cowering.

Not that I had or intended to cower since we were in my house. OMG! Was this retaliation for attempting to call her on her anniversary? She never said anything about it, and when I apologized, she told me to forget it.

Mel's memory rivaled that of an elephant's, which meant, a decade into the future, when everyone else forgot, she would remember, and that's when she would strike. I remembered when she said, "You never know when it will be, but I will get you." At the time, she had been talking to Luke's brother who accidentally spilled salsa over her head at a party. By accident!

"Why don't you tell me?" Her eyebrow quirked, and she dared me to deny...something. I was not exactly sure what I was supposed to confess at the moment.

"Tell you?" My sad attempt to move around her forced her to take a step backward to block the door. Now that my plans were foiled, I moved to the couch and sat down to throw her off my scent. See, Mel. No escaping today.

"You know." She stalked me, hovering over the arm of the couch without sitting. The coy smile that lit up her face freaked me out and made me fear the world was coming to an end.

I knew? What the hell did that mean? I knew about a lot of things, but that didn't mean I could read minds. Was I in trouble? That smile made me wonder if she wanted to throw me a party right before she killed me. Yes, Mel could be that scary.

"Why don't you tell me what it is you think I'm supposed to know, and then we can skip this whole back and forth thing?" I really had no idea what crazy idea she had gotten into her head, and this yoyo stuff was liable to get me in a lot of trouble if I guessed incorrectly.

"I'll give you a hint."

"Okaaaay." The word came out like a long note on a musical staff.

"Navy man."

"Navy man?" I questioned. Considering I associated with several different Navy men, that clue proved to be of little help. Unless...shit! The only reason she could possibly have for her cat who ate the canary grin would be if her news, secret, whatever, involved Bryan. My eyes grew wide, my pulse increased, and my hands started to feel wet and dirty.

She gave me a small nod and her smile grew. "San Diego."

CRAP! My suspicions confirmed, I warily broached the subject. "Bryan?" Yeah, I only said one word, but I figured that would open up the can of worms on its own. And it did.

"Bingo! Give the girl her prize." She flopped down onto my couch so hard it scooted backward a couple of inches.

"What? I mean he and I have talked a couple of times, but that's about it. He thinks he can give me love advice or some shit, and I called his bluff." Bryan and I chatted almost daily, but she didn't need to know that and I wasn't sure what the sailor snitch told her or what he kept from her.

"That's it?" Her smile disappeared and she looked almost disappointed.

"Yep. That's it."

"Boo. You two are no fun."

"What the hell did he tell you?" I demanded.

Crossing her arms over her chest, she huffed. "Basically, what you told me."

"Basically?"

"Well, we were talking on the phone last night, and he asked about you, but wouldn't tell me much. Then, every once in a while, he would laugh, and I sure as hell hadn't said anything funny. Finally, inquiring minds wanted to know, and I insisted he tell me who he was talking to when he was supposed to be talking to me. Can you believe he said it was the freaking TV! The TV! I called him on his bullshit and said, 'Do you have someone over there giving you a blow job? If you're laughing, then she must be doing a piss poor job of it.' Or something to that effect." The glint in her eyes told me she was hiding something.

It shouldn't surprise me when she said stuff like that, but my jaw dropped slightly and my eyes grew even larger. Unsure if it was fear over what Bryan spilled or if it was just a reaction to her proclamation, I asked, "What did he say?"

"He yelled, 'What? No! It's just Emma.' So, I ask you again, what the hell is going on with you two?"

Her confession did two things to me. First, my stomach dropped hearing that he said I was "just Emma," and second, I instantly went on the defensive, because I still felt uncertain about what she heard from him. "We've talked a couple of times, like I said. He thinks he can give me advice on catching a man, which we all know is complete and utter bullshit."

"Why do you say that?"

"Since it's true?" Sarcasm dripped off my tongue like acid, and the only thing missing was the word duh. Bryan may have helped me a little, and while I have made some strides, I still struggled to embrace all of his lessons.

Her eyes narrowed, and her expression switched from the neutral façade she had adopted after calling me "just Emma," to an expression that made me wonder if she would murder me on the spot. "What the ever-lovin' fuck does that mean?"

Rolling my eyes, I refused to cower in front of her. I would do it later in the privacy of my bedroom after she left. "It means, unless a guy is desperate, he wouldn't want someone who has MG and has to use medical equipment to get around."

She practically snarled, her lip pulled back revealing her pearly white teeth. "You're sick, not fucking dead!"

"I know. Believe me, I know that better than you." On the verge of tears, I fought for control and shifted my gaze away from her. I refused to allow her to see me on the precipice of losing it again. In the past, I had broken down in front of her a few times, and I hated it when people saw me emotionally weak and vulnerable. It was bad enough they saw me physically struggling. I didn't care if they were family, friends, or strangers. It was hard to let anyone see that part of me.

I felt the couch shift to the left of me, and then her arm wrapped around my shoulders right before she pulled me in for a hug. Unable to hold back the tears any longer, I cried on her shoulder. Talking to Bryan and allowing him to start breaking down my walls, had left me emotional and easily flustered. I blamed him for my current condition.

I wasn't sure how long I cried, or what Mel whispered to me as I bawled my eyes out, but I remembered her rambling something to me. And when I finally pulled back to wipe away the last of my tears and snot, I blubbered, "Sorry."

"Not your fault, sweetie. But it looks like Bryan still has some work to do."

What? Was she joking or serious? In my limited experience, even though Bryan managed to break through some of my defenses and get me to talk to him a little, he was far from a love doctor. Did she really think he could help me? Or was this some sort of joke because now she knew about his nefarious plan? Yes, I called it nefarious.

Sniffling and swallowing excess spit and snot, I shook my head. "He's just being nice to one of your friends. I think he honestly believes he can solve all the world's problems. You really need to have a talk with him about his over-inflated ego."

"If Bryan didn't want to talk to you, he wouldn't. Stop selling yourself short, and if he says he can help you find a date, then he can."

"I don't want a pity date!" I barked as tears threatened to engulf me again.

"He's better than that, and would never do that to you or anyone. He'll help you attract someone of your choosing, and I promise, it won't be a pity date. But honey, you have to stop doubting yourself. You are a beautiful, smart, and amazing person. Any guy would be lucky to have you."

"But no one wants me." My reminder came out as a soft whimper.

"You just haven't met the right one yet." I started to argue, but before I could utter one peep, she covered my mouth with her hand, quickly pulling it away when the liquid running out of my nose touched it. Swiping it across my jeans, she told me, "Trust me, will ya? Online dates and the losers your sister's friends hook you up with are not the right ones. People lie online and pics aren't always accurate. The good-looking men online are assholes that can't get a date any other way because no woman wants them. They are not good enough for you. I secretly have a theory they all have small dicks too, and you deserve someone better than a small dick, egocentric prick. As for the others, Ellie's friends don't know you from Adam and are probably afraid to mention your disability. The guys are begging for dates and are shallow enough to think they are going to meet a model through their friends. Sorry honey, but neither one of us are model material. We like food too much."

I snorted with laughter, nodding.

"See, much better. Look, honey, men are assholes. You have to weed out the bad in order to find the good, and the really good ones don't come around every day. You'll find your prince and he'll accept everything there is about you. He won't care one iota if you use a walker or if he has to spoon feed you. His dick will get hard when he has to bathe you, regardless if it's because you can't bathe yourself or just because you want him to do it. He'll love you for you, and he'll see the beautiful person you are both inside and out. He'll look beyond the cane, the walker, the illness, the bullshit, and see you for you. And if I know Bryan, he can help you see who you truly are, who your friends and family see, when they look at you."

"I don't know." The tears fell down my face once again.

"Trust me. This will be good for you, and when you get to the other side, you'll find the man of your dreams waiting for you…just not Bryan. Anyone except Bryan. You deserve better than a man-whore. I love him to death, but he's a slut. Great guy, but no. Just say no." She started to snigger, and it grew into a full laugh.

Unable to resist, I joined her. No, Bryan may be as sweet as molasses, hot as hell, and I my crush may be growing, but he did not hold the title of my Prince Charming.

CHAPTER FIFTEEN

EMMA

I had to say, I felt kind of irritated with Bryan. Since Mel left after lunch, I'd sat in my apartment stewing for hours. I tried to come up with good excuses on why he would talk to her, but for every one of them, I conjured two reasons that made him out to be the bad guy.

I tried to write to take my mind off of him and my anger, but I almost killed off the hero of the story. Funny how emotions wreaked havoc on a story sometimes. When that didn't work, I tried to read and managed to skim the same paragraph at least ten times. Curley was the only distraction that worked. We sat outside while I threw his toy for him to fetch, but that reprieve did not last long. After less than an hour, I walked back into my apartment, flopped down on my couch, and stewed some more.

Vegas rules? Did he need a refresher course on what the term Vegas rules meant? He said he wouldn't say anything to Mel, and then he went behind my back and asked her about me? I know I hadn't been 100% forthcoming, but this felt like a stab in the back. Why did everything have to happen when he said it did? After he told me he didn't expect me to change overnight, he decided a few online conversations should have been enough to completely remake me. It wasn't.

I'd bottled things up and kept them inside ever since I was a child. When I was younger, my sister got a lot of extra attention due to a few issues in school, and even though I wanted extra attention, I didn't say anything, even when I felt left out. But it didn't stop there. The issues I had with love, with my sister, with school, with friends—I internalized it all and held it all deep within me. Gia managed to get me to open up to her only after we had been friends for over a year, and only initially when she backed me into a corner. After that though, she became my outlet, and I still counted on her.

Maybe I was overreacting—given my anxiety issues, I probably was—but to me, Vegas rules meant he kept his trap shut. And not only that, but after the breakdown and crying fit, while she was here, my embarrassment had skyrocketed. I had to take my aggression out on someone, why not him?

I wanted to know exactly what he asked. Could it be he wanted to know how to let me down easy because he realized I was beyond help? No, if that were the case, she wouldn't have told me to let him help me.

So what then? Did I dare demand answers from him? Order him to tell me exactly what they talked about? Yes, I did.

Grabbing my laptop from the coffee table, I logged onto FaceSpace faster than ever before, swiftly found his name on my list of friends, and clicked on it. The green dot and mobile icon were both missing, which meant he wasn't available even though it was a little after 9:00 P.M. my time, but that did not prevent me from sending him a message he would see later. The problem was deciding what I wanted to type.

My point had to be made without Bryan believing I had a mental breakdown, and yet, my message had to be firm and rip him a new asshole. Decisions. Decisions.

My fingers flew across the keyboard, and before I realized what I'd typed, I hit enter and then continued my tirade.

> **Me:** *I had the most interesting conversation with Mel today.*
> *Do you know who and what we talked about? Vegas Rules? Ring a bell?*
> *Do you even know what that phrase means? What the hell did you tell her?*
> *Am I so pathetic that you decided you had to call in reinforcements?*
> *Did you have a good laugh? I hope so because now I know I can't trust you.*
> *You want me to believe that there is a good guy out there for me, but how am*
> *I supposed to believe what you say when you lie like the dog you are?*

At least it wasn't in all caps like a few of my messages from the past. Part of me wondered what he thought the night I reamed him in all caps. I kind of thought he took me seriously because he backed off slightly and gave me space, almost as if he were talking to a skittish horse. Maybe in a way, I resembled one. Trust, a concept that seemed so easy to most, was difficult for me to master. And the start of my trust issues lay further into the past than my illness.

Bryan had been right. My self-esteem problems took root way before I got sick, and I had admitted that much to him. But the lack of trust in people, I wasn't ready to face those things yet. Needless to say, if someone wanted me to trust them, they had to earn it, and I did not make it easy for them.

I waited with bated breath for my phone to alarm me to the fact Bryan had read and responded to my message. My computer had long ago fallen asleep, and yet I still waited. I wanted to know what he had to say. Would he make some sort of pitiful excuse, or would he tell me the truth?

Lolling from side to side, my head fell backward as my eyelids dropped lower and lower. My body craved sleep, but I forced myself to remain vigilant and awake—kind of. My eyelids slid closed and my head shifted to the side, placing it at a weird angle, and it mattered not. Sleep slowly shut down my brain and told my body to relax and give up its watchfulness.

Tonight would not be the night I ripped him a new one. I began to push to my feet tiredly, my brain so focused on sleep, I could already envision sinking into my bed...

A loud chime startled me, making me yelp. I fell backward onto the couch, my walker crashed to the ground, and I hissed when my elbow caught the arm of the couch. Shit that hurt! Why did they call it a funny bone when there was nothing funny about the pain? At least I didn't fall on the floor or crash into the coffee table. Both of those things could have resulted in worse injuries.

Damn phone. Damn person who decided to message me at...

With one eye shut and the other squinted so I could check the time without cursing my double vision, I saw that it was only 10:24 P.M. Okay, maybe it wasn't the middle of the night, however, I had been half asleep, and having to wake up deserved a little morsel of my irritation.

Settling my glasses back on my face, I unlocked my phone, peered at the screen, and seeing whose name appeared, my attitude changed instantly. Bryan. A little irritation? Try a bucket full of wrath. Not only had he spilled his guts to Mel—in my head he had fully betrayed me—but he had the audacity to wake me up. Never mind the fact that I was the one who had messaged him first. I didn't care about those minor details.

My thumb hovered over his face, and then I smashed it with as much ferocity as I could. It didn't do anything to him, but it gave me a tad bit of relief. My brown eyes glared back at me in the mirrored edges of my phone, almost scaring me with their intensity. I forced them to focus on the black and white message lighting up the screen, and my brow lifted. Was that how he was going to play it?

Bryan: *I have no fucking clue what you're talking about.*

Straight denial. I wished my thumb would have smashed his real face and not the one on my phone.

Me: Really? So, u didn't talk to Mel last night? U didn't ask about me or tell her u were talking to me while at the same time talking to her? U didn't have a discussion about the fact that u and I have been communicating for a while now?

If someone walked in on me now, they would've probably thought I completely lost my marbles. Deep down, I knew he didn't deserve this much anger, and I didn't know why I lashed out at him so harshly, except embarrassment. I hated knowing that one of my friends had heard that I was so hard up for a date, a complete stranger had to help me find love. And maybe, I wanted to put those walls that I had dropped around him back up. Without those walls, without his betrayal, I was vulnerable and that scared me. No, it terrified me.

Bryan: Wait. Hold up and rewind.

Me: Rewind? Y? Is it because u fucked up and want to undo what u did?

My bitchiness level raised to DEFCON 3. Not as bad as it could be, but far from safe for anyone who stood in my path. He needed to be on alert.

Bryan: Woah! You need to slow down and stop chomping at the bit to bite my head off.

Me: I'm not a fucking horse.

I refused to admit or think about the fact I had compared myself to one earlier in the evening.

Bryan: I NEVER SAID YOU WERE!

Oh, look who decided to use all caps. Before I could type anything, he continued without the caps lock on.

Bryan: Yes, I talked to Mel.

At least he admitted it. I could tell from the moving dots in the chat window, he was still typing, so I waited to see what he had to say for himself. My teeth bit my lip, digging into the flesh while I sat there impatiently. My fingers tapped out a quick rhythm on the back of my phone as he continued to type.

Bryan: I talked to her and asked about you because I wanted to know what your story is. I wanted to understand you a little more. Sometimes we don't see something in ourselves that others do, and I wanted another opinion from someone who knows you better than I do.

Me: And?

Bryan: And that's it. She asked me if I was interested in you and I told her no. She gave me hell for chatting with you, and that's it. And she gave me hell because I kept laughing during our conversation and she called me on the carpet for it like she always does.
Nothing is sacred when it comes to that woman.

Me: Uh huh.

Bryan: Don't believe me, ask her.

I wanted to hold onto my anger and irritation, but I couldn't. Reluctantly, I admitted Mel's side of the story.

Me: She basically said the exact same thing as u.

Bryan: See.

Me: And Vegas rules?

Bryan: Still intact, honey. I didn't tell her shit about how much we talk or what we talked about. I asked her about you in a casual conversation.

Slightly calmer, I pulled my computer into my lap so the small chat screen would be easier to see. And a keyboard was so much easier to type on than a touchscreen. Plus, I needed a minute after reading his "honey".

Me: You could have just asked me.

Bryan: No can do. I had to get someone else's opinion.

Me: And what did she say?

Bryan: That you've been burned in the past and she doesn't know much about it. I thought she was your close friend.

_Me:_ _She is._

Mel might have been one of my close friends, but I didn't share everything about my past with her. Gia had been there since we were younger, ergo, she knew everything. Mel came along later, and by that time, the past remained the past and the door shut tightly.

Bryan: _But?_

_Me:_ _But nothing. I trust Mel, and I do confide in her as a good friend._

Bryan: _But?_

I took a deep breath and exhaled slowly. My skin started to tingle and sweat with nervous anxiety.

_Me:_ _The past is the past._

Bryan: _Except when it intrudes on the present and future._

Squeezing my eyes shut tightly, I tried to calm my churning stomach. Without looking at my hands or the computer, I responded to him.

_Me:_ _Not discussing it with you._

Bryan: _Ever, or just today?_

_Me:_ _Probably ever. I'm not sure I trust you that much._

Bryan: _I told you what Mel and I talked about. That was it. Could it be you were looking for me to fuck up?_

_Me:_ _No._

Bryan: _That's a big yes. You answered too quickly. Don't be in such a rush to blow me off._

Taking his advice, I waited exactly three minutes before I responded next, allowing him to stew and me to calm down. My stomach still felt queasy, and I sweated bullets.

Me: *I'm not looking for you to fuck up. There, did I wait long enough that time?*

Bryan: *LOL. Yes.*

I didn't know what to say to him and thought about shutting down tonight's conversation, but before I could, he pinged again.

Bryan: *I didn't mean to put you on edge or anything like that. I only wanted to know what Mel knew about you.*
I thought I covertly asked.

Me: *She came over here demanding answers.*

Bryan: *That's because she's a curious little wench that likes to stick her fucking nose where it doesn't belong. She barges in on people whether she's wanted or not, and constantly does shit to piss me off. I swear she is worse than my sister sometimes.*

Images of him stripping down to his Captain America underwear popped into my head, and for the first time tonight, I started laughing. Thankfully, he couldn't see or hear me because my body folded over my computer and I almost knocked it to the ground. I was dying to know if there was any possible evidence. Maybe video or pictures. Oh, the possibilities…That and I could hold it over his head for a long time to come.

Bryan: *You still there?*

I took in a deep breath and straightened my body. His next response made me giggle some more. I guess he thought I was still mad at him. And the second part shocked me silent.

Bryan: *I'm really sorry. I promise not to mention anything to nosey rosy again.*
And don't listen to Mel.
Hell, she's the reason I almost got arrested before I left to report to the Navy.

Arrested? Now, this was a story I wanted details about.

Me: *What? Arrested?*

Bryan: *Not saying.*

_Me:_ _Oh no. You have to spill after that setup._

Bryan: _Actually, I don't._

_Me:_ _What if I said I forgive you?_

Bryan: _Tit for tat. Just remember that._

_Me:_ _Whatever._

I knew Mel tended to walk on the wild side and didn't always follow the rules, so police involvement wasn't a complete surprise. That said, to hear that she hadn't changed in almost a decade and that Bryan found himself in the middle of it all, I needed to know what happened. It was a moral imperative. A necessity.

Hearing this story, along with the others he had shared, was probably not the best thing for me. I absorbed everything he said like a sponge, desiring to learn all I could about him. Every little tidbit fascinated me, and that could become dangerous. I should have marked a line in the sand, poured concrete so it never disappeared, and then stayed on the other side opposite of him.

Bryan: _Fine._
I decided to join the Navy when I was 16, but didn't join up until I was 20. Since my birthday is in Dec, I actually got to start school when I was 4 and graduate at 17—a year earlier than most people. In between school and the Navy, I went to college because I promised my parents I would get a college degree before I committed myself.
I got my degree in three instead of four years, joined the NROTC. Uh, the Naval Reserve Officers Training Corps. They are like the JROTC or junior ROTC that some high schools have.

_Me:_ _I know what they are._

Bryan: _I wasn't sure._
Anyway. I joined them in college, and between them and my degree, I entered the Navy as an officer. Two days before I'm supposed to leave town, Mel gets this brilliant idea that we need to go cow tipping. She also managed to sneak out a whole bottle of Grey Goose vodka. Needless to say, we got extremely drunk, and I agreed to go with her.
The farmer called the cops. The cops came out. Even after I threw up on his

pants and shoes, we only got a warning because the chief happened to be
Mel's uncle.
We were so fucking lucky. I still hate vodka.

I snorted with laughter again, causing Curley to whimper. Cow tipping? Really? I didn't know what I expected him to type but getting drunk on vodka and cow tipping definitely wasn't it.

Somehow, I managed to quickly type two words. My dog decided to hide in the bedroom until I settled down. I couldn't help it. This whole story tickled my funny bone—so to speak.

Me: *Yep, lucky.*

Bryan: *I know you are over there laughing at me again. Live it up because I'm sure you have stories that are equally embarrassing.*

Several minutes passed since his last message, and I was pretty sure it was so I could regain some sort of control over my laughter.

Me: *Nope. Not laughing. I'm a sweet, innocent angel.*

Bryan: *I call bullshit. LOL.*

Me: *It's true. Sweet, innocent, and never does anything wrong. I thought you already knew that about me.*

Bryan: *Everyone has something hidden. I'll figure it out one of these days. ;)*

Me: *You act as if I'm going to let you remain in my good graces in the future.*

Bryan: *Now you sound like the empress. LMAO.*

Me: *Bow down to me.*

Bryan: *LOL. Sorry honey, but we're friends now and you are stuck w me forever.*

Me: *Well fuck. Can I give back my consolation prize?*

Bryan: *Nope. Stuck.*

I should have probably dropped the subject since we had already moved past it, but I still asked. I wanted an explanation.

Me: *Why did you ask Mel about me?*

Bryan: *I already told you.*

Me: *Yeah, but you didn't have to ask her about me.*

Had I pushed him too far? No typing, no nothing popped up on the screen. I sat there with my hands clenched into fists at my side, my teeth gnawing on my lip, waiting for him to respond.

When it came to Bryan, my mind had become an expert of conjuring images. I pictured him staring at the computer screen sighing, scratching his face, and shaking his head. I'd only met him in person once several months ago, and yet, his features were ingrained in my head and memories. I imagined him with scruff, without scruff, his hazel eyes crinkled as he smiled and his dimples creating divots in his cheeks. In his Navy uniform, out of it, little or no clothes as his six-pack rippled his abs. Navy, college, high school. I could imagine them all with clarity, and my mental image left me wanting. With as vivid as the memory of that karaoke night was, I didn't need to see pictures of him, I only needed to close my eyes.

I still waited. It took almost ten minutes before he started to respond, and I didn't realize I was holding my breath until the air in my lungs demanded to be released, coming out in a loud whoosh.

Bryan: *It always felt as if you were holding something back, I thought if I talked to someone who knew you it would give me some sort of clue.*

Me: *I've probably been more open with you than most.*

Trust never came easy to me, but what I told him was true. Maybe I confided in him because it felt safe to do so online, or maybe there was something else there.

Bryan: *More open is not telling me everything.*

My eyebrow quirked, and I shook my head. Greedy.

Me: *You aren't my BFF. LOL.*

Bryan: *How long have you known her?*

_Me:_ _Since my dad retired from the Navy._

Bryan: _And that's Gia?_

_Me:_ _You remembered._

Bryan: _You've mentioned her a couple of times, but yeah, I remembered. So? When did you two meet?_

_Me:_ _We were both 12 and in the same grade._

Bryan: _Long time to know someone. Where did you meet?_

_Me:_ _Texas. She was one of the first people I met in the new neighborhood. We became instant friends and were almost inseparable from day one. She knows me better than anyone. She always has my back and I have hers. Now that she's married with a kid and I live in SC, we don't see each other as often, but we talk all the time. Her family claims me, and mine does the same for her._

Bryan: _Everyone deserves a friend like that._

_Me:_ _You and Mel have been friends for a while. I have to ask, did you ever think about dating her?_

Not sure why I pried, but my curiosity got the better of me.

Bryan: _If I throw up on my computer, will you buy me a new one?_

_Me:_ _Funny. She has the same reaction._

Bryan: _Then why ask?_

_Me:_ _Because._

Bryan: _Did you ever consider dating your bff?_

_Me:_ _Hell no. She's a girl and I'm into guys. Haha._

Bryan: _To me, Mel is like my sister. I can't ever imagine dating my sister. And besides, feelings beyond friendship never came into play._

I blamed my growing incessant need to know everything about him on my next question. I needed to stop myself and was unable to do so.

Me: Have you ever been in love?

Bryan: No, but I thought I was a time or two. You?

Me: I don't know anymore.

Bryan: Ok. I have a test for you.

He changed the subject rather quickly, and for that I was grateful. That said, a test? I didn't realize I still attended school.

Me: What?

Did he sense my distress? I could not be sure, but he tried to reassure me.

Bryan: Don't worry. Mel's going too. My friend is having a party/BBQ, and you got an invite.

Telling me not to worry, made me worried and anxious. A party? A friend? I wasn't so sure about any of this. Had I met this friend?

Me: What friend?

Bryan: Doesn't matter. You're going.

That meant I didn't know this so-called friend. Great, but not really.

Me: Nope, I'm not.

Bryan: Yes, you are. Look, Mel knows him too. She's the one that told me about the party, so you don't have to worry. She and Luke will both be there as moral support. They just don't know it yet. :D

Did he really expect me to go to a party where no one knew me? Where they'd look at me like I was some sort of freak? No, thank you. I was scared. I could admit it.

After the blind date, the only time I had left my house was when my sister forced me to her cookout or brunch, or when I had to go to the store or doctor. My self-esteem took a beating that night, and while I knew Bryan had been working on helping me overcome my issues, fear held me prisoner. It shackled me and refused to let go. Most therapists would have told me to break the yoke that bound me, jump off the cliff, face my fears, and put myself out there. I've done that before, and this was the result. I had become what my granny would call plum pitiful.

Bryan: Don't think, just do it. If I could be there, I would be, but if you need me, you only need to message me. I'll make sure I'm online all day.

Easy for him to say. He had only invited me moments ago, and I already had to fight the urge to bury my head in the sand like a cartoon ostrich.

Me: You sound like a sports shoe commercial.

Bryan: Good advice can come from the boob tube. ;)

And with those simple words, he talked me down. The panic that had been welling up, threatening to drown me, only moments before, started to disperse.

Me: Fine. I'll go, but no promises on talking to anyone.

Bryan: I'm only asking you to go. First step and all that.

Shaking my head, I rolled my eyes and huffed in annoyance, pretending the grin on my face did not exist.

Bryan: In order to move forward, you have to take a chance. You won't find love sitting at home doing nothing. And sorry, but book boyfriends are not as good as the real thing.

Why had he brought up book boyfriends? Once again, my curiosity was piqued. Smirking, my fingers moved swiftly over the keyboard.

Me: How would you know? Have you compared a book boyfriend to the real thing? Do you have a book boyfriend all your own?

Bryan: NO! Don't even go there with me.

Me: You sound a little defensive. Insecure? It's all right. There are some men that write romance novels, and other men who read them. Nothing to be ashamed of.

Bryan: *Ingrate.*

Me: *Awe. Striking out? Scared I'll find out your secret?*

Bryan: *To quote you, 'I hate you'.*

Me: *LOL. :**

Bryan: *I'll send you the deets tomorrow. GTG. Bye.*

Apparently, I touched a chord and he decided to end the conversation. From what Mel told me, and my own observations, Bryan was straighter than a telephone pole, but it felt good to gain the upper hand and tease him a little.

I fell backward and laughed again. I may have a party I had to go to, even though I would have rather made an appointment with the dentist, but teasing him tonight had been the highlight of my day.

CHAPTER SIXTEEN

BRYAN

That woman knew how to get under my skin, and I couldn't believe I let her do it. Cheeky didn't even begin to describe Emma. My thoughts conjured a picture of her typing with sadistic glee and cackling at the same time. Her chocolate eyes danced as her cheeks turned pink. And I found myself chuckling. I couldn't put my finger on who it was exactly, but she reminded me of someone.

"Yo! You ready?" Evan called out from my bedroom doorway. Noticing my computer on my lap, his brow lifted and he inquired, "Talking to her again?"

"Huh?" I frowned, dropping my eyes to the slender silver piece of hardware sitting on my thighs. "Yeah. I needed to tell her about Chad's barbecue party."

"He's your friend from back home? The one you met in college?"

"Yeah."

"What's wrong?" His arms crossed over his chest, changing his countenance. His posture and the way he crossed his arms over his chest told me he would not budge until I gave him a nibble of something.

Shrugging, I said, "She doesn't get it yet."

"Do you blame her? Dude, maybe you need to put yourself in her shoes for one second." When he noticed that my scowl had turned ferocious, he held his hands up in mock surrender. "I'm just saying. She's been through a lot and has no proof any guy will actually want her. Hell, she's probably lower than plankton on the self-esteem chain."

"Watching Sponge–Bob again? Doesn't Plankton have an over-inflated ego?"

His middle finger flipped me off. "Asshole."

I chose to ignore him. Instead, I got up and ran my fingers through my hair. Tonight, we were both going to a bar to celebrate a friend's birthday, and I prayed there would be at least one decent girl there. I desperately needed to get laid.

Evan leaned against the doorjamb and snorted. "No response? That's unlike you. Are you sure that girl isn't getting to you?"

"No way in hell. She's a friend of a friend and nothing more. I only wish I knew how to fix her."

"Maybe she isn't broken." His words were an almost feral growl, and after he said his piece, he turned and walked out the door, calling over his shoulder, "Let's go before we're late."

Our discussion had been terminated, but his insight made me think. I stopped. No, I had to clear my head of Emma. In fact, once I dipped my dick into some warm pussy, all would be right with the world again. It had been too long.

Why was I hell-bent on helping one lonely girl? Why did I want to save her so badly? In the grand scheme of things, she was a nobody to me. Well, that wasn't completely true, since we were sort of friends and she was Mel's good friend, but there was nothing more to it than that. Nothing. So why had I felt it necessary to involve myself in her problems from the beginning? Why had I chosen to help someone who may be broken beyond repair, and who fought me every step of the way? Why was I torturing myself? Evan's words echoed in my mind, "Maybe she isn't broken."

No, Emma was most definitely broken. He could only say otherwise because he had never spoken to her before.

Damn it! Emma invaded my thoughts and threatened to strip my calm, cool, and collected shield from me.

Tonight, I would make myself forget about her and find a girl of my own. The sooner I found someone for Emma, the better for me. Maybe love awaited her with one of my friends in Charleston. I was sure I could get someone to date her, build up her self-esteem, and then she might believe she was worthy of love.

Maybe.

Then again, maybes equaled uncertainty. Maybe one day I would jump into my jet, fly high into the sky, and never come back. Maybe I would be called to war again. Maybe my family would pull their heads out of their asses and…

I still remembered the day I told my parents I wanted to join the Navy. After talking to a Navy recruiter at school during my junior year, I decided that as soon as I turned eighteen, I would join the ranks of our military as an enlisted man. My parents disagreed with me. They informed me that no son of theirs would ever join the military, especially not as a lowly enlisted man. Hearing their snide comments, listening to their snooty attitude, I clenched my hands into tight fists as I sat in the den enduring their endless tirade. I fought to keep my temper in check, when what I really wanted to do was to storm out of there leaving my family behind.

Why was it so wrong to want to serve my country proudly? I thought my parents would have been proud of my decision since both my grandfathers served, but like many things that came with my parents, I had been more than a little mistaken. They did everything they could to talk me out of joining and finally resorted to reluctantly agreeing if I got my degree, which allowed me to enter as an officer. They had hoped my dreams of joining the Navy would disappear while I worked toward my degree, but as they tried to crush my dreams, I crushed theirs instead. With my degree in my hand, I signed the paperwork that broke my parents' hearts and got me as far away from them as possible. I followed my own dreams.

My parents weren't bad. Dad coached my little league baseball teams. Mom organized bake sales and the like for the PTA. We were the stereotypical American family complete with two kids: one boy and one girl. Things changed in high school, and I wasn't sure exactly what had caused the house of cards to start falling. All I knew was that they suddenly stopped coming to my games, and this chasm appeared between us. Rayne, my sister, remained their little angel, but not me. And after I made my announcement concerning my wish to join the Navy, the chasm grew into a seemingly impassable gorge.

When I returned from deployment, I called them immediately and left them a voicemail. They returned my call the next day and most of the call consisted of strained conversation and awkward silence. We no longer knew how to communicate with each other.

I feared this wall would remain forever. It terrified me to think that something would happen to me, and they would not care one iota. That sounded stupid and weird because they were my parents, and I knew deep down that they loved me, even if they couldn't show it. Maybe whatever this was would never be worked out, but maybe there was a way to move forward. I didn't know. Maybe.

That word again: maybe.

One of my greatest fears was dying in my plane, and yet, as a pilot and Navy man, I would be at peace if I died protecting others while I served my country. My other greatest fear…No. I refused to go there even in my head.

Since the night Emma accidentally messaged me, I found myself questioning some of my choices, thinking about things I hadn't thought of in years. Tonight, I pushed her to the back of my mind and would do what I did best. In the crowd of wanting women, I would find a woman who would scratch my itch. Was I a playboy? Possibly, but hey, at least this time I didn't use maybe.

Evan and I arrived at the bar and immediately sought out our friend and the rest of the party. We were five minutes late and already on the prowl.

As we made our way to the reserved room far in the back, our eyes wandered around, scanning for available women in the building. Some women sat with their boyfriends. They became oblivious to anything the person next to or across from them said. Their eyes followed us as they fucked us in their minds, their partners completely forgotten. Others, who were there as a single person or maybe with a friend, stopped in their tracks, their glasses raised half way up to their lips, and they swallowed hard. Not from drink, but from the sudden unquenchable thirst for me or my roommate. And still others, searched for the reason behind the sudden lull in their conversations, and when their eyes found us, their cheeks flamed pink, and they were unable to rip their eyes away from us.

We were used to women fawning over us, and to the glares shot our way by jealous men. Both genders desired us in some way, whether they wanted in our pants or wanted to become us. We strutted through the restaurant, basking in our good fortune and future conquests. Evan and I may not be the best looking guys on the planet, however, we were far from ugly. My tall stature and muscles had girls swooning for me, but Evan put me to shame. A couple of inches taller than me, he looked as if he could compete in a Mr. Universe competition, and I firmly believed his cropped black hair (something left over from his army days) and his brown eyes, would win over male and female judges alike. He was that smooth.

Together, no one could compare or get in our way. We were two men who got what we wanted when we wanted it. Our looks, our confidence, and our bodies all ensured we had an endless supply of women...most of the time. And that wasn't cockiness, it was the God's honest truth.

I had been in the middle of a dry spell the past several weeks, and I couldn't understand why. Actually, I knew why. Every girl I met had something wrong with them. Too old—I didn't want a repeat of that woman and her daughter. Too young—the thought of someone calling me daddy made me shudder. Food in her teeth. Breath smelled. She fidgeted. Talked too much. Talked too little. And if I managed to find someone I wanted to fuck, Emma would ping me or I would think about her at the most inopportune times. Emma had royally screwed me over until now, and it was time for me to take charge again, to be the one doing the screwing.

Walking into the back room, we easily spotted our friend, and immediately noticed the eight women hanging onto every word he said. Periodically the women would shift, and that was when we noticed each girl had one hand touching him: his arm, ass, hip, and shoulder. One even boldly rubbed his crotch in the middle of the room, but at least her hands were manicured and I detected zero stench.

Those feet still haunted me.

"It's about time you assholes decided to join us!" Shane, the birthday boy, shouted, as he broke away his throng of adoring fans to give both of us a one-armed hug.

"We're less than ten minutes late." Evan chuckled and pushed him away.

Shaking my head, I laughed myself before telling him, "Happy birthday, Shane."

"Thanks, man!"

"Already starting with the harem?" I teased him. Every time we all got together, we gave each other shit, but it was all in good fun.

"I had to be sure I had some women. If I didn't, all the girls would forget I existed as soon as you two jerks arrived. How many broken hearts did you leave out there on your way in?" Shane joked standing on his tiptoes to peek over our shoulders. Whereas Evan and I were both over six feet tall, Shane had not been blessed in the height department.

Evan pushed him again, and Shane pretended to stumble backward. "Plenty for all three of us out there still," proclaimed my roommate.

One of the girls I had noticed hanging around Shane, approached us slowly, her eyes roving up and down my body, lingering on my cock. Leaning over, she whispered in his ear, but her eyes remained locked on me.

Shane snorted in amusement before making the introductions. "Angela, this asshole is Bryan. Bryan, this is the enchanting Angela."

Smirking, I narrowed my eyes and gave her body a once-over like she had done to mine. I had already sized up each woman when I entered the party room, but if she chose to be blatant, I knew how to play that game as well. "Nice to meet you, Angela."

"The pleasure is all yours," she replied, her full smile displaying her glistening white teeth with pink lipstick streaked across the front two.

One thing about me, I was loyal to my friends. Evan and Shane both counted on me, and I counted on them. So a girl who wanted to jump from the guest of honor to one of his friends, I would play with her in order to teach her a lesson, but I would never close the deal.

"I'm sure it is." I grinned. This was going to be fun. My eyes darted to Shane, who still stood next to her, and then to Evan. A silent message was conveyed before I gave Angela my full attention again. "How do you know Shane?"

She threw her head back and cackled. Her laugh annoyed me and reminded me of a hyena. Her green eyes were set wide apart, making her nose appear wider than it should. Bangs hung low on her broad forehead, and her box dyed brown hair was ratted and stringy in various spots. I could see her blond roots. She desperately needed lessons on how to apply makeup because she looked as if she got her tips from someone firmly stuck in the eighties. Bright blue eyeshadow, pink cheeks, and equally pink lipstick accentuated her round face and highlighted the mustache above her lip. Her tits were shoved into a bra too small for her, or she had tissue tits. Either way, she probably thought her boobs would stand proud and firm, and appear bigger than they were. It didn't work.

She looked about my sister's age, so why the fuck she thought she needed to dye her hair or wear that much makeup was anyone's guess. Had this been a dare gone badly? Was she hard up for a good toss in the hay?

Why the fuck had this girl been in Shane's harem? And then I realized this had been the girl brazen enough to grab Shane's clothed dick. Bold. But now that she stood closer, I detected an odd odor. Was that her perfume or a can of fishy cat food? Her hands may look manicured, but other than that, her personal hygiene left something to be desired.

"I came with my friend. She said there will be plenty of guys for both of us," Angela admitted, her tongue snaking out to wet her lips.

I wanted to cringe with disgust. Admittedly, I had been picky lately, but surely no one expected me to do this…monster. It wasn't only her looks, although that had a great deal to do with it, but it was her attitude that made her ugly. The way she jumped from one man to another so easily, like it was normal, made me squeamish.

"I see. I came with a friend too in order to celebrate another friend's birthday. The friend you were just feeling up." I still couldn't understand how she managed to get so close to him. Couldn't he smell her?

"Well, it is a party. I think we can all have a good time together. Or taking turns. Your choice."

I almost gagged but managed to keep my face impassive and hid my reaction. "I see."

"I'm just here for a good time. You know how that is?"

"I do."

"I can blow all three of you in this room if you want."

My stomach turned, making me grateful I hadn't eaten yet. If I had, I might have thrown up on her. She smelled like cat food, her makeup was too heavy, and she oozed an aura of desperation.

"Angela!" Another woman stumbled over toward us. Her tits were big, fake, and practically falling out of her halter top. Her tanned skin was clear of any blemishes, and her face and makeup made her look like she stepped out of the pages of a fashion magazine. What the fuck?

"This is my friend, Brandy." Angela introduced the newcomer.

Everything suddenly made sense. Shane wanted in Brandy's pants and put up with Angela until Evan and I showed up so that we could take her off of his hands. Either that or Shane wanted in Brandy's pants and would put up with Angela in order to succeed, even if it meant a threesome. Shane was a freak when it came to the bedroom, and had been known to sleep with anyone who had a pussy and willingly spread her legs. Angela seemed fit that requirement.

"Hi, Brandy. I'm Bryan, and this is my roommate, Evan." I made sure my tone remained even and polite.

"Hey, you're hot!" Brandy slurred as she wrapped her arms around Shane.

"Yeah, I get that a lot." My smirk grew.

Her eyes roved to Evan. "And so are you."

Crossing his arms over his chest, he nodded. "I've been told that before."

I could see the expression on Shane's face change. He knew what was coming and silently asked us to spare Brandy. We didn't.

Narrowing my eyes, I sized both of the ladies up and shook my head at what I saw. "Brandy?"

"Yeah?"

"Were you the one that did Angela's makeup?"

She giggled. "Nope. She did that on her own."

"You probably think you're the hottest woman in the room, don't you?"

"Well, yeah. I think that's pretty obvious. And I think it's also obvious that you three deserve the best. You know you want me. I'll even let you stick it in any hole you want."

Was it possible? Had my dick shriveled some more? I had yet to get hard in front of Angela or Brandy, and I think my dick just curled up inside itself. Fuck!

I turned to Angela. "You probably think you're hot stuff too, don't you?"

"I've never had any complaints. I had Shane eating out of the palm of my hand before you showed up."

"I'm sure you did," I snidely remarked.

Evan chuckled. "You want a shot at all three of us?"

Both girls answered at the same time, "Yes!" They were panting and practically drooled at the thought of having three hot men at their disposal.

"Then why don't you go home and close your eyes and start dreaming, because that's the only way you're going to get any of us in bed with you. Sorry, but we don't play pass around the pussy, and we definitely don't want what you're selling. Either one of you. So, I suggest you leave." Again, I remained patient, rational, and calm.

Angela laughed again, and I wished I had earplugs to save my ears from that horrendous sound. "You can't make us leave. We were invited."

"By who?" Shane asked.

What? Did this mean he didn't know these girls?

Angela turned to Brandy because she had received her invite from her friend, but Brandy suddenly appeared very nervous.

"Who invited you?" I demanded.

"Jill Bart," Brandy mumbled.

Did she say, Jill Bart? My crazy ex who went out with Evan, who we fought to get out of the house? The same one who I told Emma about? Her?

Shane knew the whole story about Jill the psycho, and Evan and I had less than fond memories of her. All three of us shouted, "Out!"

All eyes turned and watched the women practically run out of the bar with heads bowed low and their tail between their legs. Amazing how sober Brandy suddenly acted when the truth slapped her in the face. Fuck, I needed a strong drink.

Without waiting for our waitress, I stomped over to the bar and ordered two shots of tequila. I started to lift one to my lips when a hand stopped me. My gaze traveled from the hand, up the arm, across the shoulder and chest, and up to the face. The woman had short brown hair with sparkling brown eyes. Her makeup was light, and her teeth had a tiny gap between the front two, but they were free of lipstick and food. Her petite body appeared as if it worked out regularly and she had little to no curves–not a deal breaker though.

"Is one of those for me?" She inquired sweetly with a small trace of a southern accent.

Lifting one eyebrow, I asked with a smile, "Not from around here?"

"Georgia. You?"

"South Carolina."

She stuck her hand out to shake mine, and I enveloped her tiny hand between both of my giant palms. "I'm Jonie, and I'm a yoga instructor."

"Bryan, and I'm a Navy pilot." Her eyes glazed over when she heard what I did for a living. The smile on my lips grew. Releasing her, I pushed one of the shot glasses toward her along with the salt, which she sprinkled on her hand like I had done. "To new friends."

"Cheers." Her glass clinked against mine, we licked the salt, drink the shot, and grabbed a lime to suck on.

Tonight suddenly took a different turn. Maybe Jonie would help me out of my dry spell.

I invited her back to the back room to join the party, and she agreed to come if her friend could come too. Thankfully, her friend Michelle acted and appeared normal with light brown hair that fell to the small of her back and green eyes that instantly fell on Evan. Both girls only came to my shoulders, but where Jonie had practically zero curves except for her small breasts, Michelle had an ass a man could grab and tits that looked as if they would overflow my hands.

Evan and Michelle hit it off, leaving Jonie and me to our own devices. I didn't worry about the birthday boy because his harem—minus two—surrounded him again.

We talked, we laughed, we drank, we kissed...and I pulled back. Guilt assailed me. I tried again. Unable to continue kissing her, I took a step backward. "Sorry."

"You okay?" Jonie asked, concerned, reaching out to me.

I shook off her hand and nodded. "Yes...no...I don't know. Sorry. It's not you."

Holding up her hand, she forced me to stop. "Please don't start with that line 'it's not you, it's me.' Pathetic. If you don't want this, that's fine but don't blow me off with a bullshit line."

"Sorry. I know. I keep saying that. I've got to go," I told her, and after a quick goodbye to Shane and Evan, I called for an Uber and went home.

What the fuck was happening to me? I had the perfect opportunity to put an end to my dry spell, and I couldn't go through with it. Why? Why did I feel guilty? I had absolutely no reason to feel guilty.

Shit! My night ended horribly. I walked into the house and flopped on my bed just done with it all. Tomorrow would be a new day, and I could think about things then. Until then, I wanted to pretend tonight ended on a high instead of a low.

CHAPTER SEVENTEEN

BRYAN

"You're an asshole of the first order!" Mel screamed.

Pulling the phone away from my ear, I grimaced and stuck my tongue out at Evan before holding it up to my ear again. I'd been cooking breakfast when my cell phone rang, and he thought it would be a great idea to answer it. He was a shithead.

But for now, I needed to ignore my roommate and focus on Mel. Something told me whatever put her in a pissy mood had something to do with Emma. Had Emma told her about our argument four days ago—the very argument Mel helped instigate? Possible, but not likely. Since then, Emma and I got along great. Granted, I might have been slightly on edge since losing out on a sure thing, and I still hadn't figured out why I couldn't go through with it. I wouldn't lay that at Emma's feet or shift the blame to her, though.

What else could it be?

"Is it that time of the month?" I never liked to throw what she termed her "womanhood" in her face, however, her attitude irritated me. She chose to call me up and yell at me before a pleasant "hello" or "what's up". If she acted like a bitch, I reserved the right to act like an outright bastard to her.

"Don't even go there with me, Bryan Gorman Sampson!"

"What the fuck did I do, and who the fuck pissed you off? Is Luke withholding sex from you or something?" I snapped, throwing down the spatula I used to push the eggs around the skillet.

"ASSHOLE!" Her yell could be heard from the kitchen to the back of the house. I knew it had when Evan, who had gone to his room to grab something, came out laughing and mimicking her.

My eyes rolled on their own accord, and I pressed the heel of my hand into my forehead. "We've established the fact I'm an asshole. Now you want to pull that stick out of your ass and tell me what I did wrong?"

"I talked to your sister."

Oh shit. Everything came into focus, and I understood completely. I really was in a boatload of trouble and should have suspected Rayne would've called in reinforcements.

Rayne had called earlier in the morning and asked me to request leave so I could come home and talk to our parents. While I respected both of them, and loved them to death, they were both adults and there wasn't anything anyone could say that would change their minds about the divorce. But my sister believed otherwise. She seemed to think I lived in a bubble of denial. To her, I liked to pretend everything was all right because if I didn't see it, everything remained as it always had.

My head started to throb, and I threw the dish towel at Evan to get him to shut up, or at least try. It didn't work, but at least he left the room, the sounds of his laughter disappearing behind his closed bedroom door.

It honestly didn't surprise me that my parents decided to get a divorce. Even before I left for the Navy, things felt strained and weird. However, I still felt hurt and pissed off. The divorce made things awkward, but my own parents, the people who gave me life, never called and told me the monumental news themselves...they had left the dirty deed to my sister.

A week ago, my sister called me and informed me of the impending divorce. Not my mom or my dad. My sister called. A whole week had passed, and they still hadn't reached out to talk to me themselves. Nothing. No communication whatsoever. No emails, calls, texts, Skype, or anything. Not even a message on FaceSpace. At this point, I'd accept a Tweet or Instagram as an acceptable form of communication, but I had received nothing except complete silence from them.

Since I'd returned stateside, the only time I ever talked to either of them, was the one return phone call I received the day after I returned. I knew things were bad between us, but was I really worth less than ten minutes of their time?

We used to be a happy family. What happened? Rayne blamed me, but if I caused the rift, shouldn't I know what I did wrong? From the time I entered college through my first year in the Navy, I tried to get them to talk to me every chance I got, and yet, nothing I did ever worked. I couldn't even recall the last good conversation I had with my parents. I

My senior year in high school, I asked Rayne why she thought they stopped talking to me. Her answer shocked me. "What do you mean?

They try to talk to you all the time. You won't really talk to them, though." I couldn't believe it, Rayne actually thought I brought this upon myself.

It had gotten to the point that I tried not to broach the subject of our parents too much when talking to Rayne. It caused stress and undo strain between us when I did, therefore, it was easier to ignore.

If I understood why everything fell apart, if I heard their reasoning, maybe I wouldn't feel hurt, angry, confused, or like they discarded me. Maybe if I understood, I could try to build a bridge between us for my sister's sake, but some things truly were impossible. I understood nothing. I had zero answers. And when I asked them, they'd said, "We don't know what you're talking about, son." I would probably have an easier time getting information out of a terrorist cell than trying to get Carol and Matt Sampson to open up to me.

This was their decision and I was the last person on the planet they would ever listen to or take advice from, which was why it pissed me off that Rayne called Mel. My best friend knew the about the lack of relationship between me and my parents, and yet, she still took my sister's side. Why the hell did she call to yell at me then?

"Are you there?" Her demand sounded more like a growl.

"I'm here." My voice came out clipped and emotionless. I tried to hold it back, but her phone call irritated me.

"So, what are you going to do?"

Perplexed, I barked, "What? Do? I'm not going to do anything."

"You have got to be shitting me."

"Why the fuck does it matter? Excuse me if I'm completely off base here, but I'm pretty sure I've told you all the bullshit that's been going on with my parents. You also know that there's shit I can do to change their minds. For fuck's sake, they're grown adults and can make their own decisions about their lives and how they want to live them. Now that Rayne and I are grown and moved out, they can move on with their own lives."

"You won't do this for your sister? Won't you even try for Rayne? Look, I know your parents probably won't listen, but I'm not asking you to do this for them. I'm asking for Rayne. She's really upset and has been staying on my couch crying herself to sleep every night since your parents decided to get the divorce. I know she's acting like a toddler throwing a temper tantrum, but she never got the cold shoulder from your folks. To her, everything was always rainbows and butterflies, and now that shit has been blown to smithereens. She needs to believe that everything that can be tried has been tried. And if your parents still get divorced, then so be it, but at least you tried your best."

"Mel—" I began, however, she interrupted me before I could continue.

"Don't 'Mel' me. I agree, your parents are asshats for how they've treated you, but you love your sister, and she's your family."

"Mel, I don't know."

"Bryan, I need her off my fucking couch. She is driving me insane!"

"Is that the only reason?"

"Her crying is annoying. I love your sister, and she's a close friend of the family and all that, but damn. I've never seen someone whine so much."

"So this is all purely for selfish reasons."

"Nope."

Pinching the bridge of my nose, I sighed. "What?"

"I miss you and it'll be fun to see you again." Mel giggled, and then she turned serious again, "Rayne really does need to know everything possible was tried. I know your parents won't listen, but she needs to see your attempt to talk to them."

"She's 24, it's time she grows up. Besides, I'll be home for your wedding in about a month," I grumbled.

"And it's a month and a half until the wedding. Do you know how long that is? How long will I have to deal with her? You're right, she should grow up. So come home and tell her that, because that shit needs to come from you, not me."

Mel would harp until I gave in, which was why I decided to given in sooner rather than later would benefit me more. "Fine. But I can't promise anything. We're doing training exercises at the base and this is short notice."

Huffing, Mel told me, "I'm only asking you try your best. If you can't, then you can't. I'm not asking you to pull rainbows out of your ass."

"Whatever. I'll see what I can do, but with me getting leave for the wedding, I don't think they'll give me another leave so close to it."

"All I ask is that you try." Her perky voice grated on my nerves.

Sitting down hard on the recliner in the living room, I ran a hand through my hair and asked, "Anything else?"

"Not really. How is your little project with Emma going?" She asked offhandedly.

"It's okay." I didn't want to discuss Emma with her at all, not after it blew up in my face the last time. Erring on the side of caution, I chose to give the shortest possible answer to all questions. Even if it never got back to her, because the last thing I wanted to do was to lose Emma's trust in me again. Too many men have failed her or fallen short of the mark, and I didn't want to become one more notch on that list.

"Okay? That's all I get?" I heard the snickers she tried to muffle, and I pulled my hair in frustration.

Emma and I got along great, but there were times when I felt out of my league trying to coach a girl—not that I would ever admit that even upon pain of death—when having a girl's opinion might help. "Not much to tell. We talk and that's about it." Or all I was willing to share with her.

"She told me she's going to the barbecue on Saturday."

"Good. I kind of thought she would come up with some sort of excuse to back out of going." Relief flooded me at hearing Emma would indeed go to the party I basically ordered her to attend.

"Truth?"

That made me scared. Mel sometimes said things that didn't always help the situation, and she had been known to make it worse sometimes. "What?" I had to ask.

I thought my best friend would remain serious, but her solemn tone of voice changed when she said, "I think she was looking for me to tell her she didn't have to go." She howled with laughter. "I told her I couldn't wait to hang out with her at the party, and that if she wanted a ride, Luke and I would drive her."

"Thanks." Truth was, I didn't trust Emma to keep up her end of our deal. I fully expected her to try and bail on the party, ergo Mel was my backup, forcing Emma to follow through.

"You're making her go."

"I'm not making her do anything, but she needs to start putting herself out there." The heart of the matter when it came to Emma. She needed to learn to open up.

What I didn't say, what I feared was if Emma kept to herself and refused to meet new people, if she ran scared, she would eventually never leave her house again except when absolutely necessary. I worried she would break off ties with her friends and family and become the dreaded cat lady of the neighborhood. I don't care if she had dogs now, or if it's like she told me last night and she was allergic to cats. She would become that person. I forbade her from doing that. If my coercing her to go to a party where I knew she would know at least a couple of people prevented that image from coming to life, then so be it.

"And you're not forcing her?" Mel challenged.

"I'm not there to make sure she does or doesn't get her butt to the party," I retorted, my ego firmly in place.

"But I am?" She hinted as if she believed she was an intricate part of my plan. I hated to let her down and tell her my plans did not include her.

"You are, but this has to be all her."

"Wait a second. What?"

"You heard me. Look, I know you're there, and that you'll make sure she gets there. I also know you support her 100%, but this has to be her, or in the future, she may have to be forced into doing anything and everything. And let's be real. If the only thing she experiences is us coercing her, that would take all the fun out of it. I hated playing baseball as a kid because my parents forced me to do it. I wanted to play football, but they thought it was too dangerous. In high school, I played football and was happy as a clam."

"Good point."

"Exactly."

"You really are trying to help her, aren't you?" she muttered. She sounded as if she had come to some sort of epiphany. Knowing she didn't trust me when it came to Emma, hurt.

"What the hell did you think was happening?" I hissed. Pressing my fingers down one at a time, I felt my knuckles pop.

"Honestly?"

"Now I don't know if I want to know."

"I thought you were trying to arrange a hookup for one of your friends or for yourself when you took leave again."

"Ouch. Glad to know you have all that confidence and trust in me. I already told you that would never happen because first, she's your friend, and second, she's not my type. That's like trying to look at you in a sexual way. Bleh. NOT. GOING. TO. HAPPEN," I stressed. The sooner I got off of this call, the better for my sanity.

Sucking in her breath as if I hit her, she finally relented, "I got it."

Absolute silence stretched between us. I didn't even hear her breath. After allowing it to linger for a minute or two, I made my request. "Do me a favor and watch her."

"Of course, I will."

"Thanks." I knew she meant what she said, and I did too. We both wanted Emma to feel comfortable and safe.

If she was curious about my request or had an opinion, she kept it to herself, which made me once again grateful to her for her discreteness...for the moment. Considering this was Mel, it would be short–lived.

"You'll ask for leave?" She switched back to our initial conversation.

"I'll ask, but I'm not making promises."

"Whatever. If your ass doesn't get it, I'll come out west and kick your butt."

Chuckling at her harmless threat, I teased her. "Awe, do you miss me that much?"

"Nope. Not really. I'm just tired of dealing with your crybaby sister."

"I'll do what I can, and that's all I can do, but even if I get it, you know how my parents are with..." I trailed off, suddenly unsure of what I wanted to say.

"I know they are, but this isn't for them. It's for Rayne."

I pretended to pout. "Which is the only reason I'm doing this."

"I know." Her snickering turned to a snort.

"That's lovely. I can't believe Luke loves a pig."

"Oink oink."

"Very classy. Your grandmother would probably have a cow if she heard that."

"Probably," Mel readily agreed as she laughed.

"Okay. Look, I'll talk to you later, and I promise to call Rayne tomorrow since I'm not sure what time I'm getting home tonight?"

"Big date?" She couldn't hide it, I heard her increased curiosity over the phone.

I smirked, "Something like that."

"I got it. Have fun playing the whore and I'll talk to you tomorrow."

I knew she wasn't serious with her insults, but sometimes…I mean I was no virgin by any stretch of the imagination—lost it at 14 to a girl who was 16—but I also didn't sleep with every girl I came into contact with. I might have slept with maybe 50%, except lately. I'd felt the itch for sex, but hadn't managed to follow through. Frustrations put me on edge, and I found myself desperate to find someone…anyone. Today's date, I met at the grocery store the day before, and I figured she had to be better than stinky feet. "Please let it be better than stinky feet," I prayed.

I parked in the well–lit parking lot of the hole in the wall Italian restaurant she recommended. If I hadn't pull the address up on GPS, I would've completely missed it. The restaurant sign had several letters burned out, and therefore the name read ALF instead of ALFONSO'S. It sat situated between a dry cleaner and an insurance office. The strip center appeared small and unassuming, but standing in front of a glass door that had a potted tree on either side of it, my date, Shelly (or was it Shelby?) waited for me.

My eyes skimmed my dashboard and found my clock. I arrived ten minutes early, and she got there even earlier than I had. Punctual. I liked that in a girl. Thoughts of another girl crept to the forefront, sneaking in like a ninja. Emma and I never really had a set time we talked. It usually happened when we both wound up online at the same time, however, there were rare occasions that we would set a time. She always pinged me five minutes early on the dot. Either she was anxious to talk or all of her clocks needed to be set to the correct time.

No, now was not the time to think about Emma, or anyone else for that matter. I had a date waiting for me, and Shelby—or was it Shelly, Cindy, Shandi?—deserved my attention.

"Hi, were you waiting long?" I asked, giving her my best smile. Taking a long deep breath when I reached her side, I exhaled slowly. She smelled good. No rotting corpses or fishy cat food. So far, so good.

"Not at all. I work next door at the insurance office and got off about five minutes ago. My boss was in a hurry to close up shop, so I got the boot out the door." She giggled, and it sounded melodious and pretty. Not beautiful but pretty.

Emma's laugh sounded like a loud seal, and yet, it didn't annoy me. It probably should have, but maybe the free-flowing beer and bad karaoke singing made me deaf that night. So different from my date, whatever her name was. Another arrow of guilt hit me, and I pushed it away. I had no reason to feel guilty about going out with anyone.

Pushing all thoughts of anyone or anything else away, I chuckled and pulled open the door for the only person who mattered for the moment. "That's convenient."

"It is."

"Hey, Dana," the hostess greeted my date. Dana? I'd been way off the mark.

"Hi, Penny." Dana gave the hostess a large smile and then asked, "Can we have a table toward the back?"

"Sure. I got the perfect one for you two." Penny gave us both a conspiratorial wink and lead the way to a corner booth in the back where no one else had been seated. It was still early on a Wednesday night, so half the restaurant sat empty, but the hostess still sat us as far away from anyone as possible.

After Penny left us alone, I asked, "Are you a regular?"

Her sing-song laugh filled the air again. "You could say that. Since it's right here, I come at least three times a week." Leaning in, Dana whispered, "My figure is suffering for it."

I knew she was fishing for a compliment. She wanted me to compliment her figure, which didn't look as if she chowed down on pasta all the time. Her waist was trim and when she walked, her heels accentuated her long legs and firm ass. Yesterday at the store, her hair had been swept up in a messy ponytail, but tonight her long honey blonde hair hung down to just below her shoulders in waves. She had taken the time with her appearance tonight, I could tell, but I leaned in closely and told her, "You have an amazing figure."

Blushing, her green eyes danced as she grinned. "Thank you."

Girls were easy. They liked compliments, thrived on them in fact, and wanted to be treated with respect. I could do both of those things with ease.

Unless that girl was named Emma Taylor. Then I felt like I had to monitor everything I said. Sometimes talking to her made me feel like I was navigating a minefield. But her brown hair and brown eyes contrasted with

Dana's light hair and eyes. Even their personalities seemed to be polar opposites. I tried to picture Emma with Dana's personality, but it didn't work.

"Is something wrong?" Dana questioned.

"Wrong? No. Sorry. I was just thinking about something my roommate asked me to do." My answer sounded forced and rushed to my ears, however, she visibly relaxed and seemed to accept it as fact. *Stop it, Bryan. You don't need to think about Emma right now!*

After we ordered, I managed to keep Emma out of my thoughts the rest of the night…for the most part. On the way to Dana's house for "dessert," I might have thought about Emma briefly, and I might have checked to see if she left me a FaceSpace message, but other than that, I remained with Dana mentally.

Yes, I stayed with Dana, but the guilt started to creep in again when we got to her place and began ripping each other's clothes off on our way down the hall to her bedroom. I refused to stop though. I needed this. I needed tonight. I needed to get laid. I was on the cliff of desperation, and I jumped.

I had done nothing wrong. Dana and I were two consenting adults.

I wished I could blame the guilt on the fact I had to keep reminding myself of Dana's name, but I couldn't keep up that façade. When I closed my eyes, I imagined a set of brown eyes staring back at me. Why? Why was I plagued with thoughts of Emma? Why this guilt?

CHAPTER EIGHTEEN

EMMA

S omething felt off with Bryan today, and I couldn't for the life of me figure out why. It was only a feeling, nothing more, and nothing less, but it was like a canyon had opened between us. If I thought about it, it was ridiculous, considering all we'd ever done was to talk on FaceSpace messenger.

Me: *Are you sure u r ok?*

Bryan: *Fine.*

Every time I asked, he gave me the same answer. I knew it sounded weird or funny, but all of his responses seemed short, without humor, and clipped. What had happened in his part of the world?

Normally when we talked, Bryan harped on me about ways to better myself, to get rid of my insecurities, or he bugged me about my past. None of that had happened today...yet. I thought he would have given me a pep talk about tomorrow's barbecue by now, but that hadn't happened either. If anything, the conversation felt slightly one-sided. He asked about my day, and I told him about how I had an eye appointment and the nurse dilated my eyes. I hadn't realized I was getting my eyes dilated and wound up calling my sister to drive me home since she had stayed home to wait for the cable man today. Then I told him I tried to play with Curley, but I kept throwing the toy on the table, behind the TV, or in the water bowl. After that, my dog gave up and left me to take a nap. I expected a few LOLs or something, but I got another short response.

Bryan: _That's nice._

That was all he could say?

_Me:_ _You ok?_

Bryan: _I'm fine._

_Me:_ _How was your day?_

I hoped that would start a conversation, but my hopes proved to be in vain.

Bryan: _I flew drills, worked out in the gym, and met with my CO._

_Me:_ _Your CO?_

Bryan: _It means commanding officer._

_Me:_ _I knew that. Everything ok?_

Bryan: _Then why did you ask? And, I told you, I'm fine._

I managed to develop a deep level of hostility for the word "fine." I tried to give him an out.

_Me:_ _Need me to let you go?_

Bryan: _Nah. I can talk._

I screamed at the computer, "Then fucking talk to me!" He couldn't hear me, but it made me feel better.

_Me:_ _How were your drills?_

Bryan: _Good. I hit all my targets._

_Me:_ _So is it like that movie Top Gun?_

Bryan: _What? LOL._

That was my first "LOL" of the conversation today. Had I finally broken through to him? Maybe things were looking up. I could picture him distracted and then seeing my question. He rolled his eyes, shook his head, and laughed. Not sure if that was what he did or not, but the Bryan in my head appeared real enough to me. Then again, maybe I sat on the precipice of completely going crazy.

Cracking my knuckles and then my neck, I tried to get rid of some of my tension. I already heard plenty of stories from my dad on how Top Gun didn't come close to comparing to real life. Chris Taylor, aka "The Dad" as he liked to call himself, made it his duty to inform anyone around him exactly what Hollywood got wrong about any military movie (especially the Navy), or any movie involving planes. I had heard countless times how Air Force One couldn't possibly be accurate because shooting a gun in a plane, regardless of the plane, would cause issues with cabin pressure...after that, I usually tuned him out because by this point he sounded like the adults from those Charlie Brown cartoons.

I asked because I wanted to shock Bryan out of his funk, or whatever was going on with him.

_Me:_ _Is it like the movie Top Gun?_

Bryan: _Haha. If I say yes, will you call me Maverick from now on?_

_Me:_ _Oh please. You can do better than Tom Cruise's character. I'll call you Goose._

Bryan: _1st, Goose is the navigator. 2nd, he died. No thank you. LMAO._

_Me:_ _Iceman?_

Bryan: _Better. I'm good with Iceman._

_Me:_ _What is your pilot name?_

Bryan: _Long Duck Dong._

_Me:_ _Bwahahaha! Do not pull 16 Candles into your depravity. That is one of my fave movies._

Bryan: _U made me snort when I laughed at you._

Me: Hehe. Well? What is it?

Bryan: Something. LOL.

Me: That doesn't tell me anything.

Bryan: It's need to know and you don't need to know.

Me: Funny because I feel like I do, in fact, need to know.

Bryan: Call signs aren't like on Top Gun. Well, some are and some aren't.

Me: So, you won't tell me?

Bryan: Maybe one day, honey. ;)

Me: I'll hold you to that.
Soooo...real life isn't like Top Gun?

Bryan: Hell fucking no. It's a hell of a lot harder.

Me: Have you been to Top Gun? I know the school actually exists.

Bryan: It does and I have.

Me: Oh, so you're a hotshot.

Bryan: One of these days I may let you see how hot I can be.

Me: LOL.

His jokes still managed to make my insides clench in anticipation. No wonder I had imagined him a couple of different times as I pleasured myself.

Had I finally broken through the wall he erected today?

Me: Anything I need to know about tomorrow?

I crossed my fingers that the party had been canceled. Luck abandoned me once again.

Bryan: No. Just be you and you'll be fine.

Me: So, if I jump on the bar and perform a striptease that would be OK?

It took him a few seconds to respond, and picturing him doing a double take, had me doubling over in laughter. There was no way possible I would do something like that—now or before I got sick. Then again, before myasthenia gravis, I partied a lot more, and tequila had a way of making me do crazy things. I've kissed a stranger, made out with two men at once, flashed a bouncer so he would let me into a club without charging me, and I may have danced on a bar or four.

Bryan: WTF? You are not serious!

Me: ROFL. Of course not.

Bryan: Rolling my eyes. Just go and have fun. Mel and Luke will be there too.
This is about getting you out of the house and having fun again.

Me: Fine.

Bryan: You better go.

Me: I will. I don't want to, but I promised and I will.

Bryan: Good.

Me: Yeah. Yeah. ;)

Bryan: Hey Em?

Me: What?

Bryan had never shortened my name before. Then again, I was the only person in the chat window with him, so he hardly ever used my name to begin with. I liked it. I loved the tingly feeling when he used my nickname.

Bryan: Nothing. Never mind.

Curious by nature, I pestered him.

Me: What? I'm an open book today. Better ask while you can.

It felt as if minutes ticked by, but it might've only been seconds. When I thought he wouldn't type anything, he did, and his question shocked me. Out of anything he could have asked me, this had been the one I didn't expect.

Bryan: *What did it feel like when you got sick?*

I didn't know what I was expecting, but it wasn't this. It shocked me.

Me: *Why? Are you having weird symptoms?*

Bryan: *No, curious. One day you were fine. The next...*

Me: *Pretty much how it happened.*
I have asthma and went in for my normal checkup on a Friday morning. For the first time in a long time, everything went perfectly. My stats were great. Doc was happy.
That night, I went out when some friends to a concert and drinks. Saturday morning, I thought I had worn myself out and excused it as partying too much. I thought that's why I felt so run down and needed extra time to recoup.
Sunday I felt the same, and Monday I was tired, but I still went to work. I struggled the whole day though.
Tuesday, I couldn't breathe. I went to the ER and they thought asthma. I did too, except I got worse throughout the week. My regular doc couldn't understand it, but he knew something was wrong. I saw him the day after the ER and the day after that. And finally, he put me on what we thought would be short-term disability until we figured out what was wrong with me.
A month later, I was diagnosed with MG. From that first day in the ER to the day I got the verdict, 36 days passed. The day I ended up in the ER, my life changed forever.
LOL. Ok, that sounds more ominous and dramatic than it really was.

Bryan: *But going through it all, I'm sure it felt dramatic. Still does sometimes?*

Me: *It did, and it does.*

Bryan: *Tell me about you before you got sick.*

Me: *Me before?*

Bryan: Yes.

I paused. Me before? It all seemed like a lifetime ago, and yet, only four years had come and gone. Before…during that time in my life, everything revolved around whatever I wanted it to, and I didn't care about tomorrow as much as I did now. I never thought everything would change overnight, or that I would somehow lose a part of me.

Bryan: Hello?

My mind had wandered again, and I had left him sitting there without an answer for almost five minutes. My eyes roamed around my bedroom. They took in the walls, the pictures, the window, and finally, landed on Curley who was snoozing in between my slightly spread legs. Life had changed.

In my old apartment in Texas, the manager allowed me to paint the walls and I had covered my bedroom in a soft lilac. Pink may have been my favorite color, but I loved how the pastel purple glowed in the sunshine that shined through the big picture window. My bedroom in Charleston measured slightly smaller, and the walls were stark white. Management refused to allow me to paint them. Since I couldn't paint, my sister came over one day and we covered the walls with pictures and framed posters. We didn't cover everything, but at least the art contributed a pop of color. Something the apartment desperately needed.

Bryan: Em?

Me: Sorry about that. Dog had a potty emergency. And since I have to put him on a leash and walk outside, took me a sec. He was crying. LOL.

My cheeks turned pink as the lie rolled off my finger tips. I squirmed in bed, afraid he could see me, knowing he could not.

Bryan: NP.

Me: I loved going to school and learning, but I also liked my job. I was probably a more carefree person after I got my Master's up until I got sick.
Before I got my graduate degree, I worked my butt off so I could go to college, but I told you that whole story.
I loved playing tennis, hanging out with my friends, singing karaoke or whatever. I traveled as much as I could, watched a lot of sports (still a sports

fanatic), probably drank more than I should, and did whatever the hell I wanted to at the time.
I hate to admit it, but I didn't spend as much time with my grandparents as I probably should have. My grandfather is gone now, but my grandmother still lives in Texas right outside of Houston with a horrible relative.
I always told myself I'd have tomorrow to visit. To do things, but I didn't. I used to run, skydive, and ice skate. Not anymore.

Bryan: *You're from Texas, right?*

Me: *Yep, but not born there. I was actually born in Maryland. My dad was in the Navy and is now retired. When he retired, we ended up in Texas, and after I got sick, my family decided I needed to be closer to someone so that I had help.*

Bryan: *Where are your parents?*

Me: *Oklahoma. They both travel for work, which is why I don't live closer to them.*
I think my mom would help take care of my gma if gma didn't want to stay in Texas so bad, and if mom didn't travel as much as she does.

Bryan: *And that's where your horrible relative comes in?*

Me: *Yep. She's a first-rate BITCH.*

Bryan: *Wow. All caps.*

Me: *All caps. And if I could bold and underline it, I would.*

Bryan: *Must be pretty bad.*

Me: *She is. She treats grandma like she's an invalid and tried to forbid her from driving. Then she tells everyone that gma is senile, which she isn't. My gma is probably sharper mentally than you or me. Still sharp as a tack. On top of that, the bitch goes behind gma's back and makes decisions for her, takes her money, and has tried putting her in a home multiple times. Aunt always loses because gma still at home. LOL.*

Bryan: *Why not just let her live alone.*

Me: *Gma isn't a spring chicken anymore. Her words, not mine.*

She has some health issues, so she stays with my aunt and uncle. It's more for just in case, but aunt seems to think she is in charge and my grandma's boss. Her husband is just as bad.
They said something on FaceSpace and I called them out for it. They didn't like that, and the next morning I found myself blocked and unfriended. So needless to say, I'm on their blacklist. LOL.

Bryan: *You don't sound too upset about the unfriending.*

Me: *I'm not. They have tried to play the victim card most of my life and I'm done with them. I care about my gma, but not them. Does that make me sound heartless?*

Bryan: *Not at all.*

Me: *Good. LOL.*

Bryan: *Family can suck sometimes.*

Me: *It can.*

Bryan: *You're a strong woman.*

My cheeks burned from the compliment. Reading those words, felt like a caress to my heart and soul.

Me: *Thanks, but I don't think I am.*

Bryan: *You've learned to cope and live w your disease.*

Me: *It's either that or die. It's not my time.*

That was my philosophy in a nutshell. I could choose to not take the numerous medicines that managed all of the illnesses and effects, but if I did that, I wouldn't make it. I could live with a defeatist attitude, and if I did that, I would be miserable, depressed, and more dependent on people than I was now. I had always been independent, thus depending on someone full-time terrified me. I hated depending on my sister for little things as it was.

The life expectancy of a person with MG was supposedly normal, but they also told patients that they couldn't die from MG. I had seen the opposite to be true. In my support groups, children and adults died from the effects of MG. They would attribute the death to the lungs, heart, or anything else, but it came down to MG in the end. As with other autoimmune diseases, our bodies could not fight infection as well as a "normal" person, because our bodies were already attacking themselves. A simple cold could put us in the hospital. We had to always be careful and mindful of the people around us.

With the cards stacked against me, I had to fight for myself, my family, and my friends. I could mope, and I sometimes gave into my depression. However, if I didn't fight, if I didn't try to stay positive and continue to live an independent life, I would wither away. I believed wholeheartedly that attitude was half the battle.

Bryan: You could still live without really living.

He understood. He got it. I could live without living, but what kind of life would that be? Empty.

Me: I thought that's why you were helping me, because I'm not really living.

Bryan: You do, except in the love dept.
You don't like to complain about what you deal with. I basically have to pry it out of you. I also like how you try to remain positive.
That's some of the stuff I've learned about you.

The blush that had started to diminish, intensified once again. I fanned myself suddenly feeling very hot.

Me: Thanks. It's either adapt or else. I feel depressed and I let it get to me a lot, but I also know that it could always be worse. I'm still alive and can get out of bed most days. Sometimes I'm bed-bound because I'm too weak to get up. I can still breathe, see, walk, learn, and drive...for the most part.
I can really only drive short distances now. I get too tired and my eyes start seeing double even with special prisms in my glasses to correct the double vision. I mean I see double all of the time without my glasses, so they do help.
Walking can be touch and go. LOL. I take it all one day at a time. I think a lot of people who get a chronic illness have to shift their mentality in order to stay positive.

Bryan: Not everyone succeeds.

Me: Maybe.

I didn't want to think about those people who gave up without a fight, who were unable to alter their mentality to match their new situation. I had seen it happen to newly diagnosed patients in the support groups. They joined for answers, for a cure, only to leave disappointed. There have been cases where people with MG went into remission, but that usually only lasted a couple of years. MG was a bitch of a disease to have, and there were few strides made to find something to help the patients suffering from it. To some, it was a death sentence. To others, it was a wakeup call.

Bryan: *Were you mad?*

That sounded like a stupid question to me, but then again, he hadn't had his life turned upside down. Therefore, he didn't know. I answered as honestly as possible, still a little shocked that he continued with this particular line of questioning.

Me: *Yes. I wanted to be mad at God, my parents, the world…anything and everything. Why did this have to happen to me? I hated that I couldn't do all the things I used to be able to do with such ease. I wanted my old life back. I felt robbed. My sister has nothing wrong with her, but I won the lotto and got a fucked up disease. Where's the fairness in that?*

Bryan: *And now?*

Me: *I still get angry, but it's more at myself than anything. And I wouldn't wish this on my worst enemy. Sometimes I wish they could have a small taste though. My parents and the people around me had no control over me getting sick. I just got sick one day. No one could have predicted it.*
As for God, I figure He knows better than me. My life has completely changed, but at the same time, doors have opened for me that I wouldn't have been able to explore before I got sick. I've met great people and made new friends. In some ways, it brought my family closer together. I've learned more about myself in the last four years than in the 25 prior to that, and I've learned to appreciate the life I used to take for granted.

Bryan: *Now if we could only get you to apply that attitude to your love life.*

Me: *LOL. I'm trying.*

Bryan: *I know, baby.*
You said one time that you lost friends because you got sick?

141

UGH! That "baby." My insides quivered reading it, and I might have wished he was sitting beside me instead of on the other side of the country.

Me: I did. They didn't...appreciate the fact that I couldn't do everything I used to do and got mad about it all. My life now is a lot of day to day. I make plans, but I might have to cancel last minute if I'm having a bad day. You'd probably be surprised at how many people don't like that.
Some say they can accept it, but then you notice that the number of invitations have suddenly decreased. Then there are those that aren't quite sure how to act or what to say around someone like me. I don't look sick, but then I use a cane or a walker. The term 'walking on eggshells' comes to mind.

Bryan: *Do they ask about it?*

Me: Some do. Most don't. And when I'm out amongst the population, people stare and give me funny looks. Some look offended by my presence. My sister gets pissed off at them and grumbles that I can't help that I have to use a walker at a young age. Some look curious, but are too afraid to ask. Different is not always good.

Bryan: *Does it bother you?*

Me: It used to. I guess sometimes it still does. It's awkward more than anything. I'm 29 and use a walker like an old person. Here they see someone young using something like that and it stumps them. My sister wants to confront them all for me. She gets mad on my behalf.
There have been funny moments too. One time I went to the store to pick up some medicine. I had to go in because I needed milk. I pulled into a handicap parking space, and before I could get out of my car, an old man started yelling at me and told me to stop using my grandparents' placard. He said young punks like me were what was wrong with the world today. LOL. I had a good laugh about that one.

Bryan: *Did you tell him off?*

Me: Nah. I let my walker do the talking. I got out of the car, shuffled to the back, and carefully pulled out my walker. His mouth snapped shut, he huffed and then walked away as quickly as he could. I never said a word. Haha.

Bryan: *What do you miss the most?*

Me: *Freedom.*

Bryan: *Huh?*

Me: *Freedom to do whatever I want, whenever I want. To not have to worry how I feel from day to day and I can make plans without fearing what will happen. Freedom from using a cane or walker. From having to depend on people. Freedom.*

Tears streamed down my face as I admitted the one thing I still craved, the one thing I missed above all else. In some ways, my disease had made me a prisoner and had stolen my freedom.

Bryan: *I'm sorry.*

I loathed it with every fiber of my being when people told me they were sorry. What were they sorry about? Did they do this to me? No. I had won the genetic lottery, which unless they were a mastermind to an evil plot, they had no control over who the disease affected. There was no reason for them to feel sorry for what happened to me, and I sure as hell didn't want their pity or for them to feel sorry for me personally.

Me: *Don't be. Not your fault.*

Bryan: *Still am.*

The tears fell faster and blurred my vision, signaling an end to my conversation.

Me: *I've gtg. Bye.*

Bryan: *K. Bye.*

Shutting my laptop, my face scrunched up in an ugly frown, I allowed myself to cry. With my body wracked with gut-wrenching sobs, I grabbed my pillow and screamed, holding it tightly to my chest. Curley woke up and tried to console me, but all he could do was lick my arm. I needed to release my pain. Tonight, as I had done many times before, I mourned for everything I'd lost since myasthenia gravis swept into my life and turned it upside down.

CHAPTER NINETEEN

EMMA

B linking my eyes open, I slowly surveyed the room, noticing how bright everything appeared. Morning had come without me knowing. I grabbed my muscle pill, mestinon, and took it with a sip of water, lying there in my bed hugging my pillow for a little longer.

My eyes were crusty with dried tears, my mouth tasted like cotton had grown inside it, and my head was pounding as if someone had used it for target practice with a sledgehammer. All in all, I felt like crap thanks to my conversation with Bryan—not that it was his fault.

The first counselor I saw shortly after getting my diagnosis, told me that grieving the life I lost was a normal process. Loss hurt. She informed me that I would go through the various stages of grief, and in doing so, it would help me to heal and cope, but she also warned me that I would undoubtedly go through the various stages multiple times throughout my life's new journey. And I had. Sometimes I even volleyed back and forth between a couple different stages. Every time I thought I reached the end of the stages, something happened, and I cycled through the stages again.

I accepted that my life would never be the same. I knew everything changed the day I went to the ER; however, that did not mean I accepted everything so easily. People who had lost a loved one could accept that they would never return, but they still mourned that loss. Becoming sick held a similar loss to me. Like my counselor said, loss was loss no matter what it was.

When I felt my medicine kicking in, I opened my eyes again and stared at nothing in particular. I needed to move, and yet, I was not motivated to leave my bed for any reason. I especially didn't feel like attending the party. I didn't care about my promise to Bryan. How would he know?

Well, Mel would tell him. She was the type of person who forced me to go to karaoke "kicking and screaming," and somehow convinced me it was for my own good. Yeah right. Own good? Nope. I was convinced everything centered on Mel, and what she thought benefited her. I was 98% certain.

Did I have to go? Technically, I reached what the U.S. considered an adult over a decade ago, which meant I could make my own decisions. But thinking about Bryan and everything he had done for me, I thought it might be best if I made a small appearance. This didn't mean he was right—he was —however, if I wanted to find someone to spend the rest of my life with, I had to actually put myself out there.

Facing one's inner demons, though, was never easy. For every time I encountered rejection due to my illness, I closed myself off a little more. My walls got a little higher, a little thicker, and more impenetrable. I had gotten to the point where I hated meeting new people. And while rejection hurt, in many ways, I had come to expect it each and every time. Maybe that was the problem: expecting it. But if I anticipated it, it meant I never felt disappointed. Hurt, but not disappointed.

Bryan told me men found confident women sexy. I lost my confidence a long time ago. I could fake it with the best Oscar-winning actresses, but I didn't believe in myself any longer. Even when I had self-esteem issues prior to everything, I still carried myself well, letting most things roll off my back. My self-esteem issues were of my own making back then.

As a Navy brat, I tended to move from place to place every couple of years. For introverts, one of two things were bound to happen: they forced themselves to act like or become an extrovert, or they become a loner without friends, who didn't talk to anyone. I chose option one because moving around so much, even if I didn't make friends easily, I wanted one person who would make life a little less lonely, no matter how brief our stay in that location.

To this day, my family swears up and down I was an extrovert since at least first grade. The stress and anxiety I experienced putting on my act, the times I cried in the bathroom or quietly in my room...they witnessed none of it. If I wanted, I could talk to a room full of strangers, strike up a conversation, but I only did it because I learned to adapt and cope with my surroundings. It was the Navy way, and what all military brats did. We found ways to adapt and deal with our new surroundings. Sometimes we pretended, putting on an entire stage production, and sometimes we hid.

When my dad retired and moved us to Texas, I saw a couple of girls playing on a sand pile, but one stood out more than the other. We exchanged glares, sizing each other up. Neither broke the connection because neither of us wanted to lose our staring match, and in the end, neither of us won. I thought I might see that rude ass girl again in school, but much to my surprise, she came over to greet the new family on the street with her family. We became instant friends.

Fifteen years later, Gia and I were still best friends. From day one, she got around my walls and reached me. I never held anything back from her. It never happened to me before, and I could honestly say, it hadn't happened since. Maybe I needed that connection, or maybe I believed that since my dad retired, I could finally make a lasting friend. I couldn't say for sure, but it didn't matter to me. She was the one I shared all of my deepest, darkest secrets with. She knew all of my hopes and dreams, my disappointments and hurts, and my triumphs and little successes. I knew the same about her since we told each other everything.

My walls had been my comforter and protection for most of my life. They wrapped around me and refused to allow anyone entrance.

Until now.

Bryan had been chipping away at my walls, forcing me to expose myself. It scared me. What if the world couldn't stand the woman within? Don't get me wrong, at some point my fortress would need a drawbridge to allow that one special someone in, but I hadn't met him yet…and I really didn't believe I would. Unlike some people in my life, the very ones who constantly told me I had yet to meet the right one, I wasn't sure a man existed that could accept all of my idiosyncrasies.

I would try though. I had promised, and I never took my promises lightly.

Forcing myself out of bed, I trudged into my bathroom and started the shower. Hopefully, the hot water would rejuvenate me and make me feel less like a zombie and more like a human. And if that didn't work, coffee existed for a reason. I probably had a small addiction to the hot liquid. With a little cream and sugar, it became pure manna.

The feeling of normalcy began to return after I'd downed two cups and was sipping my third. My conversation with Bryan melted away into the steaming sweet cup of heaven, which allowed me to push everything deep inside me once again, burying it, where I could ignore it completely.

I had come a long way since the initial onset of my disease. It took me a long time to find a way to cope, but I had finally managed. Sometimes I buried some of the negative so that I didn't feel like life was trying to drag me under.

In the beginning, I tried to pretend MG did not exist in my life. Myasthenia gravis were ugly words that when spoken were worse than swearing. I eventually got to the point I couldn't pretend any longer. A trip to the hospital being unable to move could be a real eye-opening experience. I was horrified by my body and scared shitless that I wouldn't make it, or that I would be intubated for the respirator. I made it and never had to be put on the respirator, having a machine breathe for me. After two days in the hospital, they released me after giving me the name of a good counselor.

After I started seeing her, I tried to face everything head-on. Depression overwhelmed me, filling every cell in my body. I cried all the time and felt like I was drowning. I couldn't breathe because my chest felt so heavy, the weight of my world unbearable. My chains held me down, choking me, threatening to drown me. It was the only time I considered ending it all, but I hadn't been able to go through with it, and my counselor talked me down off the ledge.

Sometimes ignoring the darkness became the only way to cope. And sometimes, I had to face it in order to fulfill a promise.

I had a choice to make: go to the party or stay home. If I chose the latter, it would require complete and utter radio silence. No computer, no phone, no tablet—absolutely nothing. Easier said than done, but if I stayed home, I needed to avoid detection. If I chose the former, the likelihood of me remaining a wallflower all night plummeted. I didn't know how, why, or who, but I knew Bryan would make certain I didn't remain antisocial during my stay at the party, and his accomplice probably had the name Mel.

Really, how bad could it be?

An hour at some stranger's house meant I arrived, talked, socialized, and then I could leave. A solid plan, however, with Mel in the mix, I knew it would be difficult to stick to my guns. She was tenacious when she wanted something, and her deviousness knew no bounds. I had seen her convince a Marine to accept he was indeed part of the Navy. Not an easy feat considering there wasn't a Marine alive who wanted to admit something like that, and it wasn't exactly true. They only fell under the Department of Navy. An impossible task made possible courtesy of Mel.

My anxiety rose, making me consider staying home, but once again, I thought of Bryan. Since I had started talking to him, he never seemed very far away. If I chose to stay home or leave early, he would be disappointed, but that disappointment would be tempered with understanding. He understood me a little more than most and wanted to help me in spite of it all. I appreciated him and his concern more than he probably knew. That said, I doubted he would be too happy if I left early to go home, eat ice cream, and feel sorry for myself.

And honestly, I hated disappointing him. He wanted to help me move on and find love, and I was trying to sabotage his grand master plan. Correction. I was trying to sabotage my own life. Sitting here all day, crying about my life and about how no guy would love me, didn't change anything, and I sure as hell wouldn't find someone hidden somewhere in my apartment waiting for me.

I only had to go for an hour, and if I didn't feel comfortable, or if someone gave me that funny look when I walked in with my walker, I'd leave early without any regrets. If the opposite happened, I'd allow myself to relax a little, but the likelihood of staying longer than an hour was slim to none.

Thinking about everything, overthinking it all, my nerves were dancing a rumba in my stomach and setting me on edge. I needed something to calm me down. Alcohol wouldn't work because I had to drive.

I unlocked my phone's screen and clicked on Bryan's name in FaceSpace. I felt like throwing up, and only he held the power to talk me through this.

Me: Not sure if I can do this. What if I throw up on someone?

Bryan: You won't. You'll be fine. ;)

Me: I put on extra deodorant and am still sweating like a pig. I swear I've changed my shirt 3 times.

I slightly exaggerated my condition. I had only changed once, and that was because Curley stepped in a mud puddle right before he jumped on me. Brown paw prints on a white shirt...no one would notice, right?

Bryan: LOL. I'm sure it's not that bad. Just go and have fun. I told my friend to expect you.

Me: Did u tell him everything?

Bryan: Yes, so don't worry. He knows you might need extra help getting into the house and around.

Me: Into the house?

Bryan: There are a few steps leading to the front door. 4-5.

Me: Can I stay home?

His responses had been coming through quickly, but this time he delayed responding. He waited a full minute before he said anything.

Bryan: You can, but if you really want to find love, you won't.

Me: U saying love is waiting for me at the BBQ?

Bryan: No...maybe. But if you don't take this step, it'll be harder to take another one in the future.

Me: I guess.

Bryan: You know I'm right. ;)

Me: Maybe.

Bryan: And I'll be waiting for a report when you get home.

That struck me as strange considering Saturday night tended to be prime date night for many people. I figured he would find some girl to take out tonight, and wait until tomorrow to hear what happened at the party.

Me: Not going out?

Bryan: Date bailed on me and don't feel like going to a bar to pick up someone. Sinuses have been shit lately anyway. With my luck, I'd sneeze on her and she'd freak.

Me: LMAO.

Bryan: Not that funny. Grrr.

Me: Yes, it is. If u could see the image in my head, u'd laugh too.

Bryan: Whatever.

Me: Too bad u don't live here. We could go to the party together.
Or I could bring u some soup.

Bryan: That would be nice.

Would it or was he just saying that to placate me? Why did I even care? I had an inkling of why I did, but I didn't want to explore those feelings yet.

Bryan: Go, have fun, and report in later. Much later.

Me: I'm only staying an hour.

Bryan: _Give it an hour and if you're not having fun, leave, but if you are, stay._

_Me:_ _Yes, sir! LOL._

Bryan: _Don't get cocky._

_Me:_ _I can't. Ur the one with a cock._
I thought we already had that talk. :P

Bryan: _I've created a fucking monster._

_Me:_ _Hehe. U know u love me._

Oh no! I hit enter before I could stop myself. I didn't mean to send that, but I meant it as a joke. I wasn't serious.

Bryan: _Whatever. Have fun, Em._

_Me:_ _Will do. Sigh. I guess I have no choice._

TTYL.

Deep inside me, I felt the pull to stay and talk to him. I longed to give in to that temptation, but I couldn't. I wasn't his type, he lived in San Diego, and I desperately needed to get over my crush. The sooner that happened, the better for me, but he wasn't making it easy.

Bryan: _TTYL, Emma. :*_

Wait! Hold the presses! A kiss emoji? Had he used one before without me noticing, or was this the first time? What did it mean?

I willed myself to calm down. To him, he probably meant the emoji as a friend giving another friend a peck on the cheek. Reading any more into it, I predicted ended in disaster. But my heart didn't listen. It raced faster than NASCAR at Daytona. No. I forbade myself from overanalyzing it and getting my hopes up. If I allowed myself to think about it too much, I would somehow convince myself he returned my affections. I've had this talk with myself too many times already. It was time to move on and get over him, and this barbecue would be the perfect place to start.

CHAPTER TWENTY

EMMA

My car rolled to a stop in front of the address Bryan had supplied. In one word, the house could be described as quaint. Painted the color of redwood with white trim, it reminded me of some of the older homes located in the smaller towns of Texas. Four steps led up to a screened in porch that had a wooden white porch swing. That swing would make the perfect setting for an evening of relaxation as I watched the sunset and sipped on a cool glass of sweet iced tea, swinging back and forth without a care in the world.

And I felt nervous as hell about the fact I had to walk in there alone.

Knowing Mel the way I did, I brought my own car so that if I wanted to leave early, I could. That had been my initial intent, however, as I was about to pull out of my parking spot in my apartment complex, Mel texted me and informed me she and Luke would be an hour or two late. An hour...or two? FUCK ME!

I knew no one here, and Bryan's great idea for a buffer just abandoned me to fend for myself. I considered going back inside my apartment to wait out the two hours because I did not want to go alone to a place I knew no one, but I also knew myself. If I didn't leave right then and there, and the party would happen without me.

Before I could change my mind, I peeled out of my parking space—in my nervous excitement, I accidentally threw my car into reverse, slammed on the accelerator, and almost hit the cars parked behind me. My tires screeched when I moved my foot to the break and stomped it into the floorboards. Good news: my seatbelts worked perfectly, and I had a bruise on my shoulder for proof.

When I left the apartment, I was full of determination and gumption, but now that I had arrived and sat staring at a stranger's house, my bravery left me, leaving me feeling unsure and hesitant. I wanted to throw up, but I hadn't eaten anything this morning because my anxiety had made me too wired. Maybe a coffee run or some sort of break would give me a small reprieve before I attempted to face my fears. Great plan.

Great plans always had flaws. I reinserted my keys into the ignition and then heard a *tap tap tap*. My head whipped around to see who dared interrupt my perfect escape plan, and standing there wearing a dreaded Chicago Windstorm's baseball cap, stood a man. I didn't know who he was at all, therefore, instead of opening my door—anyone who wore a Windstorm's cap could not be trusted—I turned on the engine and opened my window a crack. Sometimes I wished I still had a crank handle in my car so I didn't have to bother going through the motions of starting it first.

"Yes?" I asked with my guard up. The words stranger danger kept flashing like a Las Vegas billboard in my head.

"Are you Emma?" His grin grew by the second, and I got the distinct impression he might be laughing at me.

This man's smile had the ability to lure in hapless females, and his slight British accent could make them melt. He was definitely not a Bryan, but I could feel the tiny jump in my heart. I was a sucker for foreign accents. That said, I wouldn't drop my guard. "Yeah, I am." Who the hell was this man?

I guessed he finally noticed I had yet to open the door or roll down the window more than an inch. "I'm Bryan's friend, Chad."

"Oh."

"I, uh, I saw you pull up. Do you need help getting out of the car?" he stammered. Suddenly, he seemed a little unsure of himself.

My defenses skyrocketed. This man knew about me from Bryan, he knew I was disabled, but the last thing I wanted was for him to think me completely helpless. I wasn't helpless. I wasn't an invalid. "No," I answered with as much attitude as I could muster.

Taking a small step backward, he held his hands up in surrender, the smile never leaving his face. "I just thought I'd offer. Bryan said you might need some assistance getting into the house, and I wasn't sure if you needed any getting out of the car as well."

I breathed in and out in an effort to calm down. Chad had done nothing wrong and didn't deserve my disdain. He wanted to help, and the only crime he committed was the hockey team he chose to support. Personally, I loved the LA Surf, and we tended to hate the Windstorms with a passion. Again, not his fault he possessed poor taste in team selection. "Sorry."

"It's all good." He moved to the side and leaned against the back of my car, giving me space to get out, however, when I made no move to roll up my window or exit, he asked, "You coming in, or do you need my help with anything? Not of people here yet. Mel telephoned to say she and Luke are going to be late, but last time she said that, they never showed up."

He sounded as if he had all the time in the world and his ramblings began to put me at ease until he got to the part about Mel not showing. "Excuse me?"

Realizing his mistake, he tried to correct himself, "Sorry. I'm sure they'll come because you're here. And if they don't, we'll tell Bryan, and he'll kick their asses. Or I can. Either way, they'll get what's coming to them."

I snorted and covered my mouth in an attempt to hold in my laughter.

"Nah, you can't cover that, I heard it. Come on. We'll get you in the house and something cold in your hand to drink. You really don't want to sit out here in the afternoon sun, do you?"

Shaking my head, I rolled up the window and shut off the engine. Time to meet my maker, or go to a party, whichever worked. "Thanks," I muttered, shifting my legs to the street and pulling myself out. "Where are you from?" My curiosity got the better of me, and as I slowly made my way to the trunk where my walker lay on its side, I thought I'd ask.

"My parents moved me and my siblings here from London when I was five, but the accent stuck." He chuckled and his smile grew. His lips curled up higher on one side than the other, and he didn't have dimples like Bryan, but he had full lips surrounded by a light brown beard.

"Excuse me, I have to get my walker out." My body got stiffer when I said that. Would Chad balk? Would he say something? Would he give me a horrified or pitying look?

He popped the trunk open, and before I could lay a hand on my walker, he pulled it out and set it in front of me. Closing the trunk, he waited patiently, his expression never changing.

"Um, thanks?" I told him uncertainly. I felt like I was floundering.

"Are you asking?" His words were not rude, but they did sting a bit. I opened my mouth to say something, to apologize, but he waved me off. "Don't worry about it. I understand. My sister has MS."

"Oh. I didn't know." Now, I felt like a total bitch. Why hadn't Bryan told me?

"She handles it like a trooper...like I heard you do."

"I don't have—"

He interrupted me before I could continue. "No, but you have another neuromuscular disease. You can't compare which one is worse. They're both bad, both do damage, both affect the body, and both suck."

For the first time since I became sick, being around a stranger didn't bother me. I wanted to cry. My nose and eyes burned, but I refused to let my tears fall. I was sure if they did, he'd panic.

"So, here are the rules. I won't baby you, but you have to tell me if I'm overstepping. Bryan said you use either a walker or a cane depending on how you feel. Since you're using your walker, I'm going to assume, it's not a great day. I know the heat bothers you and can make everything worse, and so can stress. So being thrown into the lion's den like today probably didn't help you. The same thing happens to my sister, Megan. If you need help, ask. If someone is being an asshole, tell me. If you want to leave, let me know, and I'll help you out to your car. And if you just need to lie down for a nap, I have a room ready for you."

I couldn't hold back the tears any longer, and they fell one by one down my cheeks. To have a complete stranger do all of this for me, overwhelmed me. No one ever treated me like Chad. I could overlook his choice of hockey team for this. For the first time, I didn't feel like I was drowning from the weight myasthenia gravis put on me.

"You okay?" His voice was soft and full of understanding.

Nodding, I sniffled as I attempted to stop crying. "Yeah. Sorry, I just…" Unable to continue, I swiped at the tears, wishing they would stop. His hand gripped my shoulder. He didn't pull me in for a hug or do anything that might frighten me or push my body off balance, but the pressure of his hand comforted me.

"There's nothing to apologize for. It's a lot to take on, and I bet you've had a rough go of it."

My head snapped up to meet his gaze. "Did Bryan…?" I couldn't finish my inquiry.

Shaking his head, he explained, "He told me nothing except that you might need help and that you had MG. Your secret is safe with him." His wink made me feel bad that I had jumped to conclusions. He gave my shoulder one last squeeze. "Shall we get you inside? You can take your time. I'll go at your pace."

Was I dreaming? Because everything felt like I had been transported to some make-believe world, and if that was the case, I didn't want to wake up. I took a good hard look at Chad after I had wiped away the last of my tears away. I had already noticed the well-groomed beard that covered his jawline, but he also had tufts of shaggy sandy blond hair escaping his cap in the back. His blue eyes reminded me of the ocean in Cancun, and I almost wanted to drown in them. His six-foot body was trim and built with more muscle than Bryan, making this guy look more like a bouncer than…actually, I didn't know what he did for a living. In other words, Chad was HOT! And his personality gave him bonus points. If I had to choose someone other than Bryan to crush on, Chad made the short list. However, as good-looking as he happened to be, he probably had a girlfriend tucked away somewhere, and if he didn't, I was pretty sure I wouldn't make his list.

He must have been talking to me because he shook my shoulder gently and squeezed it again. "You okay?"

"Huh? I mean, yeah. Right as rain. Sorry, I was thinking about a few things."

"Got it. Well, come on then. We'll have some fun today. Did you bring your suit?"

"My suit?"

"For swimming."

"Uh no. No one told me to, and besides, I think it's probably best if I don't. You know?" While he accepted my handicap with an open mind, others would probably not be as kind.

"That's all right. My sister left one here and you two are about the same size. If you decide to take a dip, you can borrow it." Chad outright ignored my decision not to get in the pool.

"But—"

Holding up his hand, he told me, "You never know. You might get in the mood to take a dip, and if you want to, you need to know you have that option available to you."

"Uh...thanks."

"No problem. Now let's get inside and get something to drink. I left my friend Mark manning the grill when I went to see if you'd arrived yet, and I don't completely trust him. Last year, he cooked the burgers until they transformed into charcoal. I left him with one job today, to man the fire and gave him explicit instructions not to start cooking yet. But knowing him, the meat is on the grill already."

"You can go in without—"

He kept interrupting me. If Chad had a flaw, that would be it. "No can do. I'll assist you up the stairs and we can go in together. Trust me, you'll need help. My railing is a bit loose, and I don't want you falling. Bryan will have my ass if anything happens to you."

I stopped in my tracks. "Is that why you're being nice to me?"

His eyes grew wide and round, and he shook his head. "Not at all. I'm being myself, but I've seen my sister struggle. So, I guess you could say, I'm more in tune with what you may or may not need help with. I don't need your boyfriend's threats in order to be a gracious host. My mom is big on manners and can be scarier than Bryan."

"Bryan's not my boyfriend," I said, confusion evident in my tone.

"He's not?"

"No. He's Mel's friend."

"Well, they're both my friends."

"No, I mean I met him through Mel, and he's trying to get me out of the house more." Too embarrassed to admit the real reason for Bryan's interference in my life, I decided to keep that to myself. I had yet to tell Gia. If I hadn't told her, I sure as hell wouldn't spill my guts to a stranger. I was curious though. Why did he think Bryan and I were together?

"Oh. Sorry, with the way he talked, I assumed you were more than friends."

Smiling, I tried to put him at ease. "It's okay, but we're only friends. Besides, I can't blame you. Your ability to think might be hindered by your choice of hockey team." I giggled when I saw his frown.

"Who do you root for?" I could tell he wasn't too offended by my statement, and his demand lacked intensity.

"LA."

"Fuck me! The enemy is coming into my house. Bryan will die a slow and horrible death for not telling me." He winked.

"I know. He gave me no warning either. He deserves slow and agonizing torture."

"Agreed. Come on then. We'll go inside, get a beer…uh, do you drink beer?" At my nod, he continued, "And we can plot his demise."

I had made an ally out of the enemy. This day had turned into something surprising already.

After walking up the short staircase to the porch, I was relieved I had help. One false move with that banister and I would've fallen into his bushes. If only the good feelings continued when I entered the house. Chad hadn't babied me or treated me like a broken person, but as soon as we stepped through the front door, all eyes were on me and all conversation immediately ceased. If the radio had been turned off, a pin drop could've been heard.

My body reacted to the extra attention by sending my sweat glands into overdrive and speeding up my heart rate. Was it too late to turn around and leave? I wanted Bryan or Mel, but one conveniently lived in another city and the other disappeared.

"Everyone," Chad called out, not that he needed to since we had everyone's attention. "This is Emma. Emma, this is everyone that has made it so far." I fought the urge to push him since it was probably considered rude to attack the host.

But he did remind me, this crowd would grow. "Hi." My voice squeaked in nervousness.

As if timed perfectly—they could have been synchronized swimmers—

they turned around and carried on their previously abandoned conversations.

"You'll be fine. They just have to get to know you," whispered my over-enthusiastic host.

Fine? He really believed that? "Yeah. You better go check on the meat before your friend burns it." Plastering on my best smile, I swallowed my nervous energy and fear and gestured with my chin toward the back of the house where I could see a cloud of smoke billowing.

If I could be grateful about my upbringing for anything, I knew how to pretend and perform under pressure. I might not be fine, I certainly didn't feel fine, but no one else needed to know.

I slowly pushed my walker toward the kitchen. If I was going to survive, I needed something to wet my dry throat.

The first of the hurtful words were spoken in hushed tones as I grabbed a soda from the cooler in the kitchen. "Is Chad inviting charity cases now?" They were behind me. I had thought about sitting down in the living room, but now I didn't want to turn around. I pretended I didn't hear them, put the unopened soda in my jeans pocket, and walked out the open sliding glass door to the back deck where Chad and a few others were. Some were playing a beanbag toss game, others were just talking, and blessedly, no one had noticed me yet.

"Hey, Emma!" Chad shouted from behind the grill located to the right of me.

Shuffling over to him, I said, "Hi."

"You sure you want to be out here. It's cooler in the house."

I knew for certain I did not want to be in the house. "I'm fine. Just needed to stretch my legs and get some air."

His eyes narrowed, and he looked as if he might call me on my bullshit, but instead, he pointed his spatula at the man beside him. "This is Mark. He's an asshole, but I keep him around anyway." He chuckled and winked when his friend shoved him. The push didn't even phase him. He stood his ground and only his upper body moved slightly. "Hey! Behave or I won't introduce you to Emma here. Asshole Mark, this is Emma. Be nice. She's a friend of Mel and Bryan's…and now one of mine too."

"If anyone here is an asshole, it's you," Mark teased, sticking his hand out to me to shake.

"Nice to meet you," I replied nervously.

"I'd introduce you to my wife, but I'm not sure where she is right now."

Mark's appearance was the complete opposite of Chad. Where Chad had rippling muscles, Mark looked lanky and reminded me of one of the characters in those *Revenge of the Nerds* movies. The two men were about the same height, however, if a strong breeze swept through, I was afraid Mark would blow away.

"Probably in the bathroom again." Chad's joke had his friend rolling his eyes.

"You're probably right." Mark turned to me and explained. "She's ten weeks pregnant and her morning sickness comes and goes. She's already run to the bathroom three times, and we only got here an hour ago."

"Oh. Congratulations." This time when I smiled, it felt genuine.

"You know you could have stayed home?" Chad offered.

Mark shook his head. "Nah. She wanted to get out of the house and argued when I suggested skipping it."

I stood there listening to them banter back and forth for a few more minutes until Chad lifted a silver baking dish filled to the edges with burgers and hotdogs. "You ready to eat?" His grin was infectious and I found myself smiling back. "Let's go inside and get our grub on, and if you need help making your plate, let me know. Think of me as your personal butler."

Inside meant I would be around the people who made the rude comments earlier, but then again, they could have already come outside too. I was damned if I did, and damned if I didn't. I had to pull myself together if I planned on surviving a full hour. Besides, I had heard worse things since MG took over.

No one said anything as we ate. People milled about, some walking outside and some staying in the cooler house. It was only when Chad would leave my side that people seemed to voice their disdain. While some ignored me, others chose to whisper loud enough so I could hear, but they never spoke directly to me. A couple of people pretended to run into my walker and would push it before saying, "You need to get that out of the way. It's a health hazard." When they walked passed me, they would mutter, "But then again, she is a walking disaster."

Their words and actions cut me.

When my hour ended, I started to get up to leave, but Mark stopped me. "Don't listen to others. They don't know anything. I've heard them say that Chad should get rid of me as a friend because I bring him down, but we've been friends since grade school."

"Grade school? Really? So, you know all the dirt."

"That and more. We were next door neighbors and our moms bonded over PTA and the fact their kids were only a month apart. So ignore the trash. I'm not really sure why Chad is friends with them, but I think a lot of them are clients and people he's worked with. He's a part-time personal trainer at one of the gyms in town and he is also a graphics designer. We co-own the company together."

Mark's speech helped settle my nerve a little, but I still planned on leaving. "Thanks, Mark, but I think it's about time for me to lie down and..." I stopped speaking and left my words dangling on a cliff.

"I know he set up one of the rooms for you. Not sure which one though."

It began as a small giggle and then I laughed. "Is there a reason I should stay?"

"Yep. You haven't met my wife yet."

"I don't know if she exists. I haven't seen her at all."

"Who doesn't exist?" A tall woman with bright red hair and green eyes sidled up to Mark. Her hair was curly and a little frizzy, and freckles covered her pale face. I assumed this was Mark's wife.

Wrapping the woman in his arms, Mark kissed the side of her head. "Are you all right?"

"Yeah. I was lying down in Chad's room and ate some crackers. My stomach has finally settled down."

The way they interacted, the gentleness with which Mark handled his wife, all made me a little jealous.

"Do you need anything?" Marked rubbed her back, waiting to do her bidding.

"Nah. I think the nap helped a lot."

Mark seemed so touchy-feely, and I could tell he was very attentive, but since I'd arrived, he had not been at her side. Why? Curiosity aroused, I asked, "Why didn't you lie down with her?"

"That would be me. He hovers, and when he does that, I threaten to cut off his balls for ever touching me. And then I lock him out of the bedroom." The redhead snickered.

I instantly liked this woman. "Hi, I'm Emma."

"Ingrid. You're the one Chad's been expecting. Sorry I wasn't here to greet you earlier. The baby and I had a disagreement. The baby won."

All three of us laughed.

"I guess you finally met Ingrid. How are you feeling, Emma?" Chad interrupted.

"She's ready for a nap, and I wasn't sure which room you have her in," Mark spoke before I could tell my host I wanted to leave. Why was it so important I stay? I stayed my hour. I did my penance.

Rolling my eyes, I stated, "I was actually thinking about heading home."

"If you're tired, why don't you lie down here, and then if you want to go home, you can. I'd rather you not drive when you're tired though." Chad's turn to convince me to stay had arrived.

"I'm fine. I just..." My words fell away when I noticed the way his arms were crossed over his chest. I recognized that stance and had seen it many times in people I had known throughout the years. He wouldn't budge. Sighing, I accepted my fate. "Fine. Which room can I use for a nap?"

He led me to one of the guest rooms and after shutting the door and locking out the world, I laid down on the bed and closed my eyes. Tired and emotionally bleeding, I needed to find my center again and brush off their insults. I hoped they never found themselves in my situation; however, I wished karma bit them in the ass so they could see for themselves how their words affected others.

I slept for almost an hour without interruption, and when I awoke, I felt slightly better. I still didn't like the people at the party. My nap wouldn't change their attitudes, but at least I no longer felt like I wanted to rip out their beating hearts and throw them on a grill to serve up on a silver platter.

Leaving my shoes in the bedroom, I went in search of my host and found him quickly coming down the hall headed straight for me. "Did you have a good nap?"

I nodded. "Thanks."

"Now that you've slept a little, it's time for the pool."

"I don't have a suit, and it's a pain in the ass to get in and out without help."

"Then it's a good thing I'm here. I'll help you with the pool. Although, if you want, I can also help you change?" He wagged his eyebrows.

"Maybe I should head home."

"Do you really want to head home, or do you want to have a little fun? Come on. Try it. You might like it. And if you don't, I'll drive you home myself."

This man didn't know how to take "no" for an answer. "Fine." As soon as I agreed, he draped something over my walker. He had been prepared. "Awfully sure of yourself."

"I'd like to think of it as confidence. Now, go change and let's go swimming." His finger twirled in the air before pointing toward the room I had come from.

Sucking in a deep breath, I pushed it out with a loud hiss. "Looking forward to it. Really." Only an idiot could miss the sarcasm lacing my words. He wasn't an idiot, and his laugh followed me until I closed the door on it.

When I came out of the room again, Chad stood there shirtless with only a pair of teal board shorts on. For a brief second, I forgot how to breathe. The shorts hung low on his waist showing off his deep "V," and his chest and upper arms were filled out with muscle. His muscles weren't as big as the bodybuilders you see on TV, but he wasn't small by any means. The man could probably bench press me.

"Ready?" He grinned knowingly. My eyes had moved of their own volition up and down his body, and back up again. He only needed to glance my way to know I was taking in the sights.

"Uh…" My face burned bright red at being caught looking, but I couldn't help it. A good-looking man stood in front of me only half dressed. Still, I couldn't help comparing him to Bryan. Yes, Chad was hot with his muscular body, light colored hair and eyes, and that cocky smile with his gleaming white teeth; however, there was something about Bryan that Chad lacked for some reason. I don't know exactly what that was though.

"Pool. Come on." His hand reached out and grabbed my elbow to get me started, and when I started to walk on my own, he moved suspiciously behind me, and I assumed it was so I wouldn't run away.

True to his word once again, he stayed by my side and helped me in and out of the pool. No one said anything to me, although, I swore I got splashed a few times on purpose. For the most part, everyone either ignored me or chose not to bother with me, and I was fine with that. Chad's presence kept the haters at bay until I got out of the pool, and then I became fair game again.

After changing out of the swimsuit, I walked into the kitchen in search of something to drink and someone came up behind me and pushed me. My walker skidded forward with me and hit the counter, preventing me from falling. It had been done on purpose.

I moved both hands to the counter to help me balance, and then spun my head to see who had been so classless as to run into me with the intent to hurt me. I had no doubt after seeing the scathing expression on her face, she wanted to do me harm. "Problem?" I spat and attempted to stand as tall as I could.

She sneered, her eyes moving from the top of my head to my feet. "You think you can win him, but you can't. He is so much better than you will ever be. Compared to you, he's a saint."

"What?" Did she mean Chad? I didn't want him.

Her sharp fingernail dug into my shoulder. "This is your punishment for doing something evil in your life. You must be a skank or something to have this happen to you. Maybe you should pray for healing, but then again, a girl like you won't ever repent. You deserve this and more." She took a step closer and hissed, "Nobody wants you here. Chad is only being nice because you're a pity case of Mel's. Fuck, even she doesn't really like you and only keeps you around because she feels sorry for you. So, why don't you do everyone a favor by crawling into a hole and dying? I'm sure your family would feel better because they won't have to deal with you any longer."

This wasn't the first time I'd heard something like that, but this time it cut more than ever before. I knew Mel and I were genuine friends, and this girl probably lashed out at me because she felt jealous of something. I assumed it had something to do with Chad sticking close to me and helping me most of the afternoon. And when he stepped away, I noticed this woman trying to cling to him like a second skin only to have him push her away each time.

But what scared me and made this more real and hurtful was the pure unadulterated hate in her eyes. She didn't only despise me. She hated me with her entire being. I had seen fear, confusion, and even uncertainty when people told me stupid shit before, but I had never experienced a hate of this magnitude.

Her words were still ringing in my ears. In the past, I used to question why I had been picked, why I got sick. Out of everyone in the universe, why me? I prayed for healing. I prayed for answers. I got nothing except silence. It took me a long time before I realized that this wasn't a punishment. Far from it. And yet, even though I accepted that, I still hated my body for a long time. Sometimes I still did. When I wanted it to go left, it wanted to stay put. When I wanted it to stay put, it wanted to fall to the ground. This was MG. My control had been stolen, but I still had my pride and strength. And prejudice people like this woman weren't going to tear me down or make me feel like nothing. I was worthy of this life.

"Cory!" Chad bellowed. "It's time for you to leave. Lose my number and forget where I live."

"You don't mean that," the woman tried to argue.

"Oh, I do. Now, leave."

"If anyone needs to leave, it's this ugly, fat abomination!"

"Either you leave, or I'll physically throw your fucking ass out the door and then call the police and tell them you were inciting violence. Don't think I won't do it because I will."

I stood there paralyzed. My throat wouldn't work. I couldn't scream at her. I had no way of defending myself. If I looked down, would I find blood? The wounds she inflicted felt physical as well as emotional.

"Mark, you and Ingrid help Emma lie down," Chad ordered.

I felt the pressure of someone pushing me out of the kitchen, but I barely remembered walking to the bedroom. I was in shock. How long did I lay there hearing the echo of those words? When the initial shock wore off, I asked to be left alone, and then I cried myself to sleep. And when I woke up, the sun had already set. Did I have to get up? Did I have to leave the room? I wanted to bury myself in the blankets and hide from the world.

Knock knock. Someone tapped at the door. "Yes?" I called out. My body stiffened ready to fight, or face whoever walked through that door.

Chad opened the door a crack and when he saw I was awake, he came in and sat down on the end of the bed. Rubbing the back of his neck, he sighed. "I'm sorry about her. She's been asking me out since my girlfriend and I called it quits a couple weeks ago. My girlfriend didn't want to leave behind baggage while she was deployed with the marines."

I sat up in bed, pulled my legs toward me, hugging them without saying a word.

"I guess Cory thought if she got rid of you, I'd be hers, but that wouldn't happen no matter if you came or not. I'm not even sure how she got the invite. She goes to my gym, and I think one of the other trainers invited her."

Nodding, I searched his eyes and could see nervousness and an apology, but no pity.

"You shouldn't listen to her. This is not your fault. No one knows why some people get certain diseases and others don't. If you are an abomination, then so is my sister, and trust me when I say, I have probably done more shit in my entire life than both of you combined. My older sis is probably the saint out of the three of us."

"She sounds nice." I hadn't heard much about her, but I could tell from his tone of voice that he loved and revered his sister.

He snorted with laughter. "She would slap the back of my head if I misbehaved, and then use me as her test dummy to see which Nair product worked the best. But she also had my back and would fight anyone that messed with her younger siblings."

"How much older is she than you?"

"Megan is five years older. I also have a younger brother. He's only younger by a year though."

"When was she diagnosed?"

"Two years ago. She started having some issues and when they did the MRI, they found the lesions. Her husband has been great though. You would have met them today, but he surprised her with a trip to New York for their anniversary." He paused and then asked, "How are you feeling?"

"I'm all right." I gave him my typical answer for times like this. Many people who have chronic conditions have learned to smile through the pain and say, "I'm fine. I'm okay. I'm all right." It was usually one of the three.

"So, how are you really?"

I narrowed my eyes and frowned.

"Megan tries the same thing. So tell me how you're really feeling."

Hesitating, I sat there for a moment before I said anything else. "Hurt, tired, done."

"Better. The party is still going on, but all the assholes have left. We were going to pop some popcorn and watch a movie. You want to stay?"

"I don't know."

"I wouldn't blame you if you left now, but I promise nothing else will happen to you, and I'll let you pick the movie. Whatever you want to watch."

"I think—" The sound of the front door opening followed by Mel's voice stopped me. It didn't take long before I heard the heavy sounds of her stomping down the hall before she appeared in the doorway.

"What the fuck happened?" Mel's hands were on her hips, and her anger was directed at Chad.

He got up to defend himself. "I took care of it."

"What did you take care of?"

"Mel, it wasn't his fault," I spoke up in hopes it would give him a helping hand, but it didn't.

Her eyes narrowed into tiny slits and her face turned red. When she spoke, she did so low and slow, "What exactly wasn't your fault, Chad? What did you have to take care of? And why the hell does my friend look like she's been put through the wringer? And before you say she hasn't, I can tell when Emma's been crying."

"Mel," I tried again.

"Chad?" Mel prompted.

"Cory happened," he finally answered, his shoulders slumping in defeat.

She released a string of curses. When she ended her tirade, she snapped, "What the fuck was she doing here?"

"I think one of the other trainers invited her, or she overheard us talking and showed up on her own. You know how she is."

"Yeah, and you would've thought she'd learned her lesson after the last time."

Confused, I inserted myself back into the conversation. "Last time?"

Smirking, Chad chuckled when he turned to me. "Your friend Mel here didn't like how Cory tried to hit on me or how she grabbed Luke's dick through his jeans at my last party. So, she dragged Cory outside by pulling her hair, threw her onto the ground right into a huge mud puddle, and proceeded to kick her ass. Mel fights dirty when she wants to win. I think Cory wound up with a mouth full of mud when Mel stepped on her hand and Cory screamed. When her mouth was open, Mel grabbed a handful of mud and shoved it in Cory's mouth."

"And she ran away like a scared little rat with her tail between her legs." Mel sounded awfully proud of herself, and I snickered. The anxiety and pain from the afternoon had not completely melted away, but this helped. And picturing Cory getting her ass handed to her by Mel was the icing on the cake.

"You look like you're feeling better. How about that movie?" Chad asked hopefully.

Mel pushed Chad off the bed and sat down in his place. "Hey, Chad. I'm sure Luke is famished and so am I. Go heat up some food." She waited until he left and the door closed before she pounced. "You okay? Do I need to kick his ass? What really happened?"

My head started to spin as she fired off one question after another. I felt like it needed to be sitting at a table in a dark room with the only light shining down on me like on those old crime dramas and cartoons.

"Hey. You okay?" Concern and worry laced her voice.

"Yeah. I'm fine. I... It's been a rough day."

"Rough because of Cory, or even before?"

"Cory mainly, but she wasn't the only one."

"Tell me."

I did. I opened up and told her everything that happened from the time I arrived to when Chad came in here to talk to me. By the end of it, she seethed and wanted to know names and descriptions. Even if I could, I wouldn't have given them to her. But by the time the whole Cory drama had ended, faces and voices melded together into one.

And after I confessed everything, she scooted closer to me, pulled me in for a hug, and whispered, "I know what we'll do. We'll invite everyone to a party in an abandoned warehouse, lock all the doors, and set it on fire."

"No, you wouldn't." I giggled as I sniffled and wiped my eyes on my shirt.

"I wouldn't, but it got you to smile." She sat there for a minute more and said, "People are assholes, and you can't let them get you down. You're a better human being than they are."

"Maybe."

"No maybe about it. You are. How are you feeling?"

"Better. Thanks. What happened to you earlier?"

"We had to help Luke's mom move something and then we got a flat tire, and I had forgotten to get my other tire fixed, so we had to wait for a tow truck. Do you know how long it takes for one to show up?"

"What did Luke say?"

"We got into a small fight, but we went home to change and take a shower after standing out in the heat for a couple hours, and we made up."

"Say no more."

"You going to stay for the movie? Luke and I brought over The Ugly Truth. There are others, but that one will make us laugh and make the guys suffer a little."

Laughing, I wiped my eyes again and agreed. "Sounds perfect."

After the afternoon had ended horribly, it felt good to laugh and hang out with people I felt comfortable with. Most of the guests had left and the only ones that remained were people that had either ignored me completely or had treated me kindly. I could deal with those people. Watching the movie together, I was able to almost forget the ugliness of the afternoon and focus on the good things that happened.

Much to my surprise, I wound up staying at Chad's until almost eleven. My time at his house started well, the middle was awful, and the night ended with a few laughs with friends.

And now that I was home, I had a report to make to Bryan. Truthfully, I wanted to forget about certain aspects of my day, and that meant I didn't want to talk about it at all, but I had a feeling Bryan wouldn't let me get away with an "it went all right."

Turning on my computer, I opened up FaceSpace and before I could get my fingers in place over my keyboard, he pinged me.

Bryan: *Where the hell have you been?*

What the fuck? I was pretty sure—100% to be exact—he knew I had gone to the party because he arranged the whole thing.

Me: *BBQ. Chad. Ring any bells?*

If he wanted to give me attitude, I knew how to be snarky too.

Bryan: *You were supposed to be home hours ago.*

Me: *You could have messaged me earlier. I did have my phone with me.*

Bryan: *I didn't want to bother you.*

This threw me for a loop. He didn't want to bother me, and yet, as soon as I logged on, he attacked me.

Me: *Bother me? Listen here Mother Hen. You were the one that set this whole stupid thing up. If you were that concerned about me, you should have pinged me earlier. Or do you not trust your friends?*

Bryan: *You said you didn't want to go, so I assumed you wouldn't stay long.*

Me: *You know what happens when you assume?*

Bryan: yeah, yeah. WTFE!

Me: Butthead.

Bryan: Butthead? I'm sorry. Are we in jr. high?

Me: Haha.

He waited for a few seconds and I wondered what he was thinking. Was he really that concerned? Even the mere thought of that gave me a giddy feeling deep inside me.

Bryan: I'm sorry. I've been waiting for you to get back home so I could hear how it went
I guess I was a little anxious knowing your own reasons for hesitating.

Me: You set me up.

Bryan: What do you mean?

Me: Chad's sister has MS.

Bryan: Yes, which is why I thought it'd be safe.

Me: Safe? As in no judgment?

Bryan: Exactly.

Me: He didn't judge me. He helped.

Bryan: Only him?

Did I dare tell him the truth? I hedged instead.

Me: It was fine.

Bryan: Em...tell me. I can't fix it if you don't tell me.

I admitted, at that moment, I felt a little taken aback. Fix it? What did he have to fix? People and their judgmental attitude? Newsflash, there would always be those people in the world. I coped, and when I couldn't, I hid.

Me: What do you mean?

Bryan: Nothing. Tell me.

Me: What do you want to fix? You can't force people to look at me any differently than they do. They make the conscious choice to get to know me or not. I've lived with it for over four years now. Most people form their opinions on appearance rather than getting to know the actual person. It happens in schools, in jobs, and everywhere else. It hurts, but that's reality. You can't change the world.

Bryan: Why not?

Me: Really?

My reply was pure unadulterated sarcasm.

Bryan: So are you going to tell me what happened today or not?

Though his words were typed, I almost felt and heard his frustration coming through with his message, and I honestly couldn't understand why he felt like that.

Me: Nothing much. Went to the party. Chad helped me inside. You didn't tell me he was a fan of Chicago. We might have plotted your demise for that. We drank, ate, and swam a little. I took a couple of naps, we talked and joked. Mel got there late. More laughing, watched a movie, and that's it.

Bryan: He always plots my demise. I hope you came up with something more creative than him.

Me: Of course. I got mad plotting skills. LOL. ;)

Bryan: That's my girl. What about the other guests?

His girl? I wished.

Me: Some were dicks and ignored me or told me I should get my walker out of their way. Some whispered that they didn't know why I was there, but I brushed it off.

168

Bryan: That all? What really happened? I feel like you are leaving some-thing out.

My thought inadvertently went to Cory and everything she said. Tears stung my eyes again, but I didn't want her or her actions to make me cry again.

Bryan: Em? Hello?

I must've disappeared into my own little world again because I noticed it'd been almost ten minutes since he'd sent his last response asking for the whole truth. This was turning into a bad habit whenever I talked to him.

Me: Sorry. Had to use the bathroom and forgot to tell you.
That's it. Nothing else happened.

Bryan: Why don't I believe you?

Me: Trust me.

Bryan: LOL. I've heard that one before.

Me: Can't you be happy I went?

Bryan: I am, but...

Me: But?

Bryan: I don't want you to shut out the world if people act like douchebags.

Me: I haven't done it yet.

While that statement could be considered true, in the last couple years I had become more of a hermit than I used to be.

Bryan: I don't want you to give up.

Me: And that's why I have you. You're going to help me find Mr. Right For Me.

Bryan: LOL. True.

_Me:_ _But let's start again tomorrow. I'm exhausted. I'll talk to you later._

I hit enter and waited for his response, curious to see what it would be this time.

Bryan: _K. TTYL, honey. ;)_

Not the kiss, but I'd take it. Uh. No. No, I didn't want it. He was not my Mr. Right anything. Period.

CHAPTER TWENTY-ONE

BRYAN

Signing off with Emma for the night had been difficult. Deep inside my gut, I knew she only divulged half of the real story...if that. And now Chad refused to answer his phone. Something bad went down earlier. I gave that rat bastard friend of mine one task, one simple thing to do: watch over Emma and make sure nothing or no one hurts her. How hard could that possibly have been? Someone got through the lines of defense I had set up, and now I wanted to punch someone for hurting her.

It pissed me off that when it came to Emma, I was unable to control my emotions. I hated feeling powerless, and yet, I was powerless to protect her from so far away. If I could've found a way, I would've been there for her today. Why didn't every house have a transporter like Star Trek yet?

I had this inherent need to shield her from all harm, and I did not want to dwell on why I felt that way. We were friends. She was Mel's friend. All that existed between us could be summed up in those two statements. Past, present, and future, the only thing that would ever happen between us was friendship. I ignored the small pang in my chest. She deserved better than someone who could not and would not commit to a real relationship. She lived on the opposite side of the country, and this was merely a sort of business deal. I'd drawn a line in the sand and I refused to cross it.

Shoving another t-shirt into my suitcase, a thought occurred to me... plagued me really. As of tomorrow, we won't be on different coasts. "Hell no!" I snapped out loud to my empty bedroom.

Tomorrow I boarded a plane, thanks to my approved leave, and then I'd handle the family crisis to the best of my ability. That was all I could fit into my agenda. It was all I could deal with in my life right now. My career and my family came first, and I didn't have time for anything or anyone else. That was a lie. I had my friends, and they were in some cases closer to me than my family...than my parents. Maybe, if I worked and arranged it, I may stop in to check on Emma, but I doubted I would make the effort. Our relationship needed to stay on the computer. It had to because...because I couldn't allow it to turn into more.

Relationship? What relationship? Shit. I think Evan's words were starting to permeate the air I breathed right down to my very soul. No. Once she found someone, our ties would be severed, and the bells of freedom would ring. For her? For me? I didn't know anymore.

Just not with Chad. She deserved better than to become a rebound girl. Plus, Chad fell short of the mark. He wasn't good enough for her. While he might have been committed to his last girl for the past six months, prior to that, he had a different girl every night. His fear of commitment exceeded mine. I knew I didn't have much room to talk given my track record, but not Chad. Fellow players worshiped him as a god amongst men. Emma should not be tied to someone like that.

Granted, his girlfriend did the breaking up this time, but if he expected me to believe he suffered from a broken heart, I couldn't do that. I was almost certain, he'd been plotting how to dump her for at least a couple weeks before the ax fell on him. Chad lived and breathed for Chad alone, and obsessed about himself a little too much for my liking.

It wasn't that I didn't like my own friend. I did. I'd known Chad since my freshman year at college when we pledged the same fraternity. Together we scouted for women, got into trouble, and had a grand time. If I needed him, I could call him and he would be there for me regardless of the circumstance.

But Emma was special...different. Were any of my friends good enough for her? No, definitely not. Maybe I needed to re-evaluate my pool of friends.

Emma deserved nothing less than the cream of the crop. She deserved a prince among men, even if I wasn't certain where to find such a man. I'd try for her, though. For her, I'd search the world for him, if only to prove to her someone existed that embraced everything she had to offer. Of course, I'd discovered only recently how amazing she really was through our chats. I wished she could see herself the way I did, and I wished I had seen it sooner.

And I didn't want to discuss or analyze my behavior when she first signed into FaceSpace tonight. Earlier today, I performed my flight drills, and as soon as I changed out of my flight suit, I checked my messenger app. No messages. I went home, and as soon as I pulled into the driveway, I checked again. Nothing. I started packing and checked my stupid app every thirty minutes–sometimes sooner. My focus remained on her instead of packing, and I had a 6:00 A.M. flight, which I hadn't packed for.

I guessed calling me or messaging me was too much to ask? Okay, now I sounded like a prick and an overly obnoxious, jealous boyfriend. Which I wasn't. Like any good friend who sent their friend into uncharted territory, worry settled into my gut and held on tighter than a cowboy riding a bull. Anything could've happened to her, and something did happen. Maybe I shouldn't have forced her to go.

Forced? Ha! But wasn't that exactly what I did? I sat there and convinced her that this would open the door to her future. I was an ass who tended to be a control freak. I hated not knowing. Every time I glanced at my phone, the same questions ran through my head, Was she all right? Were people treating her nicely? Did they accept her? Did she meet anyone new? Now, I sounded like an overprotective parent. Kill me now before I started imposing a curfew on her.

Zipping my suitcase shut, I threw it on the floor and sighed, before falling onto my bed. A mere girl had begun wreaking havoc on my life, and it needed to stop. I felt sorry for her, but it was starting to spiral out of control. I disliked losing control of my life—another reason a match between Emma and I wouldn't work.

I repeated my current mantra aloud, "Just a girl. Only going to help her. She's a job. I'm doing her a favor and that's it."

CHAPTER TWENTY-TWO

EMMA

I was drowning my sorrows with ice cream and diet root beer, which completely contradicted each other, and I did not care one iota. In fact, my disappointment grew when I discovered I only had cookies and cream instead of vanilla ice cream, and therefore couldn't make a root beer float.

Could someone drown their sorrows in ice cream and soda in reality? Probably not. Times like these, I wished I'd kept alcohol in the house. I imagined my best friend, Gia, rolling her eyes and shaking her head as she commented, "Drama queen much?" *Why, yes I am.*

Thinking about her made me miss her, and I wanted to talk to her. I pulled out my phone and dialed her number without scrolling through my contacts. It was probably the only number I had memorized. Any time I felt like things were falling apart, she kept me grounded and sane.

"What's up?" She picked up on the first ring and spoke before I could say anything.

"One of these day's I'll get the first word in." Gia and I had known each other for more than a decade, and in all that time, I had never spoken first on our phone calls. If she called me, she was already talking by the time I hit talk. I swore she really did that. If I called her, she hits talk and immediately spoke. I never won, and that was all right.

"Wishful thinking, sweetie. But hey, it's always good to have dream and goals and all that." She snickered, making me laugh.

"Yeah. Yeah. I get it. How's it going? You at work? How's my favorite goddaughter?"

"Last I checked, she's your only one since Ellie went and had only boys, and nope, I'm off today."

"Whatever. You know what I mean," I teasingly returned. "How's my girl?"

"She's good. Growing like a weed and a little pain in the ass right now, but this too shall pass."

"Awe. What's wrong with my little bug?"

"Just a phase. She throws her tantrums on a daily basis and expects us to cave." I could hear the love and tiredness come through the phone. Elizabeth was Gia's first and only baby so far and didn't start the terrible twos until she was three and a half. Up until recently, she had always been the sweetest baby I had ever known; however, her parents now referred to her as their demon-possessed child and constantly asked where their sweet baby had gone.

"But you won't give in to her."

Laughing, she said, "You know me so well."

"Of course. Better watch it or I'll share all your dirty secrets," I teased.

"Whatever. It's your secrets you should be worried about."

"Nah. Only when I start dating some famous Hollywood actor or some other sort of celebrity."

We both giggled, and my body relaxed. As much as I loved Mel and my sister, nothing beat the connection of a best friend. Someone who knew me better than I knew myself, and accepted everything regardless of it all.

"What's going on?"

My sigh escaped before I could stop it.

"Seriously, what's wrong?" she demanded.

I wanted to spill my guts and tell her everything I'd kept to myself, or at least what had been going on between Bryan and me. I couldn't hold back any longer and confessed everything in a rush. When I finished, I released a sigh of relief "And as of today, it's been three days since I've heard from him at all. I haven't even seen his little green dot light up on FaceSpace. Mel says she hasn't heard from him either and that he's probably busy, which I know he probably is. He is a pilot and in the Navy and—"

Gia cut me off. "Em, take a deep breath and calm down."

I did what she told me to do.

"Listen to me. I'm with Mel on this. He's probably busy and has a good reason for being on radio silence. Don't worry about that."

"You're right."

"I know I am. Now, answer something for me."

"What?" My brow furrowed in confusion, anticipation building as I waited for her question.

"Have you been cyber-stalking him?"

"Ex-Excuse me?"

"Okay, maybe not cyber-stalking, but have you been FaceSpace stalking him?"

"No, of course not!"

"Em."

Her terse tone sounded exactly like the tone of voice she used on her daughter, Elizabeth, when she managed to find herself in trouble. It was the tone only used by mothers, and made everyone within a one–mile radius to listen and obey. "Not really. I will periodically get on FaceSpace, and look to see who's online and who isn't. That's all though."

"FaceSpace stalking."

"Shut up." She might be right, but I hated to admit it.

"Real mature."

Giggling, I retorted, "Yep. I thought you understood that out of the two of us, I'm the mature one."

"In your dreams."

"Just because you're older by one month."

"Older equals wiser," Gia taunted me.

"Age before beauty."

"Beauty was the horse."

We both laughed again. I found my center during our back and forth teasing; she always made me feel better.

When she regained control of herself, she said, "He probably had something important come up and can't contact you. As for what he's doing for you, I applaud him. It's about fucking time you got over your hang-ups and started meeting new people."

"Need I remind you that I have met new people? I even went on a blind date that ended in him leaving as soon as I arrived."

"So? Listen, Em. Those assholes that people have been setting you up with were for them, not you. They don't know the real you or what you're looking for in a guy. They assume they know you, which basically amounts to a hill of beans. Hell, you'd probably get along better with an armadillo than any guy they find you. And the fact this last one wasn't even told you have MG, is total bullshit. You were set up to fail, and that pisses me off. I've told you time and time again, even before you got sick, there is someone out there for you, you just have to be patient, not give up, and keep looking. And then when you got sick, you got on this giant pity party that's lasted for four years, and it's about time it ended. You sell yourself short all the time and you don't have to. You're pretty, funny, smart, sarcastic as shit, and my best friend. If you weren't worth it, I wouldn't have stuck with you all these years. I'm ecstatic he's setting you straight and forcing you out of your comfort zone. Lord knows staying in your little bubble, you wouldn't meet any good guys. I support him 100%."

In her own way, she had just read me the riot act and griped me out completely. Gia had never been one to pull punches, especially with the people she considered special to her. "Got it," I grumbled.

"Do you? Because if not, I'm sure I can go over it again."

I snorted. "No, I'm good."

"Excellent! As for Bryan, you like him don't you? I mean, I know you always had a little crush on him since you always talked about how hot he is and stuff like that."

"A little crush. That's all."

She sat there for a moment in silence, and then said, "No, not any longer."

Since the day we met, Gia had managed to figure out when I held something back or lied. "Maybe. I don't know, but I'm not his type. Time to move on."

"What about this other guy? Chris or Chuck?"

"Chad?"

"Yeah, him. You'd think I'd remember that name since I have a cousin named Chad."

"No. He just got out of a relationship, and the last thing he wants is another one. It did feel nice to let down my guard a little though. He didn't hover too much or make me feel like less than a person because I had to use my walker while I was there. He even got a room ready so I could take a nap."

"I'm sure he understands. With his sister having MS, it helps."

"Yep."

"Have you talked to him since the barbecue?"

"Maybe."

"You bitch! You've been holding out on me. First Bryan, and now this. I should fly out there and kick your ass."

"Well, I would love to see you, but keep your hands and feet to yourself." I started to giggle.

"Spill."

I took a deep breath and finally explained. "Really, there isn't much to tell. He called the day after and checked on me and that's about it. He had to go after that, and I haven't talked to him again."

"Don't lie. Nothing else?"

"Seriously. We started to trash talk each other's hockey teams and he got another call right after I said that Chicago sucked. It was the only insult exchanged. He said he would call back, but I haven't heard from him again."

"Nice of him to check on you."

"I agree."

"If you were insulting him, who does he root for?"

"Fucking Chicago." I made a gagging sound in the back of my throat.

"Bleh."

"I know!"

She had her own team she followed, but thankfully, our friendship remained intact because it was not Chicago. "Dallas is better."

"LA."

"On this, we will never agree."

"True story," I barked, a smile lighting up my face.

"So what about asking him out?"

Odd question since she knew I loathed doing the asking. I always got tongue–tied, stuttered, and turned beet red. The two times I managed to do the asking, were a couple of my less than stellar moments that I would rather forget ever happened–even if one of the two did agree to a date with me.

"Excuse me?"

"You heard me."

"No, I don't think I heard you correctly. We must have a bad connection."

"You seriously need to get over your fear of asking someone out."

"It's not a fear…okay, maybe it is. I've just grown up believing the guy should do the asking. As far as Chad is concerned, I don't know. He just got out of a relationship and from what I understand, it was kind of serious. I doubt he's ready to date. And before you ask, those are the only two men on my radar. Is that pathetic or what?" I tried to make it sound like a joke, but my voice shook.

"Or what," she quickly answered. "You have guy friends you can date. Bryan is a good guy and is trying to help you, and Chad is a decent guy who didn't make you feel weird for being sick. You always find an excuse as to why you can't pursue someone. It's no wonder they're the only two guys on your radar, but give it time and eventually, you'll have a list a mile long."

I didn't quite believe her, however, hearing it made me feel better. "Thanks, girl."

"I'm here for you no matter what."

The conversation went from teasing to serious to teasing again. Each change happened in the blink of an eye, but this was who we were together. "Thanks. I miss you."

"I miss you too. I'm going to try and come out in a couple of months."

"I wish you could come now."

"Me too. Can you come down here?"

"Not right now. Maybe next month. I have a full schedule of doctor appointments for the rest of this month. At least one a week, and some have two or three."

"Ouch." I heard her hiss.

Whenever I went to a doctor appointment, I always had to get labs done, and each doctor wanted their own special tests run. Sometimes they only took one vial of blood, but the times I had to see rheumatology, it varied from four vials up to fourteen. My rheumatologist currently held the record for most blood sucked out of my body. "Tell me about it. I swear my rheumatologist is a vampire."

"How many vials the last time?" She chuckled with me.

"Twelve and I had to sit there because I got dizzy. I might have been better off donating blood."

"The others aren't so bad though, right?"

"Not really. I just get tired of going and dealing with it all."

"I know you do, but you have to hope and believe that one day they will come up with something that will put you in remission, or that they will find a cure."

Every person with myasthenia gravis wanted a cure, something that would end the suffering. "That would be nice."

"Yep, and then you can move back to Texas and babysit for me."

I laughed. "Ulterior motives. I should have known."

"Of course. Plus, I guess I miss you and wished you lived closer again. Girls night out just isn't the same without you there."

"I feel the same." No one compared to my best friend, although, Mel came close and we've enjoyed some fun times together.

I heard her moving, and then Elizabeth started to cry in the background. Our time had ended. Gia confirmed it when she told me, "Sorry. Elizabeth fell, and I have to take care of her. She rolled off the couch when I turned my back for one second."

"K. Give her a big kiss and hug for me."

"I will. And Em…"

"What?"

"It will all work itself out. Trust me."

"Maybe. Now, go and take care of my baby, and I'll talk to you later," I ordered and disconnected the call.

Leaning back, I stared up at the ceiling. Would everything work out? I supposed it had to, but what would the outcome be? I feared and hated the unknown in a way because it took away some of my control. I'd always been in charge of my own destiny, or so I thought, however, after I got sick, I realized how little control I really had in life. With my body failing me, I wanted a little bit of that control back.

I probably would have stayed on my couch pondering my life, or lack thereof, if someone had not rung my doorbell. Odd because I wasn't expecting anyone in the middle of the day on a Tuesday.

Slowly shuffling to my door, I reached it and leaned against it for leverage, peered out the peephole, and gasped, taking a step backward. I almost tumbled to the floor, but managed to throw myself forward against the door once again as I gripped my cane handle tightly.

On the other side of the door, appearing as casual as the last time I saw him, stood Bryan. What the hell? My field of vision narrowed due to the fishbowl effect from the peephole, but I didn't need to see clearly to tell the man clad in a pair of jeans and grey t-shirt, with slight stubble on his face was indeed him. It surprised me to see him standing there since he was supposed to be in San Diego right now. Even with the skewed view, he looked amazing. His t-shirt hugged him like a second skin and I could almost count the ridges on his abdomen. Sunglasses had been pushed up on top of his head, and he jingled a set of keys in his hands as he shuffled back and forth from one foot to the next. Damn. He looked good, and I had to swallow my suddenly very wet mouth so a puddle of drool did not flow to the floor.

"Are you okay in there?" Bryan called through the door.

Crap. He must have heard me stumble, which meant I couldn't pretend to make him wait as I ogled him, nor could I act nonchalant and cool. Busted.

Moving a couple of steps to my left, I leaned against the wall with my side and opened the door. "What are you doing here?" If my words and tone came out as accusatory, I didn't mean for them to be; his arrival had shocked me to my core.

His eyes raked me from my feet to the top of my head, taking in my neon pink cane. "I came to say hi."

"Hi," I replied a little more breathless.

"Are you…" he paused and tried again, "Are you all right?"

"Huh?"

"I heard a noise and it sounded like you fell."

"Oh. I'm fine. Just a little stumble. The wall and door caught me." I smiled nervously. My explanation made me sound like a klutz that fell a lot. I felt like such a dork.

His brow creased and pinched, forming a frown. "Are you sure?"

"Uh, yeah. Um…did you want to come in?" I swung my arm wide toward the living room.

"Sure. Thanks."

My heartbeat had increased the moment I saw him standing there, and I couldn't help my sudden nervousness. We sounded like two nervous teens who were about to go out on their first date. Tension permeated the air around us.

"Do you want something to drink?" I asked as we walked into the living room.

"I can get it," he offered.

"No!" I rushed, with probably more force than need be. Trying again in a calmer, quieter voice, I stated plainly, "I might be handicapped, but I can still be a gracious hostess. I have water, soda, iced–tea, lemonade—"

Bryan interrupted me, a grin pulling his lips upward. "And ice–cream?"

"Huh?" My eyes fell upon the half-eaten tub of ice cream slowly melting as it sat on my coffee table. "Oh. Sorry. It's been a stressful day."

His expression changed slightly and became thoughtful and concerned. "Want to talk about it?"

CHAPTER TWENTY-THREE

BRYAN

The moment I rang Emma's doorbell, I wanted to kick myself for showing up unannounced. I didn't even know why I came to see her except that something told me to do it. I had this inherent need to check on her.

And when I heard her stumble, I started to panic. Sheer willpower prevented me from banging on her door and then breaking it down. I wanted to encase her in bubble wrap so that no harm could come to her anytime she tripped or fell. Hell, if they existed, I would probably force her to live in a bubble.

While all of that sounded ideal to me, I knew she'd fight me every step of the way.

One of the things I had discovered in the last several weeks was that Emma had a fierce and independent personality. I admired her for it and wished she had that "in your face" attitude when it came to love too.

She still had days when she wanted to give up, to stop fighting, but she never did. She continued to fight for herself and others. For whatever reason, Emma felt alone, and yet, she sometimes told me about different MG Flakes—as people with MG called themselves. The words she used, I could tell she cared about them, even if she'd never met them in person. She supported and passed on information on other topics besides MG: depression, anxiety, lupus, MS, and many other diseases. Emma may not share her home with anyone, but she was never alone because she was surrounded by friends, fellow warriors, and love. No one could ever take that away from her.

She looked different now that I was seeing her again in person after almost a year. Granted we were in a karaoke bar with bad lighting, an overused smoke machine, and flashing lights. Anyone would transform when they left those conditions. Her lips seemed fuller, and her skin more like porcelain than I remembered. I always knew her hair was brown, but now I could see the strands of red and blond hiding in the mix. Her brown, twinkling eyes were sharp and noticed everything. And I didn't recall them being so intense or the color of deep dark chocolate. Weren't they only brown before?

My eyes roved over her body. Dressed in dark jeans and a black t-shirt with some sort of anime character on it, her hair pushed back in a head-band, her toes painted fluorescent pink, she looked comfortable and completely at home in her surroundings.

Her appearance wasn't the only thing that had morphed. How she carried and presented herself changed. On the night we all met for karaoke, she acted self-conscious and fidgety, unsure of herself. And now, the very air around her exuded confidence. Confidence I knew she didn't always feel. This woman would make men fight each other for the opportunity to have her at their side.

Today, she used a cane that seemed to match her toenail polish, and I briefly thought both her toes and her cane could probably glow in the dark.

Her cane brought me back to her reaction when I offered to get the drinks. It wasn't that I wanted to take away her independence, I only wanted to help her because I considered myself a gentleman, and I thought it would be difficult gathering drinks for two people. I never intended to insult her or her abilities.

Seeing the ice-cream reminded me of when my sister, Rayne, went through a break up, or when girls' night descended upon my parents' house.

"Talk about it?" she asked haltingly, confused.

Had I stuttered? Tilting my head to the side, I waved my finger back and forth between us. "Yes, talk about it. We're friends. We talk about our issues. It's become kind of our thing."

"Our thing?" Only one of her eyebrows lifted as if to mock me.

Was there an echo in here? Or maybe her brain had been taken over by a parrot and she only knew how to repeat words. Polly want a cracker? "Isn't that what we've been doing on FaceSpace?"

"Uh…yeah. I guess it has."

"You guess?" Okay, now I had transformed into the stupid parrot.

Frowning, she ignored my question and returned to her previous inquiry. "Do you want something to drink?"

I sighed and ran a hand over my face. "That would be great. Water please." Maybe I shouldn't have come. It might've been easier on me. After having yet another pointless discussion with my parents on behalf of my sister, and then another stupid talk with Rayne, I began driving toward Mel's place, only I wound up parking in front of Emma's apartment building. Luke had texted me the address the day after I got into town and told me to visit my Internet buddy.

Feeling the icy chill of something against my neck, I jumped and whipped my head around to find Emma leaning against the back of the couch I sat on. I must've really been out of it because I didn't recall sitting at all.

Her mirthful, shimmering eyes stared down at me. "A little jumpy, aren't you?"

"Not funny," I grumbled and took the water from her.

She snorted with laughter. "Actually, very funny."

The moment Emma started to talk, I began to unscrew the lid to the water bottle, pouring a little into the lid, and when she sat down on the opposite end of the couch, I tossed the capful of water at her. Wasting water wasn't normally my thing, but I needed to retaliate a little. Besides, I thought it was funny.

"Hey!" she hissed. The grin never left her face.

"Hay is for horses," I joked.

Snickering, she blew a raspberry. "That's so old. You need new material."

"But still funny."

"I suppose." She settled into her seat and took a sip of her own water before she asked, "So, what are you doing here?"

I liked this Emma. From what I could see, she acted more carefree. Her eyes danced and her cheeks blushed pink. She was real and pretty. "I was in town and I thought I'd stop by."

Squinting a little, she studied me for a moment. The wheels were turning in her head. I could practically see them spinning as she assessed me. Finally, she told me, "That's not what I meant and you know it. What's up?" She stretched her foot slowly forward to nudge mine.

My eyes roamed around the room. Where I had entered led into a short entryway hall that lead into a spacious living room. To the left as I came in, I saw a smallish kitchen and to the right a hallway where I could see two doors. I was certain one would be the bathroom and the other her bedroom. On the breakfast bar that separated the living room from the kitchen, stood numerous pill bottles. So many bottles. Did she really need all those medications? Overall her house was neat, organized, and perfect for her. But it was more than that. It felt lived in and homey. Her lair. The place she felt like she could be herself. So different from my house. Two bachelors occupying one house...ours was clean, but it smelled like two men.

"Earth to Bryan, come in Bryan." Emma nudged me again in an attempt to get my attention.

"Huh?" I grunted as I once again focused on her. Had I missed something she said?

"Are you all right?" Her brow lifted again, and this time she looked concerned.

"Yeah." I sighed and raked my hands through my hair.

"Want to tell me what you're doing on the east coast, and why you're here at my place?" Her brow furrowed as she realized something important. "How the hell do you even have my address?"

A valid question. "A friend."

"And you're here because...?" Her fingers drummed annoyingly on the back of the couch as she waited for my answer.

Sighing, I said, "Because I couldn't stand being around my family any longer."

"You could have gone to Mel's."

"I could have, but..." My words fell off. "Where's your dog?"

"Groomers. Freaking dog decided to roll around in the mud after it rained yesterday. He never does that, but I guess yesterday he decided to act a fool. So, why didn't you go to Mel's?"

"Have you ever just wanted to get away from anyone and anything that knew everything?"

"Yeah."

"That's me today. Mel knows my family, and I'm kind of done with them today."

"Sounds rough." She gazed at me in understanding. Not pity, but with an expression that suggested we were kindred spirits in a way. I should've known she'd understand more than most.

Tension and nervous energy filled me. I tilted my head from side to side, popping it in an effort to relieve some of the tightness and irritation. "My parents are in the process of separating, and my sister seems to think I can do something to prevent it. I can't. I mean it's their own fucking decision, and I can't tell them how to live their lives. Before I got here, I hadn't talked to my parents since the day after I got back from deployment and my feet touched U.S. soil again. Even that conversation was short and to the point. 'I'm back. I'm alive. I love you. Will talk to you soon.' That's pretty much it."

"Maybe they wanted to talk more, but you wouldn't let them." Her voice sounded hopeful.

She wanted to give them the benefit of the doubt, and it made me almost feel bad for crushing her happy thoughts. "Nope." I popped the P. "Their end of the conversation went something like this, 'Oh, you're back. That's good. It's bridge night. Okay, we'll talk to you later. Love you too, son.'"

"Wow. I don't know what to say to that."

"Uh huh."

"And your sister thought you could fix them?"

"I guess. Hell, I don't know what the fuck Rayne is thinking. My parents have had their share of problems for years, but I figure no marriage is perfect. They always worked through their issues."

"But?" she pressed.

"But this didn't come out of left–field for me. My sis called and asked me to talk to them, so I guess she didn't see it coming. You know what?" I chuckled humorlessly.

"What?"

"My parents didn't call to tell me the news themselves. I didn't know anything until Rayne called and told me, begging me to convince them to stay together."

"Your sister told you?"

"Yeah." I leaned back and stared up at the ceiling. "They couldn't bother to pick up the phone and call me themselves. My sister broke the news to me."

"You still came to talk to them?" When I looked at her briefly, her brow was furrowed, her eyes squinting slightly. Her head tilted to the side, and her entire expression told me she was trying to understand everything I'd unloaded.

"I told Rayne I wouldn't come, that they were grown ass adults, but then she called Mel, and Mel got onto me. Their tag teaming worked. Here I am."

Her hand covered her mouth, however, her laughter still escaped. She was laughing at me. It took her a couple of minutes before she could speak, and my eyes never left her. "Sorry, but two women who are on opposite sides of the country from you, managed to kowtow you into submission over the phone."

My eyes narrowed and I glared. I didn't think my annoyance phased her though because she continued to laugh at me. "Yeah, they did."

"And you don't find that even a little bit hilarious?" She waited until I shook my head before continuing. "You. A big Navy guy who works out and has muscles, who could probably bench press either one of them, they got you to bow down and submit. Over the phone, no less."

When she put it like that, it might have been a little odd…and funny. My lips pulled up at the corners into a smile. My first one in almost three days. "I guess I can see your point."

"And you didn't want to go to Mel's because she is part of the reason you find yourself in the middle of WWIII?"

"Yes."

"I don't blame you there. She can be a little…" Emma paused, searching for the right words to use.

Before she could, I barked, "Controlling, manipulative, irritating, vindictive, ambitious, in your face…Please, stop me any time. I'm sure I can go on for days."

She laughed again and shook her head. "No, I think you pretty much have her nailed perfectly."

A chuckle bubbled up within me as well. "It comes from being friends with her for years." For the first time since I had returned stateside, I found myself having fun with a girl, and we weren't doing anything sexual. "What are you doing tomorrow?" I blurted, unwilling to relinquish this feeling. I wanted more of it.

"Doc appointment in the morning." She frowned and stuck her tongue out as if going to the doctor were the most unappealing task in the world.

"Please, try to contain your excitement," I teased her sarcastically.

"I'm not. My sister can't take me, so my cousin will be driving me instead. Bleh."

"And you don't like your cousin? I didn't think your family was from here."

"They aren't for the most part, but I guess we actually have a little bit of family all over the east coast. Some north, and some south. This one is actually my dad's cousin."

My gut told me a story existed in there. "And?"

"I mean I like him all right. He's a good guy and everything for the most part."

Sometimes it felt like pulling teeth when I talked to her. "But?"

"He hovers without hovering. I have to tell him multiple times about things because he 'just wants to be sure.'"

"And that's bad?"

Emma sighed heavily. "Have you ever met someone that simply annoyed you by doing nothing more than opening their mouth? That's him. Adam is…well, Adam. I could actually take myself to the doctor, but for whatever reason, my parents have asked him to take me when Ellie can't. I think they're afraid I'll withhold information from them or something. I promise, I'll call them tomorrow and as soon as they get off the phone with me, they'll call whoever took me to the appointment and verify everything the doctor said."

"Got it. That's kind of…" This time I paused to figure out the right word.

"Annoying, irritating?" She supplied for me.

I laughed. "Pretty much. Okay then. How about tomorrow afternoon?"

"Why?"

"Just asking."

"Depending on the doc and how many appointments, but I'm usually beat after my appointments and have to take a nap. Curley lies down with me, and we cuddle."

Her smile took my breath away. Why did the image of her and me cuddling with her dog pop into my head? No, she was not my type. Trying to ignore the image and forget it, I cleared my throat and asked, "What time is your appointment?"

"8:30."

"Would you be able to rest up and be up to doing something at say... around three in the afternoon?"

"I guess. Why?" She seemed suspicious, and she had every right to be. I barged into her house unannounced, and now I was trying to make plans with her.

I winked. "It's a surprise." She'd gone to a barbecue where she knew only two people, the same two people who showed up drastically late, she was attempting to push herself and her boundaries, and she helped me to loosen up. This was the most I've been since my plane landed. I wanted to do something for her. From one friend to another.

She let a couple of minutes pass before she relented. "Fine. How should I dress?"

"Casually. We're going to go out and have some fun."

Snickering, she shook her head and rolled her eyes. "Got it. As long as you don't get me arrested, we'll be fine. I mean if I need to help you hide a body, make sure we're far enough away from any major roads, and we have to be way out in the country. A cornfield is best." Her smile grew and became blinding. Or maybe that was her.

This woman had listened to my gripes and kept making me laugh. "Nothing as dramatic as that...yet. I won't completely rule it out though."

"How long are you in town, Bryan?"

"Three more days, and I'm not looking forward to more 'family time'."

"So, I'm your escape?" Her eyes sparkled as if she was up to a lot of mischief.

"Maybe. It's either this or kill Mel and Rayne. I figured you were the safer bet."

Clucking her tongue at me, she tilted her head to the side and informed with a straight face, "Don't bet on it. I'm the last person they would suspect of being a mass murderer. I mean, why would they think a disabled person did it?"

My head flew backward, and I howled with laughter until my sides hurt. Trying to control my breathing at that moment was impossible. When I finally regained control of myself, I swiped at one of my eyes and told her,

"That is so true. I'll be sure to keep all sharp objects locked away when you're near."

She crossed her arms over her chest, drawing my gaze there for a brief second, and retorted, "People can kill without sharp objects."

"Should I be worried?" I couldn't stop laughing. This was probably the most outrageous conversation I had ever had with anyone in my life...and Emma and I had had some interesting ones—six-foot dicks and giants came to mind.

"Possibly, but I like you, so you're safe for now."

"Good to know, but I guess that means if I piss you off in the future, I should fear for my life? I better make sure my will and life insurance policies are both up to date."

She nodded with a smirk. "Pretty much." As soon as the words left her mouth, she started giggling with me.

It felt good to laugh. To relax and not worry about my parents, my sister, or anything else. If Emma lived on the West Coast, I might have considered exploring more than friendship with her, but she didn't and I really liked our friendship.

She was so different, and while I knew she had demons to vanquish, she was stronger than she knew. I admired her for that. I probably didn't understand a tenth of what she dealt with, but the parts I had witnessed for myself, the parts I'd gotten to know, showed me that she had an inner strength which few people possessed. Having her life changed overnight, without warning, of being no longer able to do everything she loved to do, and to have to use walkers and canes, devices typically reserved for older people—I didn't think I could have handled it like her. I flew into war zones without hesitation, but I knew I couldn't handle an illness like hers as well as she did. And while I didn't know how she acted all the time, in my eyes, she fought her disease with dignity and grace.

Her phone chimed, pulling me from my musings. I saw what appeared to be disappointment flash across her face when she checked her phone. Seeing that expression, I lifted a brow in question and asked, "Something wrong?"

"Huh? Oh. Curley is ready at the groomers. I need to pick him up soon. Do you want to come or...?" Her question dropped off and hung between us.

I felt a small thrill knowing she didn't want our time together to end, and tried to bury it. "Nah. I should drop by Mel's house. Or is it her office at this time? Then I'm supposed to meet up with some friends and we're going out tonight. But don't forget about tomorrow." Standing, I walked into the kitchen and threw my water bottle away and then strolled to the front door. I heard the clacking of her cane and knew she followed me. When I got to the door, I pulled her in for a hug and kissed the top of her head. I didn't know why I did that, but it felt right. "I'll see you tomorrow."

"Tomorrow." Her quiet voice followed me out before I shut the door behind me.

I already anticipated the next time we would see each other and the expression on her face when she figured out my surprise. She deserved this, and to find the man of her dreams.

CHAPTER TWENTY-FOUR

EMMA

Yesterday after Bryan left, I had a slight fangirl moment. I blushed and touched the top of my head where he kissed me. It took me another thirty minutes before I composed myself and left to pick up Curley, who bounced off the walls as soon as I picked him up, and crashed as soon as we walked in the door. My poor dog got tuckered out at the groomers.

I kept thinking about his surprise. As I read, Bryan transformed into the book boyfriend, or if he didn't, I compared him to the character in the book. As I worked on some of my writing, my male character started to resemble Bryan, and I had to erase him because this was a fanfiction based on a Japanese anime. Bryan in no way resembled an Asian person. As I cooked, as I brushed my teeth, as I showered, as I...everything. No matter what I did yesterday, I thought about Bryan and what he had up his sleeves, and I couldn't wait for yesterday to end.

Today, I hadn't been able to sit still at all. I bounced with nervous energy that my neuromuscular specialist noticed immediately. "Are you all right? Do you have another appointment?" He treated my myasthenia gravis for me and could tell with one glance my good days from my bad. Today was a good day.

"No. I'm just a little nervous about my labs," I replied. It wasn't a complete lie. The last time I had labs drawn, my white blood cell count, platelets, and few other numbers were out of normal range, and the doctor was slightly concerned. This time, he had me do bloodwork early so that he would have the results when I came in today. So, I hadn't lied, however, I didn't want to say anything about the real reason I seemed to be full of energy today. If I said anything about Bryan, his visit, or our future plans, blabbermouth Adam would have it spread across town before we left the doctor's office.

My doctor smiled. "Don't worry. They're fine this time. I want you to be careful about the people you're around. With your weakened immune system due to the autoimmune diseases and the medicines we have you on, it doesn't take much for you to get sick."

"I know."

"Good. Then do you have any other issues?"

The rest of the appointment went textbook. He asked about issues. I told him about how the number of days I had to use a walker had increased. He did his normal exam, testing my reflexes and strength. And then he refilled the prescriptions he was in charge of and sent me to the front desk to schedule a follow–up in four months.

Adam tried to ask me about my excess energy, but I refused to tell him a thing. I would not spill my guts to him, I hadn't told anyone about my plans for the afternoon. I didn't know what we were doing, and it was not a date. So what was there to tell? This was two friends who were going to go out and have a good time. Nothing else could be seen or read into the situation.

If only my racing heart agreed.

The moment he arrived and helped me into his navy blue Jeep Wrangler, my palms began to sweat, and my heart felt like it would either beat out of my chest or race up my throat and out of my mouth. And that all happened before he blindfolded me. To enhance the experience, make my anticipation grow, and prevent me from guessing our destination too soon, he tied a black blindfold over my eyes and temporarily took away my sight.

No joke.

Here we were racing down the highway and I couldn't see anything. The top was off, the wind blew with force across my face, and I was as blind as a bat.

I may have been blind, but everything else intensified without my sight. The feel of the wind blowing across my face, whipping my hair back and forth as strands beat me from the intensity, as it cooled my overheated skin. Sounds rushed by me, but odors surrounded me. Someone was cooking barbecue, a car needed some work because I could smell its exhaust, and I smelled Bryan. That clean and yet alluring fragrance tickled my nose.

I trusted Bryan completely.

The Jeep pulled to a stop, and I could hear something loud in the distance. A new smell assaulted my nose. It seemed familiar, and yet, I couldn't quite place it. Something on the fringes of my memory tried to make sense of my surroundings, but the memory remained out of reach.

"Bryan? Where are we?" Nervousness invaded my voice. I trusted him, and at the same time wanted answers.

I heard the smile in his voice when he responded. "It's a surprise, which by definition means I can't tell you."

"A hint?"

"You have all the hints I'm going to give by the sounds and smells in the air."

"Not fair."

"Life isn't fair." He chuckled. The sound of his deep baritone voice as smooth and silky as chocolate, enveloped me, and my breath caught in my throat. Was it wrong to want to forego our afternoon and return to my place for other activities? I didn't think he would agree with my new agenda though.

The vehicle shifted as I heard and felt him get out of the Jeep and walk somewhere. I heard his footsteps get further away and then closer, and then he appeared right next to me. His smell was even more pronounced than it was as we drove, and it made me want to breathe him in deeply, cementing the smell in my memory forever.

"Ready?" He grabbed my left hand, giving it a squeeze.

"For?" I prompted.

His hand let mine go and he slid his arm behind my shoulders as the other one slid under my knees. "Hang on tight." As he lifted me into his arms, I yelped and threw my arms around his neck.

"Wait! What about my walker?" Since waking up earlier, my legs had been less than cooperative and forced me to use my walker today.

"You won't need it."

"But—"

"Don't worry so much. I got you covered."

My body hummed with his words. If only it were true in the more physical sense. I desperately needed to stop with my line of thinking. This crush was in no ways healthy for me.

I breathed deeply again, in an attempt to calm myself and tried to reason with him again. "You can't carry me all afternoon. I'm heavy and you'll get tired. What if I have to stand or use the bathroom? Or what if—?

"First, you're not heavy. You have to stop putting yourself down. Second, I told you, I got you covered and I do. Just relax and enjoy."

His hard chest pressed against my side. I loosened my grip, but did not relinquish my hold around his neck. It felt too good to have his arms hold me close. I relaxed as much as I could and gave him silent permission to carry me anywhere.

And when he finally set me down in a chair and removed the blindfold, I found myself completely dumbfounded. My hands flew to my mouth as my eyes widened and I gasped. "Skydiving? Are you serious? Are we really going skydiving?"

He wore the biggest smile on his face that I had ever seen on anyone and nodded. "Yeah. I thought you might like to jump with me."

"Yes!" I almost threw myself at him, but behaved. Instead, I bounced in my chair unable to contain my excitement.

"I thought you might." He chuckled.

"Who will I be strapped to?" I inquired, looking around the small room searching for another person.

"Me." The pink tinge on his cheeks deepened into a blush. He'd shaved since I'd seen him the day before, and he couldn't hide his slight embarrassment from me.

"You?"

"Problem with that?" His tone didn't sound as harsh as his words did, and even if it did, I wouldn't have cared.

Did I? Hell no. However, me strapped to him...my body found the prospect of such an occurrence pleasant, and a tingle built low in my body. "Uh, no. Not at all."

"Good."

"Can I trust you though? Do you have experience?" I taunted him, and almost laughed at his gobsmacked expression. "I mean, just because you know how to fly a plane, doesn't mean you know how to jump out of one."

He leaned in closely so that our noses almost touched. "Honey, I'm fully trained to be a skydiving instructor. You aren't the only one that lives to get an adrenaline rush by jumping out of an airplane."

My jaw dropped and probably hit the floor. His smile was panty melting, and the way he called me honey ignited a fire deep within me. If he'd requested it, I would've stripped for him right then and there and begged him to take me. As it was, I tried my best to regain control over my body, but I didn't think I succeeded. "You didn't tell me that. You said you flew planes for your rush." My tone sounded accusatory as I tried to distract myself from my sexual urges.

"And I do, but I had to learn how to jump out of a plane for those situations that are classified as 'in case of emergency,' and I liked it. So are we doing this or are you going to continue to ask questions and stall?"

"Oh hell yes!" I wanted this more than ever before. My body sang with anticipation, the rush already building. Jumping out of a plane while strapped to a gorgeous man. It was a contender for best day ever.

※

BRYAN

194

As we began our ascent into the air, Emma reminded me of a kid in a candy store who had just been told she could have anything and everything in the store. And seeing her face lit up, made arranging everything for our skydiving trip worth it.

When I had visited the day before, I never planned on asking her to go jumping out of an airplane with me. Hell, my original plan never included showing up at her house unannounced. But everything happened as I sat on her couch, laughing, relaxing, and having a good time, I asked about her plans before I could stop myself. When I blurted out my question, I thought, *'Shit. Now, what the fuck am I going to do?'* But before I panicked, I remembered one of our earlier conversations and called one of my buddies as soon as I left her house. With his help, I arranged an afternoon of skydiving. I owed my friend for this one.

I knew she would love the surprise, and I didn't mind carrying her from place to place. After she described how tired she got after her appointments, I figured she would have to use her walker today, and it only made sense to carry her. It would have gotten in the way. She couldn't take it on the plane, nor could she jump with it. That said, I could picture her jumping with the walker, losing her grip on it, and the walker landing on some poor unsuspecting person, killing them in an instant.

With Emma, I felt at ease, like I could drop all pretense and be myself. I didn't have anything to prove to her, and I certainly wasn't her Prince Charming, but I wanted to do this for her. I had a desire within me to see her happy and smiling. I wanted her to be on top of the world...as a friend.

Strapped together for our tandem jump, we were ready to dive as soon as we reached our required altitude. When the altitude was achieved, the doors slid open, and we were given the signal to jump. Together we walked to the edge and began our free fall. Up there, nothing touched us except the air. Nothing bothered us. Our worries and cares fell away. It felt as if we could reach out and hold the world in the palm of our hands.

Wind rushed by, making our skin sink and flap with the pressure, but there was no other feeling in the world like the rush of skydiving, of seeing the land below you and the sky around you. Only up there, unhindered by windows or anything else, were we able to see what we missed with our feet planted on the Earth. Nothing held us back...we flew.

CHAPTER TWENTY-FIVE

EMMA

It had been a long time since I experienced this kind of rush; although some of my fellow MG Flakes seemed to think that getting our IVIG (a special IV medication) treatments gave us a rush. IVIG might make us feel stronger or temporarily hold back some of our symptoms, but this was different.

Flying through the air with the wind pressing against you, pushing you toward the earth and holding you up at the same time, creating a sort of pressure as the ground came up to meet you—nothing compared. I loved it. Something I believed gone forever, Bryan found a way to reunite me with it once again. I would forever feel grateful to him for that.

As the ground rushed ever closer, my heartbeat increased to beat even faster than when we initially jumped. It had been a while since I had jumped, even longer for a tandem jump. Would we be all right? My imagination ran away with me. I pictured us—me—falling face first with him on my back, or the wind catching the parachute and pulling us backward like in the cartoons. All of these ideas fell under the category of ridiculous, and yet, they ran through my head like a film reel that would not end.

"Don't worry," Bryan shouted in my ear, his volume toned down from the sound of the wind.

Flicking my thumb up, I signaled to him that I heard him loud and clear. His words ceased the crazy images and I allowed myself to do nothing but feel.

And a split second later, our chute deployed, and we were jerked from a free fall to a casual float. In the past, this was the time I always really studied my surroundings. The endless ocean in the distance and the vast land laid out before us. It awed and inspired me, reminded me of how small each person was in comparison, and at the same time, it overwhelmed me and scared me a little. The world was bigger than me, and I needed this reminder.

Closer and closer, the ground snuck up ready to either embrace us with a gentle landing—not that any landing was ever exactly gentle—or spit us out and make us eat dirt. On the edges of our drop zone, I saw a van waiting to pick us up and take us back to the hanger. Two men prepared to help us as soon as we touched down.

The ocean in the distance disappeared, swallowed up by the land as we neared the earth. Trees and bushes became clearer. We were no longer the rulers of the world from the sky.

Hitting the ground harder than I ever remembered doing, Bryan tried to keep us upright, however, when he realized gravity didn't want to cooperate, he wrapped one arm around my chest, right under my breasts, and twisted us so that he took the brunt of the landing with an "oomph." I kept my eyes closed until everything stopped moving, and then when I cracked them open, I peered up into a cloudless blue sky with the sun shining brightly. Up there. I had just been up there and flew down to the ground, and it was AMAZING.

"Are you all right?" the deep voice behind me inquired. Hearing it, instinct kicked in and I tried to clamber up and off of him, forgetting the impossibility of such a feat since we were still strapped together. "OUCH! Don't move. Stop wiggling."

I stilled instantly and muttered, "Sorry." My cheeks were hot enough to ignite a forest fire or glow in the dark as my embarrassed blush intensified. Then I felt it. It shouldn't have been possible, but I felt something. Maybe it was the harness or something in his suit because surely it couldn't possibly be a hard-on. I mean, I didn't remember feeling anything prior to my "wiggling," but that didn't mean it wasn't there before. Right?

I thought I heard him groan, but it might've been because I was laying on top of him crushing his liver or spleen or some vital organ. I suddenly felt hotter than I did a moment ago; my pulse raced and my breathing became shallower. Did the hard thing beneath me grow a little more?

Slowly, his hands crept up to release the harness that bound us together. Maybe it was my imagination, but he held me a little longer, a little tighter before he released it, and this time the groan sounded a little closer to my ear.

Everything—the groan, the holding me, the hardness—must've been my overly active and annoying imagination, because as soon as I heard the click, he pushed me off of him and scrambled to his feet, leaving me in the dirt. He took five steps away from me, stretched, adjusted himself—I couldn't possibly miss that one—breathed deeply a few times, and then came back for me with his hand outstretched. He acted no differently and appeared in complete control of his emotions and body, ergo, I concluded his hard-on was nothing more than a natural reaction to my unintentional stimulation when I "wiggled" on top of him. Damn! Was it so wrong to wish it was more than that?

Grabbing his hand, he hauled me toward him and swung me up into his arms in one fluid motion as the two men who were waiting for us collected the gear. This man embodied sex on legs, and I wanted to enjoy the view and my time with him as long as I could.

It did not escape my notice though, that he carried me a little higher than he previously had. Coincidence? I thought not, but I wouldn't say anything to him. Hell, in my experience, limited as it may have been, if a penis was stimulated, it reacted. A secret smile filled with private musings and enjoyment...that was safe. I could pretend, regardless of the fact that it had been a natural reaction, that he wanted me as much as I wanted him. And that was exactly what I would imagine as I lay in my bed alone at night.

CHAPTER TWENTY-SIX

BRYAN

I couldn't believe that after we landed, my dick decided to stand at attention...with Emma lying on top of me. How the hell had that happened? I mean, sure I considered her pretty and she had a great personality, but she wasn't my type. Not now, not ever. FUCK. I knew she saw it. Hell, she felt it. How could she not?

Okay. Calm down, Bryan. This was normal. Her ass hugged my dick... NO! She squirmed, and it just happened. Natural reaction. Nothing to be ashamed of or embarrassed about. Easy in theory, but in practice, I still needed more convincing.

Why was I so worked up about this in the first place? We had a good time, it happened, that was it. I dropped her off at her house, and I even gave her a hug without anything "springing" into action. So it had to have been the wiggling after we landed. Entirely her fault.

I held some of the blame because it was my penis that reacted, but no more. She was not my type.

Running my hands through my hair, both my fists grabbed handfuls and pulled. Between my family and Emma, my life felt completely out of control, and I didn't like it one bit.

I sighed and my eyes drifted to rake over the house sitting across a well-manicured lawn outside my passenger window. My parents' house. The home I lived in and loved my entire life. A perfect family with two perfect parents who had one boy and one girl. A two-story colonial where birthday parties went off without a hitch in order for my mom to impress the neighbors, where I figured out I could use the trellis as a ladder and sneak out of the house so I could meet up with my girlfriend, where my sister and I fought like cats and dogs only to make up later, and where a growth chart had been penned into the wall of the kitchen marking mine and Rayne's heights every birthday since we were one. I lost my teeth and put them under my pillow in the room on the top left corner. My sister forced me to play Barbie's with her in the room next to it.

So many memories came with that house, and now a For Sale sign had been stabbed into the ground. My parents were getting divorced. It didn't shock me; however, I could finally admit that it felt strange to think of my parents living separate lives apart from each other, and in a weird, awkward way, it hurt. Not so much as a betrayal, but in a roundabout way, maybe I thought of it as such. This wasn't about me or Rayne though. This was about them doing what they believed was best for them. Our feelings no longer mattered.

I should have gone in, but I didn't move from my car. The scheduled time to meet arrived and passed, and I still sat there. That was until my sister started incessantly tapping on my window. Not a word left her mouth. She only used her index finger to pound on the glass. *Tap, tap, tap.* It sounded more like a woodpecker at my window than it did a woman in her twenties. Aggression and annoyance built up until I rolled down the window and snapped, "What the fuck, Rayne?"

When I dropped Emma off at her apartment, I had put the top back on the Jeep since clouds had started to form on the drive to her place. I didn't want to take the chance, and as soon as I got on the highway to come to my parents' house, the skies opened up and released a deluge of water. Of course, it ended before I arrived, but at least, Rayne couldn't simply invite herself into my vehicle.

She plastered on an innocent smile, which probably had angels and demons alike running away in fear, and practically sang, "What are you doing out here?"

"Nothing." I released my pent-up breath in a gush.

"I can see that."

"What?"

"Ready to come in and do battle?" Rayne flexed her arm to show off her muscles, or lack thereof. Unlike me, my sweet not so innocent sister could be considered petite at five-three, but her height never prevented her from taking charge or giving as good as she got. I could still recall various bruises and one cracked rib I received thanks to her. And even though I could almost guarantee she was possessed by the devil or something, people seemed to believe she was this sweet woman who wouldn't hurt a fly. Men flocked to her side and wrote prose about her long wavy black hair. Or should I say, "Liquid onyx that flows like the ocean waves," or her "Deep sapphire blues eyes that glisten like the night sky full of stars." I couldn't make this stuff up even if I tried. Men actually did that for her.

I didn't get it. I've liked plenty of girls through the years, and I've had my fair share of relationships, but I DID NOT and HAVE NEVER written poetry, songs, painted a picture, or anything else, to compliment a girl's hair or eyes. Maybe I've never found a girl that moved me enough to act like a lovesick idiot. I loved my sister, and I remembered when I gave her a haircut at the age of four. I wondered what the men that waxed poetic would think of her shiny beautiful hair if they saw those pictures. I got into so much trouble for that, but she never cried about it until my mom found out what I had done, and then Rayne milked it to the moon and back. One thing that was for sure was that I never went near her hair again out of fear it would end in a death sentence for me.

"Look," I began, glancing at her hopeful, yet pleading, face. Damn. Saying no to her was like telling a kid Santa didn't really exist. It was next to impossible when I stared into her eyes. Sighing again, I shifted my gaze to look out the windshield and tried again. "Rayne, if they aren't happy, why should anyone force them to stay together? For our sakes? We don't even live at home anymore. And if this is about our childhood or holidays as a family…" I paused and glanced at her again, and wanted to moan with regret. Tears pooled in her bloodshot eyes, threatening to spill over. No backing down. Those tears could be real, or they could be a plot she used to manipulate me. Throughout the years, she had become a pro at using emotional manipulation to get what she wanted, and it usually involved getting me into trouble or stealing my candy.

I took a deep breath and pushed ahead. "We're adults now and can't act like kids anymore. For holidays, we'll work something out. Do you really want them to stay married if they don't want to? Think about it. Rob, your ex that you were with for two years. We all thought you were going to marry him, but you didn't. You dumped him the night he planned on proposing. What if we forced you to stay with him?"

"God! Ack. No." She acted as if she had a hairball stuck in her throat that needed to be coughed up. I understood the feeling well.

"Same thing, sunshine."

Stomping her foot like a child having a tantrum, she whined, "But this is our parents."

"And they deserve to be happy, to find their own way. If they stayed together simply for our sake, they would start to hate each other, might resent each other, and possibly resent us as well."

"But—"

I held up my hand to stop her. Getting out of the car, I pulled my sister into my arms for a hug. "I understand, but this is their decision and their lives. We have to respect their wishes and support them. They would do the same for us." At least, I was certain they would do the same for Rayne, however, my positivity waned when the light shined on me.

"I hate it when you're right."

"I know you do." I felt her tears soaking through my shirt as she finally let the tears free. I said nothing else as I held her, wishing I could take away the hurt and pain. Out of the two of us, she had always been the more sensitive one…and the biggest troublemaker, but she was still my kid sister, and I loved her to death.

When she finished sniffling and no longer had any tears left to cry, Rayne gave me a lopsided smile. She breathed in deeply and released it slowly. Then and only then, did she finally say, "All right. Let's go be nice little children for our parents' sake."

"That's my girl." I chuckled, tweaked her nose, and then ran away. She despised it when I did that, but hey, she began laughing.

CHAPTER TWENTY-SEVEN

EMMA

The afternoon I had spent with Bryan had been more than I ever imagined. Since I had gotten sick, I firmly believed I would never jump again, but he made it happen. He understood how much I missed it and got me back up there. And not only had I gotten to jump, he strapped my body to his as if it were an everyday occurrence.

Simply remembering the feel of us tethered together, his body pressed against mine, made me squeeze my legs together, desperate for release. After almost two days, the excitement, joy, and lust remained fresh, poignant, and new. I tried to stop it, to fight it every step of the way, but I lost. My crush grew, drowning me in the feelings I wanted desperately to subside and disappear.

How I wished those feelings would wane and vanish, but apparently, I hoped for too much. It was almost funny. After Bryan dropped me off at my apartment, he put the top on the Jeep, made sure I got into the house safely, and then left. And the rain had been falling off and on since, matching my mood perfectly.

There I was bemoaning the fact that no man wanted me, and I had already fallen for the one man who remained the most out of my reach. I stood inside the circle with him on the outside. How many times did I have to hear or read that I wasn't his type before my heart would listen? It hadn't worked so far. Instead, my feelings grew and surpassed the harmless level of a crush since agreeing to this whole stupid experiment. If only he hadn't answered. If only I'd selected the right name to begin with. If only I'd never met him. If only…

If only sounded a lot like 'what if,' and I could hear Gia's voice inside my head hollering at me. "What if my grandma wore combat boots?" I was never sure why she liked that particular saying, or what it had to do with anything, but she said it a lot. Basically, it meant the 'what ifs' and 'if onlys' didn't matter. If my parents had never met or had decided to stop at only one child, I would not be here. If I hadn't gotten sick, my life would have continued down the path it had been, and I probably wouldn't have met Bryan or any of the other people I'd met who had MG as well.

My life changed the day I got sick, and in some ways, I was still fighting the transformation, trying to decide if it had changed for the better or the worse. It was a strange argument to have with myself. Most would argue that it changed for the worse, and in many ways, I thought it had. No one should have to deal with this. Some days I could barely lift a soda can. But then again, there were many ways in which my life improved. I stopped to smell the roses now, I remembered to live, really live, as much as I could, and I tried to never take for granted anything and everything life offered me. I may not always get along with my family, however, they were there for me, loved me, and supported me. Not everyone was so lucky.

I was done and tired of it all, or maybe I was just tired of life in general. I didn't know anymore, but I had figured out one thing, I didn't want to be alone any longer, which meant I had to get over the one man I cared about romantically. It was ironic, that the one man I wanted was the one man helping me find someone else to be with. How was I supposed to get over my infatuation and feelings for him while still spreading my wings?

I stood there and no one saw me because of the throngs of people surrounding me. I needed someone who saw beyond the distractions, who could pick me out in a crowd.

I remembered watching Indiana Jones and the Last Crusade one night with my best friend. Gia had never really been into those types of movies, but I wanted to watch it and she agreed to put it in the lineup for one of our movie nights. She must've loved me or something because we watched it only two nights after I initially requested it.

In the movie, there was a scene toward the end where he made it through all of these different tasks and entered a room full of grails, and amongst them all, he had to pick which one was the real Holy Grail. So many were bejeweled and shiny, adorned with trinkets. Finally, he picked the plainest and most obscure grail. He chose correctly. I was the grail, and I wanted someone to find me amidst all of the decorated cups that surround me.

It was time to start living again. Truly living. I had been going through the motions but was always scared to really put myself out there. And my dates had left a lot to be desired, however, if I wanted to find someone to spend my life with, to love me, to find me in the sea of grails, I had to do more than sit at home complaining that no man wanted me. My walls were an impenetrable fortress which dared not open the gates. The time had come to take those baby steps Bryan suggested.

My insides quaked with pleasure thinking about him again. I still didn't know how he did it, or why, but he had the uncanny ability to break through my walls and see the real me. Too bad he didn't want that person. The time had come to move on, and if that meant throwing myself in a piranha pool, then that was what I had to do. I knew Mel would help me, but I thought of someone else who would probably help me more: Chad.

Chad had been more than a little helpful when I attended his little soiree, and he knew my current predicament. And I did have his cell phone number. Would he be willing? My stomach clenched in both nervousness and uncertainty. My inner voice yelled at me, "He's not Bryan."

I fully grasped the fact that he was not Bryan, but I couldn't keep pining for someone who did not want me. He helped, encouraged, championed, and pushed me more than anyone else in my life—past or present. For that, I felt grateful beyond measure, and maybe my heart confused those two feelings.

My heart denied the confusion, fighting against the mere thought I misunderstood myself. But could I trust my heart?

Looking around my living room, everything seemed so quiet and peaceful. Since I had woken up slightly weak and extremely fatigued, Mel came by on her way to work and picked up Curley. I had a feeling I would be seeing her this morning when she texted me last night and I told her I felt kind of blah. And at 7:45 A.M. she knocked twice and let herself in with the key I had given her. Two people had been given keys to my apartment—just in case—Mel and my sister, Ellie. Both of them used it even when I didn't want them to, but I learned to accept their sometimes overbearing tendencies. They worried about me and wanted to make sure I was all right. I appreciated the fact that they cared as much as they did.

However, this morning I missed my dog. I missed his cuddles, his barking, and his moving around. With him there, my thoughts couldn't head down paths they shouldn't.

Maybe sorting my thoughts would help me to regain control over my riotous emotions. After grabbing a piece of paper and pen from the kitchen, I flopped back down on the couch. I folded it in half, and on one side I listed all of the reasons I believed my heart was confused about my feelings for Bryan. On the other side, I wrote down all of the reasons why it might not be confused about my feelings for that Navy man. The latter started to become longer than the former, and I ripped up the paper and slammed it on the table. Fuck this shit. A list could not decide my future for me.

Bryan didn't want me, and therefore, I would have to find someone that did, and eventually, I would get over him and move on with my life. My heart would find someone new to like. No longer could I convince myself that my feelings were a mere crush, but I refused to define them any further than that.

My gut twisted with my denial, and tears welled in my eyes. I denied them permission to fall, pretending that I could actually control them, and still, they remained swimming on the surface, making my eyes glisten.

It was time to start thinking about myself and my future. My phone lay next to the shredded list, and I wondered if Bryan had maybe sent me a message. It was easy to forbid me from thinking about him, to order myself to get over him, but actually following through on either of those, was impossible. And I couldn't stop myself from checking, disappointment filling me when no message had been received. Then I wanted to slap myself when I tried to give him an excuse. He's busy with his family, and besides, it was only midmorning.

This behavior needed to stop. If I intended to find someone, to complete the mission Bryan set out to assist me with, I had to make a conscious effort to change a few things. Communication with him would come to a screeching halt. No more pinging him. No more waiting for him to message me, or looking forward to our conversations. I hated even the thought that I would never chat with him again because he made me feel normal, as if my disease did not matter. Never mattered. He had become the first guy since right before I started college that I felt I could relax and be myself around, ripping down walls he had no idea existed for a reason.

MG forced me further into my shell, but it only compounded issues that had already existed.

In high school, I was a size 16 even though I maintained an extremely active lifestyle. Winter guard/flag corps, tennis, softball, marching band, and dance. I loved it all and never got tired of my busy schedule and managed to maintain a 4.0 GPA.

And then Allen happened. I had been pushing down all of my memories of him, trying to forget that brief period of time in my life ever existed, but now without the distractions, without anything else to occupy my mind, they escaped and burst free.

I planned to use the summer between high school and college to get read ahead and start getting a jump on my studies, however, my plans changed a little when I met someone. Allen was different than any of the other guys I knew. Five years older, he had an edge to him. Bad boy personified. Drinking, smoking, partying…he did it all, and he approached me. Me, the wallflower who no one noticed. I shouldn't have wanted him. I should have told him no, but when I opened my mouth, instead of no, yes escaped, holding my denial prisoner. This man gave me my first taste of alcohol, cigarettes, and the wild side where no one cared about textbooks. And then he tore me to pieces.

My self-esteem was already shit, and I never quite understood why a guy like him would look twice at me, but at the time, I didn't care. It felt good to be wanted by someone, even if I also knew this relationship could never last. I still had plans for my future and planned on leaving for university to work on my degree. I had dreams I wanted to pursue, and I did not want to become my sister. That thought always remained first and foremost in my head. I had this violent urge to prove her wrong.

It only took two weeks for my relationship with Allen to change from giddy school girl to tortured soul.

The relationship started innocently enough, although, he tried to persuade me to sleep with him from day one, and he always pushed my boundaries when we made out, but I wasn't ready to cross the line into a more physical relationship yet. For two weeks the pressure built and increased, and on the last day, I finally gave in.

Before I could change my mind, he dragged me into his room, his hand gripping mine as he pulled me behind him with his friends cheering him on from his living room. I didn't fight him. In truth, I felt too embarrassed to even look at him. My skin prickled with heat, and I swore my whole body turned red as he stripped me and then pushed me backward onto the bed. As soon as I landed, my stiff body gave a little bounce. I tried to will my body to relax, but it remained as still as a 2x4.

Now that the memories of that time assaulted me, I could not turn them off.

Everything up until his cock slammed into me was blurred, blending into each other. He was part of the room, not a separate being, and until he rammed into me, I had no conscious thought of him above me.

It hurt. There was no foreplay, no preparation, and my pussy was dry as a bone. The moment he roughly took my virginity, I screamed. He laughed. I remembered him laughing, pulling out, pushing in…his pace picking up with each thrust, and I cried.

When he finished, he pulled out and started teasing me, calling his friends to "come in and look at the scared little girl." Sneering, he told me, "You're just like all the others, and you're not even that good. Now that I've tasted you, you can get the fuck out of my house."

One of his friends guffawed as he asked, "How were you even able to fuck her? She's a dog."

"Man, that's what a pillow over the face is for," Allen replied.

"It would take more than that to make me forget that fat ass body and that ugly mug."

Everyone in the room began to join in the fun, to make a mockery of me, and to tear me down. No one helped. I tried to ignore them as I got dressed, but I moved slowly from the shock and from the pain that lingered between my legs. Still, their taunts continued. Even Allen snapped, "Hurry the fuck up! I have a real woman on her way over. One that actually knows how to satisfy her man." It stabbed me and stung. I didn't want to cry, I tried not to, and yet, the tears fell anyway.

The torment continued until Allen's brother showed up with a buddy and they saved me. While the friend pushed everyone out of the way and threw Allen to the ground, Allen's brother, Paul, pulled me out of the room and got me into his car. Paul's friend followed a few minutes later.

They dropped me off at home, and I never heard nor saw any of them again. The rest of my time in town, I managed to avoid running into anyone present that day, but their taunts and Allen's derision stuck with me throughout the years. As many times as I tried to forget their faces, the leers and sneers, their horrifying jabs, that memory was ingrained deeply into me. I could push it down and pretend it didn't exist, but sometimes it snuck out and toyed with me. Only Gia knew what happened that day, and how it still affected me.

Maybe allowing something to chain me up like that was stupid. I allowed it to hold me in place instead of moving forward, but I couldn't help it. My sister, that experience, and then getting sick. I felt like life kept knocking me down and messed with my prospects. Finding someone always proved difficult for me, and nearly impossible after the MG. Honestly, I started to believe my future would not include love.

At least, until I began talking to Bryan.

Bryan swooped in when I had reached a low point, and helped build me back up. Now I believed, even if not wholeheartedly, that someone existed for me out there somewhere. I was scared though. Not only did that memory hold me hostage, the terror of putting myself out there still had its claws in me, wrapping me up until I could barely move.

I hated seeing the disgust, pity, indifference in people's eyes when they saw me. Of course, when I used my walker versus my cane, everyone's reactions were magnified a hundredfold. When I mentioned that to my sister, Ellie laughed it off and told me I tended to exaggerate and once again allowed my imagination to run away with me. Her words stung, but I had plenty of practice at hiding my hurt. No one ever stared at her like she was a freak. No one ever glared at her for using a walker. Her health remained intact while my body seemed like it fell apart.

After I got sick, I begged and pleaded with God or the universe to heal me. I asked for prayers from family and friends. MG remained. I wanted to give up and give in numerous times, but I forced myself to keep fighting. I could never bring myself to completely surrender. Eventually, I learned to deal with the effects of MG and adapted. Military brats excelled at adapting after all.

I accepted my life was no longer the same, and that I had a new normal. However, every time I met a guy for a date, a new wall appeared, barricading me into my own personal inner sanctuary. But by doing that, I almost lost myself without realizing it. Again, Bryan was the person who helped me realize how buried I had become.

He had yet to steer me wrong, so I would take his advice and guidance, and I would march forward, praying the chains of my past did not jerk me backward. Baby steps.

Baby steps began with calling Chad.

Picking up my phone, I scrolled through my contacts until I found his name. My heart pounded in my chest and ears. Was I breathing? I thought I was, but it hurt to breathe. I didn't know. My pulse sped up, and my face felt flush. It was time to forget my fears, jump off the cliff, and make the call.

Before I worked up the courage to hit the talk button, my phone began howling at me with an incoming call. At some point, while I tried to convince myself to hit the button, I had turned up the volume to max.

Screaming in surprise, I threw the phone into the air and it landed on the coffee table, sliding across it, and falling over the edge away from me. If I thought my pulse was racing before, nothing compared to the speed it raced now. I didn't know. Breathing deeply, I pressed my hand to my chest and felt the erratic heartbeat trying to break through my ribs and escape. The pulse point in my neck thrummed, and I felt it spazzing without touching it. Hell, anyone could probably see it and take my pulse without laying a hand on me.

I was always that person who sat on the fence about whether surprises were good or bad, and today, I despised them. My breathing came hard and fast: in and out, in and out. My lips began to feel numb and tingly. I was hyperventilating and could not control it. I needed to take in long deep breaths and settle down.

A pounding started at the base of my skull and moved forward. Bending down, I placed my head between my legs and breathed as deeply as possible. Why the fuck did I feel so panicked over a simple phone call?

Five breaths later, I felt better and the anxiety had started to wane, but the pounding grew louder behind me. It took me a moment to realize the loud noise came from my door and not my head.

❊

BRYAN

Had I followed my own advice, I would have stayed away from Emma the remainder of this trip and not seen her again until Mel and Luke's wedding. Instead, I stood in front of her door, using my fist to beat on it. Where the hell was she? Why didn't she answer?

Maybe I overreacted a little when I left my sister and mom in the middle of lunch and hurried over to her house. Maybe. But, what was I supposed to do? Chad called and asked if it would be all right if he asked Emma out on a date. My Emma!

Wait a second. Not my Emma. She was a friend and nothing more. However, she deserved a whole hell of a lot better than Chad Destin. I loved the guy. I mean he was my friend and buddy, and we hung out whenever I got into town, but there was no way on God's green earth I would allow him to date Emma. Period. End of discussion.

And when I told him those exact words, he laughed and said, "Dude, I actually don't need your permission. This is nothing more than a courtesy call because we're friends."

"She's not ready," I proclaimed, which went against everything I had been saying up until this point.

"Once she jumps on the horse, she'll be fine."

"And you want to be the horse?" My left hand pressed the phone against my ear harder as my right hand pumped open and closed as I tried to stave off the urge to punch something or someone. If Chad had been in front of me, he would have made an excellent punching bag.

His chuckle made me want to kill him. "Hey, why not? I'll make sure she enjoys herself and has a really good time. It's not like you want her, and she's hot. Just because she isn't 100% healthy doesn't mean she isn't fuckable."

I growled, the sound rumbling deep and low in my chest. "Excuse me?"

"I'm messing with you. Why don't you take a fucking chill pill and chill the fuck out? All I'm saying is, she seems like a nice girl, and I plan on asking her out."

"Over my dead body! Didn't you just get out of a relationship?"

"Bryan, remember who your friends are. I've had your back since college."

"So?"

"Come on. We both know Sarah wasn't the girl for me. Who knows? Maybe Emma is."

"You can't," I snapped again.

"You aren't her daddy or her boyfriend. I can do whatever I fucking want to, and you can't do a damn thing to stop me."

"She deserves to have someone romance her, not someone who wants to fuck and be done with her."

"Who says I only want to fuck her? You might be my friend, but you are crossing the line, Bryan."

His tone warned me to take a step back and leave this alone, but I couldn't. "I'm crossing…? Back off, Chad," I roared. "She deserves better than you can give her."

The buzzing of silence coming through my cell phone greeted me. Had he hung up? I pulled my phone away from my ear and glanced down at the screen. Call still active. Lifting the phone back to my ear, my hand ached from how tightly I gripped my cell phone, and it surprised me that it didn't shatter with the pressure.

I almost said something else, but his quiet words stopped me. "Is that your final answer? And before you say anything, you need to ask yourself why you care so much. Why are you so pissy about this particular girl?" With that, he hung up and the line went dead. I didn't have to pull the phone away to see that the call had truly disconnected this time.

ThIS particular girl? Why was I pissy about Emma? Why the hell would he ask a question like that? Obviously—maybe not to him—I was trying to watch out for her. Up until that point, Emma had some of the worse luck with men. She didn't trust easily, and the last thing I wanted for her, the last thing she needed, was to be pursued by a playboy who pretended to be a lifer. Chad would never be a lifer, and Emma deserved better in her life. My concern meant nothing more than that.

After he hung up, I placed enough cash to cover the lunch bill on the table, jumped in my car, and sped over to her place, determined to convince her to decline Chad's less than innocent invitation. The drive seemed to take longer than it should, my chest felt tight, and I couldn't stop grinding my teeth. With the way I mashed them together, they might've turned to dust, and I didn't give a fuck. I needed to get to her before he had a chance to talk to her. I didn't care that a phone call required less than a minute to make, or that my trip took almost fifteen minutes driving from the restaurant in the heart of Charleston to her apartment on the outskirts of town. I also didn't care that the only reason it didn't take longer was that I sped and might've run a couple of stop signs.

My reaction wasn't logical and I couldn't care less. I had to protect her from him and anyone else who did not approach her with honorable intentions. It was my duty to make sure she found someone who would cherish her.

By the time I arrived at the door, I was panting from the exertion and anxiety. Only friends. I only wanted to offer my friendship to her, and I refused to explore my feelings beyond that. She seemed sweet, wholesome, and amazing. And compared to her, Chad was the scum of the earth. An angel like her deserved better than the devil.

I tried to knock softly at first, in order to be as polite as possible, but she didn't answer and my stomach lurched, sending my nerves into overdrive. My fist pounded harder and louder until finally, I could hear something inside. When she answered the door, relief flooded me and I could breathe again. She appeared to be all right, and this time, her walker stood between us.

Seeing the surprise and shock on her face when she opened that door, was almost comical, and I couldn't help but chuckle a little as my body continued to come down from its nervous high. One side of her hair looked tangled and almost stood on end as if she had moments ago woken up after a night of heavy drinking or heavy sex, and her flushed face did nothing to deter from that imagery. I easily remember the feel of her backside pressed firmly against my front. How it hugged…

My throat felt tight and I cleared it. I hadn't shaved since I had gotten back in town and had a short stubby beard, and it did its job of hiding my blush. Thankfully her eyes remained focused on mine and did not move lower, otherwise, things could've gotten awkward. "Uh, hi." Well, that sounded stupid even to my own ears.

"Hi," she replied, her perplexed expression wrinkling her forehead into a frown. "What are you doing here?"

"I was in the neighborhood again…" Words failed me when she started to snicker. I felt my own smile pulling at my lips, and I rolled my eyes at my own foolishness. "Okay, not really, but I'm leaving tomorrow, and I thought you and I could grab a bite to eat and talk a little before I headed back home."

"Talk?"

"Usually happens when you open your mouth and words come out. Much like we're doing now."

She wrinkled her nose, and I couldn't help but think about how cute she looked when she did something so seemingly innocent. Then she narrowed her eyes, and her grin prevented her expression from appearing harsh. "I do know what talking is, butthead."

"Butthead again? Ouch. You wound my manly pride."

"I'm sure."

"So food?" I asked and took an ostentatious step forward. As I thought she would, she backed up and allowed me to enter her apartment.

"I suppose I can grace you with my presence. Let me grab my purse."

She slowly turned around, but the first step she took forward, she stumbled and would have fallen if I hadn't caught her. In that second, I thought my heart was going to stop. "Are you all right?"

"I'm fine." Her words didn't match her tone of voice. She sounded almost angry.

"Em—"

"I said I'm fine." She fixed her footing and stepped out of my embrace.

My arms felt almost bereft, and they tried to reach out to her again, but I dropped them to my sides before they touched her. No, this couldn't happen. We were friends. If circumstances were different, if we didn't live in different parts of the country, then maybe, but not now.

Clearing my throat, I gazed at her back as she moved into the living room and leaned against the breakfast bar separating the living room from the kitchen. If she stiffened up anymore, I could picture her body snapping like a twig with only limited force. I didn't know what I had said or done, but I had to do something to relax her. My eyes searched the small area, looking for something that might put her at ease. They found a couple of dog toys scattered around the living room. "Where's your dog? Is he all right?"

She tilted her head to the side and her frown deepened. "Dog? Curley? He's at day camp today. I've been a little weak today, so Mel came by, picked him up, and took him to doggie daycare while I slept a little longer. I barely remember her showing up."

Even talking about her dog hadn't loosened her up. I wanted to give her an escape, or if she didn't feel up to leaving, then we could stay at her apartment and order in. I knew of countless restaurants that delivered, but I didn't want to leave her alone. I told myself that it was because of her present condition, but it might have been more than that. "Are you sure you're up for going out? We can stay in..." My words tapered off when her bewildered expression turned to what appeared to be anger. What the fuck did I do now? "Em?"

"I'm fine." Those two words came out again in a clipped tone. I didn't believe she was "fine" at all.

I sucked in a breath and raked my fingers through my hair in frustration. I fought the urge to yell at her, to demand she tell me what the fuck was wrong with her. Words stuck in my throat when I noticed how red her cheeks had turned, how the defiant glimmer in her eyes transferred to her body daring me to deny her words, and how she couldn't quite meet my gaze. When she looked at me, her eyes landed anywhere except mine. Why did she look embarrassed? I wouldn't become like one of the others who she pushed away to protect herself, and at the same time, I wouldn't tear her down or hurt her. I couldn't. "What's going on?"

"Nothing. Let me get my purse then we can go."

She straightened up and took a step away from the breakfast bar, and the blush on her cheeks intensified. When she tried to brush past me, I wouldn't let her. I did not want to be shut out. My parents shut me out. My first long-term relationship started to shut me out and she wound up cheating on me. Emma was the last person on earth I wanted to shut me out.

Putting a hand on her walker, I begged, "Em, talk to me."

"It's nothing."

"Come on. We talk about everything. It's what we do. What's wrong?" It gutted me to see her shoulders sag and a lone tear fall down her cheek, leaving a wet trail in its wake.

Ignoring the tear, she spoke softly, "Maybe it would be better if I don't go."

"That's fine if you want to stay in. We can order—"

"NO! I meant, you go, and I stay."

Those words created a panic in me, and I pulled her into my arms, her walker pressing into my thighs, creating a small barrier between us. My hand rubbed her back in circles in an attempt to soothe her enough to pry her thoughts and feelings out of her. "Talk to me, honey. What's going on in that head of yours?" My question became her undoing. The tears she'd been holding back, gushed out of her, soaking my shirt. My panic grew. "Em, you have to talk to me, baby, or I won't know how to fix this."

Her body tensed up again, and she tried to push me away with one hand while holding onto her walker with the other. "Fix this? You can't fix this, Bryan. Is that what you've been trying to do? Fix me? Fix the broken woman who can't walk without assistance, who has a hard time finding her own dates? You want to fix me? You can't fucking fix me! I'm unfixable!"

"Em…" She backed up a step and would've fallen if I hadn't reached out to grab her again. "Be careful."

Shaking her head, she shrugged my hands off of her. "Thank you, but I'm fine, and I don't need fixing. You can't…MG can't….MG is incurable." Her voice caught and my heart twisted with the pain reflected in her eyes. The same pain I heard in her voice as she continued. "I'm incurable. Just go. Please."

"I don't think so." Scooping her up in my arms, her walker clattered to the ground as I carried her to the couch and sat down. "Talk to me," I insisted.

She sat there like a petulant child longer than I liked, however, she finally took a deep breath, wiped her face with her hands, and stared straight ahead down the hall, away from me. When she finally spoke, she sniffled and an occasional hiccup interrupted her words. "If you're here to fix me, it won't work."

I hated how defeated and lost she sounded, but I kept my mouth shut and started to rub her back again. I had a feeling she wasn't done.

"When I was diagnosed with MG, I kept reading about remission, but then my doctor told me that it only happened in a few cases, and no one ever goes into permanent remission. This disease isn't like the flu where I'll get better. I won't. And it isn't like cancer where some are healed and it never comes back. You can't fix me." Silent tears fell down her cheeks, dripping onto her shirt.

"I'm not here to fix you," I admitted. Evan's words came back to haunt me then. It wasn't her situation I wanted to fix. I knew MG could not be cured, but I wanted to help her overcome the things that held her back.

Her head whipped around to look at me. Her eyes narrowed as she studied me in silence as if she were trying to put together a puzzle, and trying to figure out where all the pieces fit. She must have found what she sought because she finally asked, "Why are you here?"

I came to stop her from talking to Chad, but it was more than that. I had to be there for her, and I had no fucking clue why I needed to see her, be there, or help her. Somewhere between the night we started talking and now, it had changed from wanting to help someone I barely knew just for the hell of it, to desperately needing to do this for her. Only for her. "Because you are an amazing woman, and I want to see you get the man of your dreams." Something flitted across her face, but it left as quickly as it came.

"I'm a cluster fuck of a mess," she finally said.

"You are, but you're still cute and likable." Another flitter of an expression I could not place that appeared and disappeared almost instantaneously. I almost asked, but stopped myself before the words escaped. Somehow I knew, I didn't want to hear the meaning behind the expression.

"I am?" Her voice sounded doubtful, and yet hopeful at the same time. If anyone deserved to find the right guy, to have someone love them, it was Emma.

Grinning, I lifted my hand and mused her hair even more. "Yeah, you are. Now go brush your hair, grab your purse, and let's go." In truth, Emma was probably one of the most genuine and beautiful people I had ever met. She could make those around her laugh, and also offered them comfort when they needed it, and took none for herself. In this world, she felt alone and had it in her head that no one would ever want her, but I didn't buy it. I didn't believe that there was no one out there who would want her. This girl was a catch, and I would prove it to her.

CHAPTER TWENTY-EIGHT

BRYAN

Taking Emma out in public, beyond driving directly to the airport and back, proved to be an eye-opening experience that left me scratching my head more than once.

After pulling out of my parking spot in her apartment complex, I headed straight for downtown and informed her, "I have to run by my buddy's gym, and then we can grab some grub. Is that okay with you?"

"Uh, sure," she mumbled from her seat, only briefly glancing my way before she began staring out the window again.

Needless to say, I again wondered if we should've stayed at her place and ordered in. Our last outing had been perfect, in a non-date kind of way. Seeing the smile on her face, the way her whole body lit up when she realized we were going skydiving, had been breathtaking and euphoric. And knowing I put that smile on her face, made me feel like I was a king amongst men.

Maybe I was willing to admit she tugged at my heartstrings a tiny bit. But after getting to know her, I deemed it impossible not to develop some sort of feelings for her. I could accept that about myself and my emotions, but only that.

Emma had a sharp mind that liked to challenge society and people, curves that made a man's tongue hang out, and a quick wit that could cut a lesser person down to size. Her personality welcomed everyone, even though she kept most at arm's length. She desired love, wanted to be loved, but she had convinced herself that she would never get it, and in turn, she gave up her search. The world saw her smiling face, not knowing on the inside she cried and railed against the injustices befallen her. She carried the weight of the world on her shoulders, and yet, never complained because she would rather suffer than see someone else endure the hardships she faced. A walking poetic contradiction, who completely captivated me.

When we reached the gym, I gave her a choice. "I don't know how long I'll be, but it shouldn't be too long. Want to come with me or stay here?"

Her eyes darted to the back seat, seeking her walker. Not to use though, if her glare were any indication. No, she quietly cursed it, and for some reason, that amused me. Chuckling, I covered my mouth when her glare turned onto me. "No one will say anything. Come on. I want you to meet my buddy," I pressed, unsure why I wanted her to come in and meet him when I initially put the ball in her court.

"I don't know."

"Your choice." She looked doubtful about that, but a small smile still appeared on her lips. I would take it. Anything was better than her glare or a blank expression. "Well?" I drew out my L's a little longer, and she snickered at my antics.

Rolling her eyes, she nodded. "Fine. You win." Her giggle told me her irritation was nothing more than a mere pretense at this point.

"Usually do." I shot her a wink.

"Somehow, that doesn't surprise me," quipped Emma, as she pushed my shoulder. I loved our verbal sparring whether it be on FaceSpace or in person.

It took no time to grab her walker, help her out of the car, and guide her into the building. The moment we stepped through the glass double doors, the lone man standing behind the counter gave her the once-over from head to toe. His eyes missed nothing, and I assumed by his actions, that he didn't know the definition of subtle. Glancing down at her, she remained completely oblivious to his perusal. Interesting. How many guys had checked her out, only to miss out on something because she never realized it? I apparently needed to keep my eyes open and remain alert around this woman.

"I'm here for Brandon," I announced, watching the man like a hawk.

His gaze dropped as soon as we approached him. Would he keep watching her, or would he begin to ignore her? If he chose the latter, what kind of man did that make him? Openly staring at a girl who obviously walked in with another guy. Did this guy care about that at all? Something inside told me he couldn't care less and it mattered not who escorted her. That irritated the fuck out of me. How dare he?

I stopped. My job was to help Emma find someone who wanted her, and this man most certainly wanted her. So much so, I could almost see the drool pooling on the countertop.

"Let me page him for you." He gave me a winning smile and then his eyes covertly darted back toward Emma. They didn't linger too long this time with me standing right there, but they did remain on her for a second or two.

What was it about this guy that made me want to beat my chest and tell him he better damn well back the fuck off? I didn't know him; therefore, he might be the perfect man for her, except I saw his faults. Like, why was he still trying to check her out? I'd placed my hand on the small of her back and her body had naturally leaned toward me slightly. That should've screamed her unavailability, and yet, it didn't deter him one iota. If anything, he appeared to be even more interested, which meant he was one of those guys.

Men knew other men. And this one I labeled a lurker. He lurked in the shadows, not caring if the girl had a significant other or not. If he wanted her, he tried to get her. And from what I had seen already, he wanted Emma.

Before I could say or do anything, Brandon made his appearance and asked me to follow him. After a quick introduction, Emma decided to stay in the reception area and have a seat. I had to leave her alone with the lone wolf and that did not sit well with me. However, the fact she remained practically blind to his interest, gave me a small level of relief about leaving her alone.

I glared at the other man before dropping my gaze to her. "Are you sure you don't want to come with me?"

"Nah. You two do whatever you came here to do, and I'll wait here."

"Fine, but if you need me, tell them to page me. I shouldn't be too long."

"Yeah, yeah. Go already. The longer you stall, the longer it will be before I get food, and I'm starting to feel peckish. Plus, I have to pick Curley up tonight no later than seven."

"You do realize that it's only two in the afternoon?"

"So? The longer you dawdle, the closer to seven it gets." She chortled, scrunching her nose cutely.

Secretly, I hoped it appeared we were flirting so the other man would back off. "Dawdle? I haven't heard that since my grandma."

"What can I say? I'm from Texas."

"No, you're a Navy brat who landed in Texas."

"And things rub off. Any other stupid arguments?" she deadpanned.

I was certain she did not mean it the way it sounded, however, my cock interpreted it the way it wanted to and twitched. Swallowing the spit that had collected in my mouth, I plastered on a smirk and took a menacing step forward. "I wouldn't be opposed to things…rubbing off."

Her cheeks turned a lovely shade of pink, her mouth opened and closed, and when she finally recovered, she slapped my shoulder with one hand. "In your dreams. Now, go away and take care of business."

"Not with him," I joked.

"Not even going there with you."

"Awe, honey. You wound me."

"I'll wound you when I ram my walker into you and use my cane as a battering ram on your nether region."

"Nether region?" I began laughing and finally conceded. "Fine. I'll be back as soon as I can." The teasing was innocent enough—kind of—but the receptionist didn't need to know that. Leaning down, I kissed the top of her head and whispered, "Be right back." From the moment I left her, I felt anxious to get back to her.

"You all right, Bry?" Brandon asked, his brows lifted in inquiry.

I scratched my chest and nodded. "Yeah."

"New girlfriend?"

"What? No, she's just a friend." I tried to laugh it off, but it sounded fake to my own ears.

"Friend with benefits?"

"God no!" I hissed harshly. Maybe too harshly. "Seriously, Brandon, nothing more than a friend."

Holding up his hands in surrender, he chuckled. "Got it."

"I…uh…I actually brought her up here to meet you."

"Me? Why?" His confused expression marred his normally grinning face. Brandon loved his gym, and I wholeheartedly believed he got off on torturing his clients.

"She's nice, pretty, local—"

He interrupted, "Are you trying to sell me on her or introduce us?"

"What's that supposed to mean?" It was my turn to look confused, an expression I was becoming all too familiar with lately.

"Look, dude. You do realize she has a walker, right?"

"And? She doesn't use it all the time. Sometimes she's okay with a cane."

"Cane…" His voice trailed off before he found it again. "Does she need therapy or something? Is that why you wanted to introduce us?"

"What? No, nothing like that. She has something called myasthenia gravis. Therapy won't help."

"What the fuck is that?"

"Some disease kind of like MS or muscular dystrophy."

He had started pacing after his last question and halted in his tracks.

Spinning around slowly, he commented, "Actually, some therapy will help so that her muscles don't atrophy, but why me?"

"You're a nice guy, and last I heard, you were looking for love." I grinned widely, ignoring the pang in my chest that warned me I would not like what came next.

"Have you completely taken leave of your senses?"

"What?" The warning bells rang loudly and my hands slowly clenched into fists instinctively.

Closing his eyes, Brandon shook his head back and forth sighing. "Look, I'm sure she is a nice girl, but she isn't the girl for me."

"How do you know if you don't know her?"

"I know. Call me shallow and all that shit, but I don't think I could date someone like her."

"Like her…? Oh." I should have listened to the warnings my subconscious tried to give me. Previous conversations I'd had with Emma came to mind, along with my first talk with Evan. And at that moment, I understood everything. I could call Brandon shallow, but I had done the same thing once upon a time, and so had Evan. So could I really fault him for saying and thinking the way he did? I wondered–not for the first time–if mine and Emma's situations had been different, if we had met under different circumstances, would things be different for us? If she hadn't been a friend to Mel, would I have given her the time of day? If I were the one sick, would she have ignored me? I didn't think she would've, but I would've ignored her.

Brandon's sheepish expression made me want to punch him, but I couldn't. He had done nothing wrong, but I still felt horrible for Emma. Then again, somewhere deep inside me, I felt a little relieved that he didn't want to pursue her. "I got it."

"Come on then. That protein powder I want you to try is in my office. If you like it, let me know, and I'll get some shipped out to you."

"Thanks, man."

"Too bad you aren't stationed here. It could be like old times. Hitting the clubs, picking up girls…having a good time and getting shit–faced."

The thought of that no longer appealed to me in the least. "Yeah, maybe."

"Hey."

"What?"

"Why don't you date her?" His lips had pulled up in a lecherous smirk.

"Not my type." Looking anywhere but him, I gave him my patented answer, the same one I gave everyone else that asked. And that included myself.

"See? That's what I'm saying. You want to pawn her off, but you don't like the fact she's handicap."

My head snapped back and my gaze landed on him. "I never said that."
"You didn't have to."

A scowl formed on my face, and it intensified the more I listened to him.
"Now, you're talking shit."

"No, think about it. You don't even want to date her. Why? I mean most people wouldn't want to date someone like that. She could be fucking Miss America with the best personality on the planet, but that shit is hard to get past. You know what I mean?"

"No, I don't know. She's like my sister, and that's all I see. When I say she's not my type, I mean only that. Not my type. Walker or cane, it wouldn't matter to me." Of course, my perception had only recently changed since getting to know Emma, but he didn't need to know that.

"Sorry, dude. Look, here's the powder, and if you want me to get to know her and keep an eye on her for a while, I will. But I'm telling you now, nothing is going to happen between us. Besides, I met someone last night."

I attempted to give him a friendly smile and shove, and if it happened to be a little harder than necessary, oh well. "Good for you. Why didn't you say so to begin with?"

"Because even if this doesn't work out, nothing will ever happen with that girl."

That girl. The words stung. I wanted to shove him right through the wall. Emma brought out my protective instincts and had me acting like a caveman sometimes. Taking a deep breath and letting it rush out of me, I told him, "I get it. Not everyone can deal with it." Silently I added, *"Some people are shallow pricks who wouldn't know a good thing if it bit them in the ass."*

Evan had been honest when he said if he met her in a bar he would not have given her the time of day, but he also said after he got to know her, he might actually give her a chance. Brandon's reaction had me wanting to punch his lights out, and Evan's made me appreciate our friendship, as well as respect him as a man. It wasn't Emma's fault that she had been forced to use a cane or walker, it wasn't her fault she got sick, and yet, the world punished her based on nothing more than her outward appearance. How many times had I, and others, judged the people we came in contact with on nothing except a casual glance? Judging them based solely on what we saw before us without speaking to them at all? Too many times. The world was all about the outward package. If the package looked good, it sold products and drew people in. People wanted to know anyone they thought were normal and not different.

Continuing in this fashion, the world would miss out on so much good. People would miss meeting interesting and amazing people for no other reason then because they passed judgment on the way someone appeared.

Had I ever been that blind and shallow? I was at some point. Emma changed me.

We had only known each other for a short time, and even less if we only counted the time we had really started talking, but she changed me. I didn't understand how it happened, but it had. And for that, I appreciated her so much more than I had before.

I needed to get out of here and away from him. Brandon had always been one of my closest friends, and even played football together. He was there long before I met Chad in college, and they had both managed to make it on my shit list for opposite reasons. One wanted to treat her like a pariah, and the other wanted to ask her out. "Thanks." I grabbed the sample packets and spun around, intending to leave right then and there.

"What's your problem?" Brandon's snide question stopped me, and I turned back to look at him.

"Nothing."

"Well, something has your fucking boxers in a twist. Is it because I don't like her?"

"Like I said, nothing. Not everyone can deal. I get it."

"Then what's your goddamn problem?"

My arms crossed over my chest in a clear message of 'fuck you,' but he pushed on.

"I'm not saying she isn't a great person. I just don't see any chemistry there."

I stayed silent for a moment, trying to get my temper under control before I asked, "If you were with someone and they suddenly got sick, would that change anything for you?"

"What?"

"Would it? Would you stop loving them because they suddenly lost control over their body, had to use a walker, couldn't feed themselves, had to use a wheelchair? Would you?"

"If I loved the person, then no."

"And if it wasn't love, but you'd been dating for a while and cared about her?"

"I don't know. That's a huge change. With love, you sign up for shit like that if you want to spend forever with them, but just dating…I'd like to say I'd stick around, but I'm not sure what I would do."

Once again, he answered honestly, and I could see the truth of his words in his eyes. Nodding, I turned around to leave when he stopped me again.

"I can't date her, but I never said I couldn't be her friend or never be seen with her. You're my friend, and that means I will more than likely see her around whenever you're in town."

Nodding once more, I finally left him alone. His stance on dating someone like Emma bugged the crap out of me. I needed distance from him. Emma dealt with this on a daily basis. Thinking about that made me want to stand in front of her and protect her from anything and everything. All of this solidified my belief that Emma deserved better. It blinked blaringly bright like the lights of Vegas before me.

And when I rejoined Emma in the reception area, Mr. Smooth receptionist was in the middle of striking out because she still didn't grasp the fact that this man was attempting to flirt with her. Suddenly, it felt as if a weight had been lifted off of my shoulders, and the last ten minutes never happened. Amused at the frustration I saw on Mr. Smooth's face, I laughed. Her complete obliviousness to everything was hysterical.

Their attention shifted to me. They thought I had utterly lost my mind, and maybe I had. I could see it in their expressions, in their eyes. I wanted to rip out Chad's throat for even considering asking Emma out, I wanted to punch Brandon for not wanting to ask her out, and then there stood Mr. Smooth unable to seal the deal.

"Are you all right?" Emma asked, her eyes narrowed. I thought she was trying to decide if she should call for a straitjacket.

Waving off her concern, I swiped away an invisible tear from my eye. "I'm fine. You ready to go?"

"Wait," Mr. Smooth called out. He searched his desk, and when he found his pen, he wrote something down on a white card and held it out for Emma to take. "If you need any kind of training or a good gym or advice on supplements or anything, give me a call. I'm Nick."

"I'm not really—" she began.

"Please?" His face reminded me of a sad little puppy dog, however, when she took the card, his face lit up with a smile like he had been handed the grand prize. And I did not miss the sneer he sent my way, as if to say, 'ha! I'll win her yet.' He didn't have a chance in hell. I should have rejoiced that she caught someone's attention instead of mentally patting myself—and her—on the back for escaping a close call. I silently celebrated.

"Uh, thanks...I guess," she mumbled and slid the card into her jeans pocket.

With a shit eating grin firmly in place, I approached her and the wannabe lover boy, and rested my hand on the small of her back. "Ready to go?" My deep voice rumbled through her body as I leaned in closely and spoke directly into her ear, making it appear as if we were a hell of a lot closer than we really were. Was that a shiver I felt? Probably not, but then again, it might be for the best if I didn't try to incite any sort of reaction from her.

"Yep." She beamed up at me and started shuffling toward the door. In a hurry? Maybe she realized what the guy was after, making her want to high-tail it out of there? The possibilities were too numerous to count.

I happened to glance over my shoulder at the man who had tried his damnedest to win Emma over as I held open the door for her. Seeing his forlorn face made me want to laugh again. Only she could garner this sort of reaction from me, and I had to admit, it was fun.

Regardless of all of that, seeing her throw the card in the garbage can outside the gym, shocked me a little. "What are you doing?"

Her shrug lifted her shoulders, and she admitted, "It's not like I can really use it. So, why keep it? Plus, he was kind of pushy about it all." Her head twisted this way and that, trying to spot any spies that would report her. Or maybe she only needed to pop her neck.

In all seriousness, I told her, "I get it, but Brandon said there are exercises you can do that might help with—"

"I know," she cut in. "My rheumatologist wants me to keep moving so that my muscles don't get worse. I need to move when I can, even if it's just 10 minutes twice a day."

"Okay then." I lifted one of my eyebrows.

Her feet stopped moving, and without glancing my way, she explained, "I have a gentle yoga DVD that I do when I can, and I have an exercise bike at home. I tried to go to the pool a couple times because they have a program for people with health conditions, but it's an inside pool and they heat it."

"And heat is a problem?"

"Heat makes me weaker. Neither class ended well, and the second time I tried, Ellie had to take me to the ER."

"You exercise every day?"

Shaking her head, her eyes dropped to the seat of her rolling walker. "No. Only on days I can. Some days, I can't get out of bed. Other days, I struggle to eat. On those days, I save my energy." Her feet started shuffling forward again.

I was impressed. Even with everything she dealt with, she tried to push herself, fully understanding her limits. She truly was an amazing and special woman.

"So, are you going to feed me now?" she asked, interrupting my thoughts.

"You sound like that plant from *Little Shop of Horrors*," I teased her and made my voice sound gravely when I said, "Feed me, Seymour."

"I'm not that bad," she gasped, but I could hear the trickle of mirth.

"Nah, not that bad…for now." We both laughed and I helped her into the Jeep. "Is there anything that sounds good?"

"I'm open."

"Good, because I know of this great Cajun place I've been craving, and no one in my family likes Cajun food."

Without missing a beat, she deadpanned, "Aliens. That is the only way to explain their lack of taste."

I kept a straight face when I replied, "A cryin' shame, but that would explain so much. I should have their brains dissected."

One look at her and we both lost it again. I didn't think I'd ever laughed that much with a girl. Not even Mel or my sister, but again, I didn't want to explore the whys. She needed a prince in her life, and I didn't think I fit the mold. She needed stability and someone who wanted a long-term relationship, and I was a serial dater. After my two-year relationship came to an end, the longest I'd ever dated someone was three dates, and that was only if they held out sex until then. She also needed someone who would be there for her. I lived on the other side of the country, therefore, I couldn't be here. Granted my orders were coming up and I was supposed to transfer, but that didn't mean I would be coming back to South Carolina, which was another reason we wouldn't work out. Moving and transferring, she needed one set of doctors instead of new doctors every few years. And besides all of that, I had a dangerous job and was sent into war zones. She shouldn't have to worry about whether her husband would be coming home or not. It was one of the biggest reasons I never got serious about anyone.

She deserved more than I could give her.

I didn't bring up Mr. Smooth until we sat down for our meal and she began to peruse the menu. "So, were you not interested in what the guy was selling?" I knew this menu like the back of my hand. It had always been one of my favorite places to eat, so instead of studying the menu, I chose to study her. Surprise, bewilderment, disbelief. All of them flashed across her soft creamy skin and lit up her chocolate brown eyes.

"Guy? Which guy?" She tilted her head to the side and furrowed her brow. The way she bit her bottom lip as she thought about my question, had me adjusting myself underneath the table.

Did she really not know, or was she playing dumb? "The one at the gym. The receptionist."

"What do you mean?"

Snorting with laughter, I graciously pointed out, "That guy scoped you out and tried to get your attention the entire time we were there."

The confusion never left her face. "Huh?"

"The guy. At the gym."

"Yeah."

"He stared at you like you were filet mignon and he was craving steak."

Her eyebrows scrunched together so much, she looked like she was angry. "No, he didn't."

Seriously? Was she fishing for a compliment? But I knew she wasn't because Emma wasn't that type of person. She had absolutely zero self–awareness. I had sort of clued into that during our chats, but now this assured me that was definitely the case.

Clasping my hands together, I leveled my gaze on her, and stated, "From the time we walked in until we left, he wanted nothing more than to occupy your personal space."

She had the audacity to roll her eyes at me. "Nope. That guy was only looking to expand his clientele list. That's all. He's one that will flirt and do whatever it takes to get one more customer so he can increase his bank account."

Woah! This girl happened to be even more clueless than I initially real-ized. Leaning forward, I assured her, "Take my word on this, okay? You caught his eye the moment we walked in and he hated the fact you were there with me. When he gave you his business card, he was hoping you would call him so he could ask you out on a date."

"What? No." She paused, and her face started to turn ten different shades of red. Dropping her menu onto the table, she wrung her hands together in her lap and peered down unable to hold my gaze any longer. "Really? Now I feel kind of bad for throwing it away. I mean he was a little pushy and everything, but I didn't mean to lead him on. I don't want him to think that—"

I could see her panic grow as she continued to talk. Reaching over, I grabbed her hand in order to stop her rambling. "Just be flattered. That's all you have to do."

"But maybe I should go back and tell him—"

"You don't have to tell him anything." Guys like him, he would have a new interest by the end of the day—tomorrow at the latest—but I couldn't bring myself to tell her that.

"But...I mean, when I like someone and they aren't interested, I like them to be upfront."

Her heart was a little too generous, but it made her sweetly unique. "Trust me when I say, it will be fine. Although, I think we need to work on your obliviousness."

"I'm not oblivious," she snapped.

"If you didn't pick up on his flirting, you're oblivious."

"Am not." She pouted. When our waitress left with our orders, she leaned back in her chair, crossed her arms over her chest, and repeated, "I am not oblivious."

"Keep telling yourself that, honey," I smirked and gave her a wink.

She laughed.

I hesitantly questioned her, "Has Chad called you?"

"Not that I know of, but now that you mention it, I got a call right before you knocked on my door. I never checked to see who called though after it ended up on the floor."

"How did your phone end up on the floor?"

"I threw it."

"You...Why did you throw it?"

She squirmed in her seat before finally mumbling softly, "It might have scared me."

To me, her answer sounded like one of those adults on the Peanuts cartoons. "What?"

Huffing, she barked, "It scared me. Okay?" We had moved up the evolutionary chain. Now she sounded like a teenager was in the middle of throwing a hissy fit because she didn't get her way.

"Scared you?" I bit the inside of my cheek so that I would not laugh, but my amused smile still appeared.

"I was staring at it trying to decide if I should call someone or not, and then it rang and surprised me and flew into the air."

"I see."

I saw her digging into her purse for her phone, and when she finally withdrew the small piece of technology, she swiped her finger across the screen. "Oh, it was Chad."

Hearing her say that, I had to fight the urge to grab her phone and throw it to the ground myself this time. But I wouldn't have stopped there. I would've jumped on it, breaking the damn thing into a thousand pieces.

Apparently missing the growing ball of animosity sitting across from her, she murmured, "I wonder what he wanted. Do you know why he called?"

"Em, there are some things you need to know about Chad."

"Oh? Like what?"

"He's a player. Always has been, and I bet he always will be. While it might be true that his last girlfriend broke up with him, normally he is the one to do the dumping. In fact, he had been trying to find a way to break up with her, but she managed to do the deed first. He's not a complete asshole to do it over the phone, text, or email, and she had been...somewhere with the Marines."

"Okay..." Those two syllables sounded more like four or five.

I pressed on ahead because she had to know. "He's always been a douche and always considered the girls he's dated playthings."

"And you're telling me all this because?"

With the arrival of our food, I took a deep breath, trying to give myself time to figure out the right words, but after the waitress walked away, I blurted, "If he asks you out, say no." Our eyes locked together, and I refused to drop my stare even if I wanted to, even if I began to feel uncomfortable. She had to understand how serious the situation was.

She sat there for a couple of minutes, taking a few bites of her food before she finally demanded, "Why should I?"

"Why? Didn't I just tell you about his background?"

"People can change."

I should have known she would try to defend him. Fuck that shit! "You're asking a mutt to become a show dog overnight."

"Excuse me?"

"You heard me. Look, I know him better than you do. You've been exposed to him for a couple of hours. I've known him for years."

"Has he said he planned on asking me out?"

"Maybe."

"Maybe?"

"Is there an echo in here?"

"Could be."

"Why are you so pissed off? You've asked for my advice. That's all I'm doing here, giving you my advice. He's bad news and you should stay away from him." It took all my willpower to remain calm when I really wanted to shout at her to pull her head out of her ass and listen to me.

"What if he's like that because he hasn't found the right person?"

My anger and irritation rose even higher. "You really think you're the right person for him?"

"Are you saying I can't be?"

"Yes. Yes, I am." I threw my napkin onto the table and slammed my fist down, making everything clang from the force.

She sucked in her breath and tears pooled in her eyes. After replaying our verbal tennis match over in my head, I leaned my head back and stared up at the ceiling and expelled a deep breath with a hiss. "Em, I didn't mean—"

Before I could say anything else, she interrupted. "No, I get it. It's easier to talk the talk than it is to walk the walk."

I lifted my head and gaped at her. "What the fuck does that shit mean?"

"It means, you can say I'm worthy to find love, but when it comes down to it, I'm not good enough."

"Where the hell did you get that?"

"You said—"

Holding up my hands, it was my turn to stop her tirade. I exhaled in a rush and tried to get control of my anger and irritation before I spoke again. In a softer voice, I told her, "I said he isn't good enough for you. He's a man–whore, and you don't need to be with him."

"But what if it's my one chance at love?" her meek voice questioned me further.

"It isn't." I'd lost my appetite and sank low into my chair. "Em, you are a beautiful and extraordinary woman. You'll find someone that wants more than a roll in the hay."

"Maybe he wants more."

"I doubt it, and the last thing I want to see is you hurting more."

She lifted her gaze from her lap to me and stated simply, "It's my choice to make. And if it's a mistake, it's mine to make. Not yours."

"Emma…" My words fell away seeing the determined expression on her face.

"When I threw the phone, I was trying to decide if I should call him to ask him out or not. When he called to check on me, he suggested that we should get together and hang out one night. Unlike most, he understands at least a fraction of what I have to deal with."

"I do too," I proclaimed, but I was grasping at straws. Would burying Chad six feet under satisfy my ever-growing anger at him? Maybe not, but I wouldn't know until I tried.

"No. I'll give you that unlike some, you try to understand what I'm going through, but other than the couple of days we've spent together, you haven't had to actually deal with it. And before you say I've told you what I deal with, unless you experience it on a daily basis, unless it's affected your life personally, you really don't get it."

"It hasn't affected his." Now, who was being the whiny petulant child?

"Bryan, I applaud you for trying. However, he's seen his sister get a horrible disease and watched as her life changed. He's even had to help her with mundane tasks before. He's seen the bad days and the good. You haven't. It's easy to sit there and say you can deal with it or that you under-stand when you haven't experienced it all." Reaching over, she grabbed my hand and squeezed. "You're a good friend, and you have no idea how much it means to me that you've tried to help me like you have. Honestly, I've probably laughed more in the last few months than I have since I got sick. With your help, I've faced a lot of things I tried to pretend didn't exist. You pushed me, and it's time to put myself out there. So, why not Chad? I'm not saying he's my forever, but maybe he's what I need to test the waters."

I hated her logic because it actually made sense. But I still did not want her to go out with Chad. Anyone but Chad…or Mr. Smooth from the gym. Those two were no good.

Both of us had lost our appetite with the subject of our conversation, and neither one of us wanted to concede to the other. We stared at each other, hoping the other would give up, and were interrupted by our waitress asking how we were doing. We were done. With lunch, with this conversation, with the day.

Nothing else was said between us at the restaurant or on the way to her apartment, which was sad really. There was still so much to say, and no good way to say it. But when we arrived at her apartment and I escorted her to the door, I appealed to her one last time. "Emma, I don't want you to settle for anything less than you deserve. Compared to you, Chad is scum and you should have more." I left her standing there.

CHAPTER TWENTY-NINE

EMMA

Closing my door behind me, I pushed my walker away from me and heard it clatter to the ground. My eyes burned with tears that fell as I slid down my door, landing on the floor with a thud. Something inside warned me that I should listen to him, to heed his warning, but that same part held out hope that Bryan would wake up one day and realize he had fallen in love with me. A pipe dream.

He had been right about one thing though, I deserved love. And maybe I was slightly oblivious. I honestly never realized that guy at the gym had been flirting with me the entire time I sat there. I only thought he wanted a new customer, and my budget didn't allow for a personal trainer. So I blew him off. Chad, on the other hand, understood a small fragment of my existing world. And while he might be a complete asshole, his history didn't dictate his future. People changed. My life had taken a drastic turnaround the day I got sick, and since that day people judged me by what they saw: a young woman with a cane or walker. Based on that, I owed Chad the benefit of the doubt

My biggest obstacle were my feelings for Bryan. Instead of dissipating or changing, they grew. No longer could I claim that the only thing I felt for him was a simple crush. There was nothing simple about my feelings any longer. But then, Chad could distract me from my inner turmoil and heartbreak.

Besides, there existed a small sliver of possibility that something more could develop between Chad and I. Maybe. Probably.

I knew it wasn't true, but that didn't stop me from trying to lie to myself.

And after today's lunch, I feared my relationship with Bryan sustained irreparable damage. I wanted my friend, but I had to distance myself or I risked my heart. I couldn't do it. Our conversations might continue, however, my walls needed to be erected and firmly put back in place once again. There was no other way.

My phone rang. I ignored it. The people who really mattered to me each had their own ringtone: Mel, my parents, Ellie, Gia, and even Bryan. I'm not sure what I was thinking when I decided to give Bryan his own, but the one time he called me, I snickered as The Village People's *In the Navy* blasted loudly throughout my apartment. When we made arrangements to go skydiving, he had given me his number to call him in case I wasn't up for an afternoon out. I had given him mine in exchange, and he called to make sure I still wanted to go on an adventure, as he called it. And it had been.

Whoever called now, could be dealt with later. My heart was on the verge of breaking, and I needed space. I wanted to be left alone.

Blinking my eyes open, I felt disoriented for a moment and realized I had fallen asleep at the door. Or should I say I cried myself to sleep? Something woke me up though and it dawned on me that my alarm was screaming. I had to pick up Curley, but all I wanted to do was drag myself to my bed and shut out the world. I couldn't do it, though.

Beneath my cheek, a puddle of drool had pooled and my neck had a crick in it from sleeping in a weird position for too long. My tears had long since dried and left crusty tracks on my face. I felt done with everything.

Today, after I picked up my dog, I would crawl into bed where I could cuddle Curley and forget about my heartbreak momentarily. Tomorrow, I would deal with the shambles it felt like my life had become.

CHAPTER THIRTY

EMMA

My grandmother used to tell me that if I had a bad day, not to worry, because tomorrow a new day would dawn and with it came a fresh start. In response, I always patted her hand to placate her while I secretly rolled my eyes, because I thought she had turned senile on me.

But she was never senile. It was more that I never understood the ramblings of an old woman. I finally understood what she meant back then though. Waking up today brought me a new day and a new perspective.

Bryan had his reasons for believing what he did about Chad, and all in all, he had my best interest at heart when he gave me his warning. Added to Mel's own advice to be careful around Chad, and I knew Chad was a risk. However, I at some point in time, I had to take that leap. Why not with Chad? As far as guys went, his body was the stuff of wet dreams, he understood my situation, and he always acted like a gentleman around me. Maybe he was only after a roll in the hay, but even if that was the case, no one ever said I had to give into him. And the possibility existed that he only wanted a date with no ulterior motives.

I felt almost compelled to accept Chad's invitation if he still planned on asking because it would be the first step toward a new me, a new life. It meant I could start to close the door on Bryan, I could test the dating waters again, and it would boost my confidence–something it desperately needed. After so many bombed dates from my past, I needed one to go right, and I figured going out with Chad would be a sure bet for a good date.

I picked up my phone from the bedside table, noticing for the first time that Chad had left a voicemail the day before. The butterflies in my stomach started to flutter as my thumb pressed on the button that would directly connect me with my voice mail. It was a quick message, one that only requested that I call him back. A return call sounded like an easy enough task, my finger hovering over his name, but I hesitated because my heart and my head wanted to only think about Bryan. Bryan wasn't here. Bryan didn't want me because I did not fit into his mold of the perfect woman. Chad wanted me, and even though Chad wasn't Bryan, he was there.

I had almost worked up the courage to make the call, when my vision went black. Curley, who had been lying beside me, decided it was time for breakfast. Instead of nudging me or barking like a normal dog, he laid across my eyes and nose trying to both blind and suffocate me in a bid to get me moving pronto. His needs superseded my own, at least in his head. Giggling, I pushed him off of my face and snapped my fingers. He immediately jumped off the bed, sat down, and barked, causing me to giggle some more. My little dog never failed to put a smile on my face. On days I felt down or weak, he remained at my side to make sure I was not alone. Even last night after I'd picked him up, we came into the bedroom, he jumped on the bed, and we curled up together. He hadn't tried to get me to play with him or run around like crazy. He knew I only needed him and my bed.

On the other hand, when he decided I near starved him, walking down the hall with him running circles around my feet desperate for his food, always became an adventure. As he ran around me, he stayed far enough out of reach that he wouldn't run into me, his little body leaping into the air as he whined and barked for his sustenance. On days I used my cane, he obediently stayed on the opposite side of my extra leg, and on days I used my walker, he circled the wagons in an attempt to make me move faster. It always made me laugh.

I tried to use my cane today, but the moment I stood up, I wobbled and fell backward onto the bed I had momentarily vacated. I had to have the extra support of my walker. My walker days were increasing, and I feared there would come a time when that would be the only device I used to get from place to place. I pushed that thought to the back of my mind, where I pushed everything I chose not to deal with immediately. In my current frame of mind, more walker time meant more funny looks from people, it meant it would be harder to find someone who saw past all of the issues to find the real me, and it meant my MG was not under control. Those thoughts were outrageously depressing.

Curley made it better though. After slipping my phone into the waistband of my pajama shorts, I pushed myself down the hall with Curley's yelps forbidding me from thinking of anyone or anything except him. I mixed a spoonful of wet food with a small scoop of his dry food, gave him the command to sit, and carefully set the bowl on the floor as I held onto the counter for dear life. My grip was so tight, my fingertips were turning white.

He continued to sit there, his eyes flittering between his food and me. He knew he couldn't touch it before I gave him his release command. "Okay." His release command given, he dove into his food, sucking in his stomach, and did not come up for air until he had inhaled every last crumb.

As he scarfed his food, I pulled my phone out of my waistband and stared at it. It felt hot and heavy in my hand. Chad asked me to call him back, he waited for my return phone call, but I hesitated. My gut told me if I accepted his offer—whatever that offer happened to be—things between Bryan and I would be forever changed. On one hand, given my current feelings for him, that wasn't necessarily a bad thing. On the other hand though, I didn't want to lose him completely. If I went out with Chad, I feared Bryan would be gone from me forever.

Then again, waiting for Bryan's feelings for me to change, helped no one, especially not me.

Curley whimpered and crawled into my lap, kissing my hand before curling into a ball. He supported me and somehow understood I needed him during my moment of uncertainty. Plus, he was probably exhausted from being at daycare the day before. It always wiped him out for a couple of days after.

The time had come. I slowly, almost too slowly, unlocked my phone and immediately pulled up my call log. It took me no time to find Chad's number since it remained at the top of the list. My finger lingered over the button, trembling. Before I completely chickened out, I slammed my finger down harder than needed on call. I had two choices: remain on the line, or hang up. If I decided on plan b, he would undoubtedly call me back, which meant I could answer, send him to voicemail, or block his ass.

Hearing his voice when he answered made me realize how much I had overanalyzed this whole situation. My cheeks turned pink with my embarrassment, but thankfully no one could see except Curley. "Emma?" His voice called out to me, startling me to the point I almost dropped the phone. I had already sent it flying the day before. I thought that was more than enough for the little device.

"Hey. Um. Sorry about that." My tentative voice shook slightly making me cringe. I crossed my fingers, praying he wouldn't hear how nervous and timid I felt. Because Bryan had informed me of Chad's intentions, I was more nervous than if I'd been kept in the dark. "Uh…you called yesterday?" *Way to sound nonchalant, Emma.*

"Yeah, I did. Are you all right?"

"Yeah. I mean, yes, I am. Sorry. Yesterday was a little rough for me, and this morning isn't exactly a cake walk either."

"You need anything?"

His concern brought a small smile to my lips and helped me to relax a little. "I think I'm okay. Curley went to day camp yesterday so he's tuckered out, which means I don't have to worry too much about him. I'm just going to keep it low–key today. I'll be fine."

"You sure? If you need me to pick up anything, I will."

Even though Bryan and Mel both claimed he was a player, and that he wasn't the greatest guy to know, the fact that he'd offered something so simple, made him look like one of the good ones instead of a horrible guy. Chad had his merits too. I believed under his horrible reputation, lay a truly nice guy. "I think I'm good, but if something comes up, I'll let you know."

"'Kay. So…"

"So?" Here it came. The question I knew he'd ask hung in the air. I held my breath, my skin felt hot and sweaty, and the butterflies in my stomach switched from the waltz to a salsa.

"So…want to go out with me?" He did it, he asked. I felt sick, while my heart shot into overdrive.

"On a date?" It popped out before I could prevent it.

"That's typically what it means when a guy asks a girl to go out with him."

Flustered, I stammered, "I-I-I…I know. I was just…checking?" I had to fight the urge to slap myself when it came out sounding more like a question than a statement full of conviction.

"Okay, and?"

"And?"

"Your answer. Do you want to go out with me? And to clarify, go out on a date."

"Umm—"

He more than likely sensed my hesitation, and jumped in before I said anything else. "It's only a date. Dinner, and you pick the place."

Still, I floundered, unsure of what I should say.

I heard a small chuckle, and then his smooth voice told me, "One date isn't going to kill you, and besides, aren't you trying to put yourself out there? I'm not trying to pressure you or anything, but you have to actually go out and have fun if you want to find someone. It's the only way for your little experiment to work."

Logic sucked. Chad was right, and he used the same logic I had used on myself earlier. Taking a deep breath, I shored up my courage, exhaled loudly, and then practically yelled into the phone, "OKAY."

"Does that mean yes?"

I held my breath and nodded, only to remember he couldn't see me. I swallowed hard, telling myself to be brave as I answered, "Yes."

My heart felt like it wanted to beat out of my chest while my stomach started doing flips. I hadn't eaten, but I felt like I wanted to throw up. Feelings of betrayal threatened to overwhelm me, though I beat it back as much as I could. What had I done to feel guilty about? Whom had I betrayed? No one except my own feelings. In that admission I believed I found the first step in getting over Bryan and leaving my feelings in the past. At least, I hoped that would be the case.

"Great!" he exclaimed, unaware of my inner torment. "Since you're not up to much today, how about tomorrow? If you're feeling better."

This man understood good days versus bad days, and didn't hold them against me. I told myself I should feel over the moon ecstatic. Part of me did feel that, however, the other part wept because of my decision to move on from my feelings. "I can do that." I sounded perkier than I felt.

"Okay. How about I call you tomorrow morning to check on you. If you're up for it, we can make plans then? I actually have to run. I have a meeting with a client in about an hour so I need to get moving."

"Okay."

"I'll talk to you tomorrow then."

"Awesome."

"Bye, Emma."

"Bye." My phone dropped to my side as soon as I disconnected the call.

I almost dropped it on Curley's head, but caught it before any damage had been done. The little dog in my lap continued to snooze, snoring louder than a person with sleep apnea. He dreamed while I tried to fight back the tears and trepidation caused by my upcoming date.

I couldn't believe I actually had a date.

CHAPTER THIRTY-ONE

EMMA

How was it possible that my nerves were even more out of control than they had been the previous day? This morning I woke up, got out of bed, fed my dog, and then it dawned on me that at any moment Chad would call to see if I was up for a date. Thankfully, my body decided to cooperate today, even if a cloud of foreboding and guilt still circled me. The pressure felt so intense, it wouldn't have surprised me if I looked up and saw vultures circling overhead.

Last night, I tried to ping Bryan because silly me wanted to talk to him about anything and everything, but he never responded. Even before I sent my message, I suspected he would not reply, but I had to try.

Me: *Decided to go out with Chad for one date. Now I'm nervous.*

Silly me, I crossed my fingers and watched the computer screen in the hopes he would type something, give me some sort of encouragement. I waited in vain.

Since the beginning of our odd pact, I never lied to Bryan. Maybe I withheld information, but that was different. This date was the culmination of everything Bryan and I had been working toward, and for that reason, I would not start lying to him. He knew Chad wanted to ask me out, and I believed it only right that I tell him I had agreed to the date. If he hated me for it, then so be it. But I couldn't let it—him—go completely.

I did nothing that day except lay around. Neither Curley nor I were up to doing anything. I even blew off my sister by telling her I was having a bad day. She never questioned me, only asked, "Do you need anything?"

"No, I'll be okay. Going to rest up," I told her, desperate to get off of the phone as soon as possible.

"What about Curley? Do you want me to come and get him?"

"He's fine. Mel took him to day camp yesterday, and he's tuckered out."

"Good. That'll make things easier for you. If you need me, call me. I'll call to check on you later."

"Okay," I said before hanging up. After that, I went back to bed and stayed there until morning. Periodically, I flipped through the channels on TV, however, nothing held my interest for long because I knew what I wanted to be doing. I wanted to converse with Bryan, but I never heard from him. Unable to do much more than lie in bed, I only left it to go to the bathroom, forgoing food because I had zero appetite.

Chad called around lunchtime the next day, after I'd laid down for a nap, and since I got off of the phone with him, I've had to talk myself out of canceling our date more than a dozen times. Technically, I had an easy out. An excuse I was ashamed to admit I've used in the past when I didn't feel like going out with a particular group of people, or whenever my anxiety got the better of me. I'm too weak. I took a turn for the worse. I'm too tired. My muscles don't want to cooperate. Unfortunately, with MG, things could change suddenly from good to bad, and bad to worse, however, today was not one of those days.

I could hear my granny now telling me to buck up because her great-granddaughter was no coward. That woman had raised six children during the Great Depression, could kill a chicken with her bare hands, make a meal out of scraps, and managed to make every single person around her feel special and loved. I was lucky enough to be close to her for a good portion of my life, only losing her six years ago when I was twenty-three on the verge of turning twenty-four, a year before I got sick. Through the years, her voice had developed into my conscience, and for that, I could also picture her slapping the back of my head to knock some good sense into me whenever I did something she considered wrong. Whenever I got on her shit list, her lips would always turn down into a frown, and she would demand I explain myself. In this case, I pictured her asking why I agreed to go courting with one man when I wanted a completely different man to court me. She used to call dating courting, which always made me snicker. I missed her.

So, on the one hand, I heard her voice telling me to grow a backbone, and on the other hand, her voice told me I needed to listen and follow my heart.

One date. I only agreed to go out with Chad for one date. Surely that would be all right. After dinner, I could think about what I really wanted to do about my tattered love life. Later, I would listen to my heart. Later, I would sit down and I would pray that my feelings for Bryan would leave. I wanted to be loved, I wanted to love, but caring for him made everything impossible.

Slight tremors wracked my body as my nerves got progressively worse throughout the day, and by the time the doorbell rang, my anxiety had made me so tense, I felt as if I could implode at any moment. It was probably a good thing that my phone had already been tucked away in my purse for safety reasons. I feared for its life. In my current state, it could have landed in the garbage disposal. The last thing my phone needed was another flying lesson.

Flying lessons made me think of skydiving. Skydiving made me think of Bryan. NO! Not happening. Get it together Emma! I chastised myself as I dragged my body toward the door.

Plastering on a smile in an attempt to appear more excited, I took a deep breath, grabbed the handle, and pulled the door open for my date. As soon as it flew open, I caught a waft of Chad's strong, odorous cologne. It assaulted me and could've probably been arrested for assault and battery to the nose. But it showed he put forth some effort. Right? And it could have been worse. Some fragrances out there smelled more like a garbage truck than cologne.

Nothing compared to Bryan's scent though. Fresh, clean, and crisp without being too overpowering. I never felt overwhelmed by his scent.

I had to stop comparing everyone and everything to Bryan. This was not Bryan.

When the smoke cleared, meaning I could breathe again without the smell of his scent killing me, I released my breath slowly and closed the door behind him so that Curley would not escape. Although my dog was too busy sniffing this new person to consider running out the door. "Hi. Thanks for picking me up. I hope you don't mind—"

He pressed a finger against my lip, shushing me. He actually shushed me. "Shh. Whatever you need, I've got you covered, babe."

Babe? I mean Bryan called me honey and baby, but those were southern terms people used on anyone and everyone, even people they didn't know. Babe? I kind of disliked the word. It always rubbed me the wrong way.

Already backed against the wall in the entryway, I moved my head backward and hit it against the wall. Thud. "Uh. Okay then. Well, tonight I have my walker. Is that going to be a problem?" My question was meant as a challenge because I wanted to see what he would do. Yes, he never seemed to have a problem with it at his house, but this was different–he was different. He entered my home with a completely different personality, and if it wasn't for his looks, I would have thought someone else stood before me. This man screamed gigolo, whereas the other one said caring friend and brother...man. Did he have a brain transplant? A lobotomy? Maybe he had split personality syndrome?

"Sure babe. Walker, cane, scooter, whatever. I got you covered." He tried to shake Curley off, but my dog thought the new person was playing with him and he bit down on Chad's pant leg and tugged. At that point, my date gave up, deciding to ignore my dog for now.

Scooter? Last I checked I didn't need one of those yet. Braces for my legs, walker, cane, a carryon full of meds...yes to all of the above. Not a scooter though, and as long as I was able, I would continue to walk for myself. I knew people who have had to use one and I didn't fault them for that, but I didn't want one unless it got to the point I had no other choice.

He licked his lips and leaned in closely, depriving me of fresh air and oxygen. "Or if you want, you can lean on me, and I'll help you from place to place."

Thoughts of another set of arms carrying me made me feel warm and fuzzy, while the thought of Chad with his arms wrapped around me...that image gave me the heebie-jeebies. I shuddered while picturing it. When he noticed my reaction, his smile grew and he leaned in even closer, his nose rubbing against my cheek. I knew he had misinterpreted my reaction.

This new Chad creeped me out, and I did not like the change in him at all. Knowing he could overpower me if he wanted, I still pushed him away from me, grateful that he went willingly. A point in his favor, considering he started in the hole from the moment I opened my door tonight. "What's wrong with you?"

"What do you mean?" He blinked in confusion.

Curley tried to get Chad's attention by growling as he pulled on his pant leg, but my date refused to give the little guy any attention. Did Chad dislike dogs?

Narrowing my eyes, I seethed. "At the party, you were a nice gentleman. You even acted the same way on the phone. What? Now that we are on a date, you think you should to act like you have game? Sorry, but I don't play that. And if this is the real you, I'm not in the market. You can leave. There's the door, don't let it hit you in the ass on your way out."

His eyes grew to the size of small saucers. I guessed my reaction shocked the hell out of him. "Girls like confidence," he countered.

"There's confidence, and then there's being an ass-hat."

"What the hell? Want to pull that knife out of my back?" He gripped his chest as if he had been wounded.

"Just speaking the truth. Don't tell me this is how you are with all your dates?"

"Pretty much."

"Really?"

"The ladies love what I have to offer them."

I lifted one of my brows in disbelief before I challenged him. "Yeah? Well, those girls probably wanted a couple of things. You in bed and to be seen on your arm. I mean, you're hot as hell, but your attitude sucks. I'm not impressed at all."

"Aren't you the girl who hasn't been on a date in forever? You should be happy I asked you out."

My hand reacted before I realized what it had done. **SLAP!** The cracking sound rang out loud and clear in the confines of the small space. Chad did not move a muscle, did not twitch. The surprised expression was clear on his face.

Even Curley stopped what he was doing, sat on his haunches, and watched us. If needed, he would pounce on Chad in order to protect me–not that a little pug could do much damage.

I snapped at him. "I'm sorry, but if this is nothing but a fucking pity date, you can get your ass in your car and leave. I don't need those, I don't need you, because I believe I deserve better. I've been with enough losers in my short life to know I don't want to date another one, and if a guy can't be real with me, I don't want him. I have enough bullshit that I have to deal with right now, that I don't need, or, want anymore. So if you're here only to add to my drama, leave now and lose my fucking number."

His eyes blinked in shock. "You're serious?"

"As a fucking heart attack." The ball was in his court. He had to decide his next move. Either he dropped the act, or he left. Plain as that. I might have wanted to use him to help me get over Bryan, but I refused to deal with an asshole who acted like a player. Or was that a player that acted like an asshole? Actually, they were probably the same thing. Regardless! I refused to become a pawn in his game.

I waited. Just when I got the notion to kick him out of my house, he straightened up and cleared his throat. "Sorry."

"For?" Was he leaving or apologizing for his behavior?

"Other than my family, you're the only girl that's called me on my bull-shit. Most girls I go out with don't mind me acting like that. They kind of relish the overconfident player because they like believing they tamed the bad boy." He grinned sheepishly. I noticed this time that his lips lifted higher on the right side than the left, and it was still sexy as hell.

"What about your ex-girlfriend?"

"Let's say we had an understanding."

I didn't know what he meant by that, and at this point, I didn't really care. "I see."

"How about I promise to behave if you agree to still have dinner with me?"

I knew three things: I was dressed with my hair and make-up done, hunger made my stomach growl at the most inopportune moment, and I wanted out of the house for the night so I wouldn't think about Bryan. With those things in mind, I agreed. "Fine, but if you act like an asshole, I'll call a cab and leave you wondering why I'm taking so long in the bathroom."

"Deal." He laughed, which made Curley bark and then my little dog bit his pants again. Chad must not be all bad if Curley liked him.

Dinner proved to be interesting. After figuring the best place to put my walker, since he had things piled in his trunk, he managed to shove it in his backseat, and then we took off.

Walking into the restaurant, the hostess flirted with him when he asked for a table for two. Then the waitress attempted to grab his attention when she took our orders. Actually, as I looked around the place, girls from every corner in the restaurant were gawking at him. Some of the braver single women tried to get his attention, shooting daggers at me with their eyes when nothing worked. It seemed no one was immune to his charm except me.

As we sat there eating our food, we talked about anything and everything, and that included trash talking each other's hockey teams. It felt comfortable to sit across from him. After our salads were removed by the waitress, I grinned, and he pointed out, "You have salad stuck in your teeth."

I didn't get embarrassed or flustered. I used my napkin to clear it and then asked, "Is it gone?"

"Yeah, you got it."

"Thanks. So why did you get into graphic design and then personal training?" I questioned, curious about his choices in life.

Shrugging, he started to tell me, but our food arrived before he could. After the waitress left, he explained, "Actually, I became a personal trainer first. A new gym opened up and they were hiring when I was in college. So I applied and got the job of entering in new people and cleaning up the gym. Glamorous, let me tell you." He rolled his eyes and I giggled. "So, after about six months, one of the trainers asked if I would be interested. I said yes. He helped me get me ready for the exam, and the rest is history. I liked it too much to completely give it up, but there isn't a whole lot of money in it. Some make good money, but most don't. Plus, I went to school for computer science. I love designing things and can do anything from creating pamphlets to building an interactive website. I've already created a few games. I love doing that shit."

"That's cool. So you've always known what you wanted to do?"

"No, not at all. Computers always came easy for me, but when I got into high school, my computer science teacher showed me what they could really do. Since then, I became hooked. What about you?"

"I majored in psychology."

"So you like to shrink people, or whatever they call it?" Chad asked, leaning away from me, putting a little more space between us.

I laughed. "I can. I have a Master's degree in it, but no. I actually worked for a corporation in their marketing and training department. A psych degree can be used for a lot of different things."

"I see."

"Don't sound so afraid. I'm not going to psychoanalyze you."

We ate the rest of our meal participating in only small talk, as two friends would. Maybe it was because I had made up my mind about this date and my reason for going on it before he picked me up, but I realized something by the end of it. No spark existed between us. Some would have told me that the spark would develop over time, however, I didn't agree. I wanted more, and I was certain Chad felt the same.

That old adage came back to haunt me. 'It's not you, it's me.' It really was me this time. I had a great time at dinner. We laughed, joked, talked, and enjoyed each other's company, however, nothing else existed between us. In the end, Chad was only meant to be a friend.

I dreaded telling him that when he dropped me off, but as it turned out, I shouldn't have worried so much. Like any gentleman would do, he walked me to the door, and after I unlocked it, he leaned down and kissed my cheek. "I had fun, and we should definitely do it again sometime, but…" He looked as if he could not find the right words to use, then blurted, "As friends?"

Exhaling in relief, I nodded. "Yes. Sorry."

"No, it's not your fault. I want someone who will—"

"Put up with your bullshit?" I inserted with a snicker.

Throwing back his head, he guffawed loudly before saying, "Something like that."

"Thanks for dinner, though. It felt good to be able to get out of the house."

"I can't even begin to imagine what you have to deal with, but any time you need a break, call me."

"I will." I smiled softly.

Chad gave me one last kiss on the cheek before I stumbled into my apartment, closing the door on a good night.

I briefly wondered if Bryan had responded to my message earlier, or if he might possibly be online; however, I discovered neither were true. In the pit of my stomach, a bad feeling formed. Had I lost a friend tonight? My heart cried 'no,' but my gut disagreed. If he disappeared out of my life, a small part of myself left with him.

CHAPTER THIRTY-TWO

BRYAN

I read and reread Emma's message, and had to tamp down the urge to throw both my phone and computer at the wall. They mocked me. Even though I warned her against it, she chose to go out with Chad? Why him? Sure he had a sister with MS, but that didn't make him a fucking expert on her situation. It didn't give him a Ph.D. or anything of that nature. Maybe it did give him a smidge more empathy. So? Who cared about that in the long run? A relationship depended on much more than that.

My eyes drifted to clock sitting on my nightstand. 7:59 P.M. That made it 11:59 P.M. in South Carolina. Were they still out on their date? Were they still together? Had he convinced her to go back to his place? Or maybe she invited him back to hers. I was driving myself crazy with all of these questions and speculations, which only hurt me.

But more than that, they plagued me. I trolled FaceSpace all night, waiting for an update, a sliver of news, however, neither had updated their statuses at all. Not about the date. Not even a check-in. Who didn't check-in nowadays? I felt desperate for information.

Was it unreasonable? Maybe a little, but the thought of her with him felt like a punch to the gut. I wanted to rip his head off. I didn't care if he and I had been friends for years. I didn't care that in comparison, I had only known Emma a fraction of the time. I wanted him away from her.

I...

I cared about her. That didn't sound sufficient enough.

I...

I liked her. I did, but my feelings for her surpassed that simple word.

Fuck me. No, it couldn't have happened. Not to me. I just...how the hell had this happened?

I loved her. I had fallen for Emma Taylor, and I didn't know how the fuck it happened to me. We talked online, not in person until recently. And when I'd pictured the person I might eventually settle down with, my mind conjured someone who looked more like J. Lo or Jennifer Aniston, maybe even Danica Patrick. Not that Emma wasn't pretty, she was, but I never imagined someone like her. Yet, now that I admitted my feelings, I saw no one except her in my future.

In the past, women who were more self-assured, lighter hair (Danica may not fit that part of the mold, but the woman could set fire to any man in a five-mile radius), and active. I knew Emma's activity level, or lack thereof, couldn't be blamed on her. If anything, I applauded her because she did what she could. During those few moments I thought about settling down, I never pictured myself falling for someone...well, someone sick. Again, not her fault. But who, even in their weirdest dreams, would imagine themselves falling for the girl that used a walker or cane, who had a disease that affected her life to the point she had to give up so many things she enjoyed? Who? Not a single fucking person in the whole damn world as far as I knew.

Why her?

One night out of the blue, she accidentally pinged me on FaceSpace messenger when she thought she pinged her best friend. On a whim, I talked to her, and because I found myself bored at the time, I decided to help her. Falling for her was never supposed to be in the cards. I honestly didn't want to fall for her. And yet, the mere thought of her with anyone else, tortured me, causing my soul to burn with jealousy

Now, since I was an asshole of the highest degree, and blind, she decided to go out on a date with a man who would probably hit on the Queen of England for the hell of it. Hell! He probably fucked his way around South Carolina and slipped his dick into at least half the female population in the state!

My hands slammed into my hair, pulling until the pain overshadowed my anger. Why the fuck didn't I just admit my feelings sooner? Then maybe she would... No, she wouldn't be out with me since we live on two different ends of the country...for now.

When I reported to the base today, my commanding officer gave me the good news. I would be transferred to the naval base in Charleston in three months. I knew my orders were coming up, and I had selected three different places to go, however, although I had picked Charleston, I did not think I would get it. My luck hardly ever worked that way. Was Fate trying to tell me something? Three months.

One of the excuses I kept using to convince myself it would never work out between Emma and me had disappeared, completely blown out of the water. Same side of the country. Same city. I had no reason to stay away from her any longer.

I didn't want to wait that long to talk to her. In three months, she and Chad could be engaged, but this discussion needed to happen in person. FaceSpace seemed wrong and inadequate for such a discussion. Mel's wedding was in a month. Was a month too long? Could it wait when Chad would wine and dine her, when he would have a month alone with her? Would I lose her if I waited?

Emma brought out something deep within me that I'd never felt before. Hell, she even had me doing things for her, things I would never have thought of doing before. Like skydiving. I took her the sole purpose of seeing her smile. Truth be told, I never did anything special for any girl I dated without ulterior motives. If I did something nice for a girl in the past, I expected sex. Maybe that made me as much of an asshole as Chad.

My life changed after Emma. I wanted to talk to her more than anyone else in my life. As soon as my shift finished, I turned on my phone and pulled up my messenger application. Whenever I saw a message waiting for me from her and only her, a smile instantly appeared on my face and I felt lighter. When nothing awaited me, irritation swept through me. No one has ever held that much power over me.

Maybe I should've recognized the signs earlier, but in my defense, I'd never been in love before. I had an overwhelming desire to protect her, make her smile, argue with her, and simply be there for her.

Even if I had not realized it before, I should've understood what was happening the day we went skydiving. She calmed me. With everything I had to deal with in regard to my family, I wanted to jump as much as her. As usual, the adrenaline rush consumed me, but underneath it all, the stress of my family, the worry, and anxiety melted away. With her body pressed against mine, she settled me and gave me peace. For the first time in a long time, I felt like I was home and I didn't want to let go of that feeling.

And then when we landed, my dick decided to take charge, and the more she wiggled, the worse it got. In my embarrassment and fear, I pushed her away. I'd been physical with women before, however, my reaction to her had my dick harder faster than any woman from my past. Hell, the first day I showed up unannounced, I had to adjust myself twice when she wasn't looking because my cock was hard and painful. I hadn't done anything that day, and neither had she. Her presence coaxed that kind of reaction from me.

But it wasn't only that. Emma made me laugh more than any other girl I'd ever met. She held the power to soothe me and make me feel comfortable; and before I realized what I was doing, I found myself confiding in her, telling her things I dared not spill to anyone else. Not even my family knew some of the things I shared with Emma. And up until recently, our whole relationship only existed on the computer. If she ever interrogated me in person, her brown eyes boring into me, I might confess top secret government secrets. Hell, I would probably admit to things I'd never even done. Captain America underwear and Mel came to mind. I shuddered thinking about it. Then again, with my luck, Mel had already shared that story with Emma.

I missed her. I missed Emma. The two days I spent with her, despite the argument, were the two best days of my trip, and it had everything to do with her. My chest ached and bled. If this was love, it both sucked and felt glorious.

My fingers wanted to message her, but I didn't think I could handle hearing about her budding love life with Chad. Chad and not me because I had been an ass and let her go. I kept telling her that she wasn't my type. I lied. She had burrowed her way inside me like an insect, changing my conception of the ideal woman. With a few messages, nothing more than a few typed words on the computer, I wanted to right the injustices of the world for her. I wanted to demand everyone give her a chance so they could see her the way I saw her. I wanted everyone to love her, as I loved her.

And Chad took her out. He had been brave enough to ask her for a date. Although he was my friend, I loathed him. Thinking about Emma and Chad together made me want to throw something, to punch someone. No, not someone. The only person I had the urge to punch was Chad. Growling deep in my chest with frustration, I paced my room. When that didn't work, I picked up the TV remote and threw it across the room with such force, it exploded into thousands of pieces. Okay, probably only hundreds…actually, less than twenty.

Evan burst into the room, throwing the door open hard enough that it banged against the wall and got stuck when the doorknob pushing through the plaster. I'd warned Evan that he needed those doorstop springs, or something like that might happen, but he'd ignored me.

He looked freaked out, his chest rising and falling quickly as he panted. Why was he panting if he had only been in the living room munching on a giant bowl of popcorn? His ranch styled house had a single floor layout, he shouldn't be out of breath running from the living room to my room.

"What?" I demanded.

"What the fuck is going on in here? Are you okay?" he bellowed, his voice a little higher pitched than normal from panicking. Hard to believe he was ex-Army and taught kids how to defend themselves for a living. His eyes darted around the room, and when he saw my remote, he asked, "What the fuck happened?"

"Awe, you care. That's so sweet." I blew him a kiss.

"You wish, asshole. Now, you want to tell me why there's plastic, batteries, and other shit all over the floor, or why the wall resembles a mortar hit?"

"You're one to talk. You made a hole in the wall with the door."

I guess he hadn't realized the consequences of his sudden entrance. He spun around and released a frustrated curse, "Damn it all to hell!" Glaring at me over his shoulder, he practically snarled when he said, "I don't know what the fuck your problem is, but if you won't tell me, why don't you get online with your girlfriend and message her. By the way, this is your fault too."

His comment hit too close to home.

He turned around slowly, a frown wrinkling his forehead as he studied me. "What is it? Why do you look like you want to rip my head off for kicking a puppy? Did you piss her off? Did you do something to her when you were on leave?" He crossed his arms over his chest, waiting for an answer. I knew he would not leave until I gave him some sort of explanation. His frown disappeared as his expression turned menacing. "What the fuck did you do to her?"

This would have been funny if I felt less anxious about the Chad/Emma situation. And considering Evan had never met Emma before, I wasn't sure if I should laugh or pat him on the back for defending her. Maybe if I punched him in the gut for mentioning Emma, I wouldn't feel so out of control.

"Seriously. WHAT. DID. YOU. DO?" Evan growled, his tone low and measured as he annunciated each word.

"Nothing!" I shouted, fighting the urge to wrap my hand around his neck and squeeze.

"Really? Because it doesn't look like nothing to me. You want to tell me what the fuck your problem is?"

I stood there blinking, breathing heavily. I sounded more like an animal than a man. Closing my eyes, I counted to ten...three times. When I believed I regained some semblance of control over my emotions I clenched my jaw tight, and spoke, "It's really none of your goddamn business."

"That's how you want to play this? If I need to, I'll find her on FaceSpace and message her myself. I'll tell her how much of a dick you're being."

"She's out with Chad!"

A knowing smirk appeared on his face, and once again the urge to punch him came to a boiling point, but it was his words that made me want to kill him more than I've ever wanted to before. "Jealous much? Weren't you the person who kept claiming she's not your type? You said you only wanted to help her find someone, and now that she has, you can't stand it. Hell, it's one of your friends, and you already wish they would break up. Maybe you should pull your head out of your ass and realize why."

"I know why," I yelled. Dropping to my bed, I buried my face in my hands and breathed deeply. "I know why. It's because I love her."

"It's about time you admitted it."

I snorted with disdain, lifting my head to gawk at him. "You act like you already knew."

"I kind of figured it out when you were so adamant about convincing me how great she is even if she has to use a walker and shit." His smirk grew.

"I'm only realizing this shit now, so how do you figure I've been in love with her since then?"

"Actually, I think you've been interested in her for a while. You came back from visiting your family last year and told me all about her. You kept saying that she's pretty, not gorgeous, but pretty. Then said she doesn't take shit from anyone. Your ass went on and on about how loyal she is to Mel because she was having a bad day and still came out for karaoke because it was Mel's engagement party."

"No, I didn't."

"Yes, you did. You talked about Mel, Luke, your family, and then the only other person you mentioned by name was Emma. When she sent you a friend request, you were so surprised that you mentioned it to me. It was just a friend request on FaceSpace. You have 500 friends on that thing. Why did this one matter to you? So yeah, I think you've had feelings for her longer than you realize."

Had I? It was certainly possible. I couldn't remember having feelings for her, or for that matter, when they developed, however, from the first moment I met her, she intrigued me. Had I really come home and talked about her? I honestly could not remember. Fuck me. Maybe I had. Maybe once she caught my attention, a seed had been planted which grew as I slowly got to know her.

But now, she was out with Chad on a date. I told her to stay away from him, and she hadn't listened to me. After everything she'd endured, after I promised to help her find love, did I have the right to take her from him? That was assuming she returned my feelings, but I had a feeling the odds were stacked against me.

Evan moved to stand in my doorway with a shit-eating grin plastered on his face. Silently, he challenged me, daring me to act. "What are you going to do?" he finally asked.

My own lips started to curl upward in a smile. "I'm going to get the girl."

Laughing, he slapped the doorframe. "It's about fucking time!"

CHAPTER THIRTY-THREE

BRYAN

The last month had been the hardest of my life. NROTC, training, flight school, and Top Gun combined were a cake walk compared to ignoring Emma for an entire month. Every time I saw a message from her, I thought about her with Chad and wanted to rip my computer apart. I only answered periodically with an "I'm busy" or "I'm fine, life's just crazy right now." I wanted to demand she break up with Chad, to save herself for me… I wanted to tell her that I loved her, but that shit needed to be said in person.

Luckily, I didn't have to wait until my transfer to see her again. Mel's wedding would conveniently transpire a couple of months before I moved, and Emma had been recruited to be one of the bridesmaids. The desire to see her, to talk to her again, grew with each passing day. I wanted to pull her into my arms, and punch Chad in the face, and not necessarily in that order. She had become my obsession.

Once I arrived, I had two days to convince her to drop him and choose me. I flew in a few hours before the wedding rehearsal, so somewhere between the rehearsal, rehearsal dinner, wedding, and reception, I needed to confess. The sooner the better. Would Chad be with her tonight? God, I hoped so. I wanted him to watch as I took her away from him. I wanted him to say something, and when he did, I was going to punch him in the jaw, knocking him out with one punch.

On the flight to Charleston, I had the pleasure of sitting next to an elderly woman, who did not know what to think of me at first. My eyes darted between the window and cabin, and my leg kept tapping out a quick cadence. I was nervous as hell, but only one thing filled my thoughts: I had to get to Emma.

If I had been in her shoes, I would've probably reported my suspicious behavior. I could've been a terrorist for all she knew, but she didn't report me to the flight crew. Instead, as she gently patted my arm like a grandmother would, she asked, "Scared of flying?"

I almost laughed in her face. Me? Scared of flying? I flew fighter jets for the U.S. Navy for God's sakes. Flying appeared at the bottom of the list of things I feared. "Uh, no. I'm not scared of flying, or of planes for that matter." I gave her a small smile, though I really wanted to tell her to leave me alone and to fuck off. However, the manners that had been ingrained in me as a child, would not allow me to be rude to anyone. I pictured my mother and grandmother preparing to slap me if they even thought I might be disrespectful to someone, especially a senior citizen.

"No? Are you sure? I won't think less of a big strapping boy like you if you were a little afraid. We all have something we fear in our lives." She looked to left and right, as if making sure no one was eavesdropping on our conversation. Then in a whispered voice, she told me, "I'm afraid of dying. So every month I do something on my bucket list."

This old lady...I laughed, my irritation with her melting away. "I promise, it's not the flying I'm worried about. I actually fly planes for a living."

"Which airline? Are you doing one of those where you catch a ride to go on vacation?"

Chuckling, I shook my head. "No, ma'am. I'm in the Navy. My name is Bryan."

She punched my shoulder, although, I barely felt it. "Good for you! I'm Grace. My husband, Harold, he was in the Navy too. God rest his soul. But he worked on the planes, he didn't fly them."

"I'm sorry for your loss." The response was one of those automatic things people said whenever they heard someone died.

"Why ever for?"

She had me there. I didn't know, but it felt like the proper thing to say.

Her giggle filled the awkward silence. "No need to be sorry, Bryan We were married for 61 years, and he was the love of my life. My parents weren't too sure of him, but I knew I was going to marry him the first time I saw him. I was 16 and he was 18. He had come to my church to give the sermon that day. I instantly knew. Sometimes you just know in a moment, and sometimes it takes a little longer. We got married when I turned 18. Last year, he went to sleep and never woke up. Since then, I've been doing everything on my bucket list. My Harry, he always loved trying new things. Not me. Too timid and all that. I'm a bit of a chicken. After he died, I wished I could join him, but I'm scared see, and I knew it wasn't my time. So I wrote out my bucket list and I'm doing everything on it. Last month, I took a trip to Siberia."

My eyes grew wide. "Siberia?"

"Why not? It's one of those places you always hear about it, but you never hear of anyone actually going there."

"I guess you have a point." I chuckled. When the laughter subsided, I said, "61 years is a long time."

"It is," she agreed, and rolled her eyes. "There were times when we argued, and I couldn't stand the man, but we always talked and worked it out. That's the key to everything. Good communication. If you can talk to the person you love and never get bored of it, that person is a keeper. We had our share of hard times, but the good outweighed it all."

"That's good to hear."

"Do you have someone special in your life?"

Unbidden, a smile pulled at my lips. "I do, but she doesn't realize it yet." I'm not sure why I did it, but I poured my heart out to Grace, telling her everything about Emma, about how we started talking by accident, about what happened last time I was in South Carolina, and about my own personal living hell during the past month.

"I bet she loves you too."

I wanted to believe her, but I knew better than to believe my next meeting with Emma would go smoothly. Winning her would be dangerous, difficult, and I could fail. "I hope so."

She smiled, once again patting my arm. "You really don't have a problem with her disability?"

"No. It's part of who she is. I never knew her before she got sick, so I don't really know what she was like back then."

"And now?"

"She's stronger than she probably realizes, she's beautiful, she gives me shit…uh, I mean, she doesn't take crap from me or anyone else,and gives as good as she gets."

"Good for her. She sounds lovely."

"She is. That said, she is also vulnerable and hides her pain behind a mask."

Her head nodded sharply as she proclaimed, "You better be good to her. She's been through a lot and I have a feeling her heart is fragile. In the end though, I'm sure you'll win her over."

She sounded so certain, so confident in the future. "Let's hope you're right."

"I am. No woman would share that much of herself with a man if she didn't feel something for him." Before I could argue, she held up her hand to stop me. "No woman. Trust me."

Once our plane descended, I helped Grace pull her luggage off of the carousel and we said our goodbyes, but before I could leave her, she slipped me her phone number. "When you set the date, let me know. I'm putting your wedding on my bucket list." The old woman made a lot of assumptions, and yet, I couldn't bring myself to deny her this small request. I only prayed I could fulfill it.

Exiting the airport, I found Luke waiting for me with the car running. I had two days, and I would not fail.

CHAPTER THIRTY-FOUR

EMMA

Tonight the butterflies in my belly danced the jive, making me want to throw up. Bryan would be at the rehearsal, which meant, I would have to see him. Over the past month, I'd received a total of four messages from him. They all said the same thing, he was too busy to talk.

I missed him.

Every night before I closed my eyes, I checked my phone for a message or something from him. It didn't have to be big, but I craved a smidgen of evidence that the past few months were not part of some elaborate make-believe world my imagination had concocted. I had our past conversations to prove everything actually happened as I remembered, but right now it all felt more like a dream. Even as I read through our previous discussions every night, it all seemed imaginary.

I received nothing. Zero encouragement. So why did I still want him so much? I needed to shut off my feelings and move on, but I found that to be easier said than done.

For the past month, at least once a week, Chad would pick me up, and we would go out as friends. It had become our hobby to seek out new restaurants neither one of us had been to, and try them together. I almost always thought about Bryan on those nights, wondering if he would like it or not. And maybe I posted everything on FaceSpace so Bryan would see it. I wasn't sure what I expected out of him. Maybe I hoped he had acted like an ass because of jealousy.

Chad never said anything to me, neither discouraging nor encouraging my feelings for his friend. However, he always tried to cheer me up or do things that he thought would make me happy. I had fun with him and he listened to me complain, but he could not fill that void Bryan had left.

My stomach flipped again. Maybe it'd be better if I went home and forgot about the wedding rehearsal…only, I couldn't abandon Mel. Our friendship superseded any issues I might have with one of her other friends. And at least I wasn't alone tonight. Chad volunteered to come as my friend/date. Since he had already been invited to the wedding, he decided to tag along for everything else.

No big deal.

Walking into the church, my eyes immediately found Bryan at the front of the sanctuary standing next to Luke. He threw his head back as they both laughed together, while I felt sick and heartbroken.

Chad stood next to me on my left, supporting me with his arm wrapped around my waist, as I gripped the handle of my cane tightly with my right hand. Bryan looked so handsome. His hunter green button down had been neatly tucked into a pair of black slacks. He was clean-shaven, putting his baby face on display for everyone to see. And his hazel eyes sparkled with merriment. And why shouldn't they? Two of his best friends were about to tie the knot.

My insides clenched with want, desire, and loss. I am not his type. A couple of weeks ago, I worked up the courage and asked Chad if he knew Bryan's type. My new friend had already accepted the fact my heart belonged to the Navy man, but his brow shot upward in shock and his forehead crinkled. He stared at me for a long time before he finally answered, "He mainly dates blondes who are thin and really athletic." Right then and there, I understood I truly could never be his type. First, I had never been thin. Second, while I still did as many things as my body would allow whenever possible, being athletic was not one of them. And finally, I looked god awful as a blonde. I had tried to bleach my hair in college one time–horrible mistake. Darker tones worked better with my tanned complexion and dark eyes. My pink undertones fought with the yellowy blonde, which resulted in a clash that no one would ever consider attractive.

And now Bryan and I were in the same building. I stood there gawking at him, silently begging him to turn around and notice me, but the only reason his head whipped up to look in my general direction, was due to the woman who barged into the church and screamed his name. Running around her obstacle—me—she accidentally pushed me. If Chad had not held me firmly, I would have fallen. Who was she? Who was this woman Bryan appeared so happy to see? Who was the woman who jumped into his arms and kissed each cheek before she kissed his luscious pink lips? Bryan's date? She had long silken black hair, which if Chad was right, didn't match his ideal type, but then again, she could be a fling or booty buddy.

"Rayne!" Chad snapped. Under his breath, he grumbled, "That girl has no sense about her sometimes. So fucking annoying. I swear one of these days, I will beat her ass."

Rayne? This was the infamous Rayne? Bryan's sister, Rayne? Now that I studied her a little more diligently, I could see the resemblance. Almost instantly, the rising panic began to disappear. I could breathe a little easier.

"What?" she yelled across the church, glaring directly at my own date.

"Don't give me that shit."

Narrowing her eyes, Mel growled a warning, "We're in a freaking church! Language!"

I didn't know if substituting words was considered acceptable, but given that she was the bride, I refused to point out that little tidbit to an already stressed out Mel.

My escort cursed low enough under his breath, Mel didn't hear him, and then assisted me down the aisle to the second from the front pew. After I sat down, he spun around to sneer at Rayne. "Maybe you should watch where you're going. I know you have some sort of brother complex, but the way you rushed in here without any regard for the location or people already here…Emma could've fallen!"

Rayne refused to back down to Chad, and it looked as if they hated each other. "Emma? Who the hell is Emma? Her? Oh please. I only brushed past her. Not my fault she's too drunk or whatever to stand on two feet properly."

I sucked in my breath. That hurt. More than I wanted it to. She wasn't the first person to say something like that, and I doubted she'd be the last. People who didn't understand were sometimes the most hurtful with their words and actions.

Tears burned my eyes. She didn't mean it. She didn't know me, and yet, my feelings didn't care about any of that. I wanted to tell Chad that everything was fine, but I couldn't get the words out. Hanging my head, I stared at my hands. My fingers were digging into my palms as I clenched them in tight fists, the knuckles white with the effort I exerted in trying to prevent a single tear from falling.

"Rayne!" That voice was different than the one that had only moments ago been attacking the other woman. This one sounded like Bryan's familiar and deep baritone. "Why are you acting like that?"

"What?" Her confusion was evident in that one word.

"Emma has myasthenia gravis and has to use a cane or walker to help her get around. Today it's a cane, but if Chad hadn't been there, she would have fallen," her brother tried to explain a little more calmly.

Chad jumped in, "She's definitely not drunk."

Bryan noticed me? When? I never saw his gaze shift in my direction.

Hope ignited deep within me, a small spark ready to flare into an inferno, but I couldn't lift my head. I felt their eyes on me…judging me, studying me.

"She doesn't look sick," Rayne commented.

Another stab, but unable to hold them back any longer, some of my tears escaped. So many people misunderstood my disease. An invisible illness in the eyes of many, and yet, felt acutely by the one suffering. The struggle to breathe, to walk, to move, to talk, to swallow, to see, were all invisible to the naked eye.

"Yeah, well, neither does my sister and she has MS," Chad chastised her. Out of the corner of my eye, I could see they were practically toe to toe.

"Are you all right?" A masculine voice asked, before prying the fingers of my left hand open and pressing a handkerchief into my palm. Bryan had gone the long way around in order to reach me. Going to the other end of the pew, he came around from the far end in order to avoid Chad and his sister.

I shrugged, unable to speak because I feared my tears would fall faster.

"She didn't mean it. She's not normally so insensitive."

I bobbed my head up and down a couple of times. His smell surrounded me, and I wanted to inhale as I leaned into him, but I remained on guard. I did not move a muscle, not even to wipe away the tears. One by one, they dropped down onto my forearms and hands. I wanted to reach out to him, to feel his warmth, however, if I did, I would be unable to let him go.

"Em? Em, please look at me." Did I imagine the pleading tone in his voice, or did I hear it only because that was what I wanted to hear?

Slowly, I shook my head. I couldn't look at him. If I did, my resolve would crumble. I was bound and determined to get over him.

He grabbed my chin gently and forced my face upward to face him. Shutting my eyes tightly, I still refused to meet his gaze. My heart needed to be protected, and my closed eyes provided me a small barrier.

But the slightest touch of his hand had awakened my soul. Hope and desire exploded within me.

"Em…" He whispered before his lips descended upon mine. When I felt our lips press together, I gasped in shock, my lips parting momentarily. It was enough. His tongue swept in to plunder my mouth, and I let him because this was exactly what I wanted from him. Only him. My heart would probably lie in tatters tomorrow, and yet, I couldn't stop myself. I would worry about tomorrow later.

A mewling sound came from someone, possibly me. Definitely me, and I mewled again. His tongue contained magic, forcing me to squeeze my thighs together in an effort to dampen the ache.

When he pulled back, I instinctively followed after him and heard him chuckle. The rich sound of his laugh forced my eyes open, where I found his face mere inches from mine.

I tried to escape and leaned back as if he'd burned me. Maybe he had. It certainly felt like my heart had been scorched when I saw his face so close to mine. His expression mocked me, or so I thought.

"Get away from her!" Chad bellowed, jerking me out of my seat away from Bryan.

Glaring at his friend, Bryan stood up to his full height, towering over Chad by a couple of inches, and crossed his arms over his chest. "You don't fucking own her."

"I never said I did, but she's here with me—"

"Something I intend to rectify," Bryan interrupted.

Chad pushed me behind him, however, I had left my cane in the pew and had nothing to support myself. This time, Luke caught me before I ended up on the floor. What the hell was going on here? Rectify? What did Bryan mean by that?

Holding onto Luke for dear life, I leaned over to ask Mel, "Shouldn't we do something about this?"

Instead of answering me immediately, the bride howled with laughter. "Not at all. It's about time someone decided to man up." Sighing, she grumbled, "Damn it. I wish I had some popcorn and a beer. This is going to be entertaining."

My jaw dropped open, and I was fairly certain the crash I heard came from it hitting the floor. "What the fuck?"

"Language! We're in a church!" she griped.

Normally, I would have shut up and gone along with any harebrained scheme she came up with, but not this time. "You cussed too when you said damn."

"So?"

"S-S-So?"

"Shh. I want to watch this."

"Will someone explain what's going on?" Rayne demanded.

"Your brother finally grew a pair of balls. I'm proud to say, he's no longer a pussy," Mel chirped.

I felt Rayne's gaze shift to me in order to size me up and pass judgment. I was fairly certain I came up short of the mark with her. I was sick, even if I didn't appear sick as I clung to my friend for stability. I did not fit the mold Bryan had cast.

Already on edge, my eyes met hers, and fed up with everything, I snapped. "Take a picture, it lasts longer!" This made Mel double over as she laughed hysterically. If I didn't know better, I would have thought a howler monkey had been set free in the church.

Another bang.

Craning my head around, I noticed the pews on either side of Chad and Bryan were askew. Had the whole world gone mad? They were grown men, and yet, they were physically pushing each other around in a church.

My heart skipped a beat. Was it wrong to hope Bryan fought for me? If only my brain would shut up. It wanted to argue that he kissed me because he felt sorry for me. I hated the logical side of my brain that reminded me not to get my hopes up.

As I opened my mouth to order them to stop fighting, his sister sneered, "You are so not worth it. I bet you're faking."

That sent me over the edge. I'd had enough. My feelings laid in tatters from everyone pushing me. I could take a lot, but my limit had been reached.

Spinning around too quickly, Luke grabbed me, holding me tight around the waist to prevent my fall. "You can think whatever the hell you want to. I don't give a flying fuck. I've been subjected to your kind enough to say that I don't want to have anything to do with you. I don't care if you believe me or not. I don't care what the fuck you think of me. You aren't the one using a cane. You aren't the one using a walker. You aren't the one who had to leave all her friends in Texas and move out here. You aren't the one whose life was stolen from her because one day you felt normal and the next you were in the ER and no one could figure out what was wrong with you. You aren't the one who lost friends after she got sick because you could no longer do everything you were able to before. And you aren't the one who guys look at like you're the dirt beneath their feet just because you're sick. And you know what? I hope you never have to experience any of this for yourself because it sucks! I hate being sick! I hate having to depend on others! I hate knowing that I'm going to be sick for the rest of my life because there is no fucking cure! So, say whatever you damn well want about me, but before you do, you better have your fucking facts straight!"

Tears gushed down my face as I sniffled and hiccuped. It was only then that I realized the fighting had stopped and no one was saying anything. Utter silence engulfed the church. All eyes were on me. Turning my head, I took in the scene next to me. Chad had a bloody nose and the makings of a black eye. Bryan, on the other hand, had a little blood on the side of his lip, but seemed to be none the worse for wear. Cussing in a church. Fighting in a church. Yelling in a church. My granny was probably rolling around in her grave.

"Why? Why did you kiss me?" I demanded, my eyes boring into Bryan's.

"Because I can't stand the thought of you going out with Chad." His words came out tense and rushed.

"So, you thought you'd kiss me? Bravo. That's exactly how to get me past my issues," I bit out sarcastically.

"Em…"

He took a step toward me, and I held up my hand. "Don't you dare come near me. I don't want to hear it. I thought you understood better? I thought we were friends, but I guess I should have known that isn't the case since you've hardly talked to me this past month. I'm not even dating Chad. We're only friends, which you would've known if you'd bothered to talk to me He's been trying to get me out of the house more often because…because…"

My crying overwhelmed me, making it harder to talk.

"Wait, Emma! I think you're misunderstanding something."

Shaking my head, I whimpered, "I don't think so."

"I do think so. Emma, I love you."

Had I heard him correctly? I stood there gaping at him as if he had lost his damn mind while my tears continued to fall. "I'm…I'm sorry?" My voice was nothing but a soft squeak.

BRYAN

Crap! I had everything planned. I knew exactly how I wanted to declare my feelings. But with one fell swoop, everything had been blown out of the water as I unceremoniously blurted my entire confession. In my head, everything would be said at the perfect moment in time, with her in my arms. It wasn't supposed to happen while she ranted. It was supposed to be a sweet, romantic confession. But what she got was a desperate man grasping at straws.

The moment she walked in the door, I felt her. Her very essence called out to me, pulling me toward her as if my soul recognized its other half. The only thing that marred the image of her standing at the back of the church was that Chad stood next to her with his arm dangling around her waist. Reason told me she only did that because she needed someone to steady her while she used her cane, which she probably used because it seemed less noticeable than her walker. It didn't take much to see that her stance wavered, leaving her looking a little unsteady. What killed me the most, was that I was not the person helping her Fucking Chad got the honor. Asshole.

I forced myself to keep my head straight, or else I would gape at her, but periodically I allowed myself the liberty to watch her out of the corner of my eyes. She looked breathtaking. Her black strapless sheath dress fit her figure perfectly, accentuating her body's curves. Both flawlessly done, her hair held a hint of curl, and her makeup—though not needed in my eyes— made her lips seem fuller and her brown eyes stand out a little more. The picture perfect angel...except for Chad. I wanted her, and so did my dick. Sheer willpower kept it from becoming too noticeable. Thankfully, my black slacks had some give and they helped mask my hard-on. People have said the color black made the person wearing it slimmer, and in this case, it hid my very physical reaction to her.

And then my sister had to storm in like a bat out of hell, ignoring everything around her. Before I could say anything to her, Chad tore into her, and when they went toe to toe, the distraction became my opportunity to confess my feelings to Emma. I had it all planned out right down to her ecstatic reaction in which she would confess her own feelings for me.

Unfortunately, reality and imagination very rarely coincided. Her tears pained me, twisting my gut.

She refused to look at me, thus I did what any red-blooded man in love would do: I kissed her in order to get her attention. I expected Chad to back off at that point, or at the very least to remain oblivious as he continued to argue with my sister. However, once again my expectations fell short. Upset that I dared kiss her, he yanked Emma away and threw her behind his back. Did he not realize that Emma was mine? His actions pissed me off for two reasons. First, he stood between Emma and me. Second, when he grabbed her, he had been too rough with her. She was a treasure and should be treated as such.

Unable to hold back after Luke pulled Emma to safety, I proudly threw the first punch, hitting him in his nose. Hopefully, I broke it. It didn't take him but a moment to retaliate, and he punched me in the mouth. If he thought I was done with him, he thought wrong. Throwing my fist, I caught him in the eye.

Our fight stopped there. Emma's voice carried throughout the small church, her words loud and echoing. She was crying again. All of her rage was directed at my sister, and I wouldn't stop her. Rayne had done this to herself. For Emma, though, I wanted to wrap her in my arms and shut out the world. I wanted to end her pain, her disappointment. I wanted to protect her from anything that would rob the world of her smile.

I never expected her to turn her anger on me, or to challenge my kiss. I said the first thing that popped into my head. HUGE MISTAKE! As true as it was, that wasn't the real reason I kissed her. My jealousy had spoken for me, and instead of confessing, I misspoke.

After I finally declared my love for her, she stood there with her mouth agape, stunned into silence. Everyone in the church watched us closely, waiting to see what would happen next, as if our love lives were involved in an intricate soap opera plot line. Chad's expression of disbelief was mirrored on almost everyone's face, except Mel. On her face, I saw a knowing smirk. I didn't question it, because she knew me better than I knew myself sometimes. The fact I had asked about Emma before I got into town a month ago, had probably clued her into the fact I felt something for Emma. But I ignored them all, focusing all my attention on the only girl I loved.

Her small voice questioning me felt like a slap in the face, but I understood her confusion. I had told her countless time that she was not my type. Enough that I had started to sound like a broken record, and here I stood before her contradicting myself. I had been a fool.

This time when I stepped toward her she didn't stop me. I only had one chance to convince her. "I love you more than you'll probably ever know. When you decided to go out with Chad, I got jealous. Every time I saw a status update saying you were out with him, I wanted to punch something, him mainly. He's my friend, and I hated him because he got to spend time with you. Emma, when I took you skydiving, it turned into the best day of my life—and I've had some pretty good ones. Honestly, I have more fun talking to you on FaceSpace than I have ever had with any other girl. Chad turned into my enemy because he was trying to take all of that away from me." My gaze shifted to Mel. Sending her a small wink, I shrugged. "Sorry. Em's—"

"I get it." Mel grinned. Yep, she had me completely figured out.

Focusing on Emma again, I told her, "I just want to make you happy. I want to be the one to support you when you have to lean on someone either physically or mentally. I want to protect you from anyone and everyone that would harm you or hurt your feelings. I want to love you, and I know you want the same thing."

Her brow scrunched as she regarded me before she shook her head in denial. "No, I don't."

"You do."

"No."

Sometimes her pigheadedness made me want to wring her neck...or kiss her senseless. "You do. Trust me on this."

"Oh, and how do you figure?"

Her nose resembled Rudolph's, her eyes were red and swollen, but even when she probably thought she looked her worst, she still looked beautiful to me. "You kissed me back and were ready to continue when I ended it."

Her blush intensified and moved down her neck and chest. Had her breasts also turned red? "I'll admit you're a good kisser, but it's been a while since I've been kissed, and I like kissing. That's all there is to it. I don't want you or need you."

"But you love me."

"No."

"Why don't you try looking me in the eye when you say that?" Her eyes focused on anything that wasn't my face.

She locked her gaze with mine. "I…I…I…" Huffing with annoyance, she snapped, "It doesn't matter if I do or not. I refuse to be with anyone who pities me. I want more."

"It's not pity, and I intend on giving you the world."

"I'm not your type, remember?"

Why was it when I had something important to say, people chose those moments to interrupt me? The pastor, who had been running late, ran into the church with the door slamming shut with a loud bang. Out of breath, he asked loudly, "Is everyone here for the rehearsal?"

"We're not done, Emma," I warned her.

Wiping her tears away with my handkerchief, she held it out to me. "Yes, we are."

"Bryan, take a hint. She doesn't want you. Besides, you can do better than someone who's broken." Rayne's snide remarks made me want to slap her. My sister should be supporting me, not trying to rip Emma apart again.

"Emma isn't broken! And if you can't accept her, then you can't accept me either."

"Bryan!"

Emma, the peacekeeper, said, "He doesn't mean it, Rayne. You're the little sister he adores more than anything." Her words held a note of finality to them which terrified me. And my fears were confirmed when she asked Chad, "Can you take me home? I don't feel so well."

"I'll take you home," I insisted.

Luke grabbed my arm, holding me in place, as Chad helped her toward the exit. I tried to break free, but could not. "Give her some space. After what Rayne said, and on top of everything else, she's hurt and confused. You've barely talked to her this past month, then you show up with this monumental declaration…You know, anytime we saw her this past month, she always asked about you. We knew she was pining for you. She only needs some time," he instructed me.

"He's right. Listen, I'm pretty sure she's in love with you, even though she hasn't admitted it to me. Give her some space and try again tomorrow. They say weddings can help bring people together. Maybe it'll work in your favor. If not, I fully intend to have her catch my bouquet. We'll just make sure you catch the garter." Mel snickered, getting entirely too much pleasure out of my suffering. I almost shrunk away from her in fear due to the devious expression on her face. She was plotting, which never turned out well for her victims…I meant friends.

Reluctantly, I agreed. However, when I whirled to confront my sister, my demeanor changed. I seethed with anger, and I clenched my jaw as tightly as my fists hanging at my sides. "If you ever treat her or someone else so disrespectfully again, I don't care who you are, you will regret it. Not all diseases can be seen. Mom has diabetes. You can't see that, can you?" When she didn't answer, I yelled, "Can you?"

Rayne flinched. "No."

"Then I suggest the next time you see Emma, you apologize."

The pastor appeared lost, confused, and a little scared, as if he had entered the middle of a war zone, and was trying to figure out if he should run for cover. His pews were askew, one of the members of the wedding party left in tears, and another raised his voice to a woman. This would be a wedding he never forgot.

It took Mel asking, "Are we ready to get started? I'll give Emma the rundown tomorrow," to get everyone focused on the wedding again.

Nodding quickly, the pastor agreed. "Yes, shall we?"

I honestly couldn't recall anything that happened during the wedding rehearsal or what I ate for dinner afterward, but none of that mattered as I stood on Emma's porch banging on her door at almost eleven that night. After I ditched Luke and the other guys, I drove here. She was more important than any mischief they wanted to stir up the night before the wedding. I'd given her a few hours, but now we needed to talk. I wanted to explain myself, and then I would beg her to give me a chance.

CHAPTER THIRTY-FIVE

EMMA

When he dropped me off, Chad offered to stay with me, but I wanted to be alone. My emotions were all over the place. Not necessarily in turmoil, but not jumping for joy either. I mean I felt both of those and so much more. Anger, confusion, happiness, nervousness, anxiousness, hopeful...I doubted there were enough words in the dictionary to describe how I felt the moment Bryan declared his love for me.

I wished I could believe him. I did, but, I couldn't. Why now? Why after a month of radio silence, did he confess now? Because he thought I was dating Chad? If that's all it was, he could keep his confession, his supposed love, and shove it up his ass.

Seeing him again after longing for him had been harder than I originally thought it would be. I certainly never expected to hear any sort of declaration from him tonight...his fake confession shattered my already broken heart. He didn't really want me. It was more like he didn't want anyone else to have me. To Bryan, I was the shiny new toy. He reminded me of a child that wanted not only their toy, but everyone else's as well. Eventually, my shine would fade, and he would move on to something else. The mere thought of that crushed me.

I had to clear my head of Bryan, I had to find some semblance of peace so that I could get through this weekend without breaking down. I failed. Bryan consumed my thoughts and my heart. Soaking in a bath had always been relaxing to me, even before myasthenia gravis entered my life, however, I gave up soaking after only five minutes because the longer I sat in the water, the more time I had to think. The more I allowed myself to think, the more my thoughts centered on Bryan and his confession. And the more I thought about that, the more I ached. It felt like a self-imposed torture.

Getting out of the bath had been a small struggle, but I managed it with the help of medical bars that had been installed all around the bathtub. They helped me to shower, to bathe, to soak without assistance, and gave me a lot of independence. Without them, getting in and out of the shower bath would be more difficult. On bad days though, I didn't try to bathe myself. It was too dangerous, and I never knew if I would be able to get out of the bathtub by myself, even though I used a shower chair. Tonight, my legs were a little weaker than usual, and lifting myself from a seated position on the ground was not the most graceful feat, and that was all right because I still managed it on my own.

It wasn't until I slipped on my nightshirt and shorts that I heard the first sounds of tapping. The small tapping turned into a knock, which kept getting louder and harder until the other person was essentially pounding on my door. The walls rattled. The door shook with the power. I could've pretended I didn't hear, or I didn't know who was attempting to break down my door, but I somehow knew Bryan stood just outside of my apartment. Why was he here?

"Emma, I know you're in there. Open up! We need to talk!" Bryan yelled through the door.

Talk? If he wanted to talk, he should have talked to me after he left Charleston a month ago instead of waiting until now. What was I expecting though? Bryan apparently thought everything should happen on his schedule. He tried to punish me for doing what he encouraged me to do from day one. But now I was supposed to listen to him and believe him after he ignored me? No. He always said I deserved better, he was right. I did deserve better from him.

My heart did not agree. It screamed at me to open the door and let him in because it believed in him.

On the other side of the coin sat my logic, who wholeheartedly disagreed. She reminded me that if he truly loved me, if his feelings were real, he wouldn't have shut me out for a month. To which, my heart countered that his jealousy prevented him from reacting properly. The war being waged within me exhausted me.

Pushing my walker down the hall, I shuffled to the front of my apartment and quietly placed one of my hands on the door, trying to feel him through the cool metal. He was still pounding on it, and I could feel the vibrations travel up my arm. But I refused to answer it. I couldn't. I'd left the rehearsal in order to get my head-on straight, and I still hadn't succeeded.

I loved him. I couldn't deny it, and if he actually loved me, it would make me over the moon ecstatic. But, how could it be true? For months, I continually heard him say that I wasn't his type. He told me he would help me find love, but he could never be my Prince Charming. Chad even confided in me that I was the exact opposite of Bryan's type. So how could I believe him? Why now? How was I supposed to forget everything he'd ever said, and accept his sudden confession? Did he have some sort of epiphany, because he assumed I started dating Chad? This was real life and not some dime store romance novel. I couldn't do it. If I let him through that door, my heart wouldn't survive.

My hand fell back onto my walker handle, numb and practically limp. I messed up because I fell in love with the one man I wasn't supposed to, the one man who probably knew me better than anyone. He got me to open up and exposed most of my secrets and insecurities. I didn't hate him for it. If anything, I was grateful to him. Due to his perseverance and doggedness, I'd faced a lot of my old ghosts. Bryan had done that for me.

Maybe it was a hero complex or something. Maybe I didn't really love him. Maybe it was like that Stockholm syndrome, or whatever they called it whenever the victim fell in love with their captor.

But I knew better. It wasn't. While I did feel grateful to him for what he had done for me, my feelings for him went beyond anything I'd ever experienced. Saying otherwise, was a lie. The day he took me skydiving, he handed me the world by giving me something I believed was lost forever. His body pressed into mine as we jumped out of the plane and flew through the air, the feel of his arms around me as he tried to protect me on our landing, it felt like home. Everything about him and that day felt right...utterly perfect.

The longer I stood next to the door, the more I wanted to throw caution to the wind and open it. I needed to walk away. I should walk away.

Then again, maybe it was time to stop living my life so cautiously. Maybe, it was time to start living again...

Not yet.

I walked to my couch and fell onto it, grabbed a throw pillow, and pressed it over my head to mute the sounds of Bryan's constant pounding. I wasn't sure how much time had passed, but suddenly, nothing except silence could be heard from the front door. Had he finally given up? Or was that shuffling I heard outside? Unsure, I got up, and carefully peered out of the small window next to the door. He sat on the ground, propped against the hunk of metal he'd been banging on. It almost appeared as if he was settling in for...the night? An hour? What and why? Why would he do this? Just leave! With his eyes staring out into the darkness in front of him, he sat waiting, and I sat watching him until I couldn't watch any longer.

Lightning flashed, lighting up the blackened night sky. The rumbles of thunder cracked, breaking the stillness of the night. Then the rain began. Not a mere gentle drizzle, this was a torrential downpour. Yet, Bryan remained unmoving. The rain hit him, spitting on him, but he ignored it.

I couldn't let him suffer.

Against my better judgment, already believing I would regret it in the morning, I unlocked the door. He must've heard me above the angry sounds of nature, because by the time I pulled it open, he stood there with a hopeful expression on his face, looking like a drowned rat. "Emma—"

"Come on in. I'll get you a towel. Mel will kill me if you got sick and didn't show up to her wedding," I interjected. Turning around slowly, I walked toward my bathroom where I kept the dry towels. On the short trip, I begged my heart to stop pounding, to quiet down, but it completely ignored me. Traitor.

"Here." I shove the towel in his face and told him, "I think I have a pair of basketball shorts and a T-shirt that'll fit you. We can throw your clothes in the dryer if you want." I avoided making eye contact.

"Em, I need—"

"Hurry up and dry off. You're getting my floor wet, which makes it dangerous for me. I'm a bit of a klutz sometimes. I'll go and see if I can find the clothes." When he didn't follow, both relief and disappointment duked it out within me. Logic versus heart again. This man was going to be my undoing.

It didn't take me long to find the clothes I'd offered him, but a small part of me wished it had taken longer, especially when I returned to find his shirt clinging to his chest and arms like a second skin.

I gulped. The material defined his muscles, making it look more like someone had taken a paintbrush and painted the color onto him. The visual made my mouth water. Unable to meet his gaze, I focused on his chest, fighting the small party of me that wanted to rake him from head to toe. "Here. They should fit. And before you complain about wearing women's clothes, they're men's shorts. I got them from the sports store online."

"LA Surf?"

"If you don't like my team or if you choose to complain, you can stay in wet clothes and get the fuck out for all I care."

"No, I'll change. Thanks. Where's Curley?"

"My sister's. She's watching him while I deal with wedding stuff this weekend. I was supposed to be staying with Mel tonight, but plans changed. Ellie is going to the wedding, but since she's not in the wedding, she volunteered to keep him for me since I had planned…" I cleared my throat, stopping myself before I repeated myself. My nervous energy increased around him, and I couldn't calm down. I was on edge. "There are extra towels in the bathroom if you need them." As he brushed past me, I instinctively inhaled. His scent was like an aphrodisiac. I desired him. I wanted to grab him, throw myself into his arms, and never let go until we were both tired and sated. Although, I firmly believed that I would never have enough.

I behaved. My feet remained firmly planted until I heard the bathroom door close. Then and only then, did I release my pent up breath, exhaling loudly and slowly. Stop it.

If I had to deal with him, I had to be comfortable, or at least sitting. I moved to the couch and sat down, listening carefully for him to come back into the living room. It wasn't until I heard him moving toward me that I realized my mistake. I should have sat on my oversized chair instead of the couch. The couch had too much space, gave him too many options which allowed him to sit with me. Big mistake. Monumental. 'Keep calm, Emma,' I kept telling myself.

"Where's your dryer?"

"I'll—"

"Just tell me where it is, Em. I'm a grown man. I know how to use a dryer."

Damn! There went my excuse to get up and move to a new location. "In the kitchen, behind the door on your right. The other one is the pantry."

"Thanks."

I heard him moving around before I heard the dryer come alive. Now that the dryer had been turned on, my nerves and anxiety kicked it up another notch. I should have moved anyway while he was in the kitchen.

"Thanks for letting me come in out of the rain," Bryan spoke softly as he settled on the opposite side of the couch.

See, I knew I should have moved, but even the oversized chair would not have been far enough away. "No problem. Mel would kill me if she knew you were here and I left you out in the storm. I don't want to ruin her wedding."

"I wouldn't have gotten sick from a little rain."

"What? You think you're Superman or something? People get colds all the time from getting caught in the rain. Unless you were on your way to Luke's, then you can TYA."

"TYA?"

"Take your ass."

Chuckling, he said, "No, I actually planned to stay out there all night if I had to."

"Why?" Defensively, I demanded he answer me. I was on high alert. DEFCON 1.

His body shifted until he sat on the middle cushion, a little closer to me.

I couldn't escape him. "Because we need to talk about what happened at the church."

My head shook vigorously from side to side. "Nope. Let's forget it and move on with our lives."

"I don't want to forget!" he snapped. His fingers on both hands combed through his hair in agitation, and he pulled it. I wasn't sure if he groaned from pain—I didn't realize he was a masochist—or frustration. I saw his lips moving, counting down from ten, and when he addressed me again, his tone sounded quieter and more civil. "I don't want to forget anything about you, Emma. I don't want to forget our conversations or skydiving or dinner. Until you, everything bored me except my job. Girls were fucking annoying, and anytime I had to talk to them, I wanted to rip my ears off after five minutes. You were always different."

"You're a good friend too."

"No! I mean yes, you are, but that's not what I'm talking about right now. The day you messaged about going out with Chad, I sat in my room stewing about it all day. The longer I sat there, the more pissed off I got."

"Bryan, I get it. I'm just the shiny new toy. You'll get over it." I tried brushing his confession again in order to protect my traitorous heart that wanted to shout for joy from the mountaintops. My hands ached to reach for him, my lips wanted to feel his pressed against them again, and even my logic had started to climb over the wall in order to join my heart. But I still fought. I still rejected his confession.

"I WON'T! I don't want to get over this or you." Grabbing my face in his hands, he forced it upward, and I closed my eyes so I wouldn't have to meet his stare. His thumbs brushed my cheeks softly. In a weird way, his actions soothed me, calming my racing heart. "I don't want to get over you, Em. I know you don't believe me, but I love you with all that I am."

I squeezed my eyes tighter. My body should have expelled all of the tears I'd stored, but fresh tears burned my eyes. He was too cruel.

"Em, look at me." I did not open my eyes. "Fine then. If you won't look at me, I'll just keep talking. I know I should've talked to you more after I left. I messed up. I thought you were with Chad, and I let my jealousy get the best of me."

When I still didn't do what he requested, he continued with a sigh. "Contrary to your muddled way of thinking, you're not some shiny new toy, and I didn't concoct my feelings out of thin air because of Chad. Fuck him. Take him out of the equation and I still love you. Evan believes I started falling for you the night I met you at karaoke."

That stunned me, and in my shock, my eyes popped open.

His smile took my breath away. His face was so close to mine, and once our gazes locked, his eyes held me prisoner and I couldn't escape.

"There they are. Chocolate brown eyes with flecks of gold. They're darker on the outside than they are on the inside. Full of life. I realized when I was here a month ago how expressive they are. All three times we were together, I could usually tell what you were thinking and feeling by looking into your eyes. The day we went skydiving, you were nervous, but excited at the same time. When we went to dinner after going to the gym, you were confused when I asked you about Mr. Smooth. An irritated fire bloomed in them when I told you to stay away from Chad. I knew then that you'd go out with him. I hated it. I hated picturing you and him together."

"So why didn't you stop me?" I whispered. My logic, which had climbed to the top of the wall, was on the verge of jumping to the other side to join my heart.

"I didn't realize how much I loved you until I read your message. By then, I had already gone home. I should've stopped you, though. I should've called and begged you not to go."

I tried to shake my head, but his hands held me tight. "No, you can't. I mean, I'm not your type."

"You're exactly my type. You are everything I've been looking for."

"I can't be athletic."

"I'm not asking you to be."

"I can't be blonde. I look horrible with blonde hair."

"I like you as a brunette. I can't see you as a blonde."

"What if I change to blue?"

"I would still be ok with blue hair," Bryan replied quickly, a humorous glint in his eye. He probably thought I was a little crazy.

Okay, it even sounded a little crazy to me. Suddenly, everything seemed funny causing me to snicker. We both laughed for a couple of minutes, but he never released me.

When I finished laughing, I asked, "What about all the other girls you've dated in the past. Even Chad—"

"Fuck Chad!" Bryan let me go and stood up. His hands pumped opened and closed as he paced back and forth. "I won't deny that I've leaned toward blondes in the past, but that doesn't mean I don't want you!"

"A tiger can't change its stripes."

"Really? You want to use that one on me? Then you can't change either. Are you telling me you're the same person you were before you got sick? The same person you were when we started talking?" I opened my mouth to speak, but he wouldn't let me say anything. "I know you're not. You're more open, and you've started to put yourself out there more than you did before our agreement. And if you try to say you haven't changed, then you're a damn liar."

At this point, I didn't know if he had purposely pushed my buttons or tried to make a point, but if attacking me had been his plan to win me over, he desperately needed a new one. "Excuse me?"

"You heard me. I love you, Emma, and I couldn't care less about your disease or the fact you have to use a walker or a cane. I don't care if you aren't active, or that there are days you have to stay in bed. I want to take care of you, I want to discover new things with you, and I want to love you. Yet you have the audacity to sit there and say that a tiger can't change his stripes. I guess you're in the same boat as me. If that's true, you can't change either."

Him and his fucking logic. I didn't want logic. I wanted to dig a hole to hide in and protect myself. In my hole, I would never again have to question someone's motives or words. In the past, I believed men cared about me, Allen being one of them, but all of them left me with nothing except scars and disappointment—especially after my illness. Could I give him the chance he sought?

Deep inside me, I knew Bryan was different from any other guy I'd ever been with before, but different didn't always equal better. He listened to me, made me laugh, and unknowingly lit up my world, driving away some of the darkness that consumed me. Was it possible that he really love me?

Lifting my head, I gave him a hard stare. "Why?"

I saw a split second of confusion before his eyes cleared. I wasn't sure if his knees buckled, which seemed unlikely for a man like him, or if he'd dropped to his knees in front of me on purpose, but once on the ground, he grabbed my hands, squeezing them.

"You'll get dog hair all over you if you stay down there," I warned him before he said anything.

"Then I get dog hair on me. It won't kill me." He took a steadying breath. "I love you because you are you. You're a strong woman who's had to deal with shitty things in her life, and instead of giving up, you fought and persevered. You have a strength within you born from adversity. You're beautiful, even with your brown hair and brown eyes. I don't care if you're not athletic. I think I've proven that I don't mind carrying you when you can't walk or when you need my support. Besides, you don't just lie in bed all day. You're loyal, trustworthy, beautiful, curvy—I love your curves—funny, and I love talking to you more than I love flying. I never thought I'd say that to anyone in my lifetime. You've also opened my eyes to a new world. Since we started talking, the first thing I do when I'm done with work is check for messages from you. It's also the first thing I do when I wake up, and when I go to lunch. The days I don't talk to you before going to bed, I feel like something's missing from my day. You're it. I don't care what everyone thinks my type was before you, what matters is the future. I love you."

I hadn't realized I was crying until he reached up and wiped away my tears. I found myself daring to believe in him.

The hand he used to brush away my tears, brushed my hair behind my ear before it gripped my hand once again. "You know. When we were at the gym, I wanted to punch Mr. Smooth for flirting with you, and then I wanted to wring my friend's neck for saying you weren't his type all because you had a walker. I wanted to kill Chad because I knew he would be good for you, and he could be everything you needed. I hated him for it because I wanted to be that man. I didn't talk to you because I was jealous, and because I was terrified my fingers couldn't lie to you. They would've told you what I felt, and I felt like I should save those words for when I could tell you in person. I didn't call for the same reason. I needed to be here in front of you, touching you, when I told you that I loved you. I was an ass for ever saying you weren't my type. You are exactly my type."

Crying and sniffling, I tried to wipe my face on my sleeve without releasing his hands. I hated letting him go even for a moment.

"Em?" His Adam's apple bobbed when he swallowed hard, waiting for my answer. He wanted to know his confession had not been made in vain.

"Do you want to go with me to the wedding? I need a date." My voice sounded more like a whine than a question due to my crying.

"I thought Chad..." His voice tapered off, and his bewildered expression marred his handsome face. In his eyes, I saw his hope and fear. Those were the same feelings I dealt with after he confessed.

Shaking my head, I chose my words carefully, however, I didn't offer him my full confession...yet. "No, I told you we aren't dating. Only friends. In fact, when he dropped me off tonight, he somehow knew you'd be by tonight. I'm not sure how, but he knew. He also told me that it would probably be best if I either went to the wedding alone or had you escort me."

"So, you two really aren't dating?"

I shook my head again. "No."

He exhaled in relief. "Thank God, but hell, even if you told me you were dating him, I would have found a way to take you away from him." Leaning forward, Bryan pressed his lips to mine, fulfilling one of my heart's desires. I floated to heaven. Was I dreaming? God, if I was, I never wanted to wake up.

His mouth, hot and insistent, pressed harder against mine. I wanted him to press even harder, to melt into me. I'd been waiting for this since meeting him. The night Mel forced me to attend karaoke to celebrate her engagement.

Unlike others I'd met, Bryan never gave me a funny look or treated me any differently. Granted, he hardly said much to me that night, but when he did, he never made me feel like an invalid or like I was different. To him, I was one of Mel's friends, and therefore, just another face in the crowd. God! I didn't want to think about Mel…or anyone else. Right now, at this moment, I only wanted to think about Bryan. No one else existed.

Pulling back, he growled and pressed his forehead against mine. His chest heaved as his breathing came out hard and fast, but he wasn't alone. Mine matched his. "Fuck! I planned on taking this slow and wooing you or some shit."

Snickering, I asked, "Wooing?"

"Mel said I should woo you."

Mel. I loved her more than ever before. In the past, there had been a couple of times when I mentioned I wanted someone to woo me. She remembered and had passed that information on to Bryan. However, wooing could wait. I wanted to be thrown on my bed, stripped quickly—or slowly—and for the fire that had been ignited months ago to be quenched. Not extinguished, merely sated. "But now?" I probed.

His grin…damn, it could light up the world if the sun ever went out. Standing up, he bent down, slid one arm under my legs and balanced the other on my back before scooping me up with a small grunt. "I'll woo you tomorrow."

Wrapping my arms around his neck, I told him, "I'm going to need my walker in the morning."

"You really want to worry about that right now?"

"Nope. Down the hall, the door on the left."

"That's more like it."

In the books, when the guy carried his girl to the bedroom or wherever they decided to have sex, it was a sweet romantic gesture, and nothing untoward ever happened to the heroine. In real life, I banged my feet into the doorway as he entered the hallway, which threw off his balance. He threw himself against the wall with a grunt, but he didn't drop me. My heart was racing, and I was a little scared I would fall, making me cling to him a little tighter.

"You can put me down," I suggested with a slight tremor in my voice.

"Not at chance." He grinned and kissed me quickly before shifting me, hoisting me up a little higher. With that, we continued down the hall sideways so that neither one of us would be injured before we got into bed. Afterward, all bets were off.

We were both laughing about it, but the laughter ceased when we reached my bedroom. I had clothes scattered on an unmade bed—another thing that usually did not show up in romance novels. He paid them no attention, and dropped me on the edge of the bed; I bounced

I would worry about the clean clothes tomorrow. Tonight, my desire for him outweighed any other concern. To prove that, I pushed the clothes off my bed and onto the floor.

"Laundry day?" he questioned, chuckling, but he didn't give me time to respond because his mouth claimed mine once again.

I fisted his shirt, pulling upward. I wanted it off. The elasticity of t-shirt material had some give, but the material had not disappeared. Of course, it might have been easier if we weren't connected at our lips. I felt impatient, reckless, and wanted everything to happen now. If I had magical powers like a genie, I would have blinked our clothes away, and made sure both of us were on the bed instead of me sitting on it while he stood in front of me.

He stopped kissing me long enough to get rid of his borrowed shirt. And when he was naked from the waist up, I moaned. Forget a six pack, I craved his eight. Hair covered his chest, but he was not overly hairy, it led to a trail that disappeared into his shorts. My desire urged me to follow that trail with my tongue, and his cocky smile told me he knew every single one of my thoughts and desires. Not that I tried to hide them. Not tonight, and not any longer.

Leaning down, he lifted my nightshirt off of me. His hands dropped to his sides, and he swallowed hard. I wasn't as thin as most of the girls he had been with before. Would my flab turn him off? I suddenly felt very self-conscious under his scrutiny.

"What are you doing?" he asked when I reached for the blanket.

My skin felt like it burned, when I mumbled my answer, "I'm probably not like most of the girls you've dated. I—"

His hand covered my mouth to cut me off. "If I wanted someone else, I wouldn't be here. I don't care if you don't look like anyone else because you're you, and that's the person I want. You are the most beautiful, sexy woman I've ever met. I love your curves and everything about you, Emma. You are all I want and more." He removed his hand and leaned over to kiss me again, which only lasted a second because he lifted my legs to throw me completely onto the bed, and I rolled. Laughing, he got on the bed with me and crawled over to where I landed, flopping down beside me. "You know books and movies make it seem this whole seduction thing is easy."

"Books?"

"I have a sister. She made me read some romance novels with her, but I don't want to talk about her." Lifting himself from where he lay beside me, he hovered over me and whispered, "Tonight is about us." He kissed me again. Would I ever get enough? For the first time in my life, I felt insatiable when it came to a man.

His fingers swept over my breasts, pebbling my nipples. His touch felt like pure electricity on my skin. I wanted more, and he gave it to me. His calloused palm scratched my sensitive skin as he cupped my breast. I gasped. A simple touch ignited me more than ever before, but this was no simple man and neither were my feelings for him. That had the power to change everything. I loved Bryan, which made anyone from my past melt away into nothing.

Well, that and the way he licked my neck with his teeth nipping me in all the right spots. It was like he knew all of my erogenous zones. And after every nip, his lips kissed the mark he had left, making me shudder each and every time. At that point, I was on the verge of coming and I hadn't been touched yet.

My own hands lifted to touch his chest, and I scraped my fingernails over his own nipples. The hiss that came from his lips was music to my ears. Lower and lower, my hands wanted to feel every inch of him, but they were impatient to get inside his shorts. Before I could dip my hand into his waistband, his tongue moved down my neck and he took my left nipple into his mouth to suckle as his hand played with the right. Thoroughly distracted, I grabbed his head and held him close. My nipples had always been sensitive, but the way his tongue moved, I didn't want the sensation to end. The talent in that mouth might make me come without any other stimulation.

My body arched upward to get closer at the same time I held his head down, pressing his mouth to me. Moans escaped as I laid there panting. My hips undulated, fucking the air searching for my release. They would have probably found him, but his lower half lay beside mine, and therefore, out of reach. Bryan's mouth pushed me toward the precipice, and just when I thought I would fall over, he pulled back and kissed me. He would not let me come off of my high for too long before his lips left mine and moved to the other nipple. His mouth worked me up until I wanted to shatter into a million pieces. I could see that white light, I could feel it build…and then he stopped.

"No!" I cried out.

"Baby, we have all night. I plan on savoring you and making you orgasm so many times, you'll forget your own name."

"Big promises coming from someone I'm not sure can deliver." I teased him, hoping if I toyed with him long enough, we could get back to where we were—right on the edge of coming.

"Oh, I plan on delivering." He smirked.

And he proceeded to prove to me that he had the skills to back up his words.

Kissing his way down my stomach, my muscles clenched in both pleasure and anticipation. In my haze of desire, I never felt him strip me completely. I only realized my body lay there naked when I felt his lips on the inside of my hips where my thigh and groin met. First the right, and then the left. Kiss and lick. Fuck, my previous level of desire couldn't compare. I burned for him, because of him. Each kiss, each lick, each touch made me wetter for him.

I whimpered for more, and he obliged. Moving to my pussy, he kissed one side of it then the other. Each kiss and lick brought him closer to my clit, and when he finally reached it, his tongue pressed against the nub, and he flicked it. I almost jumped off the bed from the sensation. His hands grabbed my hips, holding them exactly where he wanted them.

I was well on my way, and it didn't take much. Suck, lick, pressure, rubbing my clit with his tongue, focusing on bud, and within minutes, I cried out when my orgasm engulfed me.

Even after he pushed me over the edge into one of the strongest orgasms I'd ever experienced, he didn't stop his ministrations. I heard a small chuckle, and the vibrations stimulated my already sensitive clit more. Damn! I was almost ready to come again. One of his hands moved to my pussy, and he slid a finger inside me, pushing me toward another climax. His tongue moved lower and it entered my core along with his finger. I screamed. Another finger. Two fingers pumped into me, he curled them upward while sucking on my clit. Everything exploded as I climaxed a second time.

Exhausted and tired, I could already feel my muscles fighting me, but I still wanted more. "Bryan, I need you. Please."

"Condom?" It took a minute for his words to penetrate the haze of pleasure.

I hadn't had sex since before I got sick, but for some reason, my sister thought I should keep a box of condoms in my nightstand, and bought me some a year ago. At the time, I rolled my eyes and humored her. Tonight, I thanked her for the foresight. Pointing toward the left side of the bed, I told him, "Nightstand. Top drawer."

Getting out of bed, he found the box and threw it on the bed. Before he got back in though, he removed his shorts, and I licked my lips. His dick bobbed enticingly, and even though my experience up to that point had been limited, I knew his cock was extraordinary. I hadn't touched it, but I doubted my hand would completely encircle it. At least nine inches long, it had veins that traveled the length of it. That monster was going inside me. Would it fit? I knew logically it would, but I had to admit that while I craved it, I felt a little anxious about never experiencing anything that large before.

He rolled the condom down his length, and got back into bed, crawling toward me, and then slithering up my body. The pressure and heaviness of his body helped to push away the apprehension.

His lips moved against mine as he whispered, "You have me. Forever." Reaching between us, he lined himself up with my pussy, then thrust forward. Oh, how he filled me. Large and long, it bordered on painful, but it didn't hurt. He moved slowly, almost as if he were savoring the feel of me surrounding him.

"More," I urged him.

He gave me what I begged for. Impaling himself to the hilt hard and fast, I gasped in pleasure, my eyes closing from the intensity of everything I felt. Slowly, he pulled out, leaving only the head of his dick inside me, and held himself still for a moment. When I grunted in annoyance because I wanted him to move, and he thrust back in with a smile on his face.

The tug and feel of him gliding back and forth sent shocks of electric pleasure through me. I lifted a leg to hold him closer, digging my heel into his thigh. Unable to get it any higher, it frustrated me slightly that my leg didn't want to cooperate. I couldn't lift the other, but I had to accept my limitation. It took nothing away from the bliss I felt.

Our bodies fused together, becoming one…or that was how it felt. In and out. The feel of his cock sliding into me created a friction in my core that pleasured me more than his tongue or fingers had previously. His fullness completed me. Soon, the familiar knotted coil began forming low in my stomach. His own breathing became erratic as he moaned and moved, and his thrusts became jerky.

Reaching between us, his finger circled my clit, rubbing it, spurring me closer to orgasm. The coil wound tighter and tighter within me. And when he groaned, "Come for me, baby," I did. Hard. The world exploded in pure pleasure and bliss.

With three more short, jerky thrusts, he fell over the edge with me. Even though his dick was sheathed, I could feel his cock grow and his release.

He rolled to the side, and I instantly missed his weight. He removed the condom and tied it off, throwing it over the side of the bed. I was still out of breath when he once again gathered me to him. I felt safe, loved, and wanted. Closing my eyes, I was swathed in happiness and peace, and it didn't take long before I fell asleep to the sound of his heartbeat under my ear.

My previous sexual experiences never prepared me for this. Bryan was right in the beginning, I'd missed out on a lot of things.

CHAPTER THIRTY-SIX

BRYAN

I would love to have said when I woke up, it consisted of slowly becoming aware, pulling Emma a little closer to me as I nuzzled her hair, kissing my way down from the top of her head to her lips, where I slowly made love to her mouth, waking her up with pleasure. Afterward, we both relived one of the best nights of my life when I made love to her again. I would love to have said that, but I couldn't because that wasn't what happened.

After she fell asleep, I slipped out of bed to grab her walker for her, so that she wouldn't worry about it when she woke up. Getting back into bed, I pulled her close and watched her sleep until I succumbed to exhaustion myself.

But sometime in the wee hours of the morning, a hand accidentally—at least I think it was accidental—slapped me hard across the face. Emma had turned in her sleep. Fine. She wasn't used to someone lying down in the same bed as her. Wrapping her in my arms once again, I secured her arms to her body to protect myself and once again fell asleep.

It seemed like only minutes later, loud obnoxious music began blaring in my ear, jolting me awake. I thought it might've been loud enough to burst an eardrum. It certainly made me jump up in bed, momentarily confused about my surroundings. My eyes searched for an enemy that didn't exist until they landed on Emma, who was slowly stretching a hand toward the shelf on her headboard where her alarm caterwauled. With the press of a button, it became silent. She picked up a white pill next to it, pushed it into her pink mouth, and then she promptly buried herself back under the covers. What the fuck was that?

The whirling ceiling fan lifted the edges of the curtain ever so slightly, enough to see darkness still blanketed our part of the world. A brief glance at my watch told me it was only 6:00 A.M. Why so early? My heart still pounded out a staccato beat as adrenaline continued to race through my veins, and my breathing could best be described as haphazard. I'd panicked, afraid we were about to be attacked or something.

"Em," I called out to her.

"Hmm?" her sleepy voice asked, although, I wasn't sure if she actually acknowledged me or if she tended to talk in her sleep.

"Emma!"

"Hmm?"

"Emma!"

"What?" Now she sounded irritated, and the muffled word sounded funny to me. As annoyed as she sounded, she hadn't moved a muscle.

"Why is your alarm going off at six in the morning?" I attempted to sound calm and serene, but I wanted to cuss like the proud Navy man I was.

"Bryan?" Confusion laced her tone, but she still didn't move.

"Yeah."

"It's six in the morning."

Way to state the obvious there, Em. "It is." Should I be concerned? Her voice sounded off and her words were markedly slurred. If I didn't know better, I might have thought she was drunk.

"Am I dreaming?"

Huh? "Em? Are you—?"

"You're only here in my dreams, so I get thirty more minutes with you," she interrupted. I thought she went back to sleep, but her words still sounded weird. What the hell?

Now my pulse pounded for a completely different reason. I'd done some research on myasthenia gravis, but I was far from an expert. The disease varied from person to person, which left me wondering if I should call for an ambulance or let her sleep for another thirty minutes. I knew what I would rather spend thirty minutes doing to her. Maybe that made me a pig, but it was true…except not while she seemed out of sorts.

"Em?" My hand grabbed her shoulder and gently shook her. I hated to admit it, but I was on the verge of panicking again. I'd engaged the enemy, been in a bar fight or three, and had even gone through a pregnancy scare with one of my exes, but none of that terrified me like the thought of Emma in crisis. I'd read all about MG crisis, and it scared the hell out of me that something like that might happen to her. Unable to breathe or move, she would be placed in ICU, where they would more than likely have to intubate her to allow her to breathe. "Emma?" I practically yelled, shaking her again when she didn't respond.

"What the fuck do you want, Bryan?" It sounded more like, "Wha he uck you wan, Ryan?"

"Emma, I need you to wake up."

"I am."

But she didn't even twitch, and that scared me. Grabbing my phone, I dialed the only person I thought who might have a clue about what was happening to my Emma. "Mel!"

"Bryan, what the...? Do you know what time it is?" she growled. If she could have reached through the phone to strangle me, I was pretty sure I would be dead.

"It's Emma!"

"What do you mean?" That caught her attention.

"She's slurring her words and doesn't sound right. She's barely moving."

"Fuck! I should have known you'd end up over there. She's fine. Her medication wore off, and she needs to take another dose."

I paused and inquired, "Is it white?"

"Yes, and round."

"I think she just took it." I felt like an idiot.

"Give her about fifteen minutes for it to start kicking in, but she likes to give her morning dose thirty to really get into her system. Then, and only then, can you ask her all the questions you want, but she's supposed to be over here by nine, and I think she said something about stopping for break-fast first."

"So, why did she set her alarm for six?"

"She gets tired and needs to take breaks while she gets ready. Takes her longer and all that jazz. Listen, I'm going back to sleep. Let her explain it all."

"Fine," I grumbled. I hated waiting for answers, but I didn't have much of a choice.

Before I could hang up, I heard Mell call out to me, "And Bryan?"

"Yeah?" I asked, holding the phone up to my ear.

"Are you sure about this? This is her life, how she is every morning. She can't immediately jump out of bed like you can. Are you sure you want to take this on? Are you ready for that?"

Honestly, I didn't know what I was prepared for, but I loved Emma and I couldn't live my life without her any longer. If needed, I'd learn and adapt to her life as much as I could. "I am," I said softly, and then pressed the end button.

I could tell Emma lay there awake, and probably heard my whole conversation with Mel, but she didn't say anything nor did she try to look at me. I wanted to know what was going through her head. That said, I remained quiet until she was ready to talk to me.

As I sat there waiting, I heard nature coming to life outside. Birds were waking up, singing to welcome the rising sun. Something rustled in the bushes right outside Emma's apartment window. Somewhere in the distance, a cat meowed. And upstairs, her neighbors had started to move around.

Thirty minutes never seemed so long.

"I'm surprised you didn't leave," her voice sounded almost normal, still a slight slur, but nothing like earlier, which relieved me.

"I told you, I love you no matter the disease." My panic and emotions made my voice gruff.

"You called Mel." Not a question, a statement.

"I was scared and didn't know what to do because you wouldn't answer me."

"I don't like talking when I'm like that. I'm hard to understand, and people have accused me of being drunk when I'm like that."

"You sounded drunk, but I knew you weren't."

"No, I couldn't have been." She lay there in silence after that. Her body faced the window, so I couldn't tell if her eyes were opened or closed, therefore, I stared aimlessly at the window, waiting for her to explain what had happened, but she said nothing. The sun began to rise steadily as we laid there, penetrating the break in the curtain to light her room.

The longer we laid there, the more agitated I became. I couldn't take it anymore. "Is that really how you are every morning?"

"Yes." She sighed and started to sit up. I tried to assist her, but I quickly realized I was more of a hindrance than a help. She didn't complain though, and the small smile I received made me feel like the king of the world. Yeah, I had it bad for her. When she settled into a comfortable position, she explained, "My daily mestinon doesn't work for long periods of time. I have to take it every four hours during the day. At night I take timespan, which is a long-acting mestinon. It lasts eight hours, which gets me through the night. It's basically the medicine that helps my muscles to work and keeps me functioning like a somewhat normal person. I call it my muscle med."

"Why don't you just take the timespan all the time?"

"More expensive and not as mass produced. Usually, my alarm is set for seven so I can get my first daily dose of mestinon—a lot of us call it mesty—into my system before Curley demands food. He seems to understand that he has to wait a little bit after the alarm before he can bug me."

"So basically, we would have to wait for morning sex?" I grinned, joking with her.

She didn't seem to appreciate my jest. Narrowing her eyes, she studied me for a couple of minutes, and I almost squirmed under her intense gaze. "You aren't freaked out? You know I wouldn't be offended if you left."

I read between the lines. She might not have been offended, but she would be hurt. After all my promises, her acceptance of my feelings, it would have been a knife to the back. "I'm not going anywhere. I hate to tell you this, but you're stuck with me for pretty much fucking forever." Her eyes widened, her cheeks burned pink, and her smile grew. That reaction was everything to me. I bent forward to capture her lips in a kiss. When I reluctantly ended it, we were both out of breath. Had I ever experienced a kiss that set my whole body on fire? I couldn't think of anyone doing that to me except Emma. Damn, I sounded like a girl, but for her, I would do anything, and not care what anyone besides her thought of it.

When she had sat up, she'd tucked the sheet under her arms, but I remembered what her body looked like. I wanted that body, craved it like no other.

Beautiful, sexy, funny, courageous…how had I gotten so blessed?

"Was that your only question?" she probed.

So many questions ran through my head. Questions I'd never thought to ask before, but the first one that popped out was, "Have you ever gone into crisis?"

Shaking her head, she said, "No. I've been lucky."

Lucky. She called that lucky. I called it a miracle.

"You know, not everyone with MG goes into crisis," she stated, her head tilted a little to the side.

Had my expression changed to the point she felt it necessary to reassure me? "I realize that. It's just…" I couldn't find the words.

"Scary? Believe me, I know. It's one of the things I fear the most, but according to the doc, I'm fairly stable. Although, my legs like to take a vacation more often than they used to. We're still playing with my meds, trying to find the right combination. I have good days and bad days, I take my meds, and I get treatment every couple of weeks."

"Treatment?"

"IVIG." I guessed I appeared bewildered because she quickly explained. "It's an IV treatment and helps me function. It means intravenous immunoglobulin. The easiest way to explain it is, it is like a sponge. It soaks up the bad antibodies and helps decrease the symptoms. I go every two weeks right now, but starting next week I go every week. Insurance took their sweet time approving the treatment since it's costly. I think I got a bill once and it was over $24k for the month. When someone donates blood, one of the things that's extracted is the immunoglobulin. That's what is pushed into me."

I ran my hand over my face and huffed. "I guess I still have a lot to learn."

"You don't have to, you know."

"Why are you saying that? Of course, I do."

Picking at an invisible piece of lint on her blanket, she refused to meet my gaze. "It's a lot to take in, and I'm sure it's more than you bargained for. I accept the fact that with my MG and the stuff that comes with it, it'll take someone unique to accept everything, and—"

The irritation that had disappeared, returned with a vengeance. "You mean someone like Chad?" Apparently, my jealousy hadn't diminished as much as I thought it had.

"Not necessarily, but he's one." She stared at me as if she were trying to figure out the secrets of the universe…or just my own hidden agenda. But I had none. When it came to her, I opened myself up and gave her everything.

"You don't think I'm up for the task?"

Her eyes dropped to the blanket again as she shrugged. "It's a burden. I'm going to be a burden to anyone who decides to be with me. And it's a lot bigger commitment than it would be for a normal person. If I was normal, you wouldn't have panicked this morning. You would've probably kissed me awake and—"

"Stop it right there." Holding up my hand, I needed her to quit right there, because my imagination booted up, and thoughts of what came after the kiss were quite colorful in my head. "While that might be true, that doesn't mean I don't want you or love you." Now if only my dick would stop reacting to my wayward thoughts, this conversation might be a little easier to handle. It didn't help my situation when she started to bite her lip though. I wanted my teeth to do the biting. Damn! She made me feel like an out of control horny teenager.

And then something occurred to me. "What are you really afraid of?"

"Nothing."

"Don't bullshit a bullshitter." I'd been sitting on the end of the bed, and moved to sit next to her. Nudging her, I pleaded, "Talk to me. Please."

"I just…A lot of my single MG friends find that after they start dating someone, the other party eventually realizes they can't handle someone who's sick. Chronic illnesses don't go away. And for a lot of people, it gets really old really fast. Canceling dates last minute because I'm not having a good day. Not to mention the walker, the cane, the meds, the fatigue, and all of the doctor appointments."

"Are you trying to talk me out of being with you?"

"No, but—"

"Yes, you are." I chuckled. "We really need to work on your self-esteem. When you finally land the guy, you're supposed to sit back, enjoy it all, and be happy. I don't care about any of that. If you want me to go with you to doctor appointments, I will. Hell, it might help me understand everything a little more. If you have to cancel our dates, I'll come over and take care of you. And if you have to take a nap or lie down because you're feeling fatigued, I'll lie down with you."

She furrowed her brow in confusion. "How?"

"What do you mean?"

"I mean, how can you do all of that? You don't even live here."

Grinning, I wrapped my arms around her and lifted her onto my lap. "Well, even if I wasn't transferring to Charleston, we'd make it work somehow."

I saw the moment everything clicked. A smile slowly formed, tugging her lips upward. I loved her smile, the way her eyes seemed brighter with a little more gold when she honestly felt happy. There was so much about Emma Taylor I still needed to discover, and I estimated it would take a lifetime to find out what made the woman I loved so unique.

"You're transferring?" she asked. Eagerness lit up her expressive eyes. She wanted this, wanted me to transfer. Maybe some of her hesitations sprung out of her uncertainty over the physical distance that would've separated us.

"Yes. Two more months and I'll be here full time…or as full time as the Navy allows me to be." My own smile grew, mirroring hers, and I leaned down to kiss her again, feasting on her lips. And now that she had her medicine in her system, I could dine on her.

If only we didn't know Mel.

In the middle of our kiss, my phone started to ring. I ignored it, intent on kissing my girl. Another ring. Based on the ringtone, Mel decided to be insistent this morning. I didn't care if it was her wedding day, Emma in my arms was heaven on earth, and I was reluctant to let her go.

I ignored it again, but seconds later, another call. This time Emma's phone started to ring, and a second later, mine joined hers, this time with my sister's ringtone.

A man's ego could be a delicate thing. In other words, it hurt a man's pride when his new girlfriend laughed with his tongue in her mouth. But, that was exactly what happened when our cell phones kept ringing. As they both began ringing simultaneously for the third time, she couldn't stop giggling and our kiss was cut short.

"You know they won't leave us alone, and if I don't start getting ready, I won't make it to Mel's on time."

"Five more minutes."

"Mel will probably drive over here if we don't answer."

"We'll barricade the door."

"I'm in. We can skip the wedding."

Groaning, my forehead fell to her shoulder. "Fuck! We can't. I'm going to need help moving into my new place."

"I thought the Navy paid for all that. Always did for my dad."

"They do, but I'm going to need to buy some new furniture. I planned on putting Luke to work. Plus, Mel knows my parents. They'll kick my ass if I don't show."

"Big bad Navy man afraid of his parents."

"More afraid of Mel. She's scary. To hell with my parents."

Emma stated, giggling again. "She seriously is."

The fourth time they rang, I unwound myself from Emma's body and grabbed my phone from the floor. Fucking Mel and her demands. The fact she knew my sister, only made it worse. Before Emma's own phone sent the call to voicemail, she answered. I left her in the bedroom to deal with Mel, while I went into the kitchen to make coffee and deal with my sister. "What do you want?" I demanded.

"About time you picked up your phone." Rayne's snooty tone was not lost on me. I pushed down the urge to reach through the phone and strangle her. What exactly was her problem with Emma anyway?

"Did you need something, or did you feel like giving me attitude before I've even had my coffee?"

"Rawr." She mimicked a pissed off cat.

"What the fuck do you want, Rayne? You've got three seconds before I hang up."

"Fine! Don't get your panties in a twist. I called because Mel asked me to try your phone. Apparently, she's been trying to call you and that girl all morning. She got worried when no one picked up."

"That girl is Emma, and we're both fine. We couldn't answer because I was helping her do something, and the phones were in the other room." For the most part, I'd always been a pretty good liar when it came to my sister and prayed she bought my story.

"Yeah, sure you were."

"I'm serious about what I said yesterday, Rayne."

"It's not like she's going to stick around long enough. You've introduced me to girls before and they never lasted beyond that. What's the big deal about her?"

"The big deal is I love her and plan on spending the rest of my life with her. If you don't like that, you better start looking for a way to deal with it."

"Bryan—"

"No. That's how it is. Period." I hung up before she could say anything else.

Damn it! My emotions were all over the place this morning. Scared, relieved, happy, ecstatic, irritated, pissed off, and every other fucking emotion in between. I would've probably thrown my phone if I didn't have a use for it.

I couldn't understand why Rayne had a problem with Emma when they'd never met before. Had Mel or Luke said something to Rayne that my sister took offense to? No. I knew Mel better than most, and I believed beyond the shadow of a doubt, she'd never said anything derogatory about Emma. So then what the hell was Rayne's issue?

Pinching the bridge of my nose, I released a sigh and sagged against the kitchen counter. I loved my sister, and no matter what happened in life that would never change. But Emma…this was different. If I lost her, part of me would disappear as well.

"You okay?" her voice called out from behind me.

A slow smile appeared on my lips as I turned around. Being with her, having her here, lifted a weight off my shoulders, and my mood instantly brightened. How did she hold so much power over my mood? I neither knew nor cared. This was the effect she had on me, and I embraced it.

Walking around the counter, I carefully pulled her into my arms, holding her tightly as I kissed the top of her head. "Yeah, just a small sibling squabble."

"You sure?" she asked, her concern evident in her tone as she returned my embrace.

"I'm sure. She'll get over it."

"What happened?"

I opened my mouth to speak and snapped it closed. Finally, I admitted, "I don't know. A bee flew up her ass about something, but I can't tell you why."

"It's about me, isn't it?"

I didn't want to lie to her, but at the same time, I didn't want to tell her that yes, my sister had an issue with her for some unknown reason. I needed to navigate this properly, and I hadn't a clue as to how to manage it.

EMMA

Bryan stiffened in my arms. He said everything he didn't want to say in that one action, but I didn't blame him for his sister. I couldn't. If anything, I probably understood more than he did about his sister's behavior. First, she probably had a brother complex. Most younger sisters I had met did. Second, she probably didn't know what to think of me. She more than likely felt unnerved by the fact I was disabled and sick. Most people found it hard to deal with illnesses, diseases, or disabilities. I was different, and her brother showed an interest in me.

To Rayne, her brother had picked someone beneath him because on paper, Bryan was the cream of the crop. A Navy pilot with a killer personality and a hero complex. He was tall, dark, and handsome. Compared to him, I was average. After I got sick, I was unable to return to work, so I tried to keep busy by writing a little as a hobby and reading. Comparing both of us side by side, I wasn't exactly sure why he fell for me. That said, after last night, I did not doubt him.

His hands rub up and down my spine, relaxing me to the point that I accidentally dropped my cane. I probably should have selected my walker today, but once again I chose to pretend I'd be fine with less. I knew it was prideful, but I didn't care. I didn't want to walk down the aisle today with my walker. I didn't want all of the pictures from Mel's wedding to have a walker in them. It was bad enough that I, at the bare minimum, needed a cane. Using a walker would have called too much attention to myself, and honestly, I was slightly embarrassed to have my walker in Mel's wedding. The guests should be focused on the bride, not me.

Most of the time, I used my walker without complaint, however, there had been a few times, like today, when it bothered me to use it. People staring, whispering, pointing, and jeering. I could only ignore them for so long before the pressure got to me.

When Mel first asked me to be a bridesmaid, I gave her every excuse in the book, trying to bow out gracefully, but she was pigheaded and refused my request. Thus, I'd wear my bridesmaid dress with pride, and support her. I actually did want to stand up there with her, but my issue was with my walker and cane. It was precious moments like these that I wished they weren't needed.

He continued to rub my back, but I had a feeling it might have been more for him than for me. "I'm sure there's a lot going on right now with your parents' divorce and Mel's wedding. She probably feels like she's losing everything, and you're supposed to be her constant." I wasn't lying. That could very well be the reason.

"I hadn't thought of that. Maybe," he murmured. In his voice though, I could tell he didn't quite believe the load of bullshit I fed him, but honestly, a lot of changes were happening in the Sampson household, which was overwhelming for someone who hadn't experienced a lot of upheaval in her life. My understanding of the situation was that they never moved, their parents had always been together, same friends throughout most of their life, same schools…nothing different. Time had changed things for her. She had a friend getting married, her brother fell in love, and her parents were getting a divorce. It was a lot to process for anyone.

"Yeah," I agreed quietly.

As much as I wanted to stay right there in his arms for the moment—the day, the week, forever—if I didn't leave soon, Mel would hunt me down and serve my head-on a silver platter. Because when she wanted something, she got it. She was adamant about showing up at her house pronto. Reluctantly, I asked, "You going to be all right?"

His chuckle rumbled deep in his chest, which reverberated throughout his body and mine. "Yeah, I'll be fine. I can't say the same for my sister, but I promise not to shed any blood on Mel's big day."

"She might shed yours if you did."

"She would."

"Now, before she guts both of us like fishes, I need to get out of here and get over to the hotel. Can you bend down and get my cane for me?"

Bending down, he picked it up and handed it to me as I supported myself on the counter. We had no time for breakfast or coffee, and I wanted to stay in bed all day with Bryan. I both cursed and loved Mel today because she was a contributing factor to my new relationship.

"You got it?" He made sure I was steady before he took a step away from me.

"Yeah."

"I'll drop you off. I need to head over to Luke and Mel's place anyway. It's my job to make sure the groom is up. I was supposed to be there last night, but priorities and all that." Glancing behind him toward my coffee pot, he grumbled something that I could not understand.

"What?" I saw the coffee out on the counter, but he had not been able to start brewing a pot...sadly.

"Nothing." He faced me again with a smile and wink. "Go get your shower and start getting ready."

His broad grin made me tingle. This man knew how to make me melt and leave me breathless. Unable to say anything else, I somehow managed a nod before I shuffled off toward the bathroom to rush through my shower as much as I could. I was moving slowly this morning, a little sore and stiff after last night's events, but I wouldn't have changed anything for the world. Dressed in a pair of yoga pants and a t-shirt, I was ready to go. My hair and makeup would be done at the hotel, as well as my interrogation. I both dreaded and anticipated seeing Mel this morning.

CHAPTER THIRTY-SEVEN

EMMA

I swear Mel possessed X-ray vision or something. When Bryan dropped me off, he insisted that he walk me up to the room. I wasn't ready to say goodbye just yet, so I readily agreed, and when we made it to the room, the door swung open before I ever knocked. The second we were interrupted, my wonderful new boyfriend darted away, choosing to abandon me instead of sticking around for the Spanish Inquisition. Coward. He hightailed it to the elevator and made his escape without another word.

If I'd been anyone else, Mel would've probably jerked me into the room, however, me being me, and the fact I had my cane in my hand, she anxiously tapped her foot on the floor as I leisurely sauntered inside. I might've moved a little slower due to her impatience, but, I would never admit that even under duress or torture.

For the wedding, Mel and Luke had reserved the honeymoon suite and would be staying in it after they left the reception, which would take place downstairs in the ballroom. The room itself had a living room, small kitchen, and off to the right, there were three stairs that led to the spacious bedroom complete with king size bed, hot tub, and a bathtub big enough to fit four. If I wanted, I could use the excuse that the suite was too large and it'd take me a while to get to the couch, but I didn't think she would believe that one for a second. Her eagerness already showed on her face.

"Will you hurry up?" she snapped, losing her patience completely.

"I'm trying," I retorted. I wasn't trying that hard, but she didn't need to know that.

"Did you take your meds? Is it time for more?" Suddenly, Mel switched from annoyed and anxious for answers, to a mother hen.

"No. Just a little weak today."

"Then why the hell aren't you using your walker?"

"I'm fine with my cane!" I spat a little harsher than I intended. "Sorry, but I'll be fine."

Her eyes raked over me from top to bottom as I plopped down on the couch next to another bridesmaid, Krista, and the maid of honor, Jamie. Thankfully, Rayne didn't appear to be in residence yet. "Maybe we should call Bryan and ask him to grab your walker for later just in case?"

The worry in her voice bothered me. Plastering on a smile, I assured her once again. "It'll be all right. And besides, Bryan is one step ahead of you. He insisted on loading it into his car before we left."

"Excellent. I know you don't always like to use it, but sometimes it's necessary."

I swallowed my prideful retort. I didn't want to start anything with the bride, and I didn't want to get into it at all with anyone. I knew I needed it. I understood my limitations better than anyone. Even when I wanted to pretend they didn't exist, I understood them. And I hated it when other people reminded me about them. "I know."

And now that Mel had determined I was relatively okay, the time for my interrogation had arrived. She crossed her arms over her chest and her foot started to tap again. The countdown began in my head. Five, four, three, two, one...

"What happened last night and this morning? Bryan called and woke me up freaking out. He asked about calling for an ambulance."

"He didn't realize that's how it is in the morning."

"I could tell. I had to talk him off a ledge. Though I will admit, that part was kind of funny."

"Glad you think so." I rolled my eyes, but still giggled. "It was."

"And?"

"And what?" I played coy.

The tapping intensified, and the other two girls in the room smartly remained silent. Although, their heads did swing back and forth as if they were watching a tennis match.

Huffing, Mel demanded, "Tell me! He shows up with you, doesn't say a word to me, just kisses your head and runs away like a scared little mouse?"

"Maybe you scare him. You can be kind of terrifying at times. Plus, he said he needed to make sure Luke was awake and sober because that was the task you gave him. He also informed me you told him that you'd castrate him if Luke was late or drunk at the altar. I think he was trying to preserve the family jewels."

"You're not funny."

"I thought I was. Bryan laughed at me this morning."

"What the hell happened, Em?"

"Who says anything happened?"

"You're not funny! Just tell me already. You left last night with Chad because you were upset. This morning Bryan calls me in a panic. So tell me."

Her annoyance with me showed on her face as it turned an unbecoming shade of red. My fun was over. "Bryan showed up last night. I didn't want to talk to him, but when it started to rain I felt sorry for him, and let him inside the apartment. Then he confessed, and that's about it."

"And you believed him? What did he say?" Mel had a romantic side that craved sweet romance and everything that went with it. Her book collection could rival that of the local library.

"Eventually I did. He said that he loved me and that he wants to spend his life with me—"

She gasped. "Woah! Hold it right there! He told you he wants to spend his life with you? I mean, I knew he confessed at the church, but to hear him do all this. Wow."

I blinked in surprise. "Why?"

"I don't think he's ever told a girl anything like that before. He's never really made long-term plans with a girl." She fell into a chair, stunned.

Her reveal made me feel giddy like a schoolgirl. It also made me want him all that much more. Could it really be this easy? After years of searching for someone who would love, understand, and accept me, I'd finally found him because of a misdirected message through FaceSpace? Did he volunteer to help me only to fall in love with me? Did things like this actually happen? If I believed everything that had happened in the past twelve hours, then yes. However, I couldn't help but wonder when my bubble would burst. I hoped it never did.

After that, no one really had time to discuss Bryan and me, or the status of our relationship, any further. Rayne arrived, and right on her heels, the hair and makeup people appeared with a flourish. Ignoring the daggers Bryan's sister shot my way, we were all poked, prodded, hair pulled, face painted, and used a can of hairspray each so that our hair would not move. And then the bridal party—minus the bride—were shoved into our dresses. The whole time we were tortured...I meant, prepared for the wedding, the photographer happily snapped away, creating photo opportunities when I didn't think one existed.

I said shoved...no, we were shoved by the various people around into our dresses. Thankfully, they were fairly comfortable, long, and gorgeous. Mel had picked wisely. Her choice for our bridesmaid dresses had sweetheart necklines with one shoulder covered in a Grecian style, and they flowed down to our ankles in a lovely periwinkle color. It was pretty, unlike the dress I was forced to wear at my sister's wedding. Orange was not my color. I honestly believed some brides picked ugly dresses and ugly colors on purpose.

Once we were completely groomed and ready, everyone helped get the bride dressed. While the others assisted with the dress, I held onto the veil, and then pinned it to the top of her head when she decided she was ready for it. I had to admit, I was a little jealous. Her gown was something I dreamed of wearing. When Mel and I had gone dress shopping, I found my dream dress, announcing that was the dress I would wear if I were getting married. Little did I realize, the moment she saw it, she would insist on trying it on. It was love at first sight for both of us. White, with a sweetheart strapless neckline on an A-line frame that fell to the floor in the same light gauzy material our dresses were made of. It had pearl and silver jeweled accents which lined the top of the bodice and moved down one side to line the hips. Finally, a sash tied around the waist. Luke would appreciate the way it accentuated her curves, and then he would breathe a sigh of relief when he saw a simple zipper instead of a row of buttons. I easily pictured him pulling out a knife if the dress were difficult to remove, and then the dream wedding dress would lay dead at his feet. Then again, Mel might have appreciated his aggressive show of masculinity.

"If everyone is ready, it's time to head downstairs to the limo," the wedding planner announced.

It was time to attend Mel's wedding.

I was probably more excited to see Bryan in his tuxedo than to see the groom. Not that I didn't want to see Luke's face the moment Mel appeared at the back of the church. I did, but Bryan in a tuxedo held a certain allure for me. Plus, I was in love with the man, and couldn't get enough of him. Everything was still so new and exciting. Maybe with time, it would diminish, but until then, I would relish in these feelings...at least until I woke up and realized I'd been trapped in a damn good dream this whole time.

I should've known Mel would think of me even when it came to her wedding. As each bridesmaid stepped into the sanctuary of the church, one of the groomsmen stood there ready to escort us down the aisle. Not a normal occurrence, and when my head whipped around as the first girl took her march down the aisle, Mel gave me a wink and a thumb's up. This had been set up for me. I should be mad or irritated, but I wasn't. I needed the extra support today. I only wished I was the maid of honor so I could walk with the best man, who happened to be Bryan, instead of the bridesmaid in line right before the maid of honor.

And then another surprise.

I carefully stepped over the small bump in the doorway where the hallway met the sanctuary, ready to hold on for dear life to John's arm—the groomsman who should have been my escort—only I found Bryan waiting for me.

I frowned. "Bry—"

His smile blinded me as his finger pressed against my lips to shush me, silently telling me to ask later. I would acquiesce, but later, I wanted answers. For now, I'd bask in the joy and warmth of him escorting me down the aisle, supporting me physically the same way he did the day we went skydiving.

Slowly and carefully we marched to the front of the sanctuary. He never rushed me or tried to make me move faster. He moved at my pace, and when we arrived, he helped me into a chair that had been placed there for me. Mel thought of everything. Normally, I would have fought her on all of this. But today, I was thankful I didn't have to risk falling while they recited their vows.

As soon as the maid of honor hit her mark, everyone in the church stood up, except me. All eyes turned to the back of the church, waiting with bated breath until the doors opened. When they did, a collective gasp could be heard throughout the sanctuary. Mel was stunning.

I tore my eyes away from her and focused on Luke, enjoying the fact that Bryan happened to be in my view as well. Luke's jaw dropped open, his breath caught, and tears starting to form. Mel's fiancé couldn't take his eyes off of her. In them, the love and devotion he felt for her was on display for all the world to see.

Focusing on Bryan, I noticed he returned my stare, making my cheeks blush. Like Luke with Mel, I couldn't tear my eyes away from Bryan. I wondered…when people looked at him, did they see love shining brightly in his eyes? I could see it, but did others? Did it really matter? Despite the newness of our relationship, I knew we'd somehow manage to make it work no matter what anyone else said or thought.

The wedding was perfect. Unable to fight them any longer, Luke let a couple tears slip while he pledged his vows. Mel, on the other hand, had two raging rivers flowing down her face from the moment she placed her hands in Luke's. Bless whoever invented waterproof makeup. And in true Mel fashion, when the preacher pronounced, "May I present Mr. and Mrs. Ransom," she yelled, "Time to get this party started! Let's get our drink on y'all!" Only Mel.

After the reception, after we'd done everything we were supposed to do as part of the wedding party, Bryan, wrapped his arm around me and swept me out of the ballroom. Without my knowledge, he'd asked my sister to watch Curley for another night, which she'd planned on doing anyway.

His arm held me so tightly, he carried most of my weight, and it felt like I was floating on air beside him. After ushering me onto one of the elevators, he pressed five, swung me into his arms and carried me to one of the rooms when the doors opened. "Bryan?"

"You're tired, and I figured why drive across town when there's this big hotel right here with empty rooms," he said as he dropped my legs and I slid down his body.

"What about my medicine? I only brought enough for today."

"I grabbed everything you'd need while you were in the shower. I even brought clothes for you to wear tomorrow."

I could feel my blush coloring my cheeks. As much as I wanted him, my body didn't want to cooperate. It was too exhausted.

He must have seen my inner struggle plastered on my face because he leaned down and gave me a brief kiss. "Not tonight. Tonight, we are going to lie in bed, watch TV, and talk. Nothing else. You've been going all day, and you look like you're about to collapse. You need to rest."

I opened my mouth to deny everything, but thought better of it and in the end, simply nodded. I couldn't argue with him.

"Come on. We'll take a bath and then get into bed."

"I can bathe myself."

His grin showed off his gleaming white teeth, and his wink made the butterflies in my stomach dance. "I know you can, but this will be even more fun." He was right.

After starting the bath water and adding bubble bath to the tub, he helped me undress. Sweeping me up into his arms, he placed me in the warm water, stripped, and climbed in behind me. God how I wished I could do more than sit there with him, but having him there, feeling him behind me…I loved these moments with him too.

His hands were magic. Starting at my neck and moving to my shoulder, he massaged my backside. It relaxed me to the point, I fell asleep in the bath with him. Who did that? I had a hot man behind me and I began snoring.

Vaguely aware of him moving, he got out and then lifted me out of the tub. Setting me on the side, I woke up long enough for him to dry me off, but that was it. After that, I remember dreaming about Bryan in Batman Underoos in front of Elvis in a Vegas wedding chapel. In this dream, I'd been the bride, and I kind of hoped this one came true…not necessarily the Elvis part though.

CHAPTER THIRTY-EIGHT

BRYAN

These past two months could not have ended soon enough for me. The day after the wedding, I had to leave Emma early in the morning in order to catch my flight back to San Diego. Leaving her so soon after establishing our relationship, had been hard on both of us; however, knowing I would be back semi-permanently in a couple months—nothing was ever permanent when you were in the Navy—made things a little more bearable. Plus, we had our FaceSpace chats, phone calls, and video calls. Now that we were dating, we decided not to limit ourselves to only FaceSpace. Thank fuck. Two months with only typewritten messages would have driven me insane.

And since we could not be together in person, our imaginations became very creative.

For about a week after I returned to San Diego from the east coast, we either couldn't connect at the same time or if we did, our conversations were fleeting and short-lived. Not exactly a great start to our long distance relationship, but things eventually changed and we were finally able to speak for longer than five minutes at a time.

Damn, merely thinking about the first time we were able to have a long conversation, got me hard. It was the first of many "special conversations."

I wasn't even sure who initiated what that day. We were talking on video chat, and the next thing I knew, we were both taking off our shirts, lying back on our beds, and daring each other to take it further.

She took me up on my dare first by removing her shorts. The sight of her purple panties with little skulls and crossbones on them, made my mouth water. I desired her, but it was more than that…I craved her.

"Take yours off too." Her sultry smile demanded I follow through with her request. She was a cheeky one.

I did. Angling the computer so that she could still see me when I stood up, my fingers moved to the buttons of my jeans as I heard music start to play through my computer's speakers. She had turned on the radio. Lifting a brow in question, I asked, "What are you doing?"

"Mood music for my striptease." She snickered. My girl was in a very good mood tonight, and I couldn't blame her. I was too. Although it had only been a couple of weeks, it had been too long since we truly connected with each other, and on that particular night, we had all the time in the world.

That said, her request made me chuckle. "Striptease?"

"Yep." Emphasis on the "P". "Bow chicka bow wow."

I doubled over laughing. "What the hell have you been watching?"

"It's what happens in a lot of movies." She giggled. That sound had the power to make everything melt away. I wanted to make her laugh and smile for as long as she let me. I didn't need time or space to know this girl was the one and only one for me.

"We seriously have to talk about your movie preferences later."

"Much later. Right now, strip."

"Just wait until we're back in the same state."

"I can't wait. I'd much rather have you here than on the computer."

"Me too, honey. Me too."

We both paused for a moment. "Well…?" she pressed.

Laughing again, I shook my head, buy my hands returned to my fly. "All right! All right!"

Somehow we both wound up naked in our own beds, wishing we were with each other instead of alone, directing each other over our virtual connection.

"Grab your dick and squeeze. Move your hand up and down…not too fast. I want to draw this out." My hand did as it was ordered. Wrapping it around the base of my cock, I squeezed it gently and started pumping my fist up and down, staying away from my sensitive head because I didn't want to blow before I could make her come.

My voice sounded throaty as I gave her a set of instructions to follow. "Lick your middle finger and trail it down to one of your nipples. Circle it. Yeah, just like that baby. Now pinch it." Her soft moan almost made me come, but I let go of my dick before I embarrassed myself. If I couldn't make her come first, I wanted to come together. I refused to be the first to fall over the edge. "Now move your hand lower, between your thighs. Spread your legs for me. Press on your clit and move your finger in a circle over it." Her breath hitched. Fuck, I wanted to bury my cock deep inside her. Swallowing hard, I cleared my throat, and instructed, "Stick a couple fingers from your other hand inside your pussy. Imagine it's me thrusting inside you." She followed my directions to a T, and her soft moans were getting a little louder and higher pitched. Her head fell back and her eyes fluttered closed. Her fingers moved in and out on one hand as the others pinched and circled her clit, gradually getting faster. Her breathing became erratic, and I forgot all about my own pleasure as I watched her climb higher and higher. Lifting her hips to meet her thrusting fingers, she started to call out my name between moans.

Almost unconsciously, my hand had returned to my dick and began pumping it hard and fast, moving over the head. Up, down, and over. Up, down, and over. My own breathing felt labored. I rushed toward my own orgasm. Grunting and groaning met my ears, and I realized that those noises were coming from me, not her.

Her hands no longer moved at a steady pace. They were jerky, trying to push her over the edge as quickly as possible. If I listened closely, I could hear the sounds of the wetness as her fingers fucked her pussy. I couldn't take my eyes off of my screen. She had situated the computer at the end of the bed and I could see everything. I didn't want to miss a detail.

And suddenly, her hips lifted slightly off of the bed, her legs stiffened, and her toes curled as she screamed, "Bryan!" Her orgasm claimed her, and watching her shatter, sent me over the edge as well. My dick erupted, splattering my stomach and chest. Fuck! That had been intense.

Neither one of us spoke for several minutes. The only thing that could be heard was our labored, erratic breathing as we tried to come down from our highs.

Since that night, we'd repeated that event several times, and now in less than twenty-four hours, we'd be together again. My anticipation grew, as did the need to feel Emma in my arms. I wanted her warmth, her body... her. I needed her, only her.

One of the only downsides about my relationship with Emma: Rayne. To hell with my sister. I had hoped Rayne's attitude toward Emma would've changed over the last two months, but it hadn't. If anything, it had gotten worse. An hour ago, my sister had the audacity to ask that I break up with Emma. What the hell? I refused to give into my sister's selfish request. I wasn't sure what Rayne's problem was, but she needed to get over it quickly. Emma was staying.

CHAPTER THIRTY-NINE

EMMA

Finally! Not including video messaging or pictures sent back and forth, I hadn't seen Bryan in two months and six days.

Mel stood beside me at the airport, waiting for Bryan with me. She kept teasing me, telling me I was a combination of cute and pathetic all rolled into one. Maybe I was, but I didn't care. I wanted him to arrive so I could wrap my arms around him. Besides she had no room to talk. When it came to Luke, Mel acted the exact same way.

Didn't the plane land already? What was taking so long?

"What the fuck are you doing here?" sneered a newcomer behind me.

I recognized that voice. I crossed my fingers, hoping I was wrong, but seeing Mel's glare, my hopes were dashed. Rayne showed up even though Bryan had specifically asked her not to come. Up until this point, Lady Luck favored me. When we arrived, we pulled into the very last handicap spot, which happened to be right in front of the very doors Bryan agreed to meet me. We hit zero traffic and had gotten to the airport early. But it looked like my luck had finally run out.

"I think the question is, what the fuck are you doing here? Bryan told you Emma was going to pick him up." The way Mel's lips curled into a snarl, made her appear as if she was about to embrace her feral animal side and attack. Since the wedding, the two friends had been at odds—something I felt responsible for.

"Then why are you here, Miss…oh sorry, Mrs. High and Mighty?"

"Emma needed a ride, and I was available. So, get lost."

Talking in a baby voice, Rayne said, "Aww. Does she need you to wipe her ass as well as speak for her? Such a good mommy."

"Enough!" I growled. Slowly, I spun around to confront Bryan's sister. "Leave. Bryan doesn't want you here."

Her glare could melt paint off a house. "Trying to separate us? Trying to take my brother away from me?"

"I would never do something like that. Now, back off and go home. He'll see you later."

"You aren't worth his time or energy. You're just a broken down nobody. You really think he wants someone like you when he can have someone who's actually pretty, whole, and isn't pathetic enough to use a walker? Am I right, boys?" Rayne snarled, drawing my attention to the others with her.

I immediately recognized the shorter of the two men, the one leering at me. Allen. Fuck! I never expected to see him again, and now all of the sudden he was with Rayne. How? Why? What the hell was going on?

The other man, I now recognized as Allen's brother, Paul, chastised Rayne, "Stop it. Let's just go, and we'll catch up with Bryan later." His face appeared slightly red, almost as if Rayne's behavior embarrassed him. I was so confused. Why were they here? Why were they with her?

"Paul? Allen? What the hell are you guys doing here?" Bryan questioned. Apparently, while I had been otherwise occupied, he'd made it through the gate, and I'd missed his arrival. But it didn't matter right now. Allen was there. I stood there frozen, unable to say or do anything. My nightmare had come to life and haunted me.

Stepping past me, he greeted the two men and his sister before whipping around and sweeping me up in his arms. "God, Em, I missed you." My voice spurned me, refusing to work. Noticing, I sagged against him like a limp ragdoll—it wasn't only my voice that did not work—he carefully set me down, and his gaze swept over me. "Em?"

Allen laughed. "That's where I recognized this bitch from!"

My eyes stung with tears, but I forbade any drops to fall. No more tears would be cried because of my ex—if you could call him that. I hated him, and I hated myself for my reaction.

"I'd watch it if I were you, Allen," Bryan warned without taking his eyes off me.

"Oh, that's right. You stuck up for her that day too," he guffawed.

That day? Stuck up for me?

"What are you talking about? Rayne, why the fuck are you even here? I told you I'd see you later."

"Our cousins come all this way to see you and welcome you home, and that's how you want to act?" His sister sneered. Her attitude reeked of animosity and loathing for me. This went beyond someone who feared someone who was different. What had I ever done to her?

Wait. Did she say cousins?

Bryan glanced over his shoulder, meeting her glare for glare. "Considering I arranged for Emma to pick me up, and informed you I'd see you later tonight, yeah, I'll act this way. Secondly, I didn't know they were coming into town. Now I suggest you check your fucking attitude at the door, or else!"

"What? You going to choose her over family?"

"Every fucking minute of every fucking day. I told you, I love her."

Rayne sucked in her breath. She hadn't expected that answer.

"I see the bitch managed to do to you what she couldn't do to me." Allen's amusement about the situation made me physically ill. Bile swished in my stomach, rising up into my throat, burning it with acid.

Bryan's fingers dug into my waist where he still held me. He hung onto his temper by a thread, but I could tell he was ready to punch Allen. "What the fuck are you talking about?" he demanded.

"She's wrapped you around her little finger. This bitch tried to do that to me too, but it didn't work. After I fucked her, I tried to throw her out of my house, but you came in and took her away for me."

I gasped. Could it be true? I knew Paul had been there, but I never knew who the other man had been. As distraught as I was that day, I had zero clues as to his identity

His eyes searched mine. "Is he telling the truth? Were you with him?"

Was that the part he wanted to focus on? Did this mean if I admitted I had been, Bryan would leave me? My throat felt tight, my gaze dropping to my feet. "Yes."

"Paul, did you know?" Bryan demanded.

"No one even told me you were dating anyone new. Your sister here told us that you'd need a ride home and that we should surprise you," Paul answered, looking decidedly even more uncomfortable than he had previously.

Bryan's head bobbed up and down. "I see. Nice of her to do that for me." His was voice filled with sarcasm. His eyes never left me as he called out, "Mel?"

"Yeah?" my friend responded with an unsure tremble in her voice. Her tone told me, she had her guard up, ready to strike if required.

"You drive her here today?"

"Yeah. Her battery died, and she asked me to pick her up so she wouldn't be late."

"Where'd you park?"

"Just outside in handicap."

"Paul, can you grab my bag? Mel, grab her walker." His orders given, Bryan swept me up in his arms. I squeaked in surprise. His lips tickled my ear when he whispered, "I'd save you again and again if you needed me to. You are what matters to me. I. Love. You."

I'd been afraid. Afraid that now that he realized who I was—regardless of the fact I'd been clueless myself—he would leave me. Afraid that if his sister really pushed, he would walk away. Afraid that others' opinions might influence him. Afraid that if he knew what happened that day, he would think less of me, pity me, turn away from me, or feel ashamed of me. Some of those fears still lingered, but with that one action and a few whispered words, he calmed some of them like the sun banishing the darkness.

We waited patiently beside Mel's red four-door truck for her to unlock it. Hearing the click of the lock, Paul opened the door for him, and Bryan carefully placed me in the backseat, kissing my forehead before he turned around. Paul had already thrown Bryan's bag into the bed of the pickup, along with my walker that Mel had pushed out of the terminal.

I noticed the crazed look in Bryan's eye. Something was about to happen, but what?

"Thanks, Paul." Bryan clasped him on the shoulder, and when Allen approached him from behind, Bryan spun around and punched him in the stomach, forcing his cousin to double over and groan in pain. Lifting his knee, Bryan caught Allen in the face and sent him flying backward where he crashed onto the pavement. "Maybe she does have me wrapped, however, it doesn't look like you've done any growing up at all. I thought we taught you a lesson that day, but I guess you didn't learn shit. If you ever say anything about Emma, look at her funny, or do anything that makes her feel uncomfortable, I will skin you alive right before I stab you in the heart. You won't even get a chance to explain." His gaze shifted to Rayne, who stood near where Allen landed. "And you...I've already said this once, but I'll repeat myself one more time, back the fuck off. If you don't want to accept Emma, that's fine, but we're a package deal now. I'm not saying you have to like her, but you will respect her and treat her decently. If you can't, I have nothing more to say to you. Paul, I'll call you later. I need to get Em home. Mel, let's go." With that, he jumped into the backseat, wrapped his arms around me, pulled me tightly to him, and spared not one more word or a second of his time for the people he left behind.

CHAPTER FORTY

BRYAN

Emma and I had met in the past? Emma, my Emma was the girl I helped save? My head swam with the myriad of thoughts that assaulted me. I remembered that day very well, but I also remembered a different girl. Not necessarily as far as her appearance went, since I had never gotten a really good look at her physically, however, her whole countenance had changed. Emma, for the most part, acted confident and self-assured, and when she didn't feel it, she faked it with the best of them. The girl from my memory trembled, didn't speak, and flinched whenever Paul or I said or did anything. In other words, the girl I rescued that day had been a frightened soul that my younger cousin took advantage of, but given what we had walked in on that day, I understood why she acted skittishly.

I had been visiting family in Texas, forced there by my parents with the expectations, my aunt and uncle would be able to talk me into not joining the Navy. It wasn't a secret that as soon as I got my degree, I'd planned on signing up.

After I had been there for about two weeks, Paul suggested we find his brother and do something together. Allen had made himself scarce since my arrival, and I only had one more week before I left. If I'd had my way, I would've left Allen alone. He and I never really got along with each other, even as children, and I didn't care about spending any quality family time with him. But I went along with the plan because Paul wanted it. Unlike Allen, Paul and I got along fantastically, still did even though we only found time to talk occasionally.

Pulling up to the small house outside of the city limits that Allen had been crashing at with some of his friends, the first thing I noticed was more than ten cars were parked around the house. Some in the yard, some in the driveway. It was a rural house, so the cars parked haphazardly did not surprise me, but the sheer number did for some reason. As we stepped into the house without knocking, we heard a crowd of people. It sounded like an angry mob. I remembered looking at him right before we rushed toward the bedroom, broke through the crowd, and found their victim. We did what we could to get her out of there as soon as possible.

After we dropped her off, I never thought I'd ever see her again; and I certainly never expected her to be the girl I eventually fell in love with. I wouldn't say that I never thought about that girl or what happened to her, I had. I'd always hoped she healed and moved on to a better life without my horrible cousin. It felt fulfilling to find out what became of that scared girl. On the other hand, it filled in that missing piece about Emma and some of her self-esteem issues. Given the crowd that day, and what they were saying, it would have stayed with almost anyone, including me.

Life was funny. The day I ran into the room, I wanted to rescue a stranger because she needed it. Years later, I unknowingly volunteered to help the same girl because I wanted to save her yet again. It may have been a different type of rescue than the day Allen had taken advantage of her, but I still wanted to protect her. And in the end, I wanted to be her prince.

"You okay?" I asked Emma. Her body trembled next to mine, which made me angrier. I wanted to beat Allen into a bloody pulp again.

The day he hurt Emma years ago, after we dropped her off, Paul and I took him behind the house and proceeded to beat some manners into him. Such a shame they didn't take. Maybe another lesson was in order.

She nodded, her head resting against my shoulder.

"Em, look at me." I lifted her chin and bent down to kiss her lips. Our reunion hadn't been anything like I imagined it would be. I expected to go through the security exit, see her, run to her, and sweep her in my arms. Dealing with one bitch of a sister and one bastard of a cousin never appeared in my plan.

I'd been home less than an hour and I had an upset girlfriend, beat a bastard, yelled at my sister again, and would probably have to deal with my parents for how I treated Rayne. I was fairly certain, as soon as she got Allen and Paul in her car, she called them and told them how horrible I was to her.

For a brief second, I thought about transferring back to San Diego immediately, but this time, Emma would come with me. Then again, if she wanted to remain on the east coast, we could always transfer up to Norfolk, which was far enough away that I wouldn't have to see anyone I didn't want to see.

Releasing her lips, I noticed the dazed glimmer in her eyes. Damn, I missed her and that expression. I should've let her come out to see me when she offered, but I'd been so busy trying to get everything ready for the move, I declined because I didn't think it wise to throw her in the middle of a box jungle. Plus, I hadn't been home all that much the last couple of months. Next time, I was going to say fuck it. "You okay?" I asked again.

I didn't miss her small sigh or the way her expression changed from dazed to frustrated. "I'll be fine. Just never expected to run into my past again."

"We never do, but at least, I'm part of that past too." I winked.

Her pink lips, slightly swollen from my kiss, turned up in a tiny grin. "Yes, you are. I guess I can call you my hero or..."

Mel pulled up to Emma's apartment building, however, no one got out of the truck. "Or?"

"Captain America," she chortled.

My eyes grew, and then my head whipped around to glare at Mel. "You told her?"

Holding up her hands in surrender, she defended herself. "Before you go killing me and leaving Luke completely alone and pitiful, you need to ask her why I told her. How could I not after what she told me?"

"What the hell? Em?" Emma was laughing so hard, she had to hold her side and couldn't answer me. My eyes darted back to Mel for some sort of explanation. "Well?"

"Out! I'm not going to spoil this one for her. Besides, I need to pick Luke up. He's been at Chad's watching some game, and he's probably sloshed by now. You two have fun tonight."

Reluctantly, I got out of the truck and then helped Emma out. Handing her the walker I pulled from the bed of the truck, I waited until she felt steady on her own before I grabbed my bag. We made it two steps away from the truck before Mel peeled out of there. At least she waited until we were clear before she left.

And Emma continued to giggle. Shaking my head, I sighed. "Come on. Let's get inside so you can tell me what the big secret is."

"Maybe."

"You will."

"Maybe."

"I have ways of making you talk."

"I might like to see what you got."

Yeah, I definitely missed her, this, and everything in between. Grinning lasciviously, I swatted her bottom. I leaned close to her ear and spoke softly. "I'll show you what I've got. It's missed you." I mentally patted myself on the back when her breath hitched, and she swallowed hard before licking her dry lips.

"When do the movers show up to your apartment?"

"Tomorrow." What was she up to?

She opened the door to her place. "Oh." Why did she sound disappointed?

I dropped my suitcase and backpack in the entryway before I grabbed her from behind. Every attempt was made to ignore the jumping dog crying at my feet, because despite his cuteness, Emma required my undivided attention. Spinning her around, I bent low, threw her over my shoulder, and carried her toward her bedroom.

"Oh? You know, my apartment is a little bigger than this. It's also close to the beach and on the first floor." I dropped Emma onto the bed and enjoyed the way she bounced from the impact. Crawling onto the bed and over her, I settled on top of her, placing my arms on either side of her shoulders. They took the brunt of my weight.

And then there was Curley. I forgot to close the door, and he'd jumped on the bed with us. He sat next to us with his tongue hanging out of his mouth, staring at us. It was a bit unnerving. He demanded attention. Patting the little dog on the head, I addressed her, "Therefore, you shouldn't look so disappointed. When I went searching for a place, I made sure you would be able to maneuver it. In fact, it's a newer apartment and completely set up with handicap access. And I was thinking, since your lease ends next month, instead of renewing, you should move in with me."

Her shocked expression looked adorable on her. "What?"

"I'm serious. What do you think?" I held my breath. Like with every other plan that concerned her, my original idea to ask her in a more romantic fashion, failed. I had come to the decision, winging it was the best course of action with Emma.

"Yes!" she screamed, wrapping her arms and legs around me.

My dick swelled immediately, however, I possessed self-control, and I pushed aside my desires to ask one more question. "How did you know about Captain America?"

Her coy expression told me I might have to torture her first. "Something."

Grabbing her sides, I started to tickle her. Her laughter was a balm to my soul after everything that had happened earlier today at the airport. "Tell me." Curley began barking again and got in on the action by licking Emma's face, making her laugh more.

"AH! No!" she yelled.

"Tell me!"

"NO!"

Her legs were no longer wrapped around me but swung wildly on the bed. I grabbed one and relocated the tickle session to her feet. She screamed loud enough to make my ears hurt. "Tell me," I demanded playfully.

One minute we were both laughing, and the next she started to choke. I panicked when I saw her struggling. Falling to the side in order to get off of her, I jerked her into a sitting position so she could breathe a little easier. "Em! Emma! Are you all right?"

With a hoarse voice, she said, "Yeah. Some spit got stuck in my throat, and I guess my throat chose that moment to stop working. I'm fine." She tried to wave off my concern, but her words did nothing to tamp down on the worry and anxiety I felt. "Hey. This is life with MG. I choke sometimes when my throat chooses to rebel and the muscles don't want to do what they are supposed to do. Sometimes it's my legs, my arms, my eyes, my throat, or any other muscle in my body. If it got to the point where I needed extra help, I would tell you to take me to the hospital." She paused, giving me a hard stare before inquiring, "Are you sure you can handle this?"

I honestly didn't know, however, if it was a choice between dealing with the MG or saying goodbye to her, I would choose the disease and everything that came with it. I'd be there for her to support her, and whenever she needed me to, I'd take care of her, because I loved her. In a short amount of time, she had become my world. I always thought everyone's favorite line from *Jerry McGuire* was cheesy stupid: "You complete me." But now I understood what they meant. Emma did that for me. She was my other half and she completed me. "I can handle it because it's you."

Leaning her head-on my shoulder, she whispered, "Thank you."

"You're welcome." Holding her tightly, I fell backward and laid down with her. Curley curled himself into a ball on the other side of her and began snoring. After my scare, I didn't care about Captain America or satisfying my own needs. I only wanted to feel her in my arms, to feel her lay her head on my chest, and to know she would be all right.

We had the rest of our lives for everything else, and next time I needed to remember to shut the door to the bedroom, leaving a certain dog on the other side of it.

EPILOGUE

BRYAN

Had the temperature increased? In the last fifteen minutes, it felt like it rose by at least one hundred degrees, because I was suddenly sweating buckets while my heart raced faster than any car at NASCAR. Fuck! I felt overheated!

"Will you calm down? She'll be here soon," Luke ordered.

"I know she will!" I barked back, my nerves intensifying even further. Maybe I shouldn't have done that, but he of all people should understand how anxious I felt.

After Emma moved in with me a month ago, I finally understood exactly what she dealt with on a daily basis. It was so much more than I had been exposed to in the few nights I spent with her. There was more medicine than I had seen any one person take, walkers, canes, doctors, therapy, etc. But at the same time, I could also say that seeing it all, immersing myself in it, made it easier to deal with and understand. Even the days she deemed "bad," when she could barely get out of bed, were no longer as terrifying as they once were. That in no way meant I liked seeing her struggle; however, it made it easier to cope with it all. Now, more than ever, I wanted to spend the rest of my life with her.

"They're here!" Luke stressed, and I chuckled. I wasn't sure who seemed more nervous: him or me.

The time had come.

Mel and Emma strolled into the club. Brantley Gilbert was playing in a small local club for a special fundraiser and I managed to get tickets. Not only that, but since I knew the owner of the club, I arranged for a little surprise during the performance.

As always, Emma took my breath away. She wore simple jeans that hugged her hips and accentuated her ass, showing off those curves I loved so much. Her top was strapless, black, and gave everyone a view of her ample cleavage. I loved the way her hips swung a little bit more when she saw me no matter if she used a cane—as she did tonight—or if she used her walker. Hell, she could be in the middle of a bad day dressed in a pair of her sweats, and I'd still believe her to be the sexiest woman on the planet.

"Hey, baby." I stepped up to her, pulling her in close for a kiss. I hoped she could not tell how nervous I felt.

"Hey, sexy. You ok?" she asked, one hand holding tightly to her cane and the other holding onto my waist.

"Perfect. Lonnie put us to work when we got here. That's all." Not exactly a lie. We arrived early to talk to Brantley, and Lonnie, the owner of the club, asked for our help. Considering she had been the person who arranged my meeting with Brantley, I owed her. "You sure you're okay with just the cane?"

"Yep. My legs are actually cooperating for a change." She grinned.

I hadn't been the only one to change since we dove head first into each other's lives. In the past, she had tried to use her cane on days she really needed her walker, but after she moved in with me, she'd been doing better about not taking unnecessary risks.

A couple of weeks before she moved in, we were both at her apartment and she was using her cane when she shouldn't have been. She wobbled and the cane did nothing to steady her. Trying to take a step to the right to go into the living room so she could sit down, her foot refused to cooperate, and she would have fallen if I hadn't caught her. It scared me to death. What if something happened to her? What if she hurt herself? I couldn't handle it. My anger got the better of me and I yelled. She yelled back, and I left. I came back after I calmed down and we talked it out, but my fear still lingered. She agreed to make better choices if only to stave off my impending heart attack.

I still busted her doing things she shouldn't, like when she still tried to use a cane on bad days because "it's only five feet," but tonight she was all right. I exhaled in relief, pulling her tightly against my side. "Good." Kissing the top of her head, I breathed her in and allowed her scent to calm me.

The club had been set up for the event with tables surrounding a dance floor, and Lonnie was gracious and wonderful enough to give us a table closest to the dance floor and the stage. Finding our seats, we waited for the show to start. I grinned, seeing how excited Emma appeared to be. Bouncing in her seat, she could barely sit still as she glanced all around the club taking in everything. The sights, the atmosphere, the people. She wanted to experience and remember it all. Tonight would be extra special for her since this singer happened to be one of her favorites. She owned every single album Brantley Gilbert had released, and had been to at least three of his concerts.

When I told her I'd gotten us tickets, she gasped and then slapped me on the chest with her open palm. "You're shitting me. Are you joking?"

I almost laughed. "No. I really got tickets to Brantley Gilbert's charity concert. I got a pair for Mel and Luke too. I figured we can go on a double date. What do you think?"

"Really?" She looked as if she was going to start jumping in the middle of the kitchen, and that freaked me out. She wasn't leaning against the counter, and only held onto her walker. It turned out, I should've been concerned. She'd been wearing socks and slipped on the tiled floor, landing on her ass. Luckily, she only got a bruised tailbone that day.

It had all been worth it though, to see her happiness and over-the-top reaction, then and now. Her excitement intensified mine.

An hour later when the show began, I swept her out onto the dance floor. Like a little girl danced with adults, I held her tightly as her feet balanced on mine. I didn't want her to expend any additional energy because she needed to last through the rest of the concert…and the surprise. Besides, I kind of liked her dancing on my feet. We were on cloud nine, and the whole night felt magical.

Before the third song started, Brantley addressed the crowd. "Tonight's a special night for not only Folds of Honor, but if I can get a spotlight up front here, and ask Bryan Sampson to come on out, the floor is yours."

"Bryan? What's going on?" Emma's voice dripped with confusion.

I couldn't remember the last time I smiled so big before. Lifting her out of her seat, where we had returned after the first song, I carried her out to the center of the dance floor. Luke set a chair down and after I sat her in it, I lowered myself to one knee. "Em, when we started this journey together, I promised I'd find you someone special, someone who'd love you the way you deserved to be loved. I promised you wouldn't go through life alone. Little did I know that as I got to know you, I'd fall in love with you myself. In short order, I came to realize you were everything that'd been missing from my life. I'm not saying things will be easy, but they'll be easier together. I'm not promising I won't make you cry, because I can be a selfish bastard whose head is shoved up my ass at times." We both laughed, and I wiped away her tears. "I'm not promising we won't fight sometimes, but there is no one I'd rather fight with than you. And I'm not promising perfection, because let's face it, I'm far from perfect—even though I think I am sometimes. What I am promising, is to love you no matter what, to be there for you so we can face every challenge, every day, together. I swear that I'll support you in whatever you want to do, to cheer you on when you need it, and to carry you when you can't walk or need to rest. I want to spend the rest of my life with you. Will you marry me?" I pulled out the ring, holding it out to her as Brantley started to sing his song, Fall Into Me.

Her tears fell faster, and as soon as I wiped them away, more replaced them. I waited for what seemed like an eternity, even though I knew Brantley had only sung a few lines, before she answered, "Yes!"

Wrapping my arms around her, I stood up with her in my arms, spun her around in a circle, and shouted, "She said yes!"

The day she accidentally messaged me was the first day of my new future. The day she agreed to move in with me, I knew she would be mine forever. And today, she answered my prayers and became my dream come true. I couldn't wait for forever with this woman, and tonight was only the first step to our always.

THE END

**For Rayne and Chad's story, check out
Redeemed: Book Two of the Love Seekers**

ACKNOWLEDGMENTS

It's funny. When I started working on this book, I was in the middle of writing another book, which did not want to flow for me. I had a dream about accidentally pinging someone after a bad date, and that person responding with an encouraging message.

I love hockey, and my family will tell you that I never write during a hockey game. This dream gave me an idea for a story, and that idea would not leave me alone. I finally decided to write one paragraph even though I was in the process of watching a hockey game. One paragraph turned into one chapter...and it just kept flowing like that. I don't think I've ever written something that plagued me to write it as much as this book and the characters in it. This is my story, and I didn't know how cathartic it would be to write. A lot of my own story can be found in Emma and her situations, however, I'm still waiting on my Bryan. LOL.

In 2010, I suddenly became very sick. No one could figure out what was wrong with me. I was weak, couldn't breathe, and struggled with functioning on a day to day basis. Eventually, I was diagnosed with myasthenia gravis. As with many people with an auto-immune disease, other auto-immune diseases were found.

This book was a journey for me. Many of the feelings are my own. Some of the struggles and the horrible dates, really did happen. Not everything though. I do have to use a walker. I do have to take a lot of meds to keep me upright. I do have an army of doctors that help me. And I do hope for a cure for myself and my fellow auto-immune sufferers.

After I became sick, my family encouraged me to start writing again. I started writing fanfiction, and my fans encouraged me to write a novel. I published Another Chance in 2015. Boy did I have a lot to learn, and still do. I have come a long way, and looking back on it all, I'm glad I published that book, but there are a lot of things I would have done differently.

To my family, thank you for always having my back, for your support and encouragement, and for being there when my life completely changed. I wouldn't have made it without you.

To Shana Vanterpool, thank you for stepping in to edit the book when my editor had to back out. I was about to panic and you saved me. I'm sure it was not the easiest and you wanted to pull your hair out, but we did it. You are a lifesaver. I love your books, your spirit, your love of abs, and your friendship. You are amazing. Don't worry. Chad will get his story. You helped me get my story out there. Thank you. Spencer says hi to Bella. (Everyone reading this, if you have not read her work, DO IT!!)

To the girls at Smokin' Hot Reads Book Blog: Jamie, Krista, and Melissa. You are the best. You showed me the ropes, encouraged me, and are some of the greatest friends I could ever ask for. Krista, I want more dirty ditties. Love you. Jamie, your friendship and support me more to me than you will ever know. Thank you for inviting me to join the blog. Melissa, thank you for being my PA when I needed it, encouraging me to write the story, and telling me all about BT Urruela (the muse for Bryan).

To Melissa, Becca, Becky, Brenda, Cara, and Sharon. Thank you for beta reading for me. I couldn't have done this without you.

To Linda, thank you for proofing this one more time.

To T.E. Black and Cover Luxe Designs. The cover for Exposed turned into something amazing. I fell in love the moment you showed me the picture and you went above and beyond my expectations. T, you have helped me so much with designing everything, even when it was crunch time for the signing, and you supported me. I am forever grateful!!

To the countless blogs and people that have helped to promote Exposed, thank you!! Without you, indie authors would get little exposure. You help keep our community growing and spreading. Thank you for getting the word out.

To my high school creative writing teacher, Mrs. Shelton, you always encouraged me to go for my dreams, and I will forever be grateful. Under your guidance, I learned so much about myself and my writing.

To my true friends, you are the best. After I got sick, you were there for me, and picked me up when I felt discouraged. You helped me to remember that I was not alone, that you were right there with me.

To Joyce, we have been best friends since we were kids, and I hope we continue to be best friends throughout our life. You have always kept it real with me and told me when I was being an idiot, but with my writing, you did nothing but encourage me. You told me I could do it and when I got frustrated, you listened to me gripe. I love you.

To the MG Flakes, this disease is not easy to live with or deal with; and too many Flakes have left us too soon. This books is for them and the ones that continue to fight. You welcomed me into your community with open arms, and even after they changed my diagnosis, you still embraced and loved me. We are on this journey together. We will fall, we will struggle, and yes, at time we will feel discouraged, but we will always continue to fight. I love all of you.

To my readers of my books and of my fanfiction, thank you for reading my work and for supporting me. You will forever hold a special place in my heart.

To the ladies at SaSS, thank you for taking a chance on me and giving me a table at my very first book signing. I had so much fun and loved every minute of it!!

Everyone, thank you for believing in me. Chad's book is next in the series. Look for Redeemed coming your way in 2017.

ABOUT THE AUTHOR

Maria Vickers currently lives in St. Louis, MO with her pug, Spencer Tracy. She has always had a passion for writing, and after she became disabled, she decided to use writing as her escape. Exposed is her second novel to be published.

She has learned a lot about life and herself after becoming sick. One of the things she has learned and lives by is, life is about what you make of it. You have to live it to the fullest no matter the circumstances.

From the author:

I've always loved books. Not only creating stories, but reading them as well. Books transport me, and when I was younger, I would run into walls because I refused to put my books down even for a second. Take not, walking while reading is not advised. LOL.

With my books, I dream of sharing my stories with the world. I want others to be transported or to feel the emotions my characters feel. That is my goal. If I can do that for one person, I succeeded.

Getting sick changed me and my life, but it also opened doors that I thought were closed. Today, even though I may not be able to do as much as I once could, I still have my mind, and I can write.

Links:
Newsletter:
http://eepurl.com/cvH8tX

Join her reader group, Maria's Love Seekers.
https://www.facebook.com/groups/1362108480474447/

facebook.com/mariavickersbooks

twitter.com/mvauthor

instagram.com/authormariavickers

goodreads.com/mariavickers_author

amazon.com/author/mariavickers

ALSO BY MARIA VICKERS

MF Novels

Another Chance

Love Seekers Series
Exposed: Book One of the Love Seekers
Redeemed: Book Two of the Love Seekers
Claimed: Book Three of the Love Seekers

Siren's Song

MM Novels

By the Book

Off-Campus Setup

Unbreak Me
(see With Love From New Orleans, Found You, for the side story to this book)

My Swan Prince
Full-length MM swan shifter novel
E-Book in Fractured Fairy Tales: A SaSS Anthology

Anthologies

Live Again (An MM contemporary romance novella)
Appearing in Tempting Fate Anthology
Benefiting Cancer Research Institute

A Flashy and Frosty Christmas
(4 flash fiction stories)

Benefiting Cancer Research Institute

Kisses in the Snow (An MM contemporary romance novella)

Appearing in With Love From London

Found You (An MM contemporary romance novella)

Side story to Unbreak Me

Appearing in With Love From New Orleans

Irish Wishes (An MM contemporary romance novella)

Side story to Kisses in the Snow

Appearing in With Love From Dublin

All I Want Is You (An MM contemporary romance novella)

Appearing in With Love From Venice, Christmas

Whiskey Love (An MF historical romance novella)

Appearing in Feisty Heroines

The Brauds (A comedy about three old women who know how to have a good time)

Available on Book Funnel, but you must preorder Feisty Heroines to receive

Desperate Desires (An MF MC shifter romance)

Appearing in Dark Leopards MC Charity Anthology

Made in the USA
Monee, IL
23 June 2020